LOVE YOU FOREVER

Elizabeth's Story

Sharon K. Middleton

Black Rose Writing | Texas

ISBN: 978-1-68433-973-0
PUBLISHED BY BLACK ROSE WRITING
www.blackrosewriting.com

Printed in the United States of America
Suggested Retail Price (SRP) $20.95

Love You Forever is printed in Adobe Caslon

*As a planet-friendly publisher, Black Rose Writing does its best to eliminate unnecessary waste to reduce paper usage and energy costs, while never compromising the reading experience. As a result, the final word count vs. page count may not meet common expectations.

The heart separated from its beat,
The earth longing for the rain,
The rhyme lost to the song,
A soul denied its essence,
Its light dimmed, weakened, broken.
The two halves,
Mirroring across the dimensions.
Chaos, rage, fury,
Fire,
Restless...
But the clock chimes,
Again,
Another minute, hour, day!
Waiting in a dream
As it holds on,
For just one more breath...
Shalini K. Ahuja
2021

"Around the corner there may wait a new road or a secret gate."
J. R. R. Tolkien

Acknowledgements

I would like to express special thanks to Shalini K. Ahuja, whose lovely poem inspired so much of this story.

I would also like to express thanks to my beta readers who help me with editing and story tips. I give an enormous shout-out to Maureen Maskell for the countless hours she reviewed and edited this manuscript, besides searching the internet for dresses and jewelry. Maureen found the hieroglyphics dress, both wedding gowns, the reception gown, and the beautiful engagement ring Ari gives to Elizabeth.

Last, I would like to again thank my wonderful husband for his patience and encouragement. Gary is my twin flame, and he holds the other half of my heart. I could not write without his love and support. He inspired the title of this book. Yes, I shall Love You Forever.

Love You Forever is a work of fiction. While many of the historical depictions are accurate, archeologists have not yet found the tomb of Nefertiti. It is pure conjecture on my part to claim there was a son of Akhenaten and Nefertiti who was raised by Horemheb and Medj. However, it is believed Ay was the brother of Queen Tiye, and his wife and he had no children of their own. It is further thought they raised Horemheb as their son and Ay's wife was the nursemaid to Nefertiti and Medj. Cartouches proclaimed Pharaoh Seti I to be descended from Ay.

Cast of Characters

Elizabeth Winslow – our heroine. We met Liz first in Diary of the Reluctant Duchess as a young child and have watched her grow up. She is now an adult and owns Nefertiti's Bone Yard, a dinner club in Galveston, Texas, which Kirk O'Malley bought for her. Liz is of Egyptian, Irish, and Nubian heritage. She is a beautiful young woman with a strong physical resemblance to the bust of Queen Nefertiti.

Dr. Aristotle 'Ari' Hotep – our hero. Liz describes him as 'tall, dark and awesome.' Ari is an ophthalmologist. He and Liz met four years earlier than the beginning of this story when he told Liz she had Stargardt's disease. He now heads the department studying ophthalmic disorders at Biozyme, International, headquartered in Cairo.

Rick Jones – the medium in Galveston, Texas, where our story begins. Rick talks to ghosts.

Dr. Levi Hotep – Ari's brother, who is an archaeologist currently working at the Golden City. He was the archeologist who discovered the tomb of the Unknown Princess at Saqqara.

Anna Hotep – Levi's wife.

Theodore 'Theo' Williams - Ari and Levi's nephew. Theo is four years old at the beginning of our story. Theo lives with Anna and Levi when we first meet him.

Benjamin Williams – Theo's father. He is missing from Theo's life for most of Theo's life.

Antigone Hotep Williams – Theo's mother, who died from cancer when Theo was about two years old. Benjamin Williams abandoned them when he learned his wife had cancer.

Dr. Zain Hassan – the top archaeologist in Egypt, who is the lead archaeologist at the Golden City. Zain is handsome and charming.

Dr. Salima Mafous – another archeologist at the Golden City. Sweet, unassuming, a great person to be your friend.

Francesca 'Fancy' Winslow – Liz's mom. We met Fancy first at age four in Home to McCarron's Corner, and as a young woman in Beyond McCarron's Corner. Fancy has been the primary storyteller in the books since Diary of the Reluctant Duchess, where she wrote the story of the Duchess and changed her life. Fancy adopted Liz when Liz was three years old. Fancy was then married to Liz's biological father, Kirk O'Malley. She is now married to Dr. Richard Winslow.

Dr. Richard Winslow – Fancy's husband who adopted Liz and the other children when they understood Kirk O'Malley had been lost at sea. Richard is a cardiovascular surgeon. We first met Richard in Beyond McCarron's Corner.

Captain Kirk O'Malley – Liz's biological father, was believed to have drowned when his ship sank during a hurricane. He was missing for over a decade. He is now married to Melanie Henson. We first met Kirk in The McCarron's Daughter.

Dr. Miguel Vargas – we met Miguel in Path of the Guiding Light. Bella met him when she visited Trinity University. They married in The McCarron's Destiny. Miguel becomes the director of Biozyme, International, in Love You Forever. They will appear again in future McCarron's Corner novels.

Bella Winslow Vargas – Fancy's oldest child, who is married to Dr. Miguel Vargas. Liz and Bella are best friends. We met Bella when she was a baby in Beyond McCarron's Corner.

Mustafa Maksoud – the family law attorney who helps Liz and Ari.

Judge Jawhara Mohammed – family court judge in Cairo.

Nefertiti was the Great Royal Wife and Queen Consort to Pharaoh Akhenaten. Nefertiti is reputed to have been the most beautiful woman who ever lived.

Pharaoh Akhenaten – married to Nefertiti. Pharaoh Akhenaten established a new religion and claimed it was 'the one true religion.'

Captain Jolly Johnny English – Captain Johnny is a ghost. He continually tries to protect Elizabeth. He knew Kirk years ago and was the person who saved Kirk when Kirk's ship sank in the hurricane. Johnny was first mentioned in Diary of the Reluctant Duchess, but we never met him before Love You Forever.

Tamsin Fitz Simmons – we met Tamsin in Home to McCarron's Corner. She was Fancy's mother and is now an angel.

And of course, the Goddess Isis, who was reputed to possess great magic.

LOVE YOU FOREVER

Elizabeth's Story

Chapter 1
Galveston - Elizabeth

The striking young woman reached over to grab the phone in the busy club. She slung her long goddess braids over one shoulder and slipped off an earring as she raised the phone to her ear. "Nefertiti's Bone Yard. How may I help you?" She leveled her eyes across to a figure slumped in the shadows. "Hey, cut out the nonsense. I warned you about this before."

The older man in the shadows raised his glass to her and then slunk deeper into the darkness.

A young guy on the other end of the phone coughed as if nervous. "I hope I haven't called at a bad time. My name is Justin Black. May I speak with Miss Elizabeth Winslow? I understand she manages the bar."

"Oops, my bad. This is Elizabeth. What may I do you for?" She looked back at the character in the corner. "I'm telling you, Johnny. Cut it out, or else you need to leave."

The older man waved an insolent salute at her. "Do you intend to toss me out of your fine establishment, Elizabeth? I am devastated."

She rolled her eyes and let out a loud 'shush.' "You're devastated? I know better than to think anything I could say would devastate you. Be quiet. I'm sorry, sir. Unruly clients are the perpetual bane of the bar owner. Now, how may I help you?"

The man laughed as if embarrassed he had to make the call. "I work for the Bay Area Sun. I'm doing an investigative story on Nefertiti's in the Bone Yard. My boss suggested I talk to you."

Elizabeth sighed, already frustrated. "Another one? Good lord, don't you guys ever tire of beating this dead horse?"

The young fellow laughed again. "I'm sorry. I'm just trying to perform the job my boss dumped on me. Why is your place called Nefertiti's in the Bone Yard?"

She frowned. "The bar or the neighborhood?"

"Gosh, ma'am, I guess both." He chuckled again, revealing his nervousness.

It was clear to Liz the new reporter knew Jack Squat about Galveston history. "Oh, good lord. Did the paper assign their dumbest reporter on this? Okay, here goes. Galveston History 101. Do you know anything at all about the 1900 hurricane which decimated Galveston?"

Justin's gulp was audible over the phone. "I know it struck on September eighth of 1900, and a ton of people died."

Liz clenched her teeth as she rolled her eyes. "Clever. Well, that's better than nothing. Okay, Grasshopper, here is the history lesson for the newcomer. The Great Galveston Hurricane hit on September 8, 1900. The Galveston meteorologist was a young guy named Isaac Cline."

"You mean they had meteorologists then?"

"Apparently they did. Young Mr. Cline did not think a hurricane could seriously damage Galveston. The town had survived a multitude of hurricanes before the Great Hurricane. Cline knew the storm existed in the Gulf from about August 30th. He finally grew worried the storm might hit Galveston on September 7th. He tried to warn the townspeople an intense storm was approaching. Unfortunately, the fool failed to mention the storm barreling toward Galveston was a massive hurricane. Early the morning of September 8th, Cline drove a horse and wagon along the beach to warn people about the impending storm. He told them they should head to high ground. Unfortunately, most people elected to remain in their homes on the island. Now, bear in mind that the highest point on the island stood less than nine feet above sea level in 1900. By evening, winds up to 140 miles per hour ripped into the town. Today, winds that strong are considered a Category 4 hurricane. Many of the homes collapsed. The hurricane blew out most windows and uprooted countless trees. They estimate 3600 homes were destroyed. I'm not sure anyone knows the actual death count, but a sizable portion of the city perished. You should watch the film about the Great Storm. It will give you a perspective I cannot emulate with vivid eyewitness accounts of the hurricane and its horrifying aftermath. Dead bodies were everywhere, in the streets, under the rubble, even tied to trees. There are descriptions of babies, found dead in the arms of their deceased mothers."

Liz's voice broke. It always upset her to talk about the Great Storm. She still had vivid memories of the Dreadful Hurricane her family survived when she was small. She would never forget the howling winds as the storm passed over the house or the flooded streets the next day as Mom struggled to get them to safety. She would always remember the water rushing around her as they struggled through the flooded streets to the ship which would carry them to safety. She trembled as she remembered the shock and horror she experienced later when they were told Poppa's ship sank with no survivors. She understood firsthand the horrors of a hurricane and the aftermath. She took a deep breath.

"How horrible. You should be a writer. You weave a great tale." The shock was clear in the reporter's voice.

She snorted. "Oh, thank you. My mother is a writer. She will be delighted to learn you think I describe destruction and death well. Finally, the Galveston authorities got the brilliant idea to dispose of the unending sea of corpses by loading them onto barges, taking them out onto the Gulf, and dumping them. Unfortunately, the bloated and rotting carcasses then floated back to shore a week later."

The reporter gagged. "Are you serious?"

Liz nodded. "Oh, yes, I'm as serious as death. After that hideous debacle, the dead were burned in large pyres onshore. It took six weeks to dispose of all the corpses. Everyone watched as a sizeable chunk of the city's former population went up in smoke. The city reeked of the burning dead. Galveston had truly become hell on earth."

"It certainly sounds like it. Now, tell me how this area came to be called the Nefertiti's Bone Yard," Justin said.

She laughed, but the sound came out harsh like autumn leaves crackling beneath an angry hand. "The area is called the Bone Yard. The city built the Seawall to protect them from future storms. It raised the sea level in the city by as much as eleven feet in places. The seawall itself is 15.6 feet above sea level. The city still had to dispose of bodies and needed fill for the newly elevated city. All those burned carcasses were buried here as landfill, near the funeral home across the street, in mass graves. It raised the level of the city, but the city now lies on the bones of the dead. There are many reports of hauntings throughout this area, which is known today as the Bone Yard."

"Okay, I guess this assignment makes sense to me now."

Liz frowned. "What do you mean?"

He cleared his throat. "My boss wants me to convince you to allow a medium to come to the bar in quest of restless spirits."

Liz's jaw dropped. She glanced nervously at the shadowy figure in the corner. "He wants you to do what?"

Justin chuckled. "I'm serious. He is all into a local medium. The guy has a decent reputation, and he does not work with just anyone. Apparently, he does this EVP stuff."

"What's EVP?" Liz sounded intrigued.

"Electronic voice phenomenon. Within ghost hunting and parapsychology, electronic voice phenomena, also called EVP, are the sounds the parapsychologists claim to find on electronic recordings. Mr. Jones claims these are voices of the deceased who have been unintentionally or intentionally recorded. My editor would like me to bring Mr. Jones in so he can record voices of any spirits lingering in Nefertiti's in the Bone Yard."

Liz blinked. She glanced back at the man in the corner. He tipped his hat to her and smiled. She rolled her eyes and wagged a finger at him as she frowned. "Hmm… Well, that's a new one. I have a ghost hunter or two come in nearly every week, but I never had one want to tape-record the voices of the ghostly spirits in here before. So, if I understand you correctly, any ghosts- oops, I mean spirits- which might lurk in here could talk to this guy via these, what did you call them? EVP's?"

The gentleman in the corner sat up straighter as he nodded and grinned at Liz. She cut her eyes at him again and motioned for him to be quiet.

"Yes, exactly. I understand the procedure is widely used by credible parapsychologists. The Max Planck University in Germany recorded over one hundred thousand EVPs of spirit voices."

Liz was stunned. "One hundred thousand voices of ghostly entities? Well, I'll be jiggered."

He chuckled. "You'll be jiggered, huh? I never heard the expression before. What does it mean?"

Liz felt her cheeks redden. The reporter caught her using archaic terminology from her childhood. "I think it means 'I'm astonished.' It's an old Southern expression. My Poppa says 'well, I'll be jiggered.'"

The reporter laughed. "Parents say the darnedest things. Liz, would you allow me to bring Mr. Jones in your establishment some evening?"

Liz laughed. "Yes, but you do realize ghosts would not be restricted by the time of day, right? If they are here, they could be here any time. Heck fire, they could be here right now. It wouldn't have to be night."

Justin laughed as if self-conscious. "Huh. I had not thought about it. I guess you're right. They probably could be contacted during the day. So, can I bring him by the bar to run his EVP test in Nefertiti's in the Bone Yard?"

Liz thought for a second before answering. "Sure. Today is Wednesday. Bring him on Friday afternoon about 3, before our big Friday evening crowd arrives. Friday evening will be Krazy Kilt Karaoke Night and the place will fill up fast."

"Great! Thanks, Liz. And thanks for the info on the Bone Yard. Oh, one more question. Why is your club called Nefertiti's in the Bone Yard?"

She laughed. "It's called Nefertiti's Bone Yard. Poppa swears I resemble the bust of Queen Nefertiti. He bought the place for me and insisted on the name. I don't know, maybe a ghost suggested the name to him. I think he's full of malarkey."

The young man chuckled. "Fascinating. I have a feeling this will make one great report."

Liz smiled as she lowered the phone receiver into the cradle. "Well, this ought to be interesting, Johnny."

The man left the shadows of the corner and appeared to float over to Liz. "Righto, my girl. May I scare him?"

She shook her head as she tried to frown at the ghost. "Why don't you wait and see if this guy senses you are here first, Johnny? Most of these so-called psychics and mediums cannot sense paranormal activity if you jump up and shout 'boo' at them. Heck, they can't discern a three-hundred-year-old Irish pirate who lives in this club."

The elegant spirit scowled. "My word, Elizabeth. Don't you know it's rude to discuss one's age? I believe I have been a spirit for about two hundred years. And don't you know it's rude to call one a 'pirate?' Haven't I told you the proper term is 'privateer?'"

The corners of her gray eyes crinkled as she laughed. "My word, Captain English. I would swear Kirk told me Captain Jolly Johnny English was one of the most terrifying pirates of the eighteenth century. Besides, don't you know it's rude to scare the local ghost hunters?"

Johnny made a rude noise. "Ghost hunters, my aged ass. Not one of these so-called experts has spotted me yet."

Liz shook her head and wiped the counter. "Quit spilling the ale, Johnny. You know it goes right through you. Why do you even try to drink it? Well, who knows? Maybe this guy will be the real deal. After all, I can see you and talk with you."

"Yes, but I knew your father back in the day," the ghostly pirate said. "Oh, I suppose it is a waste of good ale, but I enjoy savoring the rich flavor of your home brewed ale."

"Oh, yeah, this little tidbit ought to be fun to explain to the reporter guy. How the ghost in my bar knew Poppa back in the eighteenth century," she fretted with a scowl. "And how my ghost loves to savor the flavor of my home brewed ale."

"Afraid the ghost hunter might learn your secret? Oh, my, my, it would be worth talking to the man to see his stunned expression when I tell him your father was once my first mate, many long years ago, and you time-traveled here from the 1700s."

"We came to the States after a horrible hurricane hit Bermuda. What did they call it?" Liz asked.

"They called it the Dreadful Hurricane," said Captain Johnny.

"Hmm. Figures. I understand over 10,000 people were killed in it, from Florida to Maine. Fortunately, you rescued my Poppa after the hurricane. That is about the seating capacity of Cameron basketball stadium at Duke University. I will be eternally grateful you saved him." Liz chuckled but refrained from saying more. One did not push the spirit of Captain Jolly Johnny English too far. The old reprobate probably would tell the parapsychologist her family history. Wouldn't it comprise a fine kerfuffle if Johnny talked about the family's travels though time? Mom would have a hissy fit. "What will you tell the ghost hunter?"

"Harrumph. Assuming his machine can detect my voice through this newfangled technique, I suppose I will tell him 'Boo!'"

Elizabeth laughed again. She shook her head as she wagged a finger at the ghost. "Okay, you behave yourself while I'm gone this afternoon. You scared off my last two assistants. I like this fellow. Behave yourself, Johnny. And don't answer the phone. No one can hear you."

Johnny glowered at her. "I swear, Elizabeth, you take all the fun out of being a spirit."

Elizabeth snickered as she picked up her purse and car keys. "Yeah, well, I'm not sure you aren't one of the undead. Now, behave yourself, or I will get my Poppa to come back over here to talk to you."

She shook her head as she struggled not to laugh. The resident spook could be fun to have around the club if he would behave like a human. She sighed. *I guess he is not human any longer. Now, he's a ghost. Oops, the correct term is 'spirit.'*

Johnny brightened up at her words. "Wonderful! I would be delighted if Kirk came back again. We could go out on a ship. I would dearly love to take the Alyssa out for a run. Jolly good, Elizabeth!"

She laughed as she shook her head once more. After a few words to her assistant manager, Liz slipped out the door and slid behind the wheel of the sleek little red convertible. Within minutes, she pulled up at the ophthalmological clinic for UTMB. She sat in the little car, clinging to the steering wheel, and taking deep breaths for several minutes as she steeled herself for the unpleasant procedure to come. With a sigh, she leaned her head into the steering wheel as she blinked away the tears threatening to spill from her eyes.

It was time for her monthly intraocular injections. She knew the process had slowed the advancement of blindness in both of her eyes. Liz still dreaded the shots more than she ever dreaded a final exam or dance audition. Who would dream a young woman would develop a form of macular degeneration and be headed to blindness? She had to quit dancing professionally because of visual deterioration. It almost killed her to relinquish her dream of being a professional dancer. Dancing had been her life.

She sighed again, steeled herself, and got out of the car. No time for a pity party. It was shot time.

Chapter 2
Galveston - Bella

"I have to go, Miguel. Liz is at the ophthalmological department for her monthly injections." Bella Vargas leaned over the table to kiss her handsome husband.

"Poor thing. I hear those are dreadfully uncomfortable. All right, *querida*. I hate to see you go, but I will see you later tonight. Only a few more hours reviewing this new data from Biozyme International. Well, this seminar enabled us to come from Boston for a working vacation while we scientists from around the world all compare notes. Have fun with Liz this evening." Miguel Vargas's eyes devoured his pretty wife silently as she laughingly leaned over to kiss her husband again.

Miguel was a board certified, infectious disease control physician and microbiologist. He worked for Biozyme, Inc., the top biochemical and microbiological think tank in the country, if not the world. He majored in biochemistry as an undergraduate at Trinity University, where he met his mentor, Dr. Kate Woodward. Dr. Woodward encouraged him to attend med school and study infectious disease control. She offered him the once-in-a-lifetime opportunity to work with Biozyme shortly before Bella and he married three years earlier. He loved his research about viruses. Through Miguel's team, the company developed the most effective and safest vaccine against COVID-19. Miguel loved his job, especially the work to protect the public from the pandemic. "Oh, Bella, the world will be our oyster if I accept this new job with Biozyme International!"

Her blue eyes sparkled as she laughed. "You silly goose, it already is. Biozyme has already been a wonderful adventure. I love being away from hurricanes and getting the Boston snow."

He grimaced. "I'm still not sold on the snow, *querida*. We can talk more about the new job Kate offered me when I get home later tonight. It's a fabulous opportunity. You better head over to ophthalmology to pick up your sister."

"Yes, Liz becomes irritable if I run late. I understand she is miserable after these shots, but she should have a little patience with me. We're supposed to be on vacation, and I'm doing her a favor."

Bella slowly raised herself from the dining room chair. At six months in her second pregnancy, it became increasingly difficult to do the things she usually could do with no problem. She winced and rubbed her back again as she straightened up. Her back had ached a lot lately. The doctor assured her back pain was typical at this stage in a pregnancy, and Bella should not worry. She grabbed a scrunchy out of her handbag and pulled her long auburn hair back into a ponytail to prepare for the trek across the campus in the Texas heat. By the time she walked across the UTMB campus to the clinic, Liz should finish her appointment. Bella would take Liz out for supper, and then drive her sister home. Bella would call Uber to transport her back to the Airbnb rental cottage from Liz's bar after she dropped off Liz.

Twenty minutes later, a sweaty and tired Bella Vargas trudged into the clinic building across the street from the main complex of the UTMB hospital. She sighed with relief as the frigid air conditioning washed over her like a healing balm. *Thank God I don't have to deal with heat and humidity like this in Boston.*

Bella had mixed sentiments about the proposed move to Cairo. Her family visited them often in Boston, but it was more challenging than she imagined living so far away from her family and friends. She realized they would have remarkable travel opportunities if they moved to Cairo, but Bella was not sold on the move halfway around the world to live on another continent. She was an introvert like Mom and her Grampa Marc. She could forget herself while she played her piano, but she could not carry her baby grand around with her everywhere she might go in her hip pocket. She snickered at the idea. It terrified her to contemplate the damage her beloved piano might suffer while being transported to Egypt.

Mom had taught her some good coping mechanisms, including 'the Duchess smile.' Mom taught her how to paste a friendly smile on her face even in the most trying circumstances. Mom even taught her how to do the royal wave. Moving to Boston had been the most trying circumstance she ever endured other than the hurricane when she was a child. The move to Boston seemed like a piece of cake compared to moving to Egypt. If only Liz would move to Egypt, too.

Liz was more than Bella's sister. Liz was her best friend. Well, that ship sailed four years ago when Liz refused to marry her handsome Egyptian doctor. Bella doubted Liz would change her mind about marriage, even to marry a gorgeous hunk of manhood like Ari Hotep. Hmm… Maybe Liz would help her convince Miguel this move to Cairo would not be the thing for them to do.

Bella pasted 'the Duchess smile' on her face and pushed the door open to the ophthalmology department just as Liz received her card scheduling her next appointment. *Okay, I can manage this*, she thought. *Liz gets the intraocular injections, not me. I just catch her anger afterward.*

"Took your sweet time getting here." Liz frowned as she flipped her braids back over her shoulder and snapped out the words at her older sister.

"Well, I'm here, and you just finished. Quit your fussing and give me the car keys." Bella reached out for the keys to her sister's snazzy little BMW.

Liz shook her head in disgust, but she handed Bella the keys. She pulled on her big, floppy hat and slipped on the dark glasses to protect her eyes from the bright sunlight outside. "Miguel seems excited about the new baby."

"He's overjoyed, especially since the obstetrician did the ultrasound and told me that I'm carrying a boy."

Liz shrugged. "It figures he would be excited about a son. I didn't realize you guys already know the sex of the baby. What, no big gender reveal? Mom will be devastated."

Bella laughed. "Mom's fine with it. Mrs. Vargas is disappointed. She wanted a big gender reveal party. She still wants one. She's excited the baby is a boy, so I'm sure Marta will get over her disappointment we are not having a gender reveal party."

At least you can have children, thought Liz. She convinced her gynecologist to tie her tubes a few months ago. She adamantly claimed she did not want to have a child after she received the diagnosis of Stargardt disease four years earlier. It devastated Liz to learn she inherited the disease from her deceased biological mother. Liz would not wish blindness on anyone. She refused to knowingly pass it on to her future children. "Fine. Let's go."

Bella adjusted the seat and steering wheel to accommodate her growing girth. "I will be so glad when this baby is born. I'm already tired of being 'fat,' and I still have three months to go until the birth."

"Girl, you are not fat. You are going to have a healthy baby. Don't complain. Not everyone is so lucky," Liz said as her lips thinned in apparent frustration and anger.

Bella looked funny and abruptly stopped fussing. She quickly pulled the elegant sports car out of the parking space and eased it into the afternoon traffic. She headed down the Seawall towards several popular restaurants. "Where shall we eat tonight? The Spot?"

Liz shook her head and leaned her head into an upraised hand. "Too busy. I'm not in the mood for a crowd. Let's go to Kritikos Grill. The food is great and even if it should be crowded, it's always a lot quieter than The Spot."

Bella nodded as she drove. "Works for me. Then we can flirt with Mr. Kritikos. He always calls me Bellissima. So, how's the resident spook treating you this week?"

Elizabeth sighed and shook her head. "Oh, good grief. Captain Johnny ran off another waiter last week. He nearly scared the living daylights out of the poor guy."

Bella laughed. "Don't you know it's politically incorrect to say, 'waitress' or 'waiter' instead of 'wait staff'?"

Liz tossed her hand in the air with impatience. "Oh, don't start on me. I am in no mood, Bella. I just got umpteen shots in both of my eyes. My eyes hurt something awful."

Bella reached over to pat Liz on the shoulder. "Sorry. My bad. I thought they numbed your eyes for those shots."

Liz glowered at her sister.

Bella cleared her throat. "Well, it sounds like classic Captain English hijinks. Did you have Kirk talk to him?"

Liz rolled her eyes. "Oh, no, Captain English refuses to talk to Kirk over the phone. Kirk yelled and fussed at him on the speakerphone, but the good Captain said not one word back to Poppa. Johnny wants Poppa to come here. Then they can talk about 'the good old days on the high seas,' he says. The damned ghost drives me batty."

Bella snorted. "Figures. That sounds like something Captain Johnny would pull. Well, look at it this way. Captain English saved Kirk's life during the Dreadful Hurricane. Johnny thinks he has an 'in' with us."

Liz shook her head. "Bella, you just aren't 'getting it.' Believe me, if I could get rid of him, I would. Hey, I've got an idea. Why don't you ask him to follow you guys back to Boston? Better yet, he could follow Miguel and you to Egypt."

Bella laughed. "No, thanks, I think I'll pass on that stellar opportunity. Are you sure you don't want to have dinner at your bar? We could chat with the good Captain."

"Oh, please, no. Let me have one evening away from Captain Horrible. Ye gods, I'm stuck with the old reprobate nearly all the time as it is. At least, I don't have to see him the evening after I have these miserable shots. He may follow me upstairs to my apartment ninety percent of the time, but he has too much good sense to go to my doctor's appointments. He figured out the one time he attempted to accompany me there that I am not receptive to his bull caca on these days."

Bella grew quiet again as she drove down the Seawall to the charming little Greek restaurant. After they were seated at a table overlooking the Gulf and ordered their favorites, the girls began talking again.

"Mom says Dara and she are coming this weekend." Bella grinned.

Liz nodded as a smile played upon her lips. "I understand they may be planning-"

"You mean they may be plotting?" Bella inquired as she arched an eyebrow and grinned at Elizabeth.

Liz chuckled. "Okay, plotting a baby shower for you. I promise to give you the heads up, so you can get your hair and nails done, and wear something pretty for the shower."

"You better give me a warning if you know what is good for you." Bella grinned at her younger sister. "But really, it will be fun. I am tired of being cooped up at home alone day after day. This trip was supposed to be a vacation."

"With another Covid-19 upsurge with this omicron variant, don't you think it's wise for you to stay out of the public as much as possible? I mean, considering your condition and all."

"Freaking pandemic. I am so sick of this mess. How many years has it been going on now?"

Liz shrugged. "The bigger question is how much longer will it continue?"

"Yeah, well, by Christmas I'll deliver this baby. I'm already the size of a barn. Oops, correction, I'm big as the side of a *bar*. "

Liz chortled. "Oh, funny, Bella. Good pun. Mom would love it. Big as a bar."

Bella smiled. "I was happy to oblige. I thought you would like my little play on words. Or maybe I should have said big as a bone yard."

Liz snorted her wine. "Oh, even better, sis. You're on a roll tonight."

Bella bit back laughter at the sight of her sister spewing her wine. "I never dreamed I could get so big. I didn't get this big before."

Elizabeth shrugged her shoulders. They both lapsed into silence at the memory of the baby Bella lost while she was hospitalized two years earlier with Covid-19. "Can you believe you have been married nearly three years now? Your wedding was so gorgeous. You must admit lavender is my color. We all looked wonderful in our 50's styled gowns. We looked like a flower-"

"Garden of beautiful girls," Bella finished for her sister. "I will never get over the reporter for the San Antonio Times who compared us all to a 'bouquet.' Then, the school here in Galveston where I taught closed for most of the spring semester, so I wasn't teaching. I take it back. I taught on-line. Teaching on-line was the weirdest experience I ever had. I cannot tell you how much I missed my one-on-one time with my students. All I have done since we moved is tread water. We moved, I lost a baby, and then I got pregnant again. You would have thought I learned my lesson the first time. I mean, who else has been through two pregnancies during this blasted pandemic?"

Liz's brow furrowed as she frowned. "Tread water? What do you mean?"

Bella shook her head. "I'm just floating along, waiting for this baby to be born and waiting for Miguel to decide if he's taking the blasted directorship in Cairo that Biozyme International offered him. I'm just treading water."

Liz frowned. "Don't you have a vote in the decision? Seems to me an important move like this one should be based on a mutual decision by you two."

Bella did not reply. She blushed as she pushed her food around on her plate while not taking a bite.

Liz frowned and pointed her fork at Bella's plate. "Why aren't you eating? You love tzatziki and dolmas."

Bella sighed and rolled her eyes. "I got fussed at today by the obstetrician I'm seeing while we are here. I gained too much weight since my last doctor's appointment. I must watch my calories now. Walk, Bella, they say. Don't walk, Bella, there's an upswing in the pandemic, the doctor warns. Don't go out of the house unless you must, says Miguel. You need to get out and walk more often, Miguel fusses. I am so tired of staying at the house and walking circles in the freaking living room. Oh, yeah, I can walk to the park or go down to the beach once or twice a day, but *nada mas*. No shopping for baby clothes. No cruising down the Strand looking for pretty dresses and shoes. I want to know we are past this wave of the blasted pandemic. It would kill me-"

As Bella's voice broke off and she pressed a hand to her mouth, Liz realized her sister felt terrified she would have another miscarriage. Liz laid a hand across her sister's arm. "It won't happen again."

Bella tried to smile at her younger sister, and patted Liz's hand. "Well, like my husband says, *ojala que no*. Let's hope not. The Texas numbers haven't spiked since Gov. Abbott opened the state and removed the mask mandate although Miguel wants me to continue wearing a mask when I'm out in public. Miguel thinks the numbers will keep going down. I hope he's right. The governor says something like 350,000 Texans were vaccinated against Covid today. I understand over sixty percent of Texas citizens have now been vaccinated, but it concerns him so few Hispanics and Blacks have been vaccinated. The governor seems to think the vaccination rates dropped with the big upsurge of immigration through the southern border. In contrast, eighty percent of the population has been vaccinated in Massachusetts. However, Texas Covid hospitalizations have dropped to the lowest they have been since June 17, 2020. I simply hope I don't catch it again while we're here."

Liz squeezed Bella's hand. "You should be safe. You have been vaccinated and received the booster."

Bella tried to smile. She patted Liz's hand. "All I know is I want this baby born, healthy and sound. I want Miguel to be with me in the hospital. And I want to be back to Boston before a blasted hurricane hits Galveston."

"No storms are in the Gulf. Hmm… Do you think Miguel will accept the job in Cairo?" Liz frowned as she chewed her upper lip.

Bella knew Liz would hate to see her move further away. Liz often called Bella her rock. Bella had been an incredible source of support to Liz since her diagnosis. It was wonderful when they lived in Galveston a few blocks from Liz. It had already been hard for Bella to be half a continent away from Liz and the rest of the family. Bella could not imagine what it would be like if Liz and she lived on opposite sides of the world.

Funny. Liz was adopted, but Bella always felt closer to Liz than the other kids, perhaps because they were closest in age.

Bella shrugged. "I don't know. I really don't want to move there, but this is the chance of a lifetime. No other doctor his age has ever been offered the position of director of any of the Biozyme facilities."

Liz continued frowning as she leaned towards her sister. "Well, none of the other doctors developed the top vaccine against Covid-19. But Cairo, Bella. My God, it's halfway around the world, in Egypt."

The older gentleman who owned the restaurant ambled over to their table, and hugged Bella. "Ah, my beautiful Bellissima, how are you tonight, my darling? When will your handsome husband finish his seminar and eat with us?"

"Hopefully by the end of the week, Mr. Kritikos. I'm fine, although I'm tired of being cooped up in the house most of the time. It has not been the vacation I hoped it would be. Mr. Kritikos, why do you call me Bellissima?"

"I call you Bella Bellissima because you are the most beautiful Bella I know. And my exquisite Elisabeth, how are you, my pet? Why do I only see you when you come here to eat with beautiful Bella?"

Liz laughed and batted her eyelashes at the flirtatious owner. "Mr. Kritikos, my love, you know it is darn near impossible for me to get away from my place. I am lucky my sister comes to visit me so often. She always insists I leave the club and come out to eat with her when she flies in from Boston. And, of course, we must make sure your wife is not here, so we can flirt with you."

The sweet, gray-haired gentleman beamed at her, his dark eyes sparkling with mischief. "I am always happy to see both of you beautiful girls and to flirt with you charming young women. You make me feel like a young man again for a little while. Bella, when is the little one due?"

Bella smiled back at the older man. She always enjoyed eating here and chatting with adorable Mr. Kritikos. "In three months, about the same time as our anniversary."

Mr. Kritikos nodded. "Yes, a birthday on your anniversary should be easy for Miguel to remember. I will miss you when you go back home to Boston, my beautiful girl."

"I will miss you, too, my friend. Thank heavens you gave me the names of some good Greek restaurants in Boston -- although no one makes tzatziki as well as you do."

He patted her on the back. "It was my pleasure to give you the names. And thank you for the compliment, my dear."

"I have to admit, I wouldn't want to live through another bad storm. The tropical depression we endured the last fall we lived here was bad enough. I never want to live through a hurricane. The fact they rarely have hurricanes in Boston was one of its strongest points for me to move there." Bella tried to smile, but she could feel her lips trembling. "Well, other than my husband works there. I love snow, but Boston winters can be brutal."

Mr. Kritikos patted her back again. "I understand Miguel has been an immense help at Biozyme through all of this pandemic. Rumor is he was the person responsible for their excellent vaccine."

Bella blushed as she shrugged. "Miguel says it was a team effort."

Mr. Kritikos chuckled. "Ah, but Miguel is the head of the team. Was the tropical storm we had here the last fall any worse than the long, tedious months you had to be sequestered because of this awful virus? Anywhere you go, anywhere you live, there will always be problems. It will always be up to you to find your happiness, as you did here."

This time, her grin was real. "Now, how could you know I found happiness here?"

"First, you married the man you love. Second, you found this fine establishment. Third, you come back often to see us." His dark eyes twinkled again with mischief as both girls laughed.

"Fair enough. And I get to see my sister whenever I visit," Bella mused, and then bit back tears again. "Could I really move all the way to Cairo? Good lord, it was hard enough to move to Boston. And how could I leave Elizabeth and Mom? And Daddy, Ronan, Sara, and Dara. I would be so far away from everyone if we move to Egypt. Heck, I'd be so far from all my friends and family."

"You are a strong woman, Bella. You could manage the move. It is the chance of a lifetime. We managed quite well when we moved here from Greece, and we spoke no English," said Mr. Kritikos.

"You might have to still fly to Galveston to accompany me to my eye appointments," Elizabeth said, her voice gravelly with unspoken emotion.

"Miguel already promised I could come back every two months if he takes the new job. Mom, Sara, or Dara will come in between. Sara lives near Houston, so it should be easy for her to come."

"If Jackson will let her come. He keeps her on a tight rein," answered Liz.

Bella gave another tremulous smile. "Well, we all know Jackson can be a controlling ass. I have no idea what she sees in him. Anyway, Miguel is supposed to decide by the weekend if he accepts the new job."

Liz frowned. "So soon? Why?"

Bella shrugged. "Biozyme needs to know whether they have a director, or they need to continue their search. And we need to get hunting for a place to live if we are going to move. I understand the housing market is smoking hot in the Cairo area right now. Miguel would make a trip over to scope it all out and conduct some preliminary house hunting. We might wind up buying a house with me touring it on zoom. I'm not sure how I feel about buying a house by zoom."

"Then wait until you get to Cairo to select a home if you guys decide to move. Buying a home is a major decision. You should be involved in making such a crucial decision."

"I agree, even if we have to rent at first. And believe me, I am not crazy about renting, nor am I wild about moving before this baby is born."

"I don't blame you. Well, if you don't find something to buy at first, you will find something in a few months. I would rent if I didn't find what I wanted. It feels like Miguel is pushing you into this move."

Bella did not reply as she began chewing on her lip.

Liz frowned. After a minute, she changed the subject. "Hey, you need to come over to the bar Friday afternoon."

Liz grinned and took a sip of her Pinot Grigio.

Bella tilted her head to study her beautiful sister. "Why? I thought Mom and Dara were coming to talk baby shower. Can I be there and listen to the talk? Or is something else happening Friday?"

Liz quickly chewed and swallowed the bite of dolmas. She washed it down with another sip of the delicate white wine. "A ghost hunter is coming."

Bella choked on her iced tea. "You've got to be kidding. Do they know— "

"I have a resident spook? The word is getting around town the place is haunted."

Mr. Kritikos sat the salad plate down before Bella and placed the fried shrimp platter in front of Elizabeth. "Oh, yes, all of the old-timers realize you have a ghost at your club. Not everyone has seen him, or talked with him, but his hijinks are well known. It surprised me when your father bought the place for you."

Bella and Elizabeth looked at each other before they burst into laughter. "Poppa was delighted to learn Johnny haunts the Bone Yard. He gets along quite well with Johnny. Captain Johnny is excited about the ghost hunter coming Friday. I expect some outlandish behavior from him."

"Oh, he'll give you outlandish if anyone would. Can you imagine? He was a pirate with Jean LaFitte," said Mr. Kritikos.

"Don't call him a pirate. Johnny will tell you he was a privateer." Elizabeth rolled her eyes.

Bella shook her head as she tapped her cheek with a finger, deep in thought. Finally, she pointed her finger at Liz. "Nope. Someone must tell the ghost hunter we think Captain Johnny was a pirate with Jean LaFitte so this fellow will ask Johnny about the LaFitte brothers. They established Campeche, which was the original name of Galveston."

Elizabeth burst out laughing. "You are so naughty, sis. You are supposed to be the sweet, serious, dependable sister, but you concoct the most outlandish stunts we pull. What a fabulous idea! Johnny loves to reminisce about the LaFitte brothers, the Battle of New Orleans, and how they came to establish a settlement here."

Bella blushed. "You give me more credit than I deserve, but I enjoy pushing limits. It's difficult to be the eldest child who your parents expect to be the 'good example' for all the other kids. Just think, Liz. Captain Johnny must have been at least ninety years old at the Battle of New Orleans."

Liz shook her head. "He told me he was ninety-five at the Battle of New Orleans. We should urge the psychic to ask Johnny how he died. Johnny never tires of telling how a whore murdered him when he was nearly one hundred years old."

Bella giggled. "Ooh, yes, we really must encourage the discussion about the LaFitte brothers. If he would only talk to Mom. She would have her next best seller."

Liz nodded. "I agree. But who knows? Maybe he will talk to her someday. He is reluctant to say much to her because Kirk is my Poppa. I write notes all the time of the stories he tells me, but I don't have Mom's flair for words. I should give Mom my notes about Johnny's stories this weekend. The ghost hunter fellow is coming to the club at 3 p.m. on Friday and should take an hour at the most. I cannot imagine Johnny would tolerate conversation with a psychic longer than an hour. Then, we can plan your baby shower from about 4 until the evening crowd comes in. We have Krazy Kilt Karaoke Night this Friday-"

Bella pushed back, shaking her head and her hands. "No. NO. I will not be the featured pregnant girl in one of your Krazy Kilt Karaoke productions again, Liz. I played the role when I was pregnant the last time. No. Can. Do. Besides, Miguel finishes this blasted seminar Friday evening. I will come, but I cannot stay too long. I want to go out with my honey. He promised me dinner at the Saltwater Grill."

"Aw, come on, Bella, be a good sport. You were so adorable the last time when we sang 'I'm getting married in the morning.' People still talk about the way you smoothed your hands over your 'burgeoning baby belly'."

"Another newspaper writer I could learn to hate," Bella said as she grimaced.

Elizabeth nodded as she continued. "You with your big ol' baby bump, singing you were getting married the next day. It was hilarious."

Bella shook her head. "Oh, good grief, girl. Look, I will come if you don't make me sing. Let Dara sing. She is the Winslow kid who has the exquisite voice."

"Don't put yourself down. You have a perfectly nice singing voice, too. At least, you don't sing like Charlie." Elizabeth snickered.

Bella made a gagging noise. "Just because poor Charlie sings like a bovine in labor. My lord, how can anyone be so tone-deaf? But don't make fun of my brother. I miss him so much. Hmm. I wonder how Kelly and he are doing in England."

She took another bite of her salad.

Liz frowned. "*Your* brother? Charlie is *my* brother, too. Even Mom says he couldn't carry a tune in a bucket."

"Well, you have a different Daddy." Bella smirked again.

"Ha! No, not really. Our Daddy adopted the three of us. However, my Poppa showed up and now I have a relationship with him, too. Jealous?"

Bella shuddered. "Yuck! Heck, no. I could never be Kirk's daughter after he kissed me like he did when we picked him up at the Beech Bottom Trailhead."

Bella wiped her lips as if she were wiping off the offensive kiss. She tossed her hand down as if to throw the unwanted kiss away. She looked at Liz, and they both burst into laughter.

"You need to tell me the story," Mr. Kritikos urged.

"Why?" asked Elizabeth as she gasped for breath.

He crossed his arms and winked at the young women. "So, I have something to hold over Kirk and Richard's heads the next time I see them."

The girls broke into laughter again. "Kirk's ship sank in a storm. Everyone thought he was dead. Mom and Daddy went to court and had him legally declared dead. And then, twelve years after his ship sank, he showed up, looking for Mom." Bella took another bite of her salad. "Anyway, the last time he saw me, I was about five years old. When he showed up, I was seventeen. I walked in, and he thought I was Mom. The dad-blasted idiot man grabbed and kissed me like there was no tomorrow. The tongue down my throat was too much."

She made a gagging sound as Liz howled with laughter.

"I never saw Bella so furious in all her life. Her face turned red as a raspberry. She reared back and slapped the snot out of Kirk. Literally. About then, Mom came in. Poor Mom had pneumonia and looked like death warmed over. Once Mom got over the shock of seeing Kirk trying to stick his tongue down Bella's throat, she explained he laid the lip lock on Bella, not Mom. I never saw a man look so kerfuffled in all my life."

The girls both laughed. Mr. Kritikos looked confused. "What is this word, kerfuffle?"

Bella struggled to stop laughing. "I should have said he looked gob smacked. Kerfuffle means it's a big mess. Gob smacked means someone looks totally stunned. Of course, the way I used 'kerfuffle' meant 'messed up.'"

"Your Southern expressions confuse me sometimes." Mr. Kritikos scratched his head as both girls giggled.

"I'm sorry, Mr. Kritikos. Anyway, Mom and Kirk tell everyone they are divorced. It's simpler than explaining 'we thought my Poppa died and he was declared legally dead, but he didn't really die and then he came here years later," said Elizabeth as she pointed her fork at Bella's plate. "Hey, Bella, can I have your last shrimp?"

Bella glowered at Liz and moved her plate away from her sister. "No. It's *my* grilled shrimp. Eat your fried ones. And I hate your metabolism. You can eat anything you want, whenever you want it, and never gain a freaking ounce. I gain weight looking at food."

Elizabeth's shrugged. "You need to dance more. It works the pounds right off me."

"Hmm. Find me a dance studio in Boston. You know, for the hopelessly uncoordinated sisters of excellent dancers."

They both grew silent, as they remembered Elizabeth's accident.

"Hey, not everyone can dance their way off a New York stage, break their leg, and learn they couldn't see the edge of the stage because they were going blind at age twenty." Liz tried to sound upbeat.

Wordless, Bella reached over and laid a hand on top of Liz's trembling hand. "It'll be okay, Liz. You'll see."

Elizabeth tried to smile. "I'll see, hmm? Interesting choice of words. Well, I used to be a great dancer. I enjoy teaching ballet to the little girls at a local dance studio here in Galveston. The doctors say I should have noticed I had trouble seeing in bright lights before I danced off the stage. The bright lights on the stage sure did a job on me the night I fell."

"Well, thank God above for these intraocular injections. You are far too young to go blind, pretty Elizabeth." Mr. Kritikos sounded subdued.

"And we pray for a cure," Bella said, as she struggled to sound upbeat. She hated it when Liz sounded so hopeless, so lost. "Miguel told me the Mankindus group received orphan designation for M1-100, to treat Stargardt disease. He hopes their receipt of orphan designation for M1-100 signals progress is being made toward a cure. Miguel works with their parent company in Boston. Biozyme has been doing important research into the disease."

Elizabeth rolled her eyes. "Oh, you make me so feel much better after the doctor used me as a human guinea pig again today. Nothing is more exhilarating than having someone stick needles full of experimental medication into my eyeballs. Besides, Miguel works with viruses, not with congenital abnormalities like Stargardt disease. And it looks like you guys will move to Cairo."

"Those intraocular shots are no longer considered experimental. They have proven to significantly slow down the progression of the disease. Miguel knows people working on Stargardt disease at both locales. And, besides, if the shots save your vision..." Bella's soft voice dropped off.

Elizabeth nodded. "Yeah, yeah, I know, I know. I've heard all the promotional pep talks about the medication. Now, let's talk about something more pleasant. What shall we do Friday when the ghost hunter comes? Should Johnny be on good behavior, or should he act outrageously?"

"Oh, he should most definitely behave outrageously. Problem is, no one can see him or hear him with any consistency except Kirk and you. Mr. Kritikos, I simply adore this salad dressing. I need to take a bottle or two back home with me." Bella closed her eyes as she savored the flavor.

"I can ship a case of bottles to you if you prefer. Some of us can see or hear your pirate ghost. I can hear Captain Johnny, but I have never seen him. Ah, I would love to see him! Ask Captain Johnny to reveal himself to the ghost hunter." Mr. Kritikos' eyes twinkled with mischief.

"Oh, sure. Like he would manifest if I asked him to do it," Elizabeth retorted. She rolled her eyes at Mr. Kritikos.

Mr. Kritikos smiled. "Then, you must tell him firmly not to manifest himself to the man. You know he can be stubborn and is likely to behave differently than you might suggest to him."

Liz's eyes lit up. "What a great idea, Mr. Kritikos! Hey, come over Friday. Maybe Johnny will get mad enough to manifest himself while the ghost hunter is there."

"I will come if I can get someone to watch the restaurant for me. I would not want to miss the manifestation of Captain Jolly Johnny English."

They all laughed.

Liz's eyes narrowed as they sparkled with mischief. "Yes, please come over Friday, Mr. Kritikos. I think you can help us push Johnny's buttons."

Davos Kritikos grinned. "I will try my best to come. It would be my greatest pleasure."

Chapter 3
Galveston
Captain Jolly Johnny English

Friday afternoon, Bella entered her sister's elite club and slipped over to the table where she knew Captain English usually sat. She nodded towards Captain Johnny and took a seat across from the ghost's favorite spot. She glanced over at the bar, where an enthusiastic older fellow stood chatting to Liz, explaining the whole kit and caboodle about this EVP stuff. Liz appeared to be studiously listening to the old fellow, but Bella could see Liz struggling to contain her grin. Bella leaned forward to hear what they were saying.

The bartender, Dave, slipped over to Bella and handed her a tall glass of mineral water. "He's been standing there and talking with Liz for a few minutes, basically explaining this EVP method. He's a captivating character."

Bella nodded as she squeezed a lime into the glass and sipped the ice-cold water. "Thanks, Dave. Has he started recording yet? Or asking any questions?"

Dave shook his head. "Not yet, but he keeps glancing over towards Captain Johnny. This investigator might be able to discern Johnny's presence for once."

Bella shrugged. "We'll see. We have certainly seen a passel of wanna-be's pass through here in quest of spirits."

Dave chuckled. "Ain't it the gospel truth?"

Dave wiped up a small spill and then returned to wait on other customers.

The paranormal investigator glanced over towards Captain Johnny again and frowned. He studied his machine for a few minutes before he walked over and sat down at the table where Captain Johnny liked to hang out. The captain arched a brow and grinned at Bella as the man took a seat. The paranormal investigator nodded towards Captain Johnny.

"My name is Rick Jones. I am a paranormal investigator and a medium. I talk with spirits. I typically communicate with spirits using this method called Electronic Voice Phenomena, or 'EVP.' I have been told one or more spirits live here at Nefertiti's Bone Yard. If there are any spirits here, I would like to talk with you via EVP."

"I think he is full of malarkey," said Captain Johnny, his voice low but audible to Bella.

Bella cut her eyes over towards the chair in the corner. "Then try him. See what he can do, Captain."

Mr. Jones whirled around to face Bella. "What did you say?"

She shrugged. "I wasn't talking to you."

He studied her for a minute. "Who were you talking to?"

"Just talking to hear myself talk, I guess. Why?"

He continued to study her. "Uh-huh. Of course."

Mr. Jones walked around to the chair in the corner and began talking again. "You and I both know the pretty girl is trying to distract me from you, sir. I would love to talk with you. A spirit named Marisa told me you frequent this place. She said you have lots of stories. She also asked me to tell you she is sorry for what happened the last time you two were here. Does her comment make any sense to you? Are you willing to talk to a student of the paranormal?"

Bella gasped as Johnny's features briefly shimmered in sight. She cut her eyes at Elizabeth. "Uh, Liz..."

Liz nodded and patted her sister's hand as she whispered her reply. "Yeah, I saw it."

"Of course, my good fellow. You say Marisa sent you?"

Me. Jones blinked. "Yes, sir, she did. I'm honored you showed yourself to me this afternoon. I understand materialization uses an enormous amount of energy. It will not hurt my feelings if you choose not to materialize again."

"Thank you, good sir. I take it you will not care if I shimmer in and out then. What did you want to know? Something about my life? Or something about the years since? Or something about your future?"

Jones smiled and pulled up the chair next to Captain Johnny. "I never want to know about my future. I know someday I will die. Eventually, I will go on to another life. Have you been here long?"

"Hmm... I'm not sure. It is hard to tell time when one is in this plane. Bella, have I been here long?"

"Yes, Captain Johnny. You have remained earthbound over 200 years."

Mr. Jones gave a sharp look to Bella. "So, you can see him?"

She shook her head. "Not with any consistency. I could see him today when he first spoke to you. Only Liz can see him anytime he manifests. However, I can hear him. You can, too, right?"

"With the machine, I can communicate with spirits and understand them any time one wishes to speak with me. But I can hear Captain Johnny's spoken words. I also saw him manifest into vision once. Is it unusual to see and hear Captain English?"

Mom and Dara nodded before Mom spoke. "I heard him once or twice when he was furious. I never saw him manifest before today."

"Me, too," Dara whispered. "He scares me."

Oh, I'm sorry, Dara, darling. But then again, aren't ghosts supposed to frighten people?" Johnny asked.

"Behave yourself, John," Elizabeth said. "I warned you--"

"Warned me? Oh, I don't think so, Elizabeth. You know I behave as I please. So, you can hear me, can you, Mr. Jones?"

Mr. Jones sat down his recorder. He leaned forward, although they figured he could not see Johnny. "Yes, sir, and my machine will record our conversation. I take it you will talk with me?"

"Clever, aren't you? Well, I am impressed the man can hear me, and he is not running out of here like a terrified child."

Mr. Jones leaned back and laughed. "I am rarely scared of spirits. Fascinated, but not afraid."

"Then I must make my best effort to scare you," Johnny said with a sly grin. He winked at Bella.

Mr. Jones laughed again. "Hit me with your best shot, man. Hey! I didn't mean you should literally hit me. And, no, I'm not scared, but I am royally pissed, you devilish old reprobate."

Mom, Dara, and Bella all grew silent at Mr. Jones' words. Only Elizabeth reacted.

"Captain English, I told you, no shenanigans today. You cut it out, or you need to leave."

"Oh, no, my dear, he is just being himself. Quite a bully when you were alive, weren't you? And you claim to be the renowned pirate, Captain Jolly Johnny English. I don't think so. Captain English might slit your throat while you both laughed over a good joke, but he was not a bully. You can't scare me. You are dead, I'm alive, and you have no power over me. Now, cut out this nonsense and leave these women alone!" Mr. Jones shouted.

Just then, Miguel walked into the bar. As everyone stared at him with blank stares, he blinked. "Uh, did I interrupt something? Richard said you guys were all over here."

Bella clamored up from the chair and rushed over to her husband. "Oh, darling, I didn't think you would finish your seminar at UTMB this early. Is Daddy in town, too?"

He shook his head. "No, but he called to make sure your mom and Dara got here okay. I told him I would come over when I got out of the research lab, and I would see what was going on." He glanced over towards the corner. "Oh, hello, Captain Johnny. Have you been taking care of our girls while I've been working?"

"Yes, indeed, Dr. Vargas. Someone must look after them, you know. Have you met Mr. Jones yet?" asked the jovial pirate specter.

"No, I can't say I have. I'm Dr. Miguel Vargas, Bella's husband. It's a pleasure to meet you, sir." Miguel extended a hand to Rick Jones.

Mr. Jones grabbed Miguel's hand with a firm handshake. "Nice to meet you, too, Doc. I am a paranormal investigator. It's interesting to see so many of you can see and hear the ghostly resident. I have been interviewing the spirit who claims to be Captain John English."

"He *is* Captain English," Bella said with a terse frown.

Mr. Jones smiled. "Thank you, Mrs. Vargas. Captain English, were you sometimes called Jolly Johnny English?"

"Oh, indeed I was, my good man. Why?"

Mr. Jones chuckled. "Well, sir, let me apologize for doubting your word and for losing my temper. I should have remembered: spirits don't lie."

"Apology accepted, Mr. Jones. You're human, and humans tend to err."

Johnny made a big flourish with one hand as he bowed to Jones.

Mr. Jones chuckled. "Well, this is the first time a spirit ever bowed to me. Thank you for manifesting in my presence. Captain, you are well known to students of privateers and pirates today. I understand you were a privateer, and you hailed from Ireland. How did you wind up on the Gulf Coast of Texas?"

As the paranormal investigator and the two-hundred-year-old ghost began chatting, Miguel slipped over to Bella. He gave her a quick kiss. "I didn't expect this. Johnny likes Mr. Jones. How long have they been chatting?"

Bella shrugged. "Not too long. Why?"

He pulled her close and kissed her again. "Are you ready to go yet? Maybe we could go grab some dinner with your mom and sister."

Elizabeth walked over and leaned down to hug Miguel. "It's good to see you, Miguel. Hey, this is Krazy Kilt Karaoke Night. Want to join in the family fun?"

He laughed, as if suddenly self-conscious. "You just love to embarrass me, don't you, Liz? What did you have in mind for tonight's humiliation?"

She laughed and hugged him again. "I thought we could perform a medley of songs about doctors. We could start with Doctor, Doctor-"

He shook his head. "I hate that song. What else?"

Her shoulders slumped as a frown slashed across her face. After a minute, she grinned. "I've got it! How about Doctor My Eyes?"

Miguel's eyes narrowed as a smile played upon his lips. "The Jackson Browne song?"

She nodded as she beamed at her brother-in-law.

"Who's singing? Bella? Will you sing it to me?" he turned to ask his wife.

Bella sighed but she nodded agreement. "Sure, I'll sing it to you. But Dara is the better singer."

"We'll all sing," interjected Dara, her tawny eyes sparkling with excitement.

Miguel grinned. "I'll make you a deal, ladies. If Bella will join in on singing the songs to me, I'll play the doctor."

"Oh, my, Jones, did you hear them? The lad is going to play doctor with our Bella. How adorable." Johnny grinned at his newfound friend.

"Yeah, you better shut up, John, unless you want to sing, too." Miguel pulled Bella into his arms for quick kiss as he struggled not to laugh at the ghost.

Elizabeth smiled broadly as she chuckled. "Now, a singing ghost would be fun."

Captain Johnny scowled at the crowd of young people. "I don't think so, Elizabeth."

"Harrumph. I could record it, Captain English. The audience would not hear you unless you wanted them to hear your voice." Mr. Jones sounded enthusiastic at the prospect of recording the ghost singing with the youngsters.

Johnny's eyes narrowed as he tapped his chin with a ghostly finger. "Hmm… your suggestion is rather tempting. I might be persuaded if I don't have to manifest myself to everyone."

Mr. Jones nodded, bouncing about in his chair as he urged Johnny to take part in the fun. "Most people don't understand presentation and manifestation take enormous amounts of energy. If you need to pop out to recharge your energy, I will understand. However, if you are interested, we could record it right over here in this corner on EVP, just like we have been recording our conversation. I will sit here with you, and we could join them singing the bits we like. I used to perform some in nightclubs in my younger days."

Johnny's eyes alit with excitement. "Now, your idea sounds like great fun! I like you, Jones."

Mr. Jones chuckled. "You may call me Rick, Captain Johnny. I would be honored."

Captain Johnny thought about Mr. Jones' words for a minute before answering. "Hmm… I think I would prefer to call you Jonesie."

Rick Jones laughed. "That'll work for me."

Liz grinned at the ghost and his new friend. "I thought we could finish with Bad Case of Loving You. What do you think, guys? Think this will set off the Krazy Kilt Karaoke Night with a flair?"

"Definitely. But tell me, must I wear a kilt? Because this Mexican laddie does not have a kilt, milady. And are you lovely ladies going to dance like the girls in the Robert Palmer video?" Miguel pulled Bella close to his side.

"Of course, we will dance the Robert Palmer routine. Dave is wearing his kilt, and I wore this little kilted skirt." Liz twirled around to show off the short skirt and her long legs. "The cocktail server is wearing one, too. Kilts are optional for everyone else, so you are safe, *amigo*. So, will you join in our performance, Miguel?"

Miguel burst out laughing. "I guess you could call the tartan mini-skirt you're wearing a kilt. I will take part on one condition. After we do those, can we perform Simply Irresistible?"

Liz clapped her hands in enthusiasm. "Oh, hell, yes! This is going to be so much fun. Hmm... Maybe we want to perform Addicted to Love after Simply Irresistible and before we sing Bad Case of Loving You."

"Sounds great, honey. Especially if you will sing with us." Bella beamed down at her husband as she rubbed his back.

"It'll be my pleasure. Anything is better than dealing with this new strand of Covid19. Hey, Liz, did you hear the mayor is talking about shutting down restaurants and clubs again next week?"

Liz nodded, suddenly all business again. "Yes, I heard the announcement, which was one reason I thought we would have Krazy Kilt Karaoke Night tonight. Plus, you guys are going back home to Boston soon, and you will not be here much longer. I wanted us to have a chance to all sing at Krazy Kilt Karaoke Night before you go home to Bean Town. So, we start with Doctor My Eyes, then go to Simply Irresistible, then Addicted to Love, before we end with Bad Case of Loving You. We have a great mix of Robert Palmer with a touch of Jackson Browne. We know the words and dance moves to all the tunes. Does anyone want to rehearse before the crowd comes in?"

As they all stood around talking about preparing for the evening performance, Mr. Jones pulled a chair up closer to where Captain English lounged. "Is it always this energized around these young folks?"

"Yes. See why I like to be here? Why would I go anywhere else when I can be here with the Winslow and Vargas families? Their energy almost gives me a new life."

Jones nodded. "Oh, yes, I get it. But tell me how you ended up in Galveston. It's a long way from Ireland. I understand you hailed from there."

"Oh, heavens, I haven't been to Ireland in hundreds of years. I swore I wasn't going home until I became rich. Tragically, I made my fortune and lost it several times over before I would reach home. But, to answer your question, I came here with the Lafitte brothers. We fought first at the Battle of New Orleans in '15. When they came to Galveston a few months later, I accompanied them."

Jones's brow furrowed. "How old were you then? I guess the better question would have been to ask when you were born."

Johnny chuckled. "I was born in 1720. In late 1815, after the Battle of New Orleans, we agreed to work as spies for Mexico against Spain. The two countries were embroiled in the Mexican War of Independence. Jean was sent here, and I came with him. Jean would be the governor over the area. In exchange, he received letters of marque from Mexico, which allowed him to attack and capture enemy ships. You understand Mexico was at war with Spain. However, Jean's letters differed from most issued."

"Oh? How so, sir?"

Johnny smiled as he rocked back in the chair. "His letters of marque gave us permission to attack ships from any nation. His admiralty counsel, of which I was a senior member, legalized all prizes."

Rick Jones' mouth fell open in surprise. "Captain Johnny, meaning no disrespect, but didn't those letters of marque essentially legalize piracy?"

Captain Johnny shimmered into view long enough to allow Jones to see him twirl his mustache and smile. "Devilishly clever plan, wasn't it?"

Jones nodded. "As an old sailor myself, I admit it was a brilliant move."

"We thought so. We developed this area as the base for our privateering. It comprised Mexican territory and was out of the authority of the United States. Lafitte named the community *Campeche*. In less than a year, the colony grew to 200 men and several women. Our headquarters was a two-story building facing the harbor where we made landings. Jean painted it red, and called the building *La Maison Rouge*, the red house. "

Jones leaned forward. "Tell me more, Captain Johnny."

Johnny paused for a minute or two before he relaxed again. "I'll tell you the truth without you having to ask the question. Jean forged those letters of marque allowing him to attack ships from all nations. Oh, Mexico gave him letters of marque all right, but they were not as all-encompassing as the letters of marque which Jean then crafted. He was a wily old sailor. But I digress. Now, to get back to your question, I died in 1817. I was 97 years old when I left my mortal shell to become a spirit."

"Johnny, your story is fascinating. How did you die? If you don't mind me asking."

Johnny shrugged and flicked more imaginary lint from his ghostly sleeve. "I died most ignominiously. I was stabbed in the brothel above this bar by one of the working girls. Marisa had no call to become so jealous that she would kill me. I told her many times I was already married. This was always one of my favorite spots. I suppose I will endlessly traverse the earth, much like I did when I was alive. However, I always liked Galveston. I've been here for a while now."

Jones frowned and leaned closer to Captain Johnny. He chewed his lip as he paused before he finally voiced his question. "Do you want to travel endlessly as a spirit? Or would you like to move on?"

"Hmm. I'm not sure I want to meet the Big Man Upstairs. I fear He might well send me south if you catch my drift." Johnny sounded regretful and rubbed his chin whiskers.

Jones shook his head with a touch of impatience. "No, no, no. The spirits above have a plan which does not include punishment. They provide each of us another chance to perform better in a future life. I guess you could say they give us each a chance to be born again."

Johnny sat up straighter, his eyes sparkling. "Born again? Hmm. I wonder if I could have another chance at love with Tamsin if I am born again. Or did I lose our relationship when I never returned to her?"

Jones' eyes narrowed as he studied the old ghost. "Who was Tamsin? Why don't you tell me more of your story?"

Johnny chuckled, but it did not sound as if he were amused. "Well, it was all a long time ago. Perhaps I should just leave it all in the past. Although, I might chance everything if I could have another day with her. Elizabeth reminds me of my Tammy. Same fire and indomitable spirit. Odd, since they are not related."

Mr. Jones' eyes narrowed. "Are you sure they aren't related?"

Johnny nodded. "Quite sure, my good fellow. Fancy – Mrs. Winslow – is related to Tamsin, as are Bella and Dara. But my fair Elizabeth is not related."

Liz wondered what the paranormal investigator and Johnny discussed with such fervor. As the two men sat chatting, Liz stood up straighter. Her mouth went dry as she noticed a tall, muscular, darkly tanned man enter the bar. Now she understood why Mom insisted she dress up tonight. Liz was glad she had her nails done and her hair braided into the fresh style before she came to work. Wow, he still gave meaning to the phrase, 'tall, dark and awesome.' He continued to wear his dark, coppery brown, curly hair cut short, although she could see the beginnings of gray at his temples. He now wore a mustache and beard which were turning gray as well. The short, neatly trimmed facial hair only enhanced his aristocratic looks. She forced herself to smile as the handsome man strolled across the bar towards her. He took off his shades, and her heart lurched at the sight of his striking hazel eyes narrowing while he adjusted to the dim lights in the bar. She always loved the sparkle in his gorgeous eyes. She used to swear he could never look any better, but the blasted man looked better than homemade chocolates on a silver serving dish. Liz straightened up and smoothed her sleek knit black crop top and her short tartan skirt. She gave her long braids a casual toss back over her shoulder.

"Dr. Hotep, what a surprise. I didn't know you were in town or that we would see you this evening. Miguel, you didn't tell me Dr. Hotep was in town."

Miguel grinned as he glanced at them. "Oops, sis, my bad. Ari is here for the medical conference I have been attending. Glad you could make it tonight, bro'. Hey, Liz, I bet you could sing 'Doctor, Doctor' to Ari."

Liz cut a dirty glare at her brother-in-law. "Hmm. Maybe so."

Ari Hotep smiled. "If Elizabeth will sing it to me, it would be my pleasure to play the Doctor."

"Oh, how adorable. Miguel will play doctor with Bella, and this handsome young man wants to play doctor with our Elizabeth." Johnny's voice sounded droll.

Mr. Jones chuckled. "So, it would appear."

Chapter 4
Galveston - Elizabeth

Liz felt her cheeks redden at Johnny's suggestive words. Incorrigible as always. Sometimes being able to hear her resident ghost was a royal pain in the northbound end of a southbound ass. She cleared her throat as she shook her head in frustration. "Dave, give Dr. Hotep a Dr. Pepper, please. Isn't Dr. Pepper your drink of choice, Ari?"

Ari Hotep nodded. "Yes, it is when I can find it. It's great to see you again after all this time, Elizabeth. I hope you don't mind Miguel asked me to join all of you here tonight. I see why your club is called Nefertiti's Bone Yard. As I told you in New York, you look enough like Queen Nefertiti to be her, re-incarnated."

Liz felt her cheeks heat again from embarrassment. It always made her feel uncomfortable to be compared to the woman who epitomized feminine beauty. "Uh, yeah. I thought I told you my Poppa claims my mother looked just like the bust of Queen Nefertiti. I understand her eyes were mahogany brown, like the Queen's eyes. Poppa says she was the most beautiful woman he ever knew. I don't see the resemblance. So, what brings you to Galveston Island?"

Ari looked shocked. "Oh, I'm sorry. I understood this pretty lady is your mother. Hello, Mrs. Winslow. And while you are beautiful-"

"I do *not* look like Queen Nefertiti, with my strawberry blonde hair and blue-green eyes," Fancy Winslow finished with a wink and a grin. She arose and walked over to the doctor, to pull him into an affectionate hug. "It's great to see you again, Ari. I thought you realized I'm not Elizabeth's biological mother. I adopted Elizabeth the week before she turned three years old. Come over here and sit down with us."

Fancy pointed to the chair beside hers, sat back down, and took another sip of her ice-cold Chablis. Ari grinned and followed her to the table in the corner.

Liz followed them over to the table and cleared her throat. "My biological mother died when I was a baby. My Poppa later married Mom and she adopted me. She is the only Mom I ever knew. Believe me, I'm lucky to have Fancy Winslow as my mom. Let me introduce you to everyone. Obviously, you know Miguel and Bella."

Miguel held up a glass of beer to acknowledge his friend. "Guilty as charged. Hey, dude."

Bella smiled and reached over to hug Ari. "It's wonderful to see you again, Ari. Miguel told me you were here at the meetings, and you might drop by the club."

Liz looked shocked. "You knew he was here, too?"

Liz's unsaid meaning hung in the air between them. And you didn't warn me? When Liz saw Bella's cheeks turn red, she knew her sister felt embarrassed. Liz did not intend to let Bella off the hook.

Bella tried not to look Liz in the eye. "Uh… yeah."

"Really? You could not bother to mention to me that Ari Hotep was in town, and he just might drop by my club tonight?"

Bella cleared her throat and tried to shift away from the sensitive subject. "Um, Ari, did you meet our little sister four years ago?"

He tried to hide the grin threatening to slide across his face. Instead, he shook his head. "No, I don't believe I did. It's a pleasure to meet you, young lady."

Dara giggled as he bent to kiss her hand. "Thank you, Dr. Hotep. I'm Dara Winslow. My friends call me Dara."

He smiled. "And my friends call me Ari."

Dara tilted her head at the handsome doctor. "How did you meet my sister?"

Liz answered before Ari could. "Ari was one of the doctors who treated me when I danced merrily off the stage and broke my leg."

Dara looked fascinated. "You didn't tell me one of your doctors was young and hot."

Ari's eyes twinkled as he smiled. "Oh, really? Young and hot? Thank you, Dara."

Dara wasn't the only Winslow girl who ever thought you were hot, Liz thought as she rubbed her forehead. Dammit, she did not want a headache tonight, much less the vertigo which often accompanied the headaches she suffered since her fateful fall.

And then suddenly, Liz found herself lost in a deluge of memories.

Chapter 5
Elizabeth Remembers
Four years earlier in New York City

Liz sat impatiently on the bed, her fingers thrumming on the bed covering. She frowned as she glanced at her watch. "When can we leave, Mom? The orthopedic surgeon already said I can go."

Mom glanced nervously at the door. She nibbled her thumb nail as she walked over to the door. She peered into the hallway. "I don't know, baby girl. We are still waiting on the other specialists to release you, too. They had a lot of specialists look you over in the past week."

Liz slumped back against the pillows on the hospital bed. She out a sigh of disgust as she thumbed through a well-worn magazine. After a minute, she tossed the magazine aside. "Well, this sucks. I fall off the damned stage and break my leg. The producer cancelled my contract because I can't dance. I had surgery to put my damned leg back together. Now it has pins, rods, screws, and a metal plate in it. My doctor says I will need at least one more surgery to fix my leg. God knows I'll set off the x-ray machines in airports from now on. I have enough metal in my leg to build the Tin Man in titanium. My professional dancing career is already dust and it just started. I'm ready to blow this joint, and now some other specialist wants to see me before we can leave. Why? What else could go wrong?"

Mom glanced at Liz with worry written all over her face. She rubbed a trembling hand across her forehead, as if to rub away a headache. "I guess we will just wait and see, sweetheart."

Just then the door swung open and in walked the most exquisitely handsome man Liz had ever seen. This guy was tall, dark, and awesome. He wore his dark, curly hair cut short. His suntanned skin shone like burnished copper and his eyes sparkled like mystical orbs of amber. *Huh*, she thought. *Mystical orbs of amber? Mom's writing skills must be rubbing off on me.* She chuckled. *Nah. Mom would say the description was overdone. Or downright corny. But gosh, he has gorgeous eyes.*

"Miss Winslow? My name is Dr. Ari Hotep. I'm an ophthalmic specialist. I've been asked to see you today."

She sat up a little taller and smiled. "Well, hello, gorgeous. And where did you get your sexy accent?"

Mom sighed as she shut her eyes and shook her head. "Elizabeth..."

The handsome man stopped and blinked, as if startled by her unexpected flirtation. He finally grinned at her. "I attended secondary school and university in England, but I'm originally from Egypt. I've been asked to review some test results with you before you are discharged."

Liz could feel her heart hammer erratically in her chest. "Uh... I hoped you just came in here to flirt with me. You said you are with ophthalmology. I broke my leg. Why are you here?"

Dr. Hotep took a deep breath, and then stepped over to the X-ray reading machine as he clutched a set of films in his hands. He slipped a film in the machine and dimmed the lights in the room. "Miss Winslow, there has been a considerable concern because a dancer of your amazing talent danced right off the stage at Carnegie Hall. There have been neurological and ophthalmic consultations to ascertain the cause of your accident, not merely the result, although you did considerable damage to your leg in the fall."

Liz glanced at her mom, who kept her eyes averted from Liz. Worse yet, Mom studied the piece of fabric between her fingers as she rubbed it back and forth. It was never a good sign when Mom rubbed fabric. It always meant Mom wanted to disassociate from a stressful situation. "Mom, what's this all about?"

Mom looked up at her daughter and gulped. She glanced at the doctor. She walked over to Liz and draped an arm around her daughter's shoulders. "Dr. Hotep can explain it better than I can, baby girl."

Liz felt the blood drain from her face. This scared Mom. Poppa swore Mom was tougher than a raccoon riding a wild hog into battle a passel of possums. As a nurse practitioner, and cardiovascular surgical nurse, her mom coped with about everything in the OR with Daddy. It terrified Liz to see this issue seemed to scare Mom. "What is it? What's wrong?"

Dr. Hotep cleared his throat. "Ahem. Allow me to show you the optical coherence tomographic results. OCT helps doctors like me get sub-surface images of translucent or opaque materials at a resolution equivalent to a low-power microscope. It is essentially an 'optical ultrasound.' OCT provides reflections from within tissue to provide cross-sectional images."

His words shook Liz. She did not know what he meant, but this sounded bad. "Okay, put it in plain everyday English, Doc. Whatever you just said sounded like a bunch of medical mumbo jumbo to me. How and why does this OCT stuff apply to me? Why are you showing me this?" She rubbed her temples. "Gosh, I'm getting a horrible headache."

"I apologize. I'm getting ahead of myself. You have the initial stages of Stargardt disease. The lights in the theatre probably distorted your vision and caused you to fall."

Liz shook her head. "No. I don't know what this Stargardt disease is, but like I told the other doctors, it felt like the room was spinning. I never had that sensation before. They called it vertigo. Yeah, I was doing a series of turns across the stage, but --"

She caught the nervous looks her mother was casting as the handsome young doctor. "Okay, what are you guys not telling me?"

Mom cleared her throat and rubbed a hand across her face. "Are you sure? Are the test results definitive?"

He nodded. "I'm afraid so, ma'am. It has been confirmed with the DNA studies."

Mom covered her face with her hands and sighed. "Oh, dear God, no."

Liz gulped and took a deep breath. "Look, I don't know what this is all about, but I'm not liking the feel of this whole conversation. You guys are about twenty steps ahead of me. Let's start over. What is this Stargardt disease? Is it what made me so dizzy when I danced off the stage?"

"Yes, it probably caused your dizziness. Stargardt disease is a single-gene retinal disease, which causes a gradual deterioration of the macula. It is like macular degeneration --" began Dr. Hotep.

Liz paled at his words and began shaking her head. "No, no, no. Macular degeneration happens in old people. I'm only twenty."

"You are correct. However, Stargardt disease is caused by an inherited genetic mutation. It usually first become noticeable in people between seventeen and twenty-seven years of age. If you look here on the optical coherence tomography --"

Liz shook her head. "No, I don't need to see whatever you called those films. I won't understand what they mean anyway. I just need to know how we fix this."

Terrified, Liz looked at her mom, who averted her eyes. Liz took another deep breath and looked back at the flustered young doctor. "Dr. Hotel? Can we fix it?"

He shook his head. "My name is Hotep. It is an ancient Egyptian word that means 'peace.' I'm sorry, Miss Winslow, I know I am not bearing peaceful tidings this morning. There is no cure for Stargardt disease."

Liz felt lightheaded. The room flicked about in a dizzying rhythm she had experienced periodically since her fall. "Uh, the room is going all topsy turvy on me again, Mom. S-s-so wh-wh-what does it mean, Doc?"

"It means your vision will worsen until you become totally blind. Of course--"

"Wait a minute. Did you say… blind?" She began trembling and grabbed for her mother's hands. She blinked repeatedly as she struggled to hold back a deluge of tears. "Jesus Christ, man, you have the bedside manner of a drunken frog. N-n-no. I don't accept this. I-I-I refuse to accept it. This cannot be happening to me. I'm only twenty years old. A month ago, I was the lead dancer in a show. Now, I have a compound fracture of my leg, I lost my dancing contract, and this damned man waltzes in here to tell me I'm going blind."

She struggled not to cry. Or scream.

The handsome young doctor nodded, obviously flustered. "I'm sorry. I'm afraid it's true."

Liz pressed her hands to her mouth to keep from screaming. A tear trickled down one cheek as she squeezed her eyes shut, desperate to shut everything out. She could never remember much of the conversation after Ari Hotep uttered the word, 'blind.' Everything he said subsequently sounded like the teacher talking on Charlie Brown.

...

"Ari helped me learn to cope with my diagnosis. He explained the disease, and the options to delay the inevitable result. He's the one who insisted I wear the glasses with the yellow lenses, and to wear a broad-brimmed hat and dark sunglasses whenever I am outside in the sunlight."

Dara tried to laugh. "And here I thought it was just vanity when you started grabbing your shades and a big hat every time we go out the door."

Liz smiled at her younger sister and reached over to squeeze her hand. "Well, I can be pretty vain. Anyway, Ari administered my first intraocular injections. He held my hand as I cried. They can be painful, you know."

Dara paled and said nothing.

Ari cleared his throat. "And then I made a fatal error."

Dara's brow furrowed. "What did you do?"

He smiled as he reached over for Liz's hand. "I fell in love with your sister."

Liz could feel her cheeks heat with color. She gently slid her hand out from beneath Ari's hand. "Yeah. He's a big dope."

She cleared her throat and arose, to start around the bar, checking if patrons needed refills.

Fancy walked over to the chair where Ari sat, still staring after Liz. She patted him on the back as she slid into the seat next to him. "Give her some time, Ari."

Fancy Winslow's words stirred Ari back from staring after the beautiful young woman. He tried to smile. "Giving her more time hasn't worked. I gave her more time four years ago, Mrs. Winslow."

Fancy nodded. "I know. She has matured a lot in those years, but she didn't expect you to walk in here tonight. We were afraid to warn her you might drop by the club. We feared she might run again. Let her come to terms with your unexpected appearance. She never thought she would see you again once you returned home to Egypt."

Miguel shrugged. "She should have known she might run into him again. She knows we may move to Egypt. She said the other night how much she would love to see the Giza Plateau and the Karnak Temple Complex at Luxor. Didn't she think she might run into Ari when she came to see us?"

Bella punched him in the arm. "What makes you think she would come to see us in Egypt? Besides, Ari is not an archeologist. Just because Ari is Egyptian does not mean she would run into him if she visited us there."

Miguel patted Bella's hand. "She knows he works for Biozyme, doing Stargardt disease research. We will work at the same location. She is a smart woman. She should have figured that one out, easy."

Bella frowned. "Hmm. Come to think of it, why didn't they offer the job to you, Ari?"

Ari chuckled. "They did. I turned it down. My team may be onto a big breakthrough about the disease. I would not give up my research even for the directorship."

Bella's eyes widened in surprise. "Wow. You guys must be onto a big breakthrough."

Ari smiled at her. "We hope it will be."

"Yeah, well, he's not working with an infectious disease he might bring home and give to his family. None of us want to mention how my Bella caught Covid-19. We all know she might have caught it when I inadvertently brought a COVID-19 germ or two into our home. She got sick before the vaccine came out, and we damned near lost her." Miguel looked sick to his stomach.

Fancy shook her head, impatient with the conversation. "We have had this conversation a million times in the past two years, young man. Bella could have caught it anywhere. She could have caught it when she went to the grocery store, to the obstetrician, or when she walked down the street. She could have caught it anywhere. You cannot blame yourself." She looked over to her daughter. "And you cannot blame yourself, little miss. You went out rarely, usually only to your doctor's appointments. You wore a mask and latex gloves everywhere you went. You kept the house impeccably clean. I swear everything got wiped down with bleach at least once every day, and you must wash your hands at least a hundred times a day. Stuff happens. You cannot blame yourselves. Case closed."

Miguel took Bella's shaking hands into his and raised them to his lips, where he kissed them. "You hear your mom?"

Bella blinked back tears as she nodded, wordless. She knew there would be no more discussion on the subject once Mom uttered 'case closed.' As she tried to smile at her husband, he winked at her and kissed her hands again.

"It's easier said than done," Bella said a little quaver still in her voice. "Even if Mom says, 'case closed'."

Miguel nodded in agreement. "*De acuerdo, mi amor.*"

Bella leaned against his shoulder and struggled to contain her tears. "Sometimes, I think the women in this family never catch a break."

Fancy shrugged. "That used to be my theme song. If it were not for bad luck, I used to swear I had no luck at all."

"Gloom, despair, and misery on ye?" asked Miguel.

Fancy grinned. "Something like it, yeah. I changed my luck. None of us is stuck with bad luck, Bella. We can all claim better luck and better times. I had heart surgery. Went to college. Became a nurse. Married the love of my life. You recovered from Covid-19. You are pregnant again. Liz is getting the shots to help control her disease, and this big handsome man might be the one who finds the cure for Stargardt's disease. And he damned sure loves your sister, no matter what."

"That's what I keep telling Elizabeth, Mrs. Winslow," interjected the ghostly voice of Captain Johnny. "She is not stuck with bad luck. She can change her luck."

Fancy looked over, surprised to hear the ghost. "Why, Captain Johnny, you startled me. You rarely speak to me. Yes, she is not stuck with bad luck even with this horrible bit of luck about her vision. That handsome young doctor adores her. If she could only open herself up to the possibility of love and marriage."

"But as you know, my dear," murmured Johnny. "She can be exceptionally stubborn."

Ari's eyes widened in surprise as Johnny materialized beside him. "My God, it's a ghost."

Fancy's laugh sounded hollow. "It sure is, Ari. Welcome to Elizabeth's haunted bar. Allow me to introduce you to Captain John English. Captain Johnny, I would like to introduce you to Dr. Ari Hotep. I can't believe I can finally hear you after all this time and Ari could see and hear you right off the bat. Ari, we are discussing Liz's stubborn streak. Yes, she is much like her father. She can be stubborn as a mule."

Johnny's eyes narrowed as he studied Elizabeth. "Kirk's stubbornness kept him alive after the hurricane until I fished him out of the drink. I imagine young Dr. Hotep knows Elizabeth is stubborn as well. They share some significant history."

Fancy nodded again as she studied her daughter and Ari Hotep. "Captain Johnny, you are correct on both issues. Yes, Ari knows first-hand my daughter can be stubborn to the max. He learned about her stubbornness four years ago."

A hint of a smile plated on Johnny's aged lips. "Really? Pray continue, Mrs. Winslow. I eagerly await you recounting their story."

"Okay, but you must call me Fancy, Captain Johnny."

The spirit chuckled, amused by her banter. "Of course, Fancy, my dear. I would be delighted."

Chapter 6
Galveston - Fancy

My name is Fancy Winslow. My family and friends call me 'the storyteller,' because I have published some books. My story has already been written in *The McCarron's Daughter*, an incredibly sad tale of gloom and despair, and *Diary of the Reluctant Duchess*, where I tell the rest of my story and how I changed my luck to get my 'happy ever after' ending. Now, I want a 'happy ever after' ending for each of my children. Charlie, our oldest son, and Kelly found there happy ever after ending, but it took a lot of challenging work for them to get there. I wrote about their story in *The McCarron's Destiny*.

Liz and Ari met the day she was being discharged from the hospital in New York City. Poor Dr. Hotep was the person sent in to break the news to Elizabeth she was going blind. She told him he had all the diplomacy and polished bedside manner of a drunken frog. I felt sorry for the young man as he desperately tried to explain to Liz what Stargardt disease entailed. As he realized how his words impacted her, he struggled to soften the blow. He explained there were treatments to slow the progression of her illness. However, I could tell poor Liz heard little after he said the word, 'blind.'

I took her back to her apartment that afternoon, thinking we would pack her belongings and take her home to Texas. I was wrong. She was determined to stay in New York City. I never much cared for big cities, but Liz loved the hustle and bustle of the Big Apple.

Did I say she is stubborn? Nope. She is bone-headed, just like her dad. She did not want to leave the city she loved, and she insisted she would remain in New York.

The next day, Dr. Hotep showed up on her doorstep, armed with flowers. The cool, suave, debonair man before us tonight stood in Elizabeth's doorway sweating with nervous energy. There were beads of perspiration on his brow and his upper lip. I even noticed his hands were damp with perspiration as he shook my hand at the door. I tried not to cringe. Sweaty palms 'get' to me. I realized he desperately wanted to make amends for the bad start.

"I am so sorry for my dunderheaded explanation yesterday, Miss Winslow. I wanted to apologize in person for behaving like – "

"Like a drunken frog?" came her pert reply as she reached out for the flowers. She inhaled the rich scent from the lilies and then smiled up at the handsome young man standing before her. "Thank you, Doctor. This really was unnecessary. Please, come in."

"I'm not at all sure how a drunken frog behaves. I've never even seen a drunken frog," he stammered.

She chuckled. "No frogs in England?"

He blinked. I thought he looked unsure if she was teasing or what. "I am sure there are frogs, but I never saw one there. I don't know if English frogs ever get drunk. I know there are frogs along the Nile. They flourish every year after the annual rains, although the flooding we used to experience is controlled since Aswan High Dam was built. I've seen many frogs in Egypt, but I never saw a drunken frog. That is where I'm from. Egypt, I mean."

Her mouth fell agape at his words. "Are you serious? Wow, I never met anyone from Egypt before. Is it really hotter than hell there?"

I swear the girl asked the man that. I thought I would die of embarrassment.

He laughed, clearly self-conscious. "Well, I'm not sure how hot it gets in Hell. It gets insufferably hot in Egypt in the summer. It can be as cool as around 50 degrees Fahrenheit in the winter and as hot as about 125 degrees in the summer. Insufferably hot. It gets ridiculously hot at Luxor where my brother currently works. He especially complained of the heat in July and August. It should cool down to a modest 100 degrees Fahrenheit there pretty soon. I think it was 106 degrees at Luxor today. Anyway, I'm not sure how the temperature compares to the temperature in hell, but it gets hot. Listen, I apologize. I totally blew explaining your condition yesterday and I feel like an utter ass."

"An utter ass, huh?" She looked over at me. "I never heard anyone, but an Englishman use that phrase. Did you, Mom?"

I shook my head. "No, I may have called your father that a few times, but I never heard anyone who was not English besides your dad or me use it."

Ari looked intrigued. "Is your husband English, Mrs. Winslow?"

I shook my head. "No. Her dad and I are divorced. I admit I have called her father an utter ass and worse a few times. He's from Ireland and he is the most bone-headed man I ever met. She's just like him."

Liz rolled her eyes. "Thank you, Mother. Way to humiliate me. So, why did you come to the States, Dr. Hotup? Did I say your name right this time?"

He chuckled. "Close. It's Hotep. It has been a common name in Egypt for thousands of years. In fact, at least four pharaohs had 'hotep' in their names."

Liz looked surprised. "Oh, really? Okay, Doc, spill the beans. Are you related to some pharaoh? Can you walk like an Egyptian?"

She slid across the floor awkwardly with her casted leg as she attempted to perform the dance move. I cringed, fearful she would fall.

Ari burst out laughing, his intriguing eyes sparkling with amusement. "My brother, Levi, can perform that dance, but I never mastered it. He's an archeologist. He currently works with Dr. Hassan at the Saqqara pyramid. Levi swears we are related to some of the old pharaohs, but I tell him he's breathed in too much funerary dust in the tombs. There has been no DNA confirmation we are related to any of the mummies recovered to date, and they have recovered the mummies of at least two of the pharaohs with 'hotep' in their names."

"Aw, darn. I thought maybe you were related to King Tut," she replied with an exaggerated pout.

"You just like the Steve Martin song." I remember I grinned at her.

"King Tut," she sang, as she stood in place and tried to move back and forth like an Egyptian again.

Ari relaxed as he burst into laughter again. "I'm glad to see you are laughing today. I understood you had a sense of humor, especially for a lady with a nasty compound fracture of her leg."

"And you did not see any evidence I had a sense of humor yesterday." Liz quit trying to perform the dance and hobbled over to the couch. She bit back a moan as she lowered herself to the seat.

"No, but that's my fault. A person does not get told they are losing their vision every day. I handled it abominably. Like I said, I was an utter ass." He ducked his head sheepishly.

"Well, maybe not an *utter* ass. Hmm… I wonder what exactly makes an ass 'utter.' "

"Utter means complete, Liz," I told her.

She shrugged. "You tried to make amends yesterday. But you ought to work on your bedside manner, Doc." Liz grinned and winked at him.

He blushed. "I was assigned to tell you to gain some bedside experience. I plan to go into research in this field. I've been doing post-doctoral studies on the disease. You might have guessed I have not had a lot of experience one-on-one with revealing the diagnosis to my patients. Oh, I have been in the room with the attending physician whilst he gave the unwelcome news."

Liz arched an eyebrow. "Did you really say 'whilst'?"

He blushed again. "Yes. I picked it up during the years I lived in England. I usually see patients in the clinic for post-diagnosis treatment. My mentors thought I needed some first-hand experience breaking the unwelcome news to a patient. Unfortunately, you landed the resident with no actual bedside experience on this extremely important matter. Ironically, I have extensive lab experience diagnosing the disease and a fair amount of experience administering the meds. I'll be the one to administer your first intraocular injections to you tomorrow."

Liz brightened up. "Oh, really?"

He tried to laugh. "Don't look so happy. You may decide to hate me after you receive the injections."

She gulped. "Why?"

He tried to smile. "I won't lie. It's not a comfortable procedure. But your mom and I will be right there with you, and we both care about you. I may have sounded like a dolt yesterday, but I care about my patients. I don't want anyone to hurt. I don't want anyone to go blind."

As his voice broke off, Liz reached out instinctively to clasp his hand. "I know you don't want me to go blind. Your concern is obvious. Otherwise, you would not have come over here today to make amends. I'll be okay. I promise. I'm tougher than I look."

He struggled to smile at her, and patted her hand still placed over his. "Thank you, Miss Winslow. Then, I will see you both tomorrow afternoon.

Be sure to bring sunglasses. In fact, you need to always wear sunglasses when you go outside during the day. It will help protect your vision."

She nodded and gave him a crisp military salute. "Yes, sir."

He chuckled. "Oh, no more of that 'sir' stuff. You make me feel older than the pyramids. Look, I realize you might want to call me Dr. Hotep at the hospital, but I would be honored if you would simply call me Ari the rest of the time."

Liz tilted her head to study him. She finally smiled. "I'd like that, Ari. Thank you. And, please, call me Elizabeth. No more Miss Winslow. It makes me sound like someone's old maid aunt who has a passel of cats."

He burst out laughing. "A passel of cats? There is that famous sense of humor again. You have a deal, Elizabeth. I'll see you both tomorrow afternoon in the clinic."

The next day, I noticed her trembling hand clung to his scrub shirt as he injected the medication into her eyes. I cringed at the thought of the needles entering her beautiful gray eyes, but I understood it would help protect her vision from further deterioration. Afterward, he held her hand as he had promised he would do. She continued to tremble from the painful injections, but she refused to cry. Like I said, my child is bone-headed. I bit back my tears as the handsome young doctor bent low to whisper words of encouragement to my daughter as she struggled to hold back her tears.

I stayed in New York City ten more weeks, until the cast came off her leg after the second surgery. By then, Ari Hotep was a regular sight at Liz's apartment. His eyes would alight with joy every time he saw her. More important to me, so did her gray ones. She would hobble over to him, using her cane for support, and he would pull her close to his chest to murmur words of love to her before he gave her a sweet, chaste kiss. I could tell they were falling in love. She might go blind someday, but what better for her in life than a doctor doing research on the disease robbing her of her vision? It seemed like a perfect match to everyone.

Except Liz.

Six months later when Ari finished his post-doctoral studies, he asked her to marry him. Liz shocked us all when she refused. She insisted she would not saddle him down with a woman who was going blind and who would never give him the children he wanted. He said they could adopt, and he pointed out there are many orphans who need homes in Egypt. She insisted a blind woman should not raise children. Even if they adopted, she could never be the mother she would want to be for her children once she went blind.

I wept. I cried again when she had her tubes tied a few months ago. They can perform DNA testing and she could know if her future children carried the recessive gene which causes her form of Stargardt disease. She loves children and I knew she would be a great mom. Miss Bone Head still insists a woman going blind should not raise children. She would not want to bring children into this world who could someday go blind from a defective gene they inherited from her.

Now Ari had returned. Was Liz being given a second chance at love? Would she dare to grab it and find her happy ever after ending this time?

Chapter 7
Galveston - Fancy

Everyone appeared pensive as I wrapped up my story. Of course, Bella, Miguel and Dara knew most of the story before I uttered a word. Captain Johnny looked contemplative – if a ghost can appear contemplative. Mr. Jones seemed rattled. He might be accustomed to conversing with spirits, but I figured he was not used to hearing the story of a young woman destined to blindness.

Mr. Jones cleared his voice. "I have macular degeneration. I get those shots, too."

He startled me. His shaken appearance must be because of the proximity with which Liz's story hit home. "Are they helping?"

He nodded. "Yes, at least with one eye. The vision in the other is minimal. Hmm... What is her birthdate?"

I could feel the corners of my eyes crinkle with laugh lines as I smiled. "Are you going to calculate her numerology status?"

He appeared surprised by my question. "Yes."

"Let me cut to the chase. Her birthday is February 1. Four years ago, was her fourth year. That was her hard year. She learned that with hard work, endurance, and self-control, she could survive. This is her eighth year. This is her power year, her strongest number. She knows what she needs what to do, and she has the strength to do it."

"Which is why she had her tubes tied," interjected Captain Johnny. "She knew what she had to do, and she had the strength to do it."

"Exactly," concurred Mr. Jones. "The numerological vibration was there for her. This is her power year."

I blinked my eyes. I expected no one to grasp the idea so quickly, but then again, I was conversing with a 300-year-old ghost and a man who routinely talked with ghosts. I should have realized they would understand what I meant if anyone would. "Well, she's a classic Aquarius, too. She's an original. She's independent, emotional, temperamental, and uncompromising. Some people view her as aloof. Her biggest problem is she feels limited or constrained by the prospect of blindness, which of course, is why she refused to marry Ari."

Ari sat in silence as I told the story, although he blushed while I described him as behaving like a 'drunken frog.' He frowned and then cleared his throat. We all looked over at him.

"So, what does it mean if I have the same number as her?"

I blinked, stunned by his question. Mr. Jones' eyes narrowed. "What is your birthday, son?"

"July 5th," came his terse reply.

Mr. Jones let out a low whistle as Captain Johnny sat up straighter. "And he's a Leo. Let me take a wild guess. Creative, passionate, generous, warmhearted."

"And Ari can be arrogant, stubborn, and inflexible," I interjected. "No offense meant, Ari."

"Guilty as charged," replied Ari. "And no offense taken. In fact, I can be rather self-centered."

My head whipped around to him at that. "I never thought of you as self-centered."

He smiled and reached over to clasp my hand. "You're a good person, Mrs. Winslow."

Mr. Jones blinked. "The same vibrational number and a Leo to her Aquarius. My god, he might be exactly the right man right for her after all."

"Why would you say that, sir?" asked Ari, his voice ripe with excitement.

"Four years ago, it was your hard year, too. You also had lessons to learn. You also learned that with hard work, endurance, and self-control, you could survive. I imagine you developed a better bedside manner than that of a drunken toad."

Mr. Jones paused as everyone laughed, including Ari, who nodded before he spoke. "I believe I have, sir."

"And like Liz, now you're in your eighth year."

"You called this our 'power year,'" reiterated Ari, his intriguing hazel eyes sparkling.

Mr. Jones nodded, excited that Ari had noticed the verbiage so quickly. "Yes, it is. This is the year when you know what you have to do."

"Ye gads, that's why the lad came now. He understands what he needs to do," chortled Captain Johnny. "He needs to marry Elizabeth."

Ari nodded, a slight smile playing across his full lips. "And I can assure you all I now have the determination and the strength to accomplish my goal."

We all fell silent as Liz walked back to the table. She frowned. "What?"

Your mother was telling us about you when you were a little girl," Ari said.

Her eyes narrowed. "You're lying."

He rolled his eyes. "That is a rude thing to say, Elizabeth. Yes, she was talking about you when you were younger. For instance, she told us you were born on February first."

"Hmm. Interesting. And did she tell you in which year I was born?"

He frowned and shook his head. "She didn't need to tell me the year. I already know how old you are."

She bit back the grin and pulled out a chair. "Yeah, sure. Hey, Captain Johnny, will you tell Dr. Hotep in what year I was born?"

Johnny shook his head. "I'm sorry, my dear. I'm not sure I know in what year you were born."

She smiled. "Take a wild guess, Captain."

The ghostly old pirate frowned, his face breaking into countless wrinkles as he did. "Elizabeth, I do not know in what year you were born. Why not ask your mother?"

She shook her head as she looked at Mr. Jones. "Did you really say ghosts can't lie?"

He nodded his head. "Yes, ma'am. If he is saying he does not know your birth year, he is telling the truth."

She snorted. "Yeah, sure. Mom, in what year was I born?"

I sat up straight. "I believe both your birth certificate and driver's license reflect you were born in 1994."

Liz shook her head. "I cannot believe you just straight out lied about my birthdate."

I felt my cheeks pale as I shook my head. "Now, Elizabeth, darling--"

"I was born on February 1, 1780, at the Seaview Plantation on Barbados. Right, Mother?"

My mouth suddenly felt so dry that all I could manage was nod as tears welled up in my eyes. I swallowed hard, but still no words would come out.

Bella's eyes were large as saucers. "Oh, my gosh, Liz, you know not to--"

"Shush! Liz, you know we aren't supposed to talk about that --" Miguel looked stunned by her words.

Dara appeared flabbergasted by her sister's outburst as her mouth fell open into a perfect 'O.' Her hands flew up to cup her face, like the little boy in that Home Alone movie. Captain Johnny looked away, pretending to pick lint off from his sleeve. His cheeks burned bright pink. *Odd*, I thought. *I never imagined a ghost could blush.* Mr. Jones appeared speechless, or as the old expression goes, aghast and agog.

"Really?" asked Ari with a tilt of his head.

Elizabeth looked triumphant. "Surprised? Yes. Really."

His eyes narrowed as he studied her. "Hmm. You used to tell me I am too old for you."

Liz looked rattled. "That's all you have to say?"

He shook his head as he struggled not to grin. I saw those lights twinkling in his eyes again. They twinkle when he becomes mischievous. "Not at all. It looks like you are the one robbing the cradle, not I. It turns out I'm not ten years older than you. Instead, you are," he paused for a second as he counted, "you are 207 years older than I am. Maybe you're too old for me."

A boyish, naughty grin spread across his handsome features.

I rarely see Liz speechless. Liz appeared flummoxed by his comment. I would have sworn she hoped Ari would be Ari's stunned speechless by her unexpected announcement.

Ari leaned back in his chair laughed.

Chapter 8
Galveston - Elizabeth

I could not believe he was here in Galveston. I never expected to see him again when I sent him away. But now he was here, looking even more scrumptious than I remembered.

Dammit. Why did my heart have to beat so rapidly at the mere sight of this blasted man? Why was I so flustered? Why was I so tongue tied? Why couldn't I act cool, suave, and sophisticated just once in my life around Ari Hotep?

I did not want to love Ari. I never intended to fall in love with him. I tried hard not to fall in love with the man four years ago. Once I accepted my diagnosis, I knew I could not marry a man like Ari. Total alpha, like my Poppa Kirk, even if Mom swears Ari is a gamma man like Daddy. But Ari is a man from another part of the world, far from my family. Of course, in the irony of all ironies, it now looked like my sister and her husband would move to Egypt, and I have always been closer to Bella than the other kids.

Bella accepted me as her sister from the moment I arrived at Waterside with Kirk and Fancy all those years ago. She smiled at me and handed me her doll. "Here, you need her more than I do. I call her Sally, but you can change her name. I have another dolly my Pawpaw gave me."

I was completely enchanted by my new big sister. I never had a doll before that. Heck, I had never even seen a doll. Kirk bent down and explained to me in Irish Gaelic what Bella had said. Bella looked surprised and then told me in Gaelic that I could keep the doll. She thought I looked like I needed one to hold. I tried to smile as I whispered thanks in Irish Gaelic. I didn't know how to say it in English. The only language I had heard before that day was

Gaelic. Thanks to Bella, Fancy, Pawpaw Marc, and Poppa, I learned English quickly.

I knew Ari wanted children. How could I be a competent parent if I went blind? Oh, yeah, I have heard all that nonsense about being 'perfectly imperfect.' That does not fly with me about raising children. Kids deserve parents who can see. How could I protect my children from harm if I could not see harm approaching? How could I snatch a bottle of bleach from their hands before they drank it, or grab them and pull them out of the street from an impending car? No, I would not risk raising children once I received the sentence of encroaching blindness. If I were going to be a mom, I would want to be the best mom I could be. A mom like Fancy Winslow, who loved her kids with all her heart. Mom might have gone to college and became a cardiovascular surgical nurse, but she never neglected us. She was always there for us when we needed her, like when I broke my leg.

My blindness may have been delayed by the injections I received every month, but the ultimate result remained the same. I would eventually go blind from Stargardt disease. My vision had already deteriorated in my left eye. I would not trust myself to raise children, given my long-term prognosis.

I realized it would be years before I completely lost my vision, although I lost most of the eyesight in my left eye over the past four years. The shots barely slowed down the deterioration of my vision in that eye. I still had some peripheral vision in it, but I had lost my central field of vision. In contrast, the right eye stabilized with the shots. The doctors concocted a way to anesthetize my eyeballs before injecting the medicine into my eyes, so it no longer hurt like it did the first time. After the initial sting, I feel nothing once the anesthesia takes effect except a slight pressure as they inject my eyes. Whoopee. Well, it stabilizes and preserves the vision in my right eye, or I might already be blind.

I lived in Blue Ridge, Georgia, for almost two years after Ari left NYC to return to Egypt. Mom wanted me to move home to San Antonio, but I knew she would coddle me. I feared she would inadvertently keep me an invalid. I had to learn how to support myself in my new life situation.

My Poppa Kirk had a different plan. He put me to work. He would not allow any 'poor pitiful me' talk. Poppa owns the Brian Boru, an Irish pub in Blue Ridge, Georgia. It is the most popular eatery in North Georgia. He trained me how to perform every job there, from washing the dishes and mopping the floors, to handling the bookkeeping and managing other employees. Then, when he thought I was ready, he bought Nefertiti's Bone Yard for me.

It shocked me when Poppa bought the bar in Galveston. We had all come on a trip with Miguel and Bella. They still love the island and visit it frequently. One afternoon, Poppa and I went walking. I walk a lot to stay fit. It is easier on my body than dancing, although it is not as physically or emotionally satisfying. Anyway, we walked into this neighborhood the tour guidebook called 'the Bone Yard,' because many people were buried here after the 1900 storm. As Kirk lengthened his stride to saunter up to a lady, I realized we were meeting a realtor to look at an old, run-down building that appeared to be abandoned. My eyes must have bulged out with surprise as the realtor told us the building had once been a car dealership with a bordello upstairs. Most recently, it had been a bar, but it had been abandoned for a couple of decades. It looked dilapidated, and I feared it was rat-infested. Poppa strolled in, looked around and grinned. Less than five minutes later, he bought the place. His rashness shocked me. He never buys real estate impulsively, and this place was a hot mess. I did not realize until after he bought it that he grinned when he looked across the empty room and spotted Captain Johnny sitting in the corner.

It about scared the tar out of me the first time I saw Captain Johnny sitting in his favorite corner. He materialized in front of me. His feet were propped up on the table, and he was leaning backwards in a chair that looked like it would topple over at any second. I was unaccustomed to having ghosts materialize in front of me, and I began screaming at the top of my lungs. Fortunately, Kirk was there. He somehow managed to calm me down. He warned Johnny not to scare me again. Johnny thought I could not see him and looked mollified to realize he frightened me. Being visually challenged makes me more 'open' to viewing ghosts. That is not a big plus in a city like Galveston, which is filled with the spirits of the dead.

Three months later, Nefertiti's Bone Yard opened for business. I am still amazed my Poppa and I converted an abandoned building, used previously as a bar, a car dealership, and a brothel, into a beautiful, brand new, and shining dinner club. We converted the upstairs into a little apartment for me. I try not to dwell on the former use of the upstairs space as a whore house, especially since I learned Johnny died there. Fortunately, no ghosts of former working girls or their clients bother me. I suspect Johnny keeps them away.

I get upstairs to my apartment through an elevator hidden in my office behind a bookshelf. I can lock it so no one else can access my apartment. There are stairs outside as well, with a tall gate and fence around the deck to keep out unwanted guests. I keep it locked, too. Now, my two cats and I live quietly in the small apartment upstairs when I am not tending to the daily functions of my club.

Oh, gosh, I guess I have become the crazy cat lady everyone laughs about.

It frightened me to be on my own at first, but Poppa kept telling me I could do it. "Hell, girl, you're my daughter. You can do anything you set your mind on doing. You can run this place. And if you stay off your toes and don't put too much stress on your leg, you can even dance now and then."

His gray eyes which are so much like mine twinkled with pride and excitement as he told me I could do anything.

Mom says I am just like him. I am tall like him, and I know I got my Irish temper from Poppa. Mom says we are both stubborn to the max. I got my gray eye color from him. However, he does not carry the Stargardt gene, so I must have received that gift from my poor dead mother, Anya, who died when I was born.

I had been warned I should not resume professional dancing since I broke both bones in my lower leg. I loved to dance *en pointe*, on my toes. My dreams of becoming a prima ballerina shattered with my poor tibia when I landed in that man's French horn. It would have been funny if it had not been so damned traumatic. I mean, I danced off the stage and landed in some poor man's French horn, for heaven's sake! I still have nightmares about it. The severity of my injuries knocked the humor right out of my memory of the event. Amidst all the pain and chaos of that night, I still remember the shrieks of horror from the orchestra and the audience attending our performance. The doctors had to piece my leg back together with all kinds of metal devices. Professional dancing would be too much stress on my leg bones. So, I cooked up the Krazy Karaoke Nights, during which I could sing a lot and dance a little.

Dave is my assistant manager. When he started, he wore a kilt for the first Krazy Karaoke Night. The locals loved it, so I changed the name to Krazy Kilt Karaoke Night. Dave tends bar for those events shirtless, changing his insane mustache, beard, and body hair for each event. Most recently, he shaved most of his body hair, so it looked like his handlebar mustache extended down his neck, onto his chest, and around his man nipples. Craziest thing I ever saw, even if it was in a haunted bar formerly used as a whore house in the Bone Yard. The man is insane enough to work as my assistant manager in my haunted bar, and sane enough to be a damned fine assistant manager. He thinks Johnny is 'cool,' adores my dad, and I trust him to run the place efficiently if I cannot work for any reason. He also gives me time to escape and do other things.

Because of Dave's efficiency, I can leave the club to teach beginner's dance classes three days a week at a local elementary school. I love working with children. I planned to add an intermediate class during the next school year until Ari showed up. Now, I am unsure what I will do or where I might do it next year.

I avoided relationships since I broke up with Ari. I dated once or twice in Blue Ridge when Kirk insisted. I let the guys know I was not looking for a relationship and I was not into sex for the sake of having sex. Neither guy called back. Let's face it: today, lots of men want a woman who is not looking for a relationship, but they think that means easy sex. Not with this gal. I might come across as a modern girl, but I was born in the eighteenth century and raised by a woman born and raised in the eighteenth century. Our mama taught us not to 'eff' around. She told us God would strike us dead and we would go to hell if we messed around, and I believe her.

I avoided relationships until I met Ari. I dated my dance partner some in high school, but we were never serious about each other. We were totally into dancing. We would go to each other's school dances because we enjoyed dancing together. Ironically, we often fought like two tomcats when we were not dancing.

Performing was my life. When I crashed off the stage, everything changed. Suddenly, I found myself vulnerable to the charms of the tall, dark, and altogether awesome Dr. Ari Hotep. I then had six months of heaven in the arms of the man I love.

Heck, maybe Mom was right. If you have sex before marriage, you go to hell. After all, I have been in hell since I refused to marry Ari. Every day away from that blasted man has been hell on earth. Now, I avoid dating altogether because I refused to fall into the relationship hell hole again.

I looked up and stared across the bar at the handsome devil sitting over in the corner, talking to my family and to the ghost who insisted it was his duty to keep watch over me. How dare that damned ghost show himself to Ari? He was *my* ghost. Ari was my… something. I swallowed hard as my throat went dry with longing. *Hmm. I wonder if he would still want me to go to Egypt with him if…*

I shook myself and took a deep breath. *No, Liz. Don't even think it.* I squeezed my eyes tight, willing the tears not to fall.

Songs about doctors are always popular at Nefertiti's Bone Yard because of the proximity of the club to the University of Texas Medical Center in Galveston. UTMB is a world-class medical school. Med students come out to eat, drink and relax when they are not on duty. Many of them seem to love karaoke. They all love our karaoke performances about doctors.

We put on our little karaoke medley of songs about doctors, with me singing to Ari, who began playing the doctor's role as a bit aloof and ended up draped over me like a warm blanket. Oh, gosh, he felt good draped around me again. Bella primarily sang to Miguel, with us doing backup, although Miguel loves to join in and sing by the end of the performances. Miguel has a decent baritone voice, and he can play the piano like a pro. He is particular about the routines in which he will perform, so we are required to make our selections for the karaoke night performances in which he will participate with great care, just as we did for this evening.

As our performance ended, I took a deep breath and smiled at my patrons as I handed them refills of their beers. "That's your third, Chuck. No more tonight."

The young med student laughed and nodded. "Yes, ma'am, Miss Liz. And I know you can't serve any liquor after midnight during the pandemic."

I smiled. "I appreciate you understand my limitations in managing the club. Shall I get you guys your ticket, or does anyone else want a refill, too? No rush to leave, but if I can start clearing out accounts now, it makes our lives easier. If you guys don't mind."

He laughed again. "No, that will be fine. We all understand. You won't lose your club because one of us left drunk and hit someone. We always have a designated driver."

"That's me." One of the guys held up his glass of Coca-Cola and smiled.

I beamed at him. "Thanks, Tom. I appreciate you."

And then Chuck shocked me. He laid his hand over mine. "So, when are you going to go out with me, pretty lady?"

I could feel my cheeks redden with embarrassment. "Chuck, you know I don't date patrons…"

He shook his head. "Yeah, I hear you tell guys that every time I come in here. What will it take to get you to change your mind and date a handsome young doctor-to-be, pretty lady?"

Just then, Ari walked over to my side. As he gave me a quizzical look, I slipped an arm around his trim waist and smiled up at him before I looked back at Chuck. "I guess it would take removing Ari from my life. Right, babe?"

One thing about Ari: he is not stupid. He smiled at me and bent me over ass backwards to kiss me. Oh, my god, did I tell you that man knows how to kiss? I swear my toes curled and my skin tingled at his touch as he slipped his tongue into my mouth. As he straightened back up, he smiled slightly before he answered. "That's right, my love."

I felt giddy from the kiss, but somehow, I laid the ticket down on the table, wink at the guys, and turn to return to the bar. I could not fathom why it did not offend me when Ari kept his arm around my shoulder as we walked to the cash register. Instead, I remembered the warm, safe, loving feeling I always had in the past when he held me close like this.

Toughen up, Liz, I thought. *Don't fall for him again. Dammit, he deserves better.*

But I feared it was too late the minute I saw those damned eyes I love so much.

Maybe I'm not good enough for him. Maybe he deserves a wife who can give him children, and who can always care for them. A wife who will never go blind. But will any other woman ever love him as much as I do? Hmm… It was time I learned to think about myself first for a change.

Oh, my God, his arms felt good wrapped around me again. I felt myself sinking deeper into his embrace. I shut my eyes and took a deep breath. *Now what should I do?*

Chapter 9
Galveston - Elizabeth

Mr. Jones and Captain Johnny were still talking as the bar closed. Elizabeth cleared her throat, and both men, the living and the dead, looked up at her in surprise.

"Did you wish to say something, Elizabeth?" asked Captain Johnny with a wry smile.

She nodded and then flashed her most engaging smile at them. "Yes. It's closing time. Mr. Jones, you are welcome back any time when we are open, but the mayor is stringent on the closing hours of establishments such as mine right now. Otherwise, I would ask you to stay past the mandated closing hour."

Mr. Jones flushed deep red. "I apologize, my dear. I had not realized it was so late. I'll take you up on the offer to return. Captain, please keep a close watch on our young lady. She seems like a special person."

Captain Johnny nodded. "Indeed, she is exceptional, Rick. I look forward to visiting with you again. I'll tell you how I came to know Elizabeth's father."

Rick Jones laughed and pushed back from the table to stand up. He winced as he struggled to straighten up. "It constantly surprises me how this old back complains if I sit too long. Captain Johnny, I doubt it will shock me as much now as it might have shocked me before our young lady mentioned her birthdate this evening. I have known many spirits, but I never met a family of time travelers before tonight."

Liz frowned as she glanced around, worrying that his comment might be overheard. "Shush! Don't talk about such things here. People might overhear you."

Ari came up behind her and slipped his arms around her shoulders again. He dipped his head to kiss her cheek. "I think you already blew that one this evening, my love."

Liz felt her reddened cheeks heat to scorching. Did she fuss at Ari and shrug away from him, or what? She shook her head. "We don't have to keep broadcasting it. It was stupid of me to raise the issue. I rarely blurt out family secrets like that. Come on, handsome. You can help me finish cleaning up in here."

He laughed as she grabbed his hand. "Sounds good to me. What did you have in mind?"

He pulled her to him, and she swatted at him. "Stop it, Ari. Behave."

He arched a brow at her. "Oh, really? You would rebuff me after I saved you from Chuckie?"

She grinned but she swatted at his hands again. "I appreciate you rescued me, too. Now, help me clean up. We can talk more later."

"Talk? Is that all you have in mind?" He arched a brow at her as he grinned.

"Hmm. We will see. Come on. Help me, or you'll never make it to second base, Doc."

He laughed as she pulled him along after her to help bus the tables.

Soon, Nefertiti's Bone Yard was empty except for Liz, Ari, and Dave. Mom and Dara would spend the weekend with Miguel and Bella before heading back to San Antonio. Dave finished cleaning his area of the club and waved goodbye to Liz. She followed him to the front door to lock the deadbolt as he left. As she turned around to Ari, he took her hands into his.

"It's time we talk."

Liz gulped and nodded. She led him into the office and locked the door behind them before she walked over to the bookcase. She pulled out a book, inserted a key, and the bookcase popped open.

Ari's eyes bulged with surprise as she opened the door to the small elevator. "Well, I didn't see that one coming."

Liz grinned. "People aren't supposed to expect the bookcase to swing open. The door is hidden for my protection. Come on, babe. Let's go upstairs."

He blinked. "What's upstairs?"

She laughed again.

"Your laughter sounds like music to my soul." He bent to kiss her again.

She sighed as the kiss ended. "My home is upstairs. Well, it's a little apartment. It's where I live these days."

He grinned and followed her into the elevator, where she pressed the button to travel to the upper level. Once there, they exited the elevator and entered the small but elegant apartment atop Nefertiti's Bone Yard.

Ari let out a low whistle. "This is impressive. I would never have imagined this sat on top of your club."

She laughed, suddenly self-conscious. "That was Poppa's plan when he designed the place. He didn't want to make it easy for anyone to break into my apartment. When I come up here, no one can enter the elevator. It remains here until I go down. No one can come up the stairs and enter through the door unless they have a key to the gate or can jump over a twelve-foot-tall fence which surrounds the deck. Poppa was all about me being safe here. I also have an alarm system, which I set downstairs before we came up, and turned off up here as we entered the apartment. I will set it again now since we are in the apartment."

"Wow. I'm impressed. Of course, Kirk and Richard both seemed protective of you when I met them in New York four years ago."

She nodded. "They are both extremely protective of me. Until Mellie and Kirk had their baby, I was Kirk's only child. He is exceptionally protective of his little girl."

Ari appeared startled by her words. "I did not realize they had a child."

Liz chuckled. "Yes, little Callan was a surprise to everyone."

Ari laughed. "They named the child Callan?"

Liz nodded. "Poppa loves NCIS, and Melanie refused to name the baby Leroy Jethro. Poppa was thrilled about her pregnancy, but they were both terrified when they learned Mellie was having a baby at her age. Mom voiced shock Mellie had the baby. Mellie had DNA testing and the baby did not appear to have any genetic issues, such as Down syndrome. That was the big question, since our friend, Baylie, had little Faith several years ago, and Faith has Mosaicism."

Ari frowned. "Who is Baylie? I don't remember the name."

"She's a Cherokee friend who is married to a Cherokee man. She was forty-something when she had their little girl. She knew the baby tested positive for Down syndrome, but Baylie refused to abort her baby. She said, 'it may be my choice, but that is not my body I would be aborting.' Her words really impacted me. Anyway, they lucked out. Faith is a beautiful little girl. She has Mosaicism, which I understand is a milder form of Down syndrome."

Ari nodded. "It is. Another group at Biozyme has done research on it."

"That's what Miguel told us. I've heard them talk about 'perfectly imperfect' children. I understand we are all perfectly imperfect, but I am not as strong as Baylie. I couldn't..."

Her voice broke off. She struggled to contain the tears threatening to fall before she resumed talking. She took a deep breath and flashed another smile at Ari. "Anyway, Callan is a healthy, happy baby, and Poppa is delighted to be raising a son."

"I imagine he is." Ari's voice sounded soft and thoughtful.

Liz gulped. "Ari, I can't give you children."

He shook his head. "No, you won't give me children. I understand why, although I will say again that DNA testing could show if a child you carried would also possess the gene for Stargardt disease."

Liz pulled her hand away from his and walked over to the window. She wrapped her hands around her arms in a protective stance. "That's not an acceptable option to me. I don't believe in abortion. I thought you understood how I feel, especially after what I just told you about Baylie's experience with Faith."

He took a deep breath and then walked over to her. He wrapped his arms around her again. "I understand. I told you years ago I didn't care if we ever had a child. We could adopt if you prefer –"

Her throat tightened with tension. She did not want to argue with him. "And I told you I would not take on such an enormous responsibility considering I am going blind."

Ari nodded. "I know, I know. Elizabeth, darling, I would love to have children. But I want *you* more than I want children. I love you. I always desired you. I still want to marry you."

She turned to face him and reached up to cup his face in her hands. "Oh, Ari, are you sure? You would give up children for me?"

He pulled her close to his chest. "I would give up anything for you, Elizabeth."

He dropped his head to kiss her. Liz felt her knees and her resolve weaken as their kiss deepened. She felt faint as he lifted his head from hers, and she gasped as he swept her up into his arms.

Ari carried her to the bedroom where he laid her on the bed. Liz lay there, with her braids spread around her, staring up at him. She raised her arms to him, and he lowered himself to the bed beside her.

"Are you sure?" His voice was hoarse with hunger as he struggled to resist the urge to kiss her again.

She nodded. "Never more so. I love you, Ari. I always loved you. If you can put up with me-"

He silenced her with kisses. She sighed and reached up to pull him close to her. "Make love to me, Ari."

He looked startled. "Are you sure? I have a condom."

She tried to smile. "You can use it. I have not been with anyone since you. I won't get pregnant."

He frowned. "I haven't been with anyone else either. I have not even wanted to be with another woman. You spoiled me, Liz. Look, you are so insistent you don't want a baby, I just want to make sure-"

"I had my tubes tied."

She cringed as the color faded from his handsome face. She pushed herself off the bed and walked across the room to stare out the window. "Yeah, I thought it would make a difference to you."

He grabbed for her arm. "Why?"

She shook her head and shrugged out of his hold. "I told you. I don't want to bring a child into this world who might go blind someday because they inherited a defective gene from me, and I don't believe in abortion. I also didn't want to wind up getting pregnant if something bad happened, and if…"

"And if someone violated you," Ari whispered as he reached over to wipe a tear from her cheek. "Oh, my dearest love. You built this fortress around you. Did someone hurt you?"

She looked at Ari, shocked by the question. "No, but Mom was raped years ago. She went through nine kinds of hell afterward. It took years of therapy to help put Fancy back together into a fully functional human being. I would not want to go through that. It had always been Poppa's biggest concern about me living in New York City. Fortunately, I stayed safe during those years. Poppa made sure I would be safe here, too. Galveston is a wonderful place, but it has an unsavory side."

Ari ran a hand down her arm. "I understand. Well, kind of. It might have been an extreme means to avoid conception in case of a possible sexual attack, but… No matter. It is done. I already knew how you feel about bringing a baby with Stargardt disease into this world. I love you, Elizabeth. If you want me in your life, I will be eternally grateful to God above. If you want me in your bed, I will be the happiest man in the world. If you just want me as a friend, I will accept it. But I need you back in my life."

She tried to smile. "You do?"

He nodded. "Absolutely."

She reached up to him and pulled his shirt into her hands. "I want you in my life, too. Make love to me, Ari."

She pulled his shirt again. She did not have to ask twice. Ari swung her up into his arms and quickly carried her back to the bed.

She sighed as he laid her on the bed again. "You cannot imagine how often I longed for this."

He chuckled. "I imagine I can. Being away from you is like my heart has been separated from its beat. Like I have been living half a life."

Her smile was tremulous. "I felt like a dancer who lost her song."

"Well, to be honest, I guess you had, my love," he replied.

She shook her head. "No, you goose. It was like I was the earth, during a drought, longing for the rain of your touch to slake my thirst."

"Oh, believe me, darling, I will quench your thirst tonight."

She giggled. "You're terrible."

He shook his head. "No, Elizabeth, I'm serious. We have been separated far too long. It is like our souls have been denied their essences, their lights dimmed, weakened and broken."

Her eyes widened in surprise. "You remembered."

He smiled. "Of course, I remembered the poem your friend wrote. I read Shalini's poem so many times that I know it by memory now. It perfectly describes how I felt these past few years. But now we need wait no longer. No more rage. No more chaos. No more waiting in a dream, holding on for one more breath."

He lowered his head to kiss her again.

She sighed as the kiss ended. "No. No more holding on for one more breath. No more waiting in a dream."

It was different and yet it was the same. They both remembered the moves each other loved the most. Ari was gentle and playful, forceful and yet giving, not merely taking. Liz was demanding and impatient, taking and receiving. Both became lost in the passion that enveloped them as they rode to new heights they never reached before.

And yet, Elizabeth felt acutely aware this was different. Perhaps she was breathing this time, for the first time. Maybe she was learning to cope with her diagnosis. She no longer felt filled with rage and chaos. Maybe this could really work this time. She thought she had finally accepted that she counted, too. Her desires counted. Her wants mattered. Not all of this was about Ari. Her desires should matter as much as Ari's did.

He had been telling her that she mattered all along.

And for once, Liz felt freed from worrying about pleasing Ari. She let him please her. She felt liberated from fearing the conception of a child doomed to blindness and freed from her fear she would upset Ari by not wanting to give birth to his child. Once freed, Liz soared on the clouds, exulting in the love of the man she held most dear.

Chapter 10
Galveston - Elizabeth

Liz stretched out on the bed the next morning, still smiling with the afterglow of their lovemaking from the night before. Ari pulled his jeans back on, and then bent over to kiss her. She grabbed his hand before he zipped the jeans. "When are you going back to Cairo?"

Ari paused from dressing and leered down at her. "Why?"

She shrugged, as she pulled the sheet over her breasts. "Just wondering how much time we have before you go home."

He leaned back over to kiss her again and then sat on the edge of the bed. "I can stay another week. Maybe two. However, we have as much time as you want. Come with me to Egypt."

She smiled at him, bittersweet. "I think we had this discussion about four years ago, Ari."

"Yes, we did. And yet here we are, again sharing a bed. We resolved some of our differences last night. I still want to marry you, Elizabeth. I am not looking to marry a broodmare. I long for you to be my partner in life, my helpmate. You are the other half of my heart. Please, Elizabeth, come to Egypt. See my country firsthand. I have it on good authority you would like to see the Giza Plateau and Luxor. I can arrange personal tours with Dr. Hassan."

Liz felt her cheeks heat as she blushed. "Tours guided by Zain Hassan?"

He nodded. "The one and only Dr. Zain Hassan himself."

"You silver-tongued devil. You would tempt me with tours lead by Dr. Hassan. Miguel talks too much. What if I hate it there? The worst thing about Galveston is the heat, and it gets a lot hotter in Egypt than here. What if I don't want to stay?"

Ari's face looked serious. He gathered both her hands into his. "Then don't stay. Just come to visit. Check it out. It gets hot there, but it is a dry heat. We don't have this awful, unbearable humidity, and we don't have hurricanes. In 2019, we had an extremely rare October storm labelled a 'Medicane,' due to its location in the Mediterranean. The last tornado occurred in 1981. Enjoy visiting the archeological sites. I know my brother would be delighted to show you the Giza Plateau, Saqqara, and the new digs at Luxor. The recently discovered City of Gold is reputed to be amazing. I'm sure we can wangle a private tour or two by Dr. Hassan if you come. They hope to locate the tomb of Queen Nefertiti at the Golden City. Admit it. You would love to help the team locate the mummy of Queen Nefertiti. If you come back with me, you can help Miguel find a house for Bella, the baby and him to live in when Bella and the baby come to Egypt in a few months. You could email photos of houses and objective descriptions of them to Bella. You can find her another obstetrician-gynecologist and a pediatrician before she arrives. We can find doctors for you as well. Believe me, I know a few who have excellent credentials who work with Stargardt patients."

She giggled but continued to chew on her upper lip.

He took a deep breath. "We can look for a house for us, too. I have a beautiful home, but it is small, with only two bedrooms and one bath. It's big enough for me, but we might feel crowded living there long-term. It is only three blocks from Biozyme, but it is in the old part of the city. I am not sure you would like the area."

"Why? Is the neighborhood dangerous?" She lifted his hand to kiss it, and then rubbed it across her cheek.

He chuckled and pulled her hand to his lips to kiss it. "Not at all. It's one of the safest neighborhoods in the city. However, the houses are quite old-fashioned. You won't find an open concept design there. The houses are plain on the outside, with inner courtyards. That way, no one knows how nice your house is inside. It stays cooler in the house with the inner courtyard, which is surrounded by the thick walls of house. However, my little house is quite pleasingly remodeled inside. The kitchen and bathroom were redone two years ago. The house next door just came on the market, and I told my neighbor I might want to buy it to expand my house. We could break through the connecting wall and go from a two-bedroom, one-bath home to a four-bedroom, two-bath home within a three-minute walk of my work."

She grinned. "You told him that before you came to the convention, hmm?"

He laughed. "Yes, I did. Otherwise, if you want to stay but want a different house, we could find a home near wherever Bella and Miguel settle. There are some lovely, new neighborhoods built on canals close to the city. They are further from Biozyme, but they are still within a reasonable distance to work. Please, my love, see if you like my country, the people, the food, the music, the culture, the history, even the interminably hot summers."

She looked worried as she nibbled her upper lip. "And if I don't like it?"

Ari shook his head and tried to chuckle. "Then I guess you come back to the States."

She reached out for his arm. "But what about you? What about us?"

"Would you want there to be an 'us,' Elizabeth?"

She blinked, suddenly uncertain. "I hope so. I mean, of course. Don't you know that after last night?"

Ari grabbed her hands and pulled her close to him again. "Oh, my love, I hoped you felt that way, too. You have no idea how elated I am you have returned to my arms with love and passion. Don't think for a minute I intend to let you escape me again. If you cannot stand Egypt and decide you must return to live in the United States, I shall find work here."

Liz's heart leaped at his words. She raised up, and the sheet dropped from her chest as she grabbed his arms. "Are you serious? You would move here for me?"

"I am as serious as life and death, my love. I would move to the States for us. I want you. I need you. Without you, I am like a heart which has been separated from its beat. I need you in my life to be complete. Oh, that sounded like bad poetry."

She chuckled. "My poet who doesn't know it."

He joined her laughter and then became serious again. "Elizabeth, I would be delighted for you to come to Egypt and to love it, but if you hate my country-"

"But what about your research? You said your team is close to a breakthrough." She frowned.

"Ah, so you want the Stargardt research completed? We are close to a breakthrough. However, I can work for Biozyme anywhere in the world with computers. It's a new world, Elizabeth. The pandemic has taught us much can be accomplished from home with a top-notch computer."

Liz threw her arms around him. "You're serious? They would let you work from here? You would move here for me?"

He grinned as he hugged her close. "I'm here, aren't I? Darling, I would move here for us. I could have attended this conference by zoom, but I came to see you again. To win you back."

Liz squealed with excitement as she showered his face with kisses. "Oh, Ari, you are the most wonderful man I ever met."

Ari began laughing as he lost his balance and fell onto the bed again. "Now, hold on, my love. First, you must come to Egypt and see how you like it. I would appreciate it if you gave my country a fair trial. if you love it-"

"We stay there," she said as she sat on the bed beside him and kissed him again.

He grinned and kissed her back. "And if you hate it, I am sure I can work for Biozyme from here, or I can go to work for UTMB. They were sounding me out about a job offer this week. Fair enough?"

She showered his face with kisses again. "You are decidedly the most wonderful, sexy, fantabulous man in the entire world. I don't know why I ever let you go four years ago. I have no idea how I ever let you go. I missed you so much, Ari."

He fell beside her on the pillows laughing. "Only for you, my love, could I ever be the most wonderful, sexy or fabulous –"

"Fantabulous," she said as she kissed the tip of his nose.

Ari struggled not to laugh. "I beg your pardon, my love. Fantabulous – was that right? Fantabulous? Is that a word?"

She nodded. "It is now because you are most definitely fantabulous. You are fantastic and fabulous. When I put those together, you are best described as fantabulous."

She snuggled up close to him.

He stopped trying to control his laughter as he pulled her closer to him. "Fine. I'll take your word for it. I am the, ahem, most 'fantabulous' man in the world. But, darling, if that's true, it's because you bring joy to my life. You are my queen, my beauty who comes. I need you in my life to be a complete person. Without you, I am only half a man. I need the other half of my soul with me."

"That must be the most romantic thing I ever heard."

He chuckled. "Well, you inspire me. Will you show me around Galveston today? All I have seen so far is UTMB, a sliver of the beach beyond the seawall, and your club."

"I would love to show you around."

For the next four hours, Liz took Ari to all her favorite places in Galveston. He stared in awe at the glorious opulence of the Bishop's Palace. They laughed in childlike delight at the antics of the precocious monkeys and the walk-through jungle at Moody Gardens. They strolled down the Strand before Liz finally took him to eat at The Spot. After dinner, they walked barefooted down the beach at dusk. As the setting sun flared red across the darkening sky, Ari pulled her into his arms for another long kiss.

She sighed. "I love you, Ari. You know I love you, don't you?"

He smiled as he ran his hand over her braids. "So, does this mean you will marry me?"

She gulped and then nodded. "We can plan a wedding for when Bella arrives with the baby. The baby is due in December, and she will want to wait until he has been inoculated to come to Egypt. That might be late February or early March. Mom already said she will come to Egypt with Bella and the baby. We can convince everyone else to come then, too."

He laughed, suddenly self-conscious. "To be honest, my love, I think we should marry before then if we want to live together when you arrive in Egypt. I am not Muslim, but Egypt is a Muslim country. They disapprove of couples living together without the benefit of marriage."

She gulped. "You mean you want us to get married in the next week?"

The corners of his eyes crinkled as he laughed. "I mean let's get married this week, or the week after. We have had almost four years to think about this, Elizabeth. If you are serious and want to come to Egypt, then let's get married in a civil service before I return to work. We can register it in Egypt, and then have a formal church wedding after Bella, the baby and everyone else can come in a few months."

Liz's eyes narrowed as she quickly thought about his idea. "Maybe Mom and the others could stay a few more days. Daddy could fly over from San Antonio, and Poppa and Mellie could fly in from Blue Ridge. They would all have conniption fits if we married, and they were not included."

He smiled and stroked down the side of her face. "Whatever you want, my love. As long as you will come with me and try to love my country even half as much as I love you and yours."

She grabbed his hand. "Oh, my gosh, Ari, does this mean we're engaged?"

He laughed and reached into his shirt pocket. He pulled out a little ring box, opened it, and fell to one knee in the sand beside her. "Elizabeth Winslow, will you marry me? If you will accept this ring, it means we are officially engaged."

Liz gasped. Her hands automatically reached out for the beautiful ring. Each side was shaped like a lotus blossom. Green emeralds flanked the sides of the amethyst stalk to the tanzanite lotus blossoms which wrapped around a cabochon emerald. "Oh, Ari..."

"Will you marry me, Liz? Will you come to Egypt and love me forever?"

Silent, she bit back tears as she nodded. Finally, she nodded as she whispered to him. "Yes, of course."

Ari's eyes sparkled as he slid it onto her ring finger on her right hand.

She giggled. "Ari, I think you are so rattled that you put the ring on my wrong hand."

He shook his head. "Not at all. Egyptian Coptic Christian women wear their engagement rings on their right hands. It is moved to the left hand at the wedding ceremony."

"That's so romantic. Oh, Ari, how did you know my ring size?" she whispered as she stared in awe at the beautiful ring. "It's the most beautiful ring I ever saw. I never saw anything like this in my life."

"I have my sources. Does this mean you like it? I know it is not traditional. I understand it is an antique. I thought we could add a narrow gold band to go with it to serve as the wedding band. Or, if you would prefer, we could add a narrow band of emeralds, to match the emeralds in the ring."

She nodded as she continued to stare at the beautiful ring. "It's exquisite, Ari. I love it."

"Okay. Now, answer the question. Will you marry me?"

She blushed and she threw her arms around his neck again. "Of course, I will. I love you, Ari." When they got back to the house, she pulled him back to the bed and slid her hands into the waist of his jeans. "Let me show you again how much I love you..."

Later, Liz showered and dressed to go downstairs to the club. Ari chuckled as she pulled on the unusual ensemble. "Where did you find that?"

She chuckled, suddenly self-conscious. "I bought it in SoHo, four years ago. I was going to wear it with you back then, but I never did. I figure my beautiful ring deserves an equally beautiful, Egyptian-styled gown for this evening at my club."

She twirled around so he could better see the exquisite fabric.

"It is hard to look both modest and daring at once, Elizabeth, but you always manage. A high neckline, long sleeves, and a bare midriff with a long, straight skirt slit up both sides. For easy dancing?"

She nodded and grinned as she spun around again. "Yes, exactly. I have running shorts on underneath it for spins."

He chuckled. "Figures. The fabric looks like you bought it in Cairo, with the copies of Egyptian hieroglyphics on it. Those earth tones flatter your exquisite complexion immensely. Not to mention the fabulous neckline looks like an ancient Egyptian gold and lapis necklace fit for a queen."

She threw her arms around his neck again. "For your queen. So, you like it? It's not too daring?"

"It's beautiful. Do you know what this cartouche spells?" He traced over a section of the hieroglyphics.

She shook her head. "I don't have the foggiest idea."

He smiled as he traced over the ancient name again. "It says 'Nefertiti,' which means 'Beauty Has Come'. I always called you 'my beauty' because you resemble the Great Royal Wife so much. Yes, my love, you could even wear this ensemble many places in Egypt. Of course, you might want to wear a wrap over it to cover your bare midriff until we arrived at our destination. You could wear it at the December Christmas party at Biozyme."

"It really says that?" She tilted her head. "Wait a minute. Will Biozyme Cairo have a Christmas party?"

"We call it the Winter Ball, to avoid offending anyone. There will be a big Christmas tree and Santa always hands out presents to all the children. Many of our employees are from the United States and expect a Christmas celebration. While the entire country may not celebrate Christmas, we will at Biozyme. We will also celebrate Christmas at my family's church in Cairo. The Coptic Orthodox religion celebrates Christmas. Coptic Christians comprise about 10% of the Egyptian population."

Her eyes narrowed as she tapped a finger against her cheek. "Hmm... Will the Coptic priest let us get married at the church in Cairo when everyone can come?"

He laughed and pulled her close for another kiss. "I imagine so. We will find out when we arrive in Egypt. Our services are in Coptic, you know."

She frowned. "What is Coptic? You told me before, but I don't remember."

He smiled and dipped his head to kiss her forehead once more. "Coptic is the ancient language of the Egyptians. It preserves Egypt's original language, which the Arabic invaders forbade us to use when they took over the country. St. Mark established the Cairo Coptic Church in 42 A.D. Today, the Coptic language is written with the Greek alphabet. That's supposed to be easier to learn than hieroglyphics. The hymns and the liturgy have been passed down for two thousand years. We call the Nicene Creed 'the Symbol of Faith.' It was mainly based on the teachings of St. Athanasius of Alexandria, who was the Bishop of Alexandria and a Pope according to Coptic traditions."

"Really? I didn't know that. It sounds like the Episcopal church I grew up attending in Georgia."

He nodded. "Yes, they are much alike. The priest may require you to learn some Coptic before we marry, but you are a quick learner. You can learn the rudiments of the language before the formal wedding."

Her brow furrowed with thought. "Should we check with the Episcopalian priest and see if we could be married there in the next two weeks? Or, hey, I have an idea! There is a Coptic church in Clear Lake. Let's go there tomorrow and talk to the priest."

He beamed at her and pulled her close for another kiss. "You are the most amazing woman. That is a wonderful idea. If he says no, then we can talk to the Episcopal minister."

"Sounds like a plan, babe." Liz snuggled close to him.

He sighed with relief. "Then... when will you come to Egypt?"

She took a deep breath. "We can have our wedding service here as soon as everyone can come. If neither church will perform it, we can simply have a plain old civil service at the justice of the peace. I need to call Poppa and Daddy tonight after we tell everyone and see when is the best day for them, assuming there is any flexibility to the date. Probably next weekend or the one the week after. Then, maybe we can squeeze in a little honeymoon for a couple of days before you have to go home and go back to work."

"Wait… You won't come back with me?" He looked stricken.

She bit her lip again. "I'll see if I can manage it. I need to bring my cats, and I'm not sure what that entails. I want to make sure Dave is comfortable taking over, and that Poppa approves of Dave to manage the bar when I leave. Let's face it. If I love Egypt, I won't be coming back here permanently. Once I get those things done, I could come to Egypt. If I can get it all done before you leave, I'll go with you. Otherwise, I don't think those things would take over a month at most."

"And you promise you won't change your mind?" He nibbled on his thumbnail.

She cringed. He didn't say the words 'like before,' but it hung in the air unspoken. She crossed her heart and then held up two fingers. "I promise I will not chicken out again. I will either go home with you when you return to Egypt, or I will come as soon as possible."

He smiled. "Go home with me, hmm?"

She nodded and gave him a crisp salute. "Yes, sir, Dr. Hotep."

He struggled to smile. Liz leaned close and kissed him. "I promise I'll come, Ari."

He pulled her into his arms and leaned close to her. He sniffed her hair as he rubbed a strand of hair between his fingers. It would kill him to lose her again. He forced a smile and nodded. "Okay. If you promise."

That evening, Liz called her family to come back over to the bar. When they arrived, she called everyone into the office. With Ari standing beside her, they announced they planned to marry as soon as possible.

Bella looked stunned but thrilled. "You told me she would accept this time."

Miguel grinned and pulled Bella to his chest. He kissed her forehead and hugged her tight. "I figured she had four years to think it over. I'm glad she accepted his proposal this time. Feel better about going to Egypt now, knowing your sister will be there, too?"

Bella beamed with excitement. Leaving Liz had been her greatest worry about moving to Egypt. She nodded. "Oh, yes. Much better."

He leaned over to kiss her once more, this time on her cheek. "Then I will tell Dr. Kate I accept the job."

Bella giggled as she gave his arm a light pop. "Pish… You and I know you were going to accept the job no matter what Liz said."

Fancy grabbed Liz and hugged her. "Baby girl, I'm so happy for you. I hate for two of my girls to move so far from home, but I am delighted you will marry the man who loves you and who you love, too. Congratulations to you both."

Dave grinned and slung a bar towel over his shoulder. He walked over to Ari and shook his hand. "Congratulations, dude."

Margaret, the waitress, hugged Liz and wished them every happiness, too, before she and Dave returned to work.

Once the evening crowd was in the club, Liz walked onto the stage. She turned on the karaoke machine and sang and danced to 'Walk Like an Egyptian.' As everyone clapped afterwards, Ari joined her on the stage, and they sang "Hooked on a Feeling." When they stopped, everyone cheered as Ari swept her into his arms and kissed her.

As the kiss ended, Ari cleared his throat. "I have the great honor to announce tonight Elizabeth Winslow finally agreed to become my wife. Now, it only took me four years to convince her to agree. She had some reluctance at first to moving to Egypt. Fortunately, she relented, and we plan to marry soon."

Everyone seemed pleased for them except Captain Johnny. Liz glanced over at the surly ghost several times, dismayed he continued to glower at them both. He sat in his favorite chair, arms crossed, his fingers tapping with nervous energy. She finally slipped over to the corner he favored.

"What's wrong, Johnny?"

He sniffed disdainfully. "Why Egypt?"

"He lives there."

The ghost shrugged and turned halfway from her. "I live here."

She giggled. "Well, Captain Johnny, I can't give up love for the spirit of a privateer who passed away in the early nineteenth century."

Johnny turned back towards her, with frustration written across his face. "You don't understand, Elizabeth. There are limits to what I can do. I am not sure I can travel to Egypt. Even if I can follow you, I am unsure whether I can protect you from certain evils which might befall you there."

Her eyes narrowed as she studied the ghost. "What are you trying to say, Johnny? Did my Poppa ask you to watch over me? to protect me?"

He shrugged again with a disdainful sniff. "Perhaps. In any case, I am uncertain if I can protect you in Egypt."

She laid her hand beside his arm. She knew from experience she could not touch him. "Why not?"

"They have strange and powerful gods in Egypt. Did you know they worship frogs?"

Liz tried not to shudder. She had an inordinate fear of frogs. She took a deep breath. "No, I didn't know that. Anyways, I bet they worshipped frogs a long time ago. Well, Johnny, perhaps it's time for you to go on to your eternal reward."

He glowered at her. "Who said anything about 'going on?' I said I am uncertain if I can protect you there. I will need to make certain inquiries."

She struggled not to laugh at the idea of a ghost 'making inquiries' about whether he could protect her if she moved halfway around the world. Sometimes he made the funniest comments. "I would appreciate that, Johnny. Thank you."

She paused. "Would you materialize a bit more solidly for me for a minute?"

He frowned at her unusual request. "Full body?"

She shook her head. "Just your cheek."

His eyes softened, as his cheek temporarily solidified. Liz chuckled as she leaned over to kiss the scruffy cheek of her favorite reprobate pirate.

Ari looked at her quizzically as she returned to his side. "What did your friendly ghost have to say?"

She shook her head and chuckled. "That darned old reprobate is unsure if he will be able to keep his promise to my father and continue to protect me if I move with you to Egypt."

Ari looked startled and glanced over to Johnny. "Why not?"

"He says there are 'strange and powerful gods in Egypt,' and he will have to 'make certain inquiries' if it is possible for him to go someplace where he has never been before. He is not all too crazy about moving to Egypt."

Ari struggled not to laugh. He glanced over at Johnny and gave him a smart salute. "Afraid of the heat, hmm?"

Liz chortled. She nodded as she struggled not to laugh. "Something like that would be my guess. Come on, let's greet my patrons."

Liz could see that her patrons making their way to congratulate them. Even Chuckie came forward to wish them happiness.

Ari shook the resident's hand. "I thought you wanted a date with Liz?"

He shrugged as his cheeks reddened. "Hey, you can't blame a guy for trying."

After an hour of congratulatory comments from the crowd, Ari and Liz slipped away before closing. They knew they had to get to church early the next morning to talk to the priest at the Coptic Church.

Chapter 11
Eighteenth Dynasty – Egypt
The Great Royal Wife

"Look, my beloved, the little frog eats out of my hand!" The beautiful woman stroked the frog's head as she fed it a dead fly.

Akhenaten shook his head reprovingly at his wife. He loved her with all his heart, but sometimes she acted as if she lacked common sense. "Nefertiti, you know not to handle a frog. It will make you sick."

She laughed, the sound sweet as a bird's song. She smiled at him. "Don't be silly, my love. She represents the fertility of our land. See? She wishes me to hold her, to caress her. In doing so, she will guarantee we will have a son."

Akhenaten rolled his eyes and shook his head in disgust. "Nefer, you know there is no god but the Aten. That is nothing but a dirty frog that hopped out of the Nile. It cannot guarantee us a son. Only Aten can give us a son."

Nefertiti smiled at her husband, amused by his comments. She composed her countenance so it would not distress her husband. She worked hard to always appear to agree with Akhenaten. "Of course, my lord, you are correct. That means my petting the little frog will have no adverse effect upon me. Humor this silly woman and allow me to pet my little frog friend."

She fed another dead fly to the frog.

Her husband grimaced with disgust as he shook his head. "To feed the frog, you must touch the dead. You must allow her to catch her own food. Don't touch the dead flies. They carry corruption and disease."

Nefertiti always struggled to support her husband in his belief of Aten, who he called the one true God. She stood by his side as he pronounced the other gods to be nothing and drove the priests out of the temples for all but Aten. She helped him when he insisted to build the new city to honor Aten. However, she still found it difficult to ignore the sweet little frog. For untold centuries, Egyptian women worshipped the Egyptian symbol of fertility and water, the little Nile frog goddess called Heket. The Nile was still high from the annual flooding. Everyone knew the frogs symbolized the fertility of the land and the people. Egyptians called the annual Nile flooding the 'Hapi.' Nefertiti longed to be rewarded by Heket and the Hapi this year with a son for her beloved husband.

With the body of a woman and the head of a frog, every woman in Egypt knew from an early age that Heket, their goddess of fertility, had the power to give them the babies they wanted. Human children were made at a potter's wheel from clay. After being shaped into human form, Heket breathed life into the child and then placed the baby into its mother's womb to grow. Heket was present at the birth of every child as an attending midwife.

Her husband did not know Nefer always wore a little turquoise amulet of Heket hidden within a secret pocket in the folds of her gown. She knew Heket would protect her when she went into labor with this seventh child, as she had done with the daughters Nefer gave her husband previously. Nefertiti quickly kissed the little frog and uttered a silent prayer. She slipped her little friend back into the garden waters which ran through the new palace at Akhetaten, the beautiful new city her husband built to honor the Aten and for her. She would not distress her husband with what he mocked as her old-fashioned beliefs. My heavens, he did not even acknowledge that Isis was the Giver of Life, or that she possessed great magic! What could her beliefs hurt anyway? She was merely one woman. And perhaps this time, Isis and the little frog goddess would give them the son they both desperately desired.

Ptah was another frog-headed god. Nefertiti could not imagine how any faithful Egyptian could ignore the great god, Ptah, who made his transformation to rise as the one who opened the lower world. He symbolized rebirth and reincarnation. He was the god of creation because he constructed the world in ancient Egypt using his heart and tongue. The world was built based on the power of Ptah's word and his command. All the gods who followed were given work based on what Ptah's heart devised and his tongue decreed. How could her husband ignore the words of Ptah? She feared

Akhenaten's rejection of the old gods would cause rage and chaos which could destroy their land.

And what would happen if Ptah denied their son his vital essence? How could a child be born without his *ka*?

Nefertiti ran her hands over her growing belly, worried anew that her husband's denial of the old gods might be why they did not already have a son. She bit her lip, praying that her husband's denial of Ptah, Isis, and little Heket would not result in her again giving birth to a daughter. She loved her daughters dearly, but she understood the Great Royal Wife and Wife of Aten had an obligation to provide a son for Pharaoh and Egypt.

She only had a few more months to pray for the birth of a healthy son. It was imperative that she give birth to a son this time. The priests and counselors already exhorted Akhenaten to take another wife into his bedchamber. Akhenaten was the love of her life. She had loved him since she first saw him when she was a child. It would kill her if she lost his favor to another woman. He had already wed and bedded Kiya. The Royal Princess was his sister. She had born four children, three daughters and a son. Tutankhaten was a good lad, but he was not born of her loins. She longed to give her beloved husband a son born of his Great Royal Wife who he would proclaim to be his heir.

Odd. She was never supposed to marry Akhenaten. When she came from Mitanni, her sister and she were young girls. Both were pledged to marry the old pharaoh, Amenhotep III. Her father sent the two girls with the agreement that she would become the Queen Consort. Pharaoh Amenhotep was already wed to Queen Tiye, who was his Queen Consort and Great Royal Wife. Even as a young girl, Nefertiti knew she could never replace Queen Tiye in Amenhotep's favor. Tiye was a wonderful queen, loved by the pharaoh and the people. It pleased Nefertiti when Pharaoh Amenhotep refused to put his beloved wife aside to marry her. She was only a child named Tadukhipa when she arrived from Mitanni. Queen Tiye had loved Amenhotep since she was a little older than Nefertiti was then and gave him many children.

Nefertiti smiled as she remembered the day she was called into the chambers of Vizier Ay. Her sister and she had been placed into the care of Vizier Ay and his wife until they were old enough to marry. She still chuckled that the official records showed that his wife was their nursemaid. She was more like a loving yet stern foster mother.

Nefertiti remembered how her heart leaped into her throat with terror at her first sight of Pharaoh Amenhotep. She shook her head and chuckled at the memory. Pharaoh Amenhotep seemed ancient to her when she first met him. Now, she realized he must have been about thirty-five. Her beloved Akhenaten was nearly that old.

Pharaoh Amenhotep brought two boys with him that fateful day. One was Thutmose, who was expected to be his heir. Although short and stout, the boy had a high opinion of himself. He barely wasted a glance at the girl standing before them. Nefertiti felt her cheeks flush with embarrassment as Thutmose sniffed and looked away from her.

The other lad was a tall, gangly boy called Amenhotep, like his father. He already had a rugged handsomeness that promised unusual looks as he matured. He gazed upon her with eyes of longing. It surprised Tadukhipa the young prince could not keep his eyes from her.

Vizier Ay ordered her to stand tall for the pharaoh and his sons to inspect her. Heart pounding with fear, she stood upright, as regal as possible for a ten-year-old princess. She was sent to Egypt to be a queen. She must impress Pharaoh Amenhotep and his sons. She wanted them to realize she would be a wonderful queen someday.

Finally, Pharaoh Amenhotep nodded his head. He cleared his throat and then spoke. "She is a beautiful child. She will be an excellent Queen Consort for you someday, my son."

The older boy deigned to smile at her. "I suppose she will do."

She blushed and lowered her eyes. She understood the pharaoh was pledging her to his son rather than marry her himself. For the first time since she came to Egypt, she felt relief. She would not have to marry an old man or compete with his beloved queen for his affections. Thutmose might be rude, but he was not an old man.

The younger boy frowned at his rude older brother. His disapproval of his brother's behavior was palpable. He leaned forward and impetuously lifted the long, plaited lock of her hair to sniff it. "Your hair smells like attar of roses, Princess Tadukhipa."

She raised her eyes to his. "It is my favorite scent, my lord."

He smiled. "This girl should not be called Tadukhipa. She should be called Nefertiti, for surely beauty has come to Egypt from Mitanni."

His older brother scowled at him. "She will be *my* queen, brother. It is not for you to name her."

The young Amenhotep chuckled. "Perhaps. We shall see. This beautiful girl should be honored with a name as impressive as she is."

She looked at him, surprised and thrilled by his words. As he smiled at her, she blushed and modestly lowered her eyes again. It was not seemly for a young maiden to stare at a young man, especially one who was not intended to become her husband someday.

Not long after that, the old pharaoh's older son died of a flux. Pharaoh Amenhotep died soon after his son's death. The tall, handsome, younger son became the new pharaoh. When he became pharaoh, he changed his name to Akhenaten, which meant 'Effective for the Aten.' He had chosen the Aten to be his primary god.

Four years later, she married the young man. As she reached him in the marriage ceremony, he bent to sniff her hair. He smiled. "I smell attar of roses."

She blushed as she smiled. "Yes, my lord Akhenaten. It is still my favorite scent."

"And because you wear it, it is now my favorite as well. This woman was previously known as Princess Tadukhipa of Mitanni. She shall henceforth be known as Nefertiti, for surely when she came to Egypt, beauty came to dwell amongst us. It shall further be recorded that Nefertiti shall be my Great Royal Wife and the Queen Consort of Upper and Lower Egypt. Send forth the royal announcements to all the lands accordingly. A messenger should leave for Mitanni within the hour to advise her father she has become Queen Consort to the Pharaoh of Egypt."

But since then, Akhenaten turned religion upside down in their country. He proclaimed only Aten would be worshipped to the shocked disbelief of many citizens. He declared Aten was the one true God, creator of the heavens and earth, and the giver of life.

Nefertiti diligently supported her husband in all his endeavors. She stood beside him at the altar of Aten and prayed with him there every day. Yet she often wondered if Akhen's rejection of the old gods, of the old ways, might be the reason she could never give him a son.

She secretly rubbed the tiny amulet of Heket in the hidden pocket in the lining of her gown. *Please, beloved Heket, give us a son this time.*

Chapter 12
Galveston to Cairo
Elizabeth

They arrived at the Coptic church early before the morning services began. Ari introduced them to the priest and explained they wanted to marry before Elizabeth moved to Egypt with him. They both looked disappointed as the Coptic priest stated he could not conduct a wedding within the next two weeks. Liz smiled as the priest offered to teach Liz the Coptic language immediately. He offered to tutor her for an hour a day via zoom meetings. Their lessons could continue via zoom when Liz went to Egypt.

Liz was not sure where to turn next when the Episcopal priest also stated he did not have availability in the next two weeks to hold even a small wedding. Bella saved the day. She called a judge she knew when Miguel and she lived in Galveston. Judge Nicholson readily agreed to hold the ceremony the following weekend. Liz hurriedly arranged for all her family to be in Galveston for the wedding ceremony. Bella and Fancy somehow found a wedding planner who quickly assisted them to set up the wedding at a covered pavilion on the beach.

The next few days were spent in a flurry of shopping. The wedding planner took them to a small wedding boutique to search for a simple wedding dress. Liz fell in love with a pretty, chiffon gown with a swirly skirt. The gown had a sweetheart neckline, and the lace above the neckline looked like an Egyptian collar. A delicate lace belt accented her trim waistline. The skirt fell to just below her knees, perfect for a beach wedding. Mom and Bella laughed when Liz selected a pair of sandals that looked like pearl encrusted starfishes crossed the instep of each foot. "What better for a beach wedding, Mom?"

Bella and Dara found gauzy dresses with swirly skirts they felt worked well with Liz's beach-worthy gown. Bella chose a soft blue and Dara selected pale lavender. Sara chose pale rose for her gown.

Fancy drew the short straw and had to call both Rick and Kirk to tell them Liz intended to marry the following weekend. Liz grimaced as Fancy held the phone out from her ear when she called Kirk. They could both hear every word as Kirk shouted the wedding was happening too soon and they needed to wait. Somehow, Mom convinced Kirk the wedding would happen with or without him. He continued to grumble, but finally conceded Mellie and he would come for his only daughter's wedding. "At least, she didn't elope like Sara did."

Fancy said nothing in response to his mention of Sara's recent elopement with Jackson Talbott. The unexpected elopement remained a sore spot with all of them. Jackson was ten years older than Sara and tended to put on airs and flirted with any woman he met. When Melanie learned about her daughter's elopement, she warned Sara she might well rue her rash decision to elope with Talbott. She told Sara 'if you marry in haste, you repent at leisure.'

Liz located a vet who could examine the cats, confirm their shots were in order, and sign their international travel permits. The vet provided mild tranquilizers to give the cats before the flight. He urged Liz to grind the pills and mix the crushed pills with some canned cat food. "You don't want to try stuffing pills down their throats the morning of your flight."

Liz cringed. She remembered the debacle which ensued the last time she had to give a pill to one of her kitties.

It thrilled Ari when Liz managed to obtain the international travel permits for her cats in a matter of days. He arranged for each of them to take a cat into the plane's cabin in its little cat carrier. That ensured Liz's beloved kitties did not have to be checked as freight.

Rick brought a pale pink sheath for Fancy to wear at Liz's wedding. He also brought Liz's passport from the safe in the house in San Antonio when he arrived for the wedding. He greeted Ari warmly, and the two men talked quietly away from the women. Liz bit back a grin as she noticed her dad slip an envelope to Ari.

The morning of their wedding, Liz ran to the hairdresser, who removed Liz's braids from her hair. The hairdresser styled Liz's chestnut brown hair to stream over her shoulders in loose waves.

Liz borrowed a pearl necklace from her mother and pearl earrings from Bella to wear at the ceremony. She wore no veil, but wore a wide-brimmed, white hat which would help protect her eyes in the afternoon sun on the beach.

Kirk continued to glower, although he gave Liz away in the lovely, small ceremony. As he handed her over to Ari, he muttered, "You had best treat her right, Hotep."

Liz huffed up and started to respond to Kirk. Ari laid a hand on her arm and smiled before he replied to Kirk. "It is all right, my love. Your father loves you. He only wants the best for you."

"That's right," growled Kirk.

Ari smiled and put an arm around Liz's shoulders. "I shall always treat her well, sir. I love your daughter more than life itself."

After a short ceremony, Judge Nicholson pronounced Ari and Liz man and wife. They enjoyed a small, intimate reception on the beach with her family. Later, they held another reception at Nefertiti's Bone Yard so Liz could bid farewell to her patrons and employees.

She frowned as she noticed Johnny and Kirk speaking quietly in the corner, frequently glancing at Ari and her. What was the troublesome old pirate saying to Poppa? Kirk was having a hard enough time with this quickie wedding. She could not believe how annoying Johnny had been all week long since he learned they were going to marry today. She did not need Johnny fueling Kirk's anger. She finally shrugged, determined not to let the worrisome ghost ruin her wedding day.

The following day, Liz gave the cats their medication to help them remain calm on the long flight. Bella and Miguel drove them to Bush International Airport since they would return to Boston on the same airline that morning. Bella and Liz hugged before Bella and Miguel boarded their flight to Boston.

Bella struggled to hold back tears. "You call me when you get to Cairo."

Liz hugged her sister again. "I will. And I promise to send you links to houses I think you will like."

Bella tried to smile. "I'll like anything that is near your home."

An hour later, Ari and Liz caught a plane for Cairo, with each lugging a carrier containing a sleepy cat. As they settled into their seats, Ari leaned over to her. "You know, my love, we could have found cats on the streets of Cairo and saved hundreds of dollars."

She stuck out her tongue at him. "Machi and Otto were my biggest emotional support for the past two years, Ari Hotep. I refuse to abandon my sweet kitties now."

Ari laughed and pulled her to him for a quick kiss. "I would never separate a mama from her babies."

Fifteen hours later, two nervous kitties and two exhausted humans arrived in Cairo. Three hours later, they had cleared customs and finally arrived at Ari's house. By then, the cats were howling to be released from their carriers. Ari and Liz were both way past tired of hearing the cats fuss. Ari commented he wished they had obtained anxiety medications for humans to take on the long trip. Liz sighed and nodded. "Me, too."

Once they moved all the bags into the house, Liz released the kitties from their carriers. Ari and she stood back to watch as the cats explored the courtyard. Once the cats found their food, water bowls, and their litter boxes, they appeared to relax and to settle into their new environment. Liz smiled as she watched Machi play with a large moth. Otto sighed and curled to go to sleep in the shaded courtyard. Finally confident the cats were adapting to their new home, Liz and Ari trudged upstairs. They collapsed into each other's arms on Ari's bed for some well-deserved rest.

The next morning, Ari brought Liz a cup of coffee as she stared out the window into the courtyard, deep in thought. "A penny for your thoughts. Are you already having second thoughts about this move?"

She shook her head and took a long sip of her coffee. "Of course, not. I'm tired, but I expected to feel fatigued. That's why we wanted to come back now instead of next weekend. It gives you a week to rest before you return to work. But, Ari, I had the strangest dream last night."

Ari glanced back at her as he walked to the kitchen. "What did you dream?"

She shrugged. "Some woman who looked a lot like me was playing with a frog."

Ari stopped flipping the pancakes he was preparing for his bride and stared at her. "It probably was you. Why would that surprise you?"

Liz could feel her cheeks redden. "I told you before. I have a ridiculous, phobic fear of frogs. I understand it is silly. Frogs won't hurt me. Not most frogs, anyway. There are some tree frogs in South America which are poisonous, but we are not in South America. Anyway, I doubt I would ever play with a frog. Heck, I can't imagine voluntarily touching a frog."

Ari burst out laughing as she shuddered. "You're serious? You are afraid of little bitty frogs? This move to Egypt might not work out too well then."

Her head whipped around to stare at him. "Why not?"

He struggled to control his laughter. "Like I told you in Texas, my love. Several of the ancient gods were reputed to have the heads of frogs. Ptah, the giver of life, had the body of a man and the head of a frog."

Liz paled. She hoped Ari could not see her hands trembling. "Uh... why would ancient Egyptians worship a frog man? I think frogs are repulsive."

Ari struggled not to laugh again. "But, darling, frogs are so ugly that they are cute. Every year when the Nile would flood, the frog eggs laid the year before during the summer season hatched and became tadpoles. Soon after, the Nile Valley would be overrun with thousands of little frogs. We no longer have annual flooding since the Aswan High Dam was constructed. However, my people have long considered frogs to bring good luck. Frogs really frighten you?"

Liz nodded. She struggled to keep her revulsion out of her voice and off her face. "Yeah. I understand it is not a logical fear, but... your people actually worshipped frogs as gods?"

Laughter burst out of Ari's mouth again. His eyes twinkled with mischief. "Yes, I'm afraid so. Don't worry. I'll keep you safe from the big, bad froggies."

She glowered at him as she slugged his arm. "Oh, shut up."

They drove to the registry office with the documents from Judge Nicholson and Galveston County about their marriage. The clerk did not look thrilled to be registering a civil ceremony, but duly recorded the marriage of Dr. Aristotle 'Ari' Hotep and Miss Elizabeth Ann Winslow. They assured the clerk they would have a religious ceremony as soon as the Coptic Orthodox minister could schedule it. Ari explained Liz's Coptic had to improve before they could hold a wedding in Egypt. They did not mention they were already living together. The clerk politely refrained from asking the question.

Later, Ari took her to the Cairo Museum of Antiquities. Liz listened to the tour guide, fascinated by the beautiful exhibits and the vast array of mummies. "It's incredible."

Ari nodded. "I agree. Levi helped move the mummies to this new location. It was an enormous honor for him to be allowed in the procession."

"Wow. That would have been something to see."

Ari grinned. "It was, and you can still see it on YouTube."

Liz's eyes lit with excitement. She grabbed his sleeve. "Oh, Ari, we'll have to find it. I would love to see the procession."

He patted her hand. "We'll watch it tonight, my love."

The following morning, they drove around Cairo with Ari pointing out various sites to her. They stopped by the Coptic Church so Ari could introduce her to the priest. Father Andreas sounded thrilled she was studying their religion and language.

Afterward, they drove to several of the newer neighborhoods. Ari showed her the areas where he thought Bella would be most interested in living. She snapped photos of several houses she thought Miguel and Bella might like and texted them to her sister.

"Miguel comes in two weeks. It would be nice if I could narrow down the house search for him before he arrives. Maybe I could get a realtor to show me a couple of these and conduct zoom tours with Bella."

"That's an excellent idea, my love. I bet Miguel would appreciate you doing that for Bella."

Ari called his brother that evening. It thrilled Levi to learn they were back in Egypt and that Liz was enjoying it so far. He urged Ari to bring Liz to see Luxor. "There is much to show her here, Ari."

"I agree. The problem is there is so much to show her in our country that it is hard to know where to begin."

Levi suggested they go first to the Giza Plateau. He assured them Anna, his wife, would be thrilled to have them as overnight guests and show them around the Giza Plateau. After a call to Anna, Liz and Ari decided to drive to their home on the Giza Plateau the next morning.

Ari convinced her that the cats were settling into the new house well, and that Machi and Otto would be fine while they went on their trip. "The cats have food and water. They should be fine until we come back in a few days. I still cannot believe you named them Machi and Otto. Hilarious names."

She grinned. "What? You don't love caramel macchiatos? I do. Of course, they are both the color of caramels. Hmm. I guess I could have named them Coco and Chanel."

Ari groaned. "Only my wife would have thought of those names for cats."

Liz smiled as her eyes softened. "Your wife. I like the sound of that, Dr. Hotep."

He beamed back at her as he pulled he into his arms. He answered her after a long, lingering kiss. "I am glad you do, Mrs. Hotep."

Ari's next-door neighbor came over to meet her and offered to watch the cats for them while they went on their mini honeymoon. He would make sure they had fresh food and water every evening.

"There is plenty of cat food and water out for them in the automatic feeders. They should be fine for a few days, but I appreciate your offer to check on them, Mr. Maksoud."

He bowed slightly. "It is my pleasure, Mrs. Hotep. Enjoy the rest of your honeymoon."

The following day, the temperature soared before they left the house. Despite the soaring heat, Ari urged Liz to wear a something cool yet modest. She pouted, but she realized she needed to learn how to live in Egypt like an Egyptian. She pulled off the halter top and shorts and pulled on a sleeveless print tunic and tan slacks.

Ari complimented her on her clothing selections for the day. "You look beautiful, as always. However, you might regret the lack of sleeves. I know it's hot today. The linen tunic will wick perspiration and will have a cooling effect. However, long sleeves would also protect your beautiful silken skin from the unforgiving Egyptian sun."

Liz glowed at the compliment. Her husband was one sweet talker. "My beautiful silken skin, hmm? Thank you for the lovely compliment, Dr. Hotep. Maybe tomorrow. Right now, I'm hot as the blazes. I don't think I could bear to wear long sleeves today. Besides, I never sunburn. I'll just tan darker."

He laughed, his intriguing eyes twinkling with mischief. "Don't say I didn't warn you."

Liz pulled on her floppy hat and sunglasses before they went outside to the car. She sighed as she settled back against the tan, butter-soft, leather seat of Ari's Mercedes Benz SUV while they sped down the highway to the Giza Plateau. Ari laughed as she bounced up and down at the sight of the Great

Pyramid in the distance. "Oh, my gosh, Ari, I can see the pyramids! Look, babe!"

"We will see the Great Pyramid and the Sphinx later today, my love. Anna plans to take us to visit them."

"And Saqqara?" Her voice sounded eager. Her eyes twinkled with excitement as she pulled on his shirt sleeve.

He laughed as he shook his head. He pulled his shirt from her fingers as he reached around her shoulders. He bent over to give her a quick kiss. "No, we will see Saqqara another day. I am sure Levi will want to show it to you. He discovered the burial tomb of the unknown princess who was buried there. He is one of a handful of archeologists authorized to show you those."

Anna Hotep seemed thrilled to see them when they arrived at the Hotep home. She ushered Ari and Elizabeth into her home for pastries and coffee. Afterwards, she left the children with their live-in nanny to take Ari and Liz to see the Great Pyramid and the Sphinx. "Levi can take you inside to tour the Great Pyramid and Saqqara. I lack those credentials. You can go without a guide, or I can show you all around the outside and in the adjacent museum."

"That sounds fine, Anna. You be our guide today." Liz beamed at her sister-in-law.

Anna reached over and squeezed Liz's hand. "Wonderful. The Great Pyramid was built for Pharaoh Khufu during the Fourth Dynasty. It stands 481 feet tall and was the tallest man-made structure in the world for over 3800 years. White limestone originally covered the exterior, with a gold capstone, or pyramidion. Unfortunately, the gold capstone and gleaming, white limestone were removed long ago. The archeologists say it required 2.3 million large blocks weighing a total of 6 million tons to build the Great Pyramid. They wondered for many years how the Egyptians moved the limestone to this location, but they recently discovered a canal dug from the Nile over here to make transportation of the limestone blocks much easier."

"You should be a tour guide, Anna," Liz said.

Anna beamed at Liz. "I was a tour guide before we had children. Now, the children take most of my time. I am lucky to have a live-in nanny to help me, but this way I can home school the children. It would be difficult to have to drive into Cairo every day to take Theo and Naomi to the Coptic school. They were elated to have a holiday from their studies today. Theo won't enter first grade until the fall term, but he loves to read. He already reads better than Naomi, and she is three years older than Theo."

By the time they returned to Anna and Levi's home, Liz's cheeks and shoulders were turning red from the sun. She winced as she slipped out of the sleeveless blouse that evening.

Ari struggled to bite back a grin. "I tried to warn you."

She glumly nodded. "Yes, you did. You earned the right to 'tell me so' – this time. Believe me, I learned my lesson. I'll wear sleeves tomorrow if I can bear to have sleeves over my sunburned skin. I don't think I ever sunburned before, Ari. I usually just tan darker."

He laughed. "Ah, but now you are in Egypt, near the equator. The rays of the sun are more direct here. Even skin kissed by the sun since birth like ours will darken and burn under the Egyptian sun."

She pouted. "Okay, I get your point. Here. Help smooth this moisturizer on my shoulders."

She handed the little jar of the expensive cream to him. He bent over, kissed her shoulder, and then smoothed it onto her skin.

"Better?"

"Much. Now, make love to me, Dr. Hotep."

He sat the little jar on the nightstand by the bed. "Of course, Mrs. Hotep. I thought you would never ask."

He reached over and turned off the light as she giggled.

Early the next morning, Liz donned a long-sleeved, pale blue, linen blouse over a soft, knit crop top. If the linen blouse proved unbearable on her sunburned shoulders, she figured she could get away with the crop top in the car or in tourist areas. She could button the blouse to appear more modest if needed although the crop top was much more her normal style. The softened linen shirt paired nicely with a pair of blue linen slacks. She understood now why Mom insisted she bring linen and cotton garments. She took the linen shirt off when she slipped into the passenger seat. Liz folded the linen shirt neatly and placed it on the back seat so it would not wrinkle on the trip south. Ari turned the air conditioning on full blast as the sleek SUV hurried south along the Nile toward Luxor. Liz slept in the comfortable leather seat until he awakened her to see Amarna.

"There is not much to see there now. The city was originally called Akhetaten. They call it Amarna now. This is where they discovered the bust of Nefertiti. They found it in the workshop of an artist named Thutmose. The bust is in the museum in Munich."

She sniffed in disdain. "The Munich Museum should be required to return that bust to Egypt. It is a national treasure."

Ari laughed. "Now you sound like an Egyptian, my love. Yes, they should be required to return the bust. Dr. Hassan has argued for the return of the Nefertiti bust for years. Did you know Germany changed its law to justify keeping the bust? Their law now says if they have had an artifact over twenty-five years, it becomes the property of Germany."

She sniffed again, this time in disgust. "That is so low class."

They arrived at Luxor a little after noon. Ari parked the car as Elizabeth buttoned her linen blouse to cover the crop top, touched up her lipstick and ran a brush through her hair. She hurried to pull her thick, curly hair into a ponytail. Ari quickly found his brother working beside another archeologist as they examined a mummy. The brothers hugged, and then Ari introduced Liz to Levi.

Levi scowled. "Am I to understand you are the woman who refused to marry my brother four years ago in New York?"

As Liz stammered, Ari and Levi burst into laughter. Ari pulled her into his arms. "He's teasing you, Elizabeth."

Liz frowned at Levi. "I thought I made the right decision for Ari back then. I was wrong. Thank heaven, we have another chance at love. Be happy for us, Levi. Don't make fun of me."

Levi pulled his new sister-in-law into his arms for a hug. "Ari is correct. I am teasing you, little sister. Let me introduce you to my boss. Dr. Hassan, this is my brother, Ari, and his wife, Elizabeth."

Dr. Hassan wiped the dust off his hands before he walked over and shook their hands. "I met Dr. Hotep at Saqqara last year. However, I did not realize you were married. Why have I never seen this exquisite young lady before?"

Liz smiled. "I met Ari in the United States four years ago, Dr. Hassan. We married in Galveston, Texas last weekend. I am delighted and honored to meet you, sir. I believe I have seen all the shows on television in which you were featured. You taught me a great deal about Egypt and its remarkable history before I arrived. I want to see all of Egypt's treasures, but I am especially eager to see this Golden City your team recently discovered here at Luxor. Ari has been telling me about the remarkable finds your team has made so far. How many undisturbed tombs have you found? Ari thought you have found about thirty."

Dr. Hassan beamed with pride at her words of praise and her enthusiasm for their dig. "It has been a team effort, Mrs. Hotep. Levi has been especially helpful here, as he was at Saqqara. He is one of our finest archeologists. We have found thirty-five undisturbed tombs in our Golden City so far."

"Why is it called the Golden City?" asked Liz.

Dr. Hassan chuckled. "That is an excellent question, Mrs. Hotep. I call it 'the Golden City' because it was built during Egypt's Golden Age. Amenhotep III was Pharaoh when Egypt was richest. He named this city 'tehn Aten,' which means 'dazzling Aten.' The Golden City is easier to remember than is 'tehn Aten.' When ancient Egyptian kings built a city, they dedicated it to a deity to whom they associated. Aten is usually associated with Amenhotep III's son, Akhenaten, who worshipped Aten and banned the worship of the other Egyptian deities. Akhenaten later built the city of Akhetaten, which today is known as Amarna. Amarna is much easier to remember and to say than is Akhetaten. It is about 250 miles north of here."

Liz nodded. "Yes, Ari pointed it out to me as we drove here from Levi and Anna's house this morning."

Dr. Hassan smiled. "Excellent. Now, allow me to show you around."

Liz could barely contain her enthusiasm. She realized people paid big bucks for tours of the Egyptian archeological sites led by Dr. Zain Hassan. She hung on every word as the world-famous archeologist guided them through the Golden City. They passed the tented area in which archeologists cataloged newly discovered mummies. Dr. Hassan permitted them to enter the tent to glimpse at the mummies. They next passed walls of ancient buildings which were being uncovered for the first time in countless centuries. It amazed Liz to discover some of the walls were nine feet tall.

"How could people have missed all of this for so many years, Dr. Hassan?" Liz inquired.

He smiled again, thrilled by her interest. "It was covered with sand. The sands of Egypt hide many treasures we have not yet found. We are finding much more with the use of radar. Many sites have been found using radar from planes flying above as well as new land-based techniques. One of our graduate students came up with that idea several years ago."

Liz nodded. "I remember a television documentary about that technique. I recall the student was a woman. Wasn't her name Selma? No, I think it was Salima. I remember she was a pretty woman, and I loved her name."

He chuckled. "Her name is Salima Mafous. She is a lovely lady, and now she is one of the excellent archeologists working on the team here. Let's find her."

They entered another tented area which covered the steps leading down to a cluster of underground tombs. The newly discovered tombs were about five feet below the surface of the ground. As they approached a group of archeologists working on unearthing another tomb, Dr. Hassan called out to Dr. Mafous. "Salima, come here for a minute. I want to introduce you to Levi's new sister-in-law, Elizabeth Hotep. She is interested in our Golden City."

The two women chatted for a few minutes while Ari spoke with his brother and Dr. Hassan. "I can see she is getting tired. She is not accustomed to our heat yet."

Dr. Hassan studied Elizabeth's movements. "Yes, she appears fatigued. Ari, take her a bottle of water. You don't want her to dehydrate."

Ari nodded. "That's an excellent idea, Zain."

Zain Hassan showed him where an ice chest held bottles of water. He pulled out a bottle and handed it to Ari. "Take this to her. Ari, I feel certain she will adjust. She exudes enthusiasm about Egypt and loves our antiquities. She will love our country as well. I cannot get over her resemblance to the bust of the Royal Queen Consort, Queen Nefertiti."

Ari nodded. "I agree. It stunned me the first time I saw Elizabeth. I made quite a muddle out of our conversation that day. Her resemblance to Queen Nefertiti is uncanny. However, Elizabeth has a vision problem, Dr. Hassan. We keep her out of too much direct sun. She sunburned yesterday. She claims she never sunburned before in her lifetime. So much exposure to the sun could not have been good for her eyes. We have been up since six this morning. It was a five-hour drive from Levi's home. She napped for part of the ride, but she is fascinated by our land, and did not want to miss a thing. We have been out here for several hours. She appears to be tiring rapidly. I'll run the water over to her. It should help."

Dr. Hassan's eyes narrowed. "What sort of vision problem does she have?"

Ari never took his eyes off Liz. "Stargardt disease."

Dr. Hassan looked shocked. "Oh, that is a shame. She is so young, so full of life."

Ari nodded. "She would not marry me at first because of the diagnosis. She felt I deserved better than a woman going blind. I finally convinced her she is the woman I love, and I deserve no less than love. Nor does she. Her vision is fairly stable in her right eye, but it is rather poor in her left eye."

"Ah, that explains why I noticed she holds things up to her right eye," observed Levi.

Ari nodded. "I hope she has her magnifying glass with her. I'll be right back after I take her the water."

He caught Liz's hand before she descended into the crypt. "Here's some water, darling. Don't get dehydrated."

She caught the bottle he handed to her and blew him a kiss. "Thanks, babe."

Elizabeth opened the water bottle and drank it as she walked down the steep steps into the crypt where the tombs were located. She placed the empty bottle into a basket for recyclables. She bent down beside Salima, who lifted a soft brush and gently brushed away dirt from the surface of the ancient tomb.

"We think this may be the tomb of a person of some importance. The tomb is more elaborately carved than most, from what I have cleaned away so far. It appears to be from eighteenth dynasty or close to it. You brush it like this, Elizabeth. Here. Now, you try."

Liz squatted beside Salima and took the small brush the archeologist offered to her. Following Salima's directions, she gently eased dirt and sand from the exterior of the tomb. The two women worked side by side in silence for about an hour. Finally, Liz lifted her magnifying glass to peer at an inscription carved into the side of the tomb. Her eyes narrowed as she peered at the engraving. "Salima, isn't this a cartouche?"

Salima frowned. "Oh, I doubt it, Elizabeth. A cartouche usually showed the name of a monarch."

Liz leaned closer to examine the engraving on the side of the tomb as she uncovered it of the centuries of dirt and sand. "Salima, I would swear that this is a cartouche. I think it reads N-F-R-T-T. Doesn't that mean 'Nefertiti'?"

Salima looked surprised. She bent over, and carefully traced the ancient carving with her finger. She raised up, excitement radiating from her face.

"Elizabeth, you are correct. How did you know the meaning of this cartouche?"

Liz chuckled, suddenly self-conscious. "Well, Ari says I look like Queen Nefertiti. He showed me what her name looks like when written in hieroglyphics."

"You could almost be her twin. Your eye color is different, but other than that, the resemblance is astonishing."

Liz felt her cheeks turn red with embarrassment. "I honestly don't see the resemblance. My eyes are gray, and my skin is darker than the bust of the Great Queen. I think a person would have to be incredibly vain to claim she resembled the woman who has been heralded as the epitome of feminine beauty. Anyway, Ari taught me the cartouche for my 'look-alike'."

She made air quotes around 'look-alike.' She did not want anyone to think she was vain enough to compare her looks to those of the incomparable Queen Nefertiti, reputed to have been one of the world's greatest beauties.

"Ah, but your bone structure is identical to that of the woman in the bust. If they changed her eye color and slightly darkened her complexion, it could be you." Salima looked up and smiled when she spotted Dr. Hassan talking with Ari and Levi near the tomb. "Dr. Hassan, please come here. You must see what Mrs. Hotep discovered!"

The three men hustled over to the women, and Dr. Hassan bent down to examine the carving. He let out a low whistle of surprise. "Mrs. Hotep-"

"Please, Dr. Hassan, you must all call me Elizabeth," Liz interrupted with an embarrassed grin.

He smiled. "Elizabeth, I understand you are studying Coptic, which is our ancient language. Can you tell me what this says?"

She grinned and nodded. "Well, Coptic is supposed to be the language ancient Egyptians spoke, but it is written with Greek letters. However, unless I am mistaken, that is the cartouche for Queen Nefertiti."

Dr. Hassan looked surprised and pleased. "You are correct. Gentlemen, I believe our Elizabeth has found the tomb of Queen Nefertiti. As you know, Nefertiti's tomb has never been discovered elsewhere. We think Tutankhamun was buried in the tomb intended for her, and his famous funerary mask was made for her. We had reason to believe we might find her tomb here. Beauty has indeed come to the Golden City today."

Elizabeth continued carefully working with Salima through the afternoon. By late afternoon, they meticulously removed countless decades of sand from the front of the exterior of the tomb. The two women talked about their families as they worked. Liz told Salima she grew up in Georgia and went to New York City to study dance. She told Salima about the horrific accident which ended her professional dancing career. She was telling Salima how she met Ari when Salima grabbed Liz's hand.

"Stop." Salima's voice sounded harsh, almost fearful.

Liz's hand stooped midway back to the face of the tomb. "Why? What's wrong?"

Salima pointed to another engraving they had just cleaned. "This tomb is protected by a curse. This was placed on the tomb to serve as a powerful amulet of protection for her tomb for all eternity. We must not open the tomb yet. Mustafa, send for Dr. Hassan. He must see this immediately."

Liz stared wide-eyed as Salima sent for the head archeologist. After Mustafa left, she whispered. "Are you serious? It's cursed? What does it say?"

Salima looked grim. "The engraving says whoever opens this tomb will give their *ka* to the one who lies herein. We must call the religious leaders to pray over this."

Liz bit back laughter of disbelief. "It says a dead woman will steal the soul of the person who opens the tomb. But how could a dead person take the soul from a living person?"

Salima shrugged. "I don't know. However, archeologists have opened cursed tombs in the past and fell victim to the curses. Nowadays, we have a Coptic priest come out to pray protective prayers before opening tombs bearing a curse."

Liz didn't know whether to laugh or scream in terror. "Uh… why a Coptic priest instead of a Muslim imam? That's the right word, isn't it?"

She nodded. "We have both the Coptic priest and the Muslim imam come out to the site in cases such as this. However, members of the Coptic religion speak a version of the Egyptian language which the ancients spoke. If the spirits of ancient Egyptians can hear the prayers, we believe the prayers in Coptic will touch their hearts before those in Arabic, which they would not know."

Liz looked around and then leaned close to Salima. "But they are dead."

Salima shrugged. "Are they? They believed they would be in suspended animation until called back to life. Their belief is not dissimilar from the Christian belief in resurrection and life after death. Her tomb is protected with a curse. We will call the priest and the imam to say the prayers before we go on."

Liz shrugged and sat her tools down. She brushed the sand off her hands before she arose. "Well, all righty then."

Liz helped Salima stretch warning tapes across the top of the tomb and across the partially exposed side. They had put away their tools as Dr. Hassan and two teenaged girls entered the covered area where they had been excavating.

"And we believe this is the tomb of the royal queen, Nefertiti." He frowned. "Salima, what is wrong? Why have you called for me?"

She pointed to the front of the exquisitely carved tomb. "It is cursed."

He scowled. "Again? Did you send for the Coptic priest and the imam?"

She shook her head. "We just taped it off. I was about to make the calls. Zain, Elizabeth is proving to be a wonderful help. You should talk to her about joining our graduate research program."

He beamed as he patted Liz on the shoulder. "I agree. Elizabeth, you have already contributed significantly to this dig. I would like to invite you to apply to our graduate program. I guarantee you will be admitted."

She laughed. "Sir, we only arrived here. Ari has not even gone back to work yet. I need to speak and write Arabic with some fluency before I consider going to graduate school. And, to tell the truth, I have a vision problem."

He shrugged. "I know, my dear. Ari mentioned it. We can talk about graduate school more later after you have settled into life in Egypt. Girls, you may not touch this tomb. Elizabeth Hotep discovered the cartouche for 'Nefertiti.' With the warning of a curse attached to the tomb, we feel certain this tomb houses the mummy of Queen Nefertiti."

One of the girls reached toward the tomb. "Oh, Dr. Hassan, are you sure we can't touch it? I would really love to have my photo taken sitting on it."

Salima grabbed the girl's hand. "No, Marjorie. It would be an insult to the one in the tomb for you to sit on it. Such ill-mannered behavior could prove dangerous. That is why we have now taped it off from casual touch. We must move with caution now."

The petite blond-haired teen named Marjorie sniffed, shrugged, and began looking around at the other work in progress. "So, what is going on over here? Are there any tombs of other famous dead people down here?"

Dr. Hassan frowned. "We do not know yet. Christina, stop leaning against that tomb. It is the final resting place of a human being. It is not a lounging chair. You must not disrespect the dead."

The taller brunette girl frowned. "My daddy said that I could see anything I wanted to see."

Dr. Hassan glowered at the girl. "That is incorrect. You may see anything I allow you to see, and you may do what I allow you to do. Now, stop leaning on the tombs or this tour will terminate immediately. And let me add that if you climb on top of any of these tombs to get a selfie, you will be permanently banned from my sites. You must not disrespect the dead. Do you understand?"

"Yes, sir," came the grumbled reply from both girls.

Liz struggled not to laugh. Finally, she spoke. "Where do you girls live? I swear I hear a little bit of Georgia in your accents."

Marjorie gasped. Christina shrugged. "Savannah. Why?"

"I grew up in Blue Ridge. I always loved going to Savannah and to Tybee Island. It's nice to hear that accent again."

Christina stared at her. "So, where did you stay at Tybee Island? Or did your family camp out on the beach?"

Both girls snickered.

Liz ignored the intended slur and laughed. "Oh, no. My parents own a beach house there, right where the Savannah River runs into the Atlantic. I love to go to Tybee Island. My dance group, the Cohutta Queens, used to hold our summer camps there every year."

"You were a Cohutta Queen dancer?"

"Yes, I was a Cohutta Queen until I went to Juilliard in New York. After Julliard, I danced with the Joffrey Ballet."

The two girls looked stunned.

Christina arched a brow. "And you say the group used to hold summer camp at your parents' house?"

Liz nodded. "Yes. It's a large residence. And like I said, it's right on the Atlantic."

Christina snorted. "Uh, honey, those houses are kind of pricey."

"Uh, honey, you think I don't know that? My dad's a cardiovascular surgeon. He could afford it."

Christina blinked. "*Your* dad is a cardiovascular surgeon?"

Liz smiled. The girl's condescension was wearing on her last nerve. "Yes. Perhaps you have heard of him. My dad is Dr. Richard Winslow. He and Dr. Dan Smith created the Smith-Winslow valve and minimally invasive valve replacement procedure."

"Holy crap, Chrissie, your dad was talking about Dr. Winslow a few days ago," Marjorie blurted. "He invented the valve they put in your mom's heart."

Chrissie shrugged her friend's hand off her shoulder. "Well, here's a news flash for you, sugar. Dr. Winslow is white. I don't think he has any blackish kids."

Liz bit back her initial inclination to beat the little racist brat into the ground. Instead, she smiled. "Well, here's a news flash to you, sugar. Dr. Winslow is part black. His wife is part black. My five siblings are all part black. And I'm part black. We're all blackish, although I think we all look like various shades of tan in color."

About then, Ari walked over and slipped an arm around Elizabeth's shoulders. "Are you having fun this afternoon?"

"Um... the writing on the tomb says it is cursed," Elizabeth replied, without taking her eyes off Christina.

"Holy Christ on a stick! Vavavavoom!" Marjorie appeared to be salivating over Ari.

Elizabeth wondered if she should wipe the drool off Marjorie's receding chin. Her eyes narrowed as she frowned at the teen. She had not expected to run into such poor representatives of the United States.

As Ari frowned at the girl's crude comment, Salima spoke up. "Girls, this is a Muslim country. We believe Jesus was a prophet. We do not say things like 'Holy Christ on a stick.' It is vulgar."

As both girls giggled, Ari replied. "I agree, it is vulgar, and at that, ten percent of us are Christians. I take it personally when people say such crude things."

Liz cleared her throat. "Um, girls, allow me to introduce my husband, Dr. Ari Hotep."

"Are you an archeologist, Dr. Hotep?" Marjorie tossed her long, straight, blonde hair over her shoulder flirtatiously.

Ari rolled his eyes. "No, I am an ophthalmologist. Elizabeth, we need to leave soon. I promised Levi and Zain that we would meet them later for dinner."

"Of course, darling." She beamed at her handsome husband. "Let me help Salima finish this, and I'll be right there."

As Ari walked away to go locate his brother, Salima grinned at Elizabeth. "I must agree with Marjorie. He is definitely worthy of a 'vavavavoom'!"

Liz laughed and hugged her new friend. "I agree. He is one fine hunk of chocolate thunder."

"Elizabeth!" Salima sounded shocked by Liz's comment.

Liz laughed again. "Well, he is, Salima. And believe me, girls, I don't share my chocolate thunder with anyone."

Marjorie pouted as Christina chortled at her friend's embarrassment.

"So, can we see inside the tomb of this old dead queen tomorrow?"

Salima shut her eyes as she counted to twenty under her breath. Liz forced a smile. "Perhaps you can get a closer look tomorrow. It depends when the priest and the imam come out to pray over the tomb. Why?"

Christina pouted. She sighed aloud as she flipped her hair back over her shoulder again. "We want to see it before we have to leave. It's the most interesting thing out here. Gosh, it is so hot and dirty. All we have seen is just a bunch of crumbling old buildings, broken pots, and a few old, moldy mummies. Is it always so hot here?"

Liz smiled again. "Well, it's Egypt, and it's September, so yes, it's always this hot during this month. It was supposed to hit 105 degrees Fahrenheit today. It is not as hot as it was last month. What did you girls expect? Air-conditioned tombs?"

Christina shrugged. "With all the money my dad donates, I kinda expected air conditioning out here. I sure expected something nicer than a bunch of creepy old dead bodies and tombs out in the middle of nowhere in the desert. Come on, Marjorie. Let's find my dad. I'm ready to blow this dump."

Liz stared after the girls in disbelief. She could not get over the poor impression the two spoiled brats made of Americans.

Salima let out a long sigh of relief. "Thanks be to Allah that the teens are now leaving."

"I am so sorry that visiting Americans act like those ill-mannered brats. Believe me, Salima, not all Americans behave like those cretins. "

She laughed. "Oh, believe me, I know. I did my graduate work in the United States. I found the people frank, but usually honest and quite interested in crumbling old buildings, broken pottery, and moldy old mummies."

Liz chuckled. It pleased her to know Salima realized the girls were not typical representations of American teens. "Like I said, cretins."

Chapter 13
The Eighteenth Dynasty
Nefertiti

It was a beautiful, clear night, although it was still painfully hot. Nefertiti moaned as she rubbed her temples. "My head pains me dreadfully tonight, my love."

Pharaoh Akhenaten chuckled as he he sat beside his queen on her bed. "You were probably out in the sun too long today playing with your frogs."

He reached over to caress her breasts, but she swatted at his hands. "Don't, Akhen, I am not in the mood. My head aches horribly, and my feet are so swollen. I kept them in the cool water this afternoon, but the swelling remains. What could it be?"

Her husband frowned as he bent over to look at her feet. He next examined her hands. He winced at the sight of her swollen extremities. "I do not know, my love. I never noticed swelling in your feet or hands like this before during one of your pregnancies."

She shook her head as she laid down on the bed and covered her face with her hands. "A little right at the end, but I still have two months to go before this child is born. And I cannot remember ever having a pounding headache like this before today."

The Pharaoh frowned as he straightened up. He motioned for her Majesty's slave girl. "Miriam, fetch a cool, wet rag for her Majesty's face. Scent it with the attar of roses she likes."

The girl bowed low. "Of course, Great Pharaoh."

"Not too much, Miriam. Just a drop or two of the scent, please."

"Yes, of course, my Queen. Right away." The girl bowed to both and quickly backed out of the room.

Akhenaten waited until the slave girl left to say anything else, but Nefertiti felt sure her husband seethed with anger. "Yes, my lord?"

He shook his head. "You are far too easy on your slaves, my love."

She patted beside her body on the bed. "Yes, my beloved. I know. You have told me this many times. Please, my love, sit beside me. Perhaps you might rub my temples and say a little prayer for me. My slaves are eager to please me, while yours run because they fear you."

He snorted as he crossed his arms. "A little fear is a good thing in a slave."

She smiled up at the man she adored. "Perhaps so, my love. Will you rub my temples for me?"

His face softened as he stared down at his Great Royal Wife. They had been married fourteen years, and she was still the most beautiful woman he had ever known. He bent over to kiss her. "Of course, I will, my Nefer. But you must promise me that you will get better. I cannot have the mother of my son feeling unwell."

She laughed softly as she trailed a finger down his face. "Of course, my lord. It would be unbecoming for the wife of Pharaoh Akhenaten to feel ill during her pregnancy."

He nodded as he gently rubbed her temples. "I agree. I shall pray to ask Aten to protect you and heal you this evening, my love. I know that He shall see you safely through your pregnancy again."

She sighed and smiled as he gently rubbed her temples. "Of course, my beloved."

She slipped one hand to her side and gently caressed the tiny amulet of the frog in the hidden pocket of her dress. Akhenaten could pray to his Sun God. She would continue to pray to Heket as she had with all her pregnancies. She came through all those pregnancies just fine. What a man did not know would not hurt him, would it?

Miriam quickly returned with the cloth. She held it out to Pharaoh. "Here is the linen, my lord. Shall you need the clay crocodile? I brought two, one for her forehead, and one for her nape."

He frowned but nodded. "Yes, I will use both. While I do not believe the crocodile can cure her, the cool linen rag held in place with the water-cooled clay will put pressure to her scalp and ease her pain."

"Of course, Great Pharaoh. Both have already been soaked so the wet, cool clay should help ease her Majesty's headache." The slave girl bowed in obeisance and backed away from Akhenaten, who then bound the clay crocodiles against Nefertiti's forehead and nape.

"Oh, that feels so good, my beloved. I am certain the touch of the Pharaoh who is one with Aten shall heal my headache pain now. Please continue, my love."

She fell asleep smiling as the Pharaoh gently rubbed her temples. He never noticed her fingers clutching a bit of fabric, within which lay hidden the small amulet of a frog.

Chapter 14
Egypt – Elizabeth

Liz lay her head against the headrest of the car as they drove to the Hotep family home in Luxor. "Ari, I have a horrible headache."

Ari frowned as he reached over to stroke her face. "I feared you stayed out in the sun and heat far too long today. Let's get you into the cool house and a dark room. I can get you some Ibuprofen and a glass of water. That should help."

She nodded. "That sounds like a plan. A cool, wet rag over my face might feel good, too."

Minutes later, they pulled into the courtyard outside the Luxor home of the Hotep family. Ari quickly helped Liz out of the car and into the darkened home originally built of mud bricks.

Liz shivered. She expected the thick walls of the house to cool the interior, but the house was nearly cold. She ran her hands up her arms. "Is this house air-conditioned?"

Ari nodded. "Yes, and Levi has it ridiculously cold in here. I will adjust the temperature. Here, darling, let me cover you with this throw while the temperature warms up a little bit. I cannot imagine how he works outside in the desert heat all day and then come home to a house this cold."

She struggled not to laugh. She could not get over the way Ari was carrying on about the temperature. "Will he mind if we stay here overnight?"

"Oh, no, it was his idea. He is living here while they work on this site. Anna and he have a lovely home on the Giza Plateau, but it is too far for him to drive back and forth every day. He goes home on the weekends."

Liz laid down on the couch and pulled the throw around her. A few minutes later, Ari handed her a glass of water and a couple of Ibuprofen. After she swallowed the pills, she sighed and laid back on the couch. "Thank you."

He laid a cool, wet wash cloth across her forehead. "This should help, too. I put a couple of drops of the rose scent you liked in the museum shop on the cloth. I bought it as a surprise for you. It is supposed to be wonderful to ease headaches. We are supposed to meet Zain and Levi at eight. Get some rest. I'll awaken you about seven to get ready."

She smiled at him and laid the wash rag across her face. "Thank you, love. Hmm. This fragrance smells wonderful. It should help. What is it called?"

"Attar of roses. It is reputed to have been favored by ancient Egyptian queens."

She tried to bite back her grin. "Really? How charming. Your wife is scented like one of the ancient queens of Egypt."

Two hours later, Ari gently shook Liz's shoulder. "Darling, it's time to wake up. We need to get ready to meet Levi and Zain at the restaurant."

She stretched and yawned. "Okay. I feel better. My head still aches, but the horrible throbbing pain stopped. I can cope with this."

Ari scowled. "You probably need to eat. I don't think you ate a bite since we left Anna and Levi's home early this morning. We won't stay out too late tonight. We need to get you back home to get some rest before tomorrow. I warn you; Zain will try to convince you that he needs you to work on this dig. Wait and see."

Liz sat up and laughed as she reached for her brush. "That must be the silliest idea I ever heard. Dr. Hassan needs *me* on a dig? Why?"

Ari frowned and shook his head. "The American brats."

Liz stopped brushing her hair to gape at her husband. "Oh, please, no. Ari, darling, please tell me those horrible, ill-mannered girls are not coming back tomorrow."

He shook his head. "I would bet good money those brats will sashay their sweet, pampered, spoiled, little butts right back to the site in the morning. You are going to have to keep a close eye on those two if you continue helping Salima. That Christina girl is an annoying little twat."

Liz began laughing. "Did you actually call her a twat?"

He nodded. "It's the nicest thing I could think of calling her. My heavens, that girl is enough to give a strong man a heart attack. I almost feel sorry for her father."

Liz began brushing her hair again and winced as her brush caught on a snarl. "Darn it. I'm regretting my brilliant decision to take my braids out before our wedding. Well, she is most definitely a brat. She called me 'blackish', and commented she figured my family must have camped on Tybee Island when we used to visit there. She inferred that a black – or 'blackish' – family could not afford a house there."

Ari's eyes widened in surprise. "Oh, my merciful heavens! Does she not realize she is in Africa now? Besides, you primarily have Egyptian and Irish ancestors according to your DNA study."

Liz giggled. "Well, I'm part black, too. The Egyptian DNA was totally unexpected. I'll never forget how shocked Kirk looked when he learned my birth mother was more Egyptian than black. Christina does not realize Egypt is in Africa, or that such comments might be construed as obnoxious, much less racist. Of course, she might not give a tinker's damn. She was completely flummoxed when I told her who Daddy is."

Ari laughed. "I imagine she was. I was pretty shocked when I realized who your father is, too."

Liz's laughter escalated. "I remember when we went for my first intraocular injections and Daddy stood glowering at you."

Ari took the brush from her hand and began working the snarl out of her hair. "I overheard some of the residents discussing the famous Dr. Richard Winslow was visiting the hospital earlier that morning. Everywhere I went people were whispering, '"Dr. Winslow is here today. Maybe he will demonstrate the Smith-Winslow procedure. ' It never occurred to me that Dr. Winslow, of the renowned Smith-Winslow valve and procedure, was *your* father. I might have died of shame had I known."

She giggled and grinned impishly in the mirror at her husband. "He thoroughly enjoyed embarrassing you."

"I'm sure he did. Here, I got the snarl out. You can finish fixing your hair the way you want it styled. Now, don't let Dr. Hassan railroad you into helping him tomorrow. He is looking for someone to ride herd on the brats."

She giggled as she gave him a fake salute. "Yes, sir, Dr. Hotep!"

She pulled her hair up into a messy bun, and refreshed her makeup with smoky eyes and sultry red lips. She pulled two dresses out of the closet and turned to Ari. "Okay, I brought these dresses. Which should I wear tonight? The blue or the purple?"

The corners of his eyes crinkled as he laughed. "Purple is your favorite color."

She shrugged. "Yes, but the blue is more modest. It has sleeves and the skirt is longer."

Ari gathered her into his arms. "We are eating at a rather touristy restaurant this evening. Wear the purple halter dress. In fact, if you had brought the one made with the Egyptian fabric, I would say wear it."

Her eyes lit up. "Really?"

He began laughing. "Why? Did you bring it? I thought you only brought the other two."

She grinned. "Well, a girl never knows when she can dress up for her fellow. We are in Egypt about to dine with renowned, world-famous archeologists. Okay, Dr. Hotep, I'll wear it!"

He burst into laughter as she snapped another saucy salute to him.

Minutes later, she came out clad in the dress made with the Egyptian fabric. Ari laughed to see she wore a black bodysuit under it to cover her midriff. Matching leggings covered her legs where the skirt was slit up the sides. She finished the look with black stilettos. As she walked into the living room, she tossed a linen scarf around her shoulders.

Ari pulled her into his arms for a quick kiss. "You look scrumptious. It is a beautiful outfit for a beautiful woman. Okay, my beautiful queen. Come on. Let's go."

It only took a few minutes to drive to the upscale restaurant overlooking the Nile. They were quickly seated with Levi and Dr. Hassan. It pleased Liz to see Salima also joined them for dinner. "I'm so glad you joined us this evening."

Salima smiled as she reached over to hug Liz. "It seems more normal by Egyptian standards if I joined the group for dinner. This allowed me to join friends for dinner tonight and not eat take-out in my quarters."

Liz felt embarrassed. "Oh, Salima, I'm sorry I didn't think of that earlier. I should have invited you."

Salima laughed and shook her head. "It is not something a person newly arrived in our country would be expected to know, and I recall you had a horrendous headache when you left this afternoon. I am here, and I am delighted to be in this wonderful group of friends. I love your gown. You look absolutely fabulous."

Liz blushed. "Oh, thank you."

Zain nodded. "I agree. Your dress is perfect for our Nefertiti look-alike to wear the evening she discovered the tomb of Queen Nefertiti."

Since Liz was unfamiliar with Egyptian food, she suggested the others order a variety of dishes. They ordered koshari, which she learned was a mix of rice, brown lentils and macaroni topped with fried onions and a spicy tomato sauce. They also ordered lamb kebobs, grilled pigeon stuffed with bulgur wheat. Ari requested baba ghanoush, which she learned was a dish made primarily from mashed eggplant and olive oil. Salima added a tomato and cucumber salad. Liz then ordered bottled water, but Ari suggested coffee might help to ease her headache. They all ordered coffee and sparkling water to accompany their meals. They completed their meal with baklava.

About halfway through the meal, Dr. Hassan broached the subject Ari had warned her would come during the evening. "Elizabeth, you were an amazing asset to us today. I hope you will come back and help us again tomorrow."

Liz smiled and reached for Ari's hand. "Dr. Hassan, my husband and I will both be there tomorrow morning. I look forward to seeing the rest of the Golden City. Afterwards, I think we will probably go home. We will come back another weekend so I can see more of Luxor."

"But, my dear, there is so much more to see. We call Luxor 'the world's greatest open-air museum.' It is one of the oldest inhabited cities in the world. You need to spend at least three days here. It was one of only three ancient Egyptian cities ever known as 'the city.' The other two were Memphis and Heliopolis. It was also called 'the city of a hundred gates,' and 'the southern city.' Later, ancient Egyptians called the city 'Waset,' which meant 'city of the scepter.' It was considered the city of the god, Amun-Ra and was the capitol of Egypt for many years. The great temple of Amun-Ra at Karnak was the most important temple in Egypt throughout antiquity. They called the city 'Karnak' for years because of the importance of the temples at Karnak. Later, the city was called Thebes. Some believe a Hittite prince met and married the widow of Pharaoh Tutankhamun here. She was called Ankhesenamun, and she was the daughter of Queen Nefertiti and Pharaoh Akhenaten."

"I never thought about the fate of Tutankhamun's queen after he died. I hope she had a happy life."

He smiled at her. "I hope so, too. She was young when her husband died. They had already lost two children, who were most likely stillborn."

'Poor girl. I wonder if she had other children later," Liz mused.

Zain shrugged. "We do not know. As you said, I hope she found happiness in her second marriage. Elizabeth, you cannot leave tomorrow. You must see the Karnak temple, the Colossi of Memnon, the Necropolis, which includes the Valley of the Kings, and the Mortuary Temple of Hatshepsut. Those are just a few of the incredible treasures here in Luxor. The city remained a site of spirituality into the Christian era. Levi will tell you about the Christian monasteries established here. There is so much to see in Luxor. I hoped you could stay a few more days so I could show you around. I could even take you into the tomb of Pharaoh Tutankhamun."

Levi turned red in his face as he choked on his coffee. "You would take them into Pharaoh Tutankhamun's tomb?"

Zain smiled and nodded. "Of course, Levi. It would be my pleasure to take your brother and his charming bride to see the tomb of Tutankhamun."

Liz struggled not to laugh. She understood it was virtually impossible to see Tutankhamun's tomb unless you were an archeologist. *You get special treatment if you discover the tomb of a Great Royal Wife.* She glanced at Ari and quickly winked. "It's up to you, Ari. What would you prefer?"

Ari shut his eyes. He rubbed his free hand across his face as if his head now throbbed painfully. "It's entirely up to you, my love. I've seen them all before, except for Tutankhamun's tomb. I realize this is all new to you."

She bit back laughter as she noticed that neither Levi nor Salima could look either of them in the eye. "Levi, what would you suggest?"

Levi's eyes flew to her in shocked surprise. He looked quickly from her, to Ari, and then back to Liz. "Uhm, Elizabeth, I think that is a decision for you and your husband to decide."

Ari nodded. "I agree, Levi."

"But don't you agree, Levi, that they could enjoy their vacation here a bit longer? Or are you eager to be rid of them?" asked Zain with a sly smile.

Levi paled as he glanced nervously from Zain to Ari. "Oh, of course, I am not eager for them to leave, Zain. My brother and his beautiful wife are welcome to stay if they desire. It is Ari's house as much as it is mine. However, I understood that my brother intended to show Elizabeth some more of Egypt before he returns to work next week."

Liz saw Ari cringe. Levi's ill-thought comment made her cringe, too. She knew as soon as Levi stated that Ari did not need to return to work until the following week that they were stuck in Luxor through the weekend. There would be no escape.

She only hoped the brats would not be there the entire weekend.

"That is correct." Ari's voice sounded low and controlled, but Liz could hear the edge of tension in each word.

Zain leaned back in his chair and smiled. "Wonderful. Then you must stay a few more days with us. I know you will want to see the prayers over the tomb to remove the curse. And tomorrow Elizabeth can assist us some more after the curse is removed from the tomb of Nefertiti. Our Nefertiti-look-alike should assist us in opening the tomb."

Ari cleared his throat and laid his napkin across his plate. "I must admit, Dr. Hassan, that I had some other surprises for my bride. Elizabeth does not know that I planned for us to fly to Marsa Alam. She loves the ocean and we both love to dive. I knew she would adore diving in the Red Sea with the pristine coral reefs there. I made reservations at a diving resort, the Costa Del Mar."

"But nothing could compare to assisting with the excavation of the Golden City, much less opening the tomb of the Great Royal Queen Nefertiti, could it?" interjected Dr. Hassan. "No, of course not. Besides, it is mating season for sea snakes, and they have been known to attack during mating season."

Ari chuckled and shook a finger at Dr. Hassan. "Zain, you know there are no sea snakes in the Red Sea. The salinity it too high for them to survive there."

Zain Hassan waved a dismissive hand in the air. "That is unimportant."

Liz touched Ari's arm. "Are you sure there are no sea snakes there?"

He patted her hand. "Yes, my love. There are no sea snakes in the Red Sea. Look, it's up to you. What do you say? Diving in the Red Sea or Tutankhamun this weekend?"

She smiled, her gray eyes sparkling. "I think diving on the coral reef in the Red Sea sounds wonderful, but let's stay, darling. Dr. Hassan is right. We can go diving any time. We might never get another opportunity to see the tomb of Tutankhamun."

Zain leaned back in his chair and smiled. "Fine. It is agreed. You will cancel the reservations at the Costa Del Mar and stay here through Sunday. We should be able to make some short trips to some of the other remarkable archeological sites here at Luxor before you return to Cairo."

Liz felt her anxiety level rise again. She tugged on Ari's sleeve. "Ari, I just thought. Oh, my god, my cats. What about my kitties?"

Ari nodded as he struggled not to grin at Zain Hassan. "Yes, Elizabeth has two cats who just arrived from the United States with us. The cats must be nervous without her."

Dr. Hassan smiled and waved a hand in the air again, as if he could somehow make it all work out magically. "I am sure Ari arranged for a neighbor or a co-worker to check on the cats for you, to ensure they have adequate food and water while you would be gone. See? There is no problem. Ari already arranged to be away until Sunday evening. Now, there is no reason for you two not to stay."

Ari nibbled his upper lip. "Zain, I prepaid the resort and the plane tickets from Luxor to Marsa Alam."

Zain waved his magical hand in the air again. "I will call them. They will allow you to change the reservations. Like your beautiful wife said, you can go to the Red Sea to dive any time. See? It is all settled. No problem."

Ari looked at Liz and slowly nodded his head. "Then I guess we will stay."

As they left that evening, Liz laughed. "You told me not to cave into him, and then you folded to his wishes like a piece of origami paper. It was hilarious."

Ari frowned as he helped her into the car. "Oh, shut up, woman. I did not want to cause Levi any problems at his job. And my neighbor already said he is most willing to assist with the cats. He knows we won't be home until Sunday evening. Besides, you want to see the tomb of King Tutankhamun."

Liz laughed until she cried. She continued to laugh when they arrived at the house. Ari stormed inside as Liz trailed behind, holding her side as she continued to laugh.

Ari glanced at her scornfully. "You won't be laughing tomorrow if he makes you babysit those horrid teenagers."

She stopped laughing. "Now, that's just mean. You caved in, not me. How about you babysit the little witches? They think you are the sexiest thing they've seen in Egypt."

He shook his head. "Oh, no. I would probably say something incredibly rude to them and cost Zain a big donation from their rich father."

"Well, heck. You're no fun," Liz muttered as she kicked a clod of dirt while they walked into the house.

"I'll show you fun," he said as he swung her over his shoulder.

Liz let out a little shriek and then laughed again as he carried her into the house.

Chapter 15
Egypt – Ari

As Liz disappeared into their bedroom at the Luxor house, Captain Johnny materialized, reached out and grabbed Ari's arm.

The ghostly touch rattled Ari. "Hey! I didn't know you could touch a person. Don't grab me, Captain. How did you get here anyway?"

Ari shuddered as he rubbed his arm where Johnny had touched him. The spot felt so painfully cold Ari would have sworn he had been touched with dry ice if he had not realized the ghost caused it.

Johnny frowned as he shook his head with obvious impatience. "That is unimportant. Doctor, you cannot allow our Elizabeth to go back to that place tomorrow."

Ari felt his brow wrinkle with concern as he frowned. There was a new tone that neared hysteria in the old pirate's voice. Ari never expected panic from Captain Johnny. "Why not? What concerns you?"

Captain Johnny looked as shaken as he sounded. "I warned Elizabeth before we came to Egypt. I cannot protect her there. This place they call the Golden City is laden with curses and protections. I am powerless to protect her there. Promise me, Dr. Hotep. Please don't let her return there tomorrow. Something horrible will happen if she goes to that place again."

Ari shook his head. This was insane. The ghost sounded almost hysterical. Was he really arguing with a ghost? "I wish I could avoid returning to the Golden City. Unfortunately, we promised Dr. Hassan we would return to the dig again tomorrow. What rattled you so badly? What happened there today? What do you suspect will happen if Elizabeth returns to the Golden City?"

Johnny stood there, wordless, but tried to project something to Ari. Ari suddenly had a terrifying thought. "Johnny, do you know something unpleasant is going to happen to her at the Golden City?"

Johnny appeared shaken. "I… I am uncertain. I heard rumblings there today. The spirits sounded most agitated. Several are extremely powerful. They said one awaited Elizabeth's arrival for eons…"

Ari glowered at the ghost. "Are you joking? What spirits? Who? Dammit, Johnny, this is one of those moments when I want to shake your ancient teeth out of your long dead head."

Johnny blinked. He reached toward Ari again, his ghostly hands trembling. "No, I am not joking. If it would help keep Elizabeth safe, I would most happily have my teeth shaken loose by you, Dr. Hotep. No one will say the names of these spirits. When I inquired, they seemed stunned I did not know who they were. In the background, I could hear a beating of drums, archaic prayers, and screams of terror. Some chanted about one they called 'the Betrayer.' They seem terrified of that spirit. They whispered that the female entity is exceptionally powerful. They call her The Great One, and they said she has waited an eternity for the right *ka*. I know not what that word means. What is a *ka*? Dr. Hotep, I know deep down in my blackened soul that it would be gravely dangerous to return there with Elizabeth tomorrow. I fear for her safety – nay, for her eternal soul - if she returns to the blasted Golden City tomorrow."

Ari's frown deepened. "Why couldn't you figure out who these spirits are? I don't understand, Captain English."

The old ghost sighed. "These spirits are far older than I am. They know how to shield themselves from strangers such as me. No one will even utter the name of the female. They seemed stunned – nay, horrified – that I knew not who the Great One is."

Ari's mouth went dry with fear. He wet his lips and tried to swallow. "Come on, Captain. Could a curse be real? Could a spirit harm Elizabeth? Excuse my crudeness, but spirits are dead. How can the dead harm the living? Why would these spirits seek to harm my beloved wife?"

Johnny shook his head. "I have never encountered the power of this place before. Their secrets are well guarded. All I know is that there are curses on those tombs. If the tomb of this Queen Nefertiti is opened before the curse is removed, I fear for Elizabeth's safety. The other spirits say that one of immense importance awaits the *ka* of the new beauty who comes. They say beauty shall be restored when she receives the *ka*. What does this word, *ka*, mean? I never heard it before."

Ari went cold with concern. "They say she awaits the new beauty who comes. The word, *ka*, means soul. Are you sure those were their words, Captain? How could a ghost somehow rip a soul from a living person to give to one who has already passed?"

Johnny began fading in and out. "I'm sorry, Dr. Hotep. I don't know. The spirits whispered, 'the Great One possesses powerful magic.' They view her as a goddess. No one would say her name. They all thought I should know it. I will try to find out who she is."

Suddenly, the ghost disappeared.

Ari tried to swallow, but his throat felt as parched as the sands of the Egyptian desert. Captain Johnny claimed the unnamed spirit might be a powerful goddess who possessed great magic. How could he protect Elizabeth from the unseen dangers of not merely a powerful spirit but an ancient goddess who sought to snatch Elizabeth's soul?

Ari believed he and his wife were true twin flames. He loved Elizabeth with a passion so profound and so never-ending that it astounded him. Was it normal to love another human being with such intensity? But then, how could he not love her? As her mother said, Elizabeth held the other half of his heart. Ari often wondered if Elizabeth and he had been together through multiple lives. He sighed as he raked his hands through his usually impeccable hair. If he allowed himself to believe in reincarnation, he would assume they had been together in other lifetimes.

He knew he would protect Elizabeth at all costs. He would allow no one to harm her. She was his life. She held his essence, part of his soul, or as the ancient people in his land called it, his *ka*. He realized in the last four years that he was only half a man without Elizabeth by his side. He needed her in his life. No, he would not allow anyone or anything to harm his beloved wife. Mr. Jones swore the dead could not harm the living. If some errant ancient spirit foolishly believed she could snatch Elizabeth from him, that spirit would have the fight of her undead life on her hands. Ari would not easily relinquish the woman he cherished.

He straightened his shoulders and walked upstairs to the bedroom. He smiled as he entered the quietly elegant room. He stopped to watch his wife sitting cross-legged on the gray linen duvet covering the king-sized bed.

Elizabeth grimaced as her brush caught a new tangle in her long hair. "Ari, darling, will you help me braid my hair again? I can't stand it down. I was so hot at the Golden City today. I think I might have suffered a heat stroke."

He strode across the room and slid onto the bed beside her. "That's probably why your head hurt so horribly when we returned here this afternoon. You became overheated. You could easily have a heat stroke out there. The temperature hit 40 degrees Celsius today. It was hotter than that in the trenches."

Liz quit struggling with her hair and frowned. "What would that be in Fahrenheit? Something like 120?"

He chuckled as he pulled her to him for a kiss. "No, darling, more like 104, maybe 105. Here, give me the brush. Of course, I will help you, my love. I braided the hair of Levi's daughter, Naomi, many times before. She claims I braid hair perfectly. Tell me how you want me to braid it."

He bent over and kissed her nape.

She trembled and she sighed at his touch. It was as if she melted against him. She turned halfway around and smiled up at her husband. "Let's braid my hair first thing in the morning. I just changed my mind about doing anything with it tonight. I can do a simple braid now to keep it from snarling too badly. We can braid it again in the morning so it will still look fresh and neat for the day."

She quickly braided her long hair and threw the braid over her shoulder. She smiled seductively as Ari as she slipped the loose neck of the silken caftan off from her shoulders, allowing the silken fabric to pool around her waist. Ari grinned and pulled her into his arms for a long, lingering kiss. As the kiss ended, she sighed and smiled up at her husband.

He chuckled. "Yes, we can braid your hair in the morning. First things first. We're on our honeymoon."

Elizabeth giggled as she placed her arms around his shoulders and pulled him down to her again. "I agree. We have more important things right now."

For just a moment, Ari thought of Johnny's warning, but Elizabeth's kisses soon drove thoughts of the specter's dire prediction from his head. *Oh, well, tomorrow is another day. We will address Captain Johnny's concerns in the morning.*

The alarm clock went off at 7, as they had planned. Ari groaned as he reached over and slapped it off. Two hours later, he awoke as his cell phone rang incessantly. He grabbed the phone. "Hello?"

"Where are you?" Levi sounded frantic.

Ari yawned as he struggled to awaken. "We're at the house. Why?"

"Dr. Hassan is concerned because you guys are so late. Hurry up."

Ari frowned. "Well, remind the good doctor that we *are* on our honeymoon, and we *don't* work for him. We will get over to the dig as quickly as possible, but we are going to bathe and eat breakfast before we come. We should be there in about an hour."

Ari groaned again as he rubbed his face, and then glanced at the time on his phone. "My heavens, Elizabeth, no wonder they are freaking out. It's already 9 o'clock. I must have turned the alarm clock off when it rang at 7. We need to get moving, darling."

Liz replied something unintelligible from beneath the pillow covering her face. Ari chuckled and pulled the pillow away from her face. "I beg your pardon?"

She jerked the pillow from his hands and whacked him with it. "Oh, come on, Ari. We are on our honeymoon. Can't we sleep late just one morning?"

He laughed as he reached over to tickle her ribs. As she squealed and swatted at his hands, he answered her. "We did. Besides, your favorite archeologist demands your esteemed presence. We need to hurry along."

"I could learn to hate archeology. Fine. Give me five minutes. I want a shower."

He snapped a towel at her butt as she started for the bathroom. "Forget something?"

She turned back and snatched the towel from his grasp. "I bet you're oodles of fun at parties."

"That's what all the girls say. Hurry up. You wanted me to help you braid your hair again this morning, although I think it's rather charming as it is."

She groaned again. "You like the 'JBF' look, hmm? Nope. I'm not going anywhere looking like we just tumbled out of bed, fresh from making love."

Ari laughed. "Why not?"

She glared at him as she shook her head. "You'd like that, hmm? For the whole dig site plus the priest and imam to know what we did most of the night? You are incorrigible. Sheesh, I had no idea that archeology was so exhausting or that I married a sex fiend. I'm not sure which made me hurt more, but my legs haven't ached like this since I danced professionally."

He laughed. "Well, that could be from marathon lovemaking as much as working at the dig, my love. Here, take the towel and dance your beautiful body into a piping hot shower. I'll run down the hall and shower in Levi's room. Let's get going."

A few minutes later, she came out of the shower, clad in a lavender linen tunic top over patterned leggings. She pulled a long, tiered, lavender skirt over the leggings. She slipped her feet into a pretty pair of gold and lavender sandals and fastened a gold link belt around her trim waist. She unwrapped the towel from around her head and began brushing out the snarls and tangles. "I think you have the right idea with your short hair. I may cut this mess off."

She let out a loud sigh of exasperation.

"I didn't realize you intended to wash your hair. I'm impressed you managed it so quickly. I hope you leave your hair long. I love your beautiful hair. Here, let me help." Ari took the brush from her hands, spritzed her hair with her leave-in conditioner, and gently worked the snarls from her hair. He then sectioned her hair and began French braiding it. He soon completed the task and Liz stood admiring her new hairdo in a hand mirror.

Liz smiled. "Naomi's right. You are first-rate at braiding hair. I love this style."

Ari kissed her neck. "You should. You look like Beyoncé with your hair braided like this."

Liz giggled. "I thought I looked like Nefertiti."

Ari grinned. "That, too, but she probably kept her head shaved and wore a wig. Hey, where did you get the leggings?"

"At the archeology museum gift shop in Cairo the other day. I thought they looked quintessentially Egyptian. Why?"

"They are Egyptian. They picture Isis and something from the Book of the Dead."

Liz lifted her skirt to study the pattern across her legs. "Hmm. Seems appropriate I wear them today. It's a shame Nefertiti isn't on them."

Ari leaned closer to examine her leggings. "She's right here. And look, darling. Here's the cartouche for her name."

She leaned down, enthralled, and traced the cartouche on her leg. "Wow. That's kind of spooky."

"I thought perhaps it's prophetic. You are meant to wear them there today."

She nibbled her lip, her brow scrunched in worry. "Maybe so. Well, I'm wearing the skirt over the leggings until after the de-cursification of the tomb. Is that a word?"

Ari laughed. "I don't think so, but I got the idea."

She shrugged. "Oh, well, *sea lo que sea.* "

Ari tilted his head as he studied her. "What does that mean?"

She blushed. "Oops, my bad. It's Spanish, for 'what will be, will be.' Anyway, after the priest and the imam leave, I intend shuck the skirt. It should be easier to help remove the dirt off the tombs in leggings and a sports bra than a light-colored linen ensemble."

Ari laughed and pulled her close for a kiss. "Leggings and a sports bra, hmm? Now, there's an outfit that the Golden City has not seen in several millennia, if ever. Sounds like a plan."

They grabbed some fruit and bread before they headed to the front door. As he opened the door, Ari frowned. He turned around to look at the house as he scratched his head. "Hmm. I would swear I'm forgetting something."

Liz grabbed his hand. "You're forgetting we need to go. No more time to dawdle, Dr. Hotep. Come on, babe. The Grand Vizier of Archeology commands our presence."

He bit back a laugh and raised her hand to kiss it. "I guess we better get moving then since the Grand Vizier awaits our arrival."

They ran out of the door laughing all the way to the car. Ari opened the door for Liz, bent to give her another kiss, and then hurried around to the driver's side. Minutes later, they parked at the Golden City and soon walked up to Salima. Ari kissed Liz's hand and turned to go locate his brother.

Salima struggled not to laugh as she shook her head. "He surprises me with his public displays of affection. He's Egyptian. He should know better. You two need to be careful or the morality police will scold you."

Ari stopped and turned back towards the two women. "Oh, Salima, don't frighten her like that."

"For kissing my hand?" asked Liz. "You're joking, right?"

Salima shook her head. "I'm afraid I'm not joking. You live in a new world now, Elizabeth. You know that, Ari. Behave yourself. Elizabeth, come with me. We need to guard the tomb until the priest and the imam arrive. Those bratty teenagers keep trying to get to it. They want to take selfies sitting on the tomb."

"Sheesh. Couldn't we let them climb on top of the tomb to get their selfies? If the hooligans crack it open, they could be the ones who get cursed."

Salima laughed. "Don't tempt me. Come on. Hannah has been guarding the tomb for three hours now and she is tired of dealing with Frick and Frack."

"For three hours? When did those brats show up? Frick and Frack. Hmm... Great nicknames for the Terrible Twins," muttered Liz as she followed Salima towards the steps down to the tomb. "Hey, Ari, did I tell you I had that crazy dream again?"

Ari stopped at the exit, startled by his wife's words. She caught his attention just before he would have left to go after Levi. He turned and stared at his wife. "What dream? About the frog?"

She nodded. "Yes. I swear, she followed me wherever I went."

Ari gulped. "Why do you call it 'she'? Did the frog speak to you?"

Elizabeth looked uncertain. "I'm not sure. It seemed like she was sending me some sort of warning, but it was in Coptic. She might have been speaking frog language. I didn't understand all of it."

"Did it seem to be a warning or a threat?"

She paused, pondering his words. "A warning, I think. I'm usually afraid of frogs. That little frog never seemed threatening to me. She seems concerned about my safety. Why on earth would I dream about a protective frog?"

Ari frowned as a cold knot of fear gripped his belly. "Be careful today, my love. Be wary. Listen to Salima."

"Of course." Liz glanced over at Salima, worried anew about the plan to open the cursed tomb.

Ari bit back his next thought. *And heed the warnings of your little frog friend.* No, he could not say that. It would sound silly.

She gulped as she nodded and forced a smile. "I'll pay close attention to Salima. I promise."

Ari glanced at his watch. It was only 10:30 a.m. The heat already rolled off the desert floor like waves of fire from the depths of hell.

Chapter 16
Eighteenth Dynasty – Egypt
Nefertiti and Akhenaten

Nefertiti fanned herself as she sweltered in the shade of her garden. She slipped her swollen feet into the cool waters of the pool beside her. "Ah, the coolness of the water feels wonderful. It seems hotter than usual today, my lord."

Akhenaten frowned. "Where is your slave girl? She should fan you."

Nefertiti made an elegant yet dismissive motion with her hand. "I sent her to fetch me a glass of fresh squeezed pomegranate juice. I told her to be sure the cook sweetens it. I thought the juice might refresh me and help to ease my horrible headache. My feet are so swollen, and my head hurts beyond belief. Even my hands and face are swollen today. This child must be a boy. I never felt like this during my other pregnancies with our daughters."

She pressed a hand to her temple as she shut her eyes and laid her head against her other arm. If it were a boy, she would not need to worry about Akhenaten continuing to sleep with his other wives. Kiya continually attempted to get him back into her bed. Just the other day, Nefertiti heard Kiya whisper a promise to Akhenaten that she would give him another son if he would come back to her bed.

Akhenaten looked around for his man servant. "Go fetch her Majesty's slave girl. Tell her to bring the juice for her Majesty immediately. And send two other slaves to fan us. It is unbearably hot today. Her Majesty is suffering from the heat. This is unacceptable. The wife of Aten must not suffer."

Only the Great Royal Wife of Pharaoh could be the Wife of Aten.

He reached over to gently caress her face as his brow furrowed with worry. He loved Nefertiti beyond all reason. She was the most important person in his life. Only Aten meant more to Akhenaten than his beloved wife. He had loved her since the moment he first saw her beautiful countenance when he proclaimed her name should be Nefertiti, Beauty Has Come. Yes, he had other wives, but none that he loved the way he loved, cherished, and adored Nefertiti. Kiya was special, but she still could not replace Nefertiti in his heart, even though Kiya gave him a son.

He believed Nefertiti was the most exquisite woman ever created by Aten. He often asserted her beauty was more than physical. She was beautiful of spirit as well as physically beautiful. She was kind, loving, caring, and an intelligent helpmate to the pharaoh. She often assisted him by governing the affairs of the country as his co-regent while he attended to the country's spiritual needs. She led their troops into battle while he prayed to Aten for their success. She loved their daughters and taught them how to behave as the daughters of the Pharaoh. She guaranteed they understood what their duties and responsibilities would someday be when they married kings and princes in other nations. Aten could not have given him a better or more talented Great Royal Wife.

He winced as he felt her cheek. She felt hotter than the desert winds that blew through his city each blazing summer afternoon. He reached down to the little pool and scooped up a handful of water to bathe her face.

She sighed. "Ah, that feels better. Thank you, my beloved."

Akhenaten relaxed as he alternated between stroking her face and bathing it with the cool water from the pool. His heart lurched as he realized her body also felt like it smoldered with the fire of fever. He began bathing the rest of her exquisite body with handfuls of water as well. He grabbed a linen cloth from her bed. He soaked it in the water and laid it over her body. "If the pond was bigger, I would place you in it."

Nefertiti smiled as her husband tended to her with such loving care. "Oh, this feels wonderful. You are most considerate, my lord."

His angular face broke into a loving smile as he continued to drench her with the cool waters.

Suddenly, Nefertiti pushed up from her arm, gasping with pain. "Akhen…"

Her eyes rolled in her head as she collapsed into his arms. The seizure did not last long, but it terrified Akhenaten. He had never witnessed a person have a seizure before. Akhenaten clasped her close to his chest. "Fetch the court physician at once! Her Majesty is grievously ill!"

The servant paled. He immediately turned to run from the garden, calling out as he went, "Fetch the court physician immediately! Her Majesty is ill!"

Nefertiti roused as the court physician rushed into the garden. "My Queen, how may I assist you?"

Akhenaten scowled at the terrified man. "She had some sort of a convulsion. She never did this before. She complains of a horrible headache, and I noticed that her hands, face, feet, and legs are all painfully swollen. She burns with fever, also."

The physician looked askance. He gently prodded the queen's swollen legs, hands, feet. He stared at her swollen face, fearful to touch her royal countenance. "She may have had a heat stroke. The heat may have caused the convulsion. We must reduce her body temperature immediately. You were doing the correct thing when you wet the cloth to put on her. We must lower her temperature right away. Girl, run to the kitchen and fetch some willow bark tea for her Majesty. It will help ease her headache and will reduce her fever."

Miriam bowed to the physician. "Yes, my lord. With your permission, my Lord Pharaoh."

She bowed, backed away to the door, and then hurried to fetch the medication.

The physician frowned and pointed to another slave girl. "And you, girl, keep bathing her Majesty with the cool water. How long have your extremities been swollen like this, your Majesty?"

Nefertiti nibble her lip. Her eyes clouded with worry. "Two days, I think. Perhaps three. What does it signify?"

The physician shook his head. "And when did your headache begin, my Queen?"

She gulped and glanced from the physician to her husband. "About then as well. The headache worsened today until I began shaking all over. Then I fainted. I try not to take the willow bark tea. It made me vomit the last time I drank it. Please tell me, doctor. What could these symptoms signify?"

He shook his head. "It probably signifies a heat stroke, but I sometimes see women suffer similar symptoms in late pregnancy. The willow bark tea was too strong if it made you vomit. We will weaken it with some wine. We – uh - Pharaoh must pray that Aten allows this baby to come soon."

"Why?" demanded a scowling Akhenaten. The pharaoh sat beside his wife as he continued to stroke her face with a cool, wet rag.

The physician gulped. It was apparent the man dreaded informing Pharaoh of the significance of her Majesty's symptoms. He cleared his throat. "If the baby does not come soon, it could bode poorly for her Majesty and the child. You must pray Aten allows her to be safely delivered of a healthy son soon."

Akhenaten's dark skin paled at the ominous words of the physician. He nodded. "Then I must pray immediately for her safe delivery."

"Yes, your Majesty." The court physician wiped a hand wet with nervous perspiration across his long white robe.

Akhenaten stared at the physician. "She must not die. You shall forfeit your life if the Great Royal Wife dies. She is the Wife of Aten. You know the Great Royal Wife has been selected to also serve as the Wife of Aten. The child she carries is the Child of Aten. She must not die."

The court physician bowed low to the Pharaoh. "Yes, my lord. I understand."

Akhenaten motioned for his man servant. "Come. We must help her Majesty into her bedchamber right away. We must continue to keep the linen cool and wet to reduce her fever."

As Akhenaten helped Nefertiti to her chambers, he did not notice the small frog hopped along behind them, watching their movements.

Chapter 17
The Golden City – Elizabeth

"Come, Elizabeth. Dr. Hassan wants us to stand guard at the tomb. The ceremony starts soon to remove the curse, but Frick and Frack have arrived down by the tombs and are acting like fools, as usual." Salima slipped her cell phone into her pocket, put her tools aside and rinsed off her hands.

Liz rolled her eyes. "Oh, for the love of — someone needs to sit those two girls down for a good, long, 'time out.' It's a shame their parents did not teach them some manners."

She set down the little brush Salima had given her to clean the surface of the tomb, rinsed the desert dust off her hands, and then quickly splashed some water on her face. It was hideously hot excavating in the tombs below the ground level today. She grabbed a bottle of water and quickly drank the contents. The two women began walking up the walkway between the excavations towards the tent which covered Nefertiti's tomb as they continued their discussion.

Salima nodded. "I agree. Neither girl comprehends common boundaries. They both need to learn respect for other people."

"They also need to learn to respect things which belong to other people. Neither one has an iota of respect for things which belong to others. These tombs are priceless relics of the Egyptian people. The whole attitude of those two little snobs is they are rich. If there is a problem, Daddy can fix it."

Salima nodded. "Exactly."

Liz frowned. "Oh, good lord, what are those crazy girls doing now?"

Salima shrugged. "It appears to be some sort of a dance."

Liz shook her head in dismay as she realized the girls were going around the tent performing a popular Fortnite dance that her younger brother,

Ronan, loved to dance. Called the Glyph It, the dance emulated moves often associated with dances of the ancient Egyptians. Liz knew several Egyptian-styled dances and had danced them in the past. However, it felt obnoxiously sacrilegious to Liz for the girls to do the silly Glyph It dance in the Golden City. Only a few minutes remained before the religious ceremony would be performed at an archeological site which was at least 3500 years old. Liz rolled her eyes and let out a long sigh of disgust. "Not all Americans are like those brats."

"I know. Most American tourists are much more respectful of our history than are these girls. Christina's father is a huge donor, and Zain puts up with more foolishness from these girls than he usually tolerates from tourists. However, their absurd behavior must stop, the sooner, the better. Come on. Let's go guard the tomb of our Queen Nefertiti. I would hate for Frick and Frack to provoke the ancient spirits and create chaos and confusion today of all days. With the curse on her tomb, we do not need to unleash fury which could deprive a soul of its essence."

Salima shrugged and rolled her eyes. "The curse says if the tomb is opened, the *ka* of the one who opens it will be forfeited to the Great Royal Queen. The *ka* is the essence of the soul. It is what makes a person that unique person."

Liz felt an uncomfortable tickle run down her spine at Salima's words. "You mean to say that could happen?"

Salima shrugged. "In archeology, we have found that virtually anything is possible."

Liz realized with a start that she was living proof anything could happen. She was born the daughter of a slave on the island of Barbados in 1780, time traveled to the present when she was four years old and lived in the present since then. She realized everyone in her family was proof anything could happen. Daddy traveled back in time to find Mom. Mom came forward in time when Daddy returned here without her. The kids all came to the present to be with Mom. Years later, even Kirk came forward in time to find his future. Hmm. She grinned as she wondered what Salima would think if she heard the story of her time-traveling family. It might be worth her mother's fury to see Salima's face if she told the archeologist about her family. "Well, we mustn't let that happen. It would be horrible to have your *ka* ripped out and sent to a woman who died 3500 years ago."

Salima nodded as they continued walking. "Exactly. I cannot imagine a more unpleasant fate. I don't want to say I believe in these old curses, but bizarre things have happened when tombs are opened without the prayers of protection. The tomb must be opened with proper decorum and respect for the spirits of the deceased."

Liz nodded her head as she still considered telling Salima about time travel. No, she had better save that conversation for a future day. She did not want to wind up being studied in a laboratory like a rat for the rest of her life. "I agree. I would not want to cause chaos, anger or rage by attempting to open this tomb without the proper protections."

Salima smiled and patted Liz on the back. "You are a wise young woman. We can stand here on ground level, just inside the warning tape, to guard the tomb from the idiot girls as they dance around this tent. Honestly, I must talk to Zain. Their behavior is completely inappropriate. I don't want the girls around this site. They comprise a safety hazard. They could easily dance off the ground level and fall into the trenches. I would much prefer they were sent off the site until the priest and the imam complete the ceremony."

Liz snorted. "I would much prefer to never see either one of those idiots again."

Salima struggled to control her laughter. She nodded. "I would say something to the girls, but Zain gave explicit instructions only he should correct the girls."

Liz rolled her eyes. "Oh, for the love of… Well, let's not piss off Mr. Moneybags or his little juvenile delinquents."

Salima giggled and reached into a pocket to pull out an extra hijab. "Exactly. Here, let me help you cover your hair with a scarf. This imam can be testy about such things."

Salima quickly tied the cotton scarf to cover Liz's hair. She tucked the last wayward strand under the scarf and smiled. "That looks good. I like your French braid."

"Oh, thank you. Ari braided it for me this morning. I don't know how you wear a hijab all the time, Salima. It's so hot. I feel like I am being baked alive."

"Females wear hijab from the time we are small children. I began wearing one when I was five years old. The Islamic dress code requires a woman to cover her entire body except her hands and face with loose clothing. 'Hijab' refers to modestly covering your head, neck, body, legs and arms. However, most non-Muslims use the term to refer to the head covering alone. I have worn a hijab over my hair for so long now that I feel naked without one. I wear scarves made of cotton or linen, so they help wick the perspiration from my head and they have a cooling effect while it keeps my hair and neck from showing. You get used to wearing hijab if you dress this way all the time. However, *you* are not Muslim, and you will not need to wear a hijab. There is no law requiring women to wear a head covering in Egypt. I only suggested you wear a scarf now because the imam who is coming for this ceremony is traditional and can be rather fussy about such things."

Liz blinked, startled by her words. "It doesn't offend me to wear a scarf. Ari says Coptic women often wear one in church as a sign of respect. I need to know how to wear one. I'm glad you thought to suggest it. I don't want to offend anyone."

Salima smiled at Liz and patted her on the back. "You are a good woman, Elizabeth. Ari is a lucky man."

Liz laughed. "I think I'm the lucky one. He's a dish!"

Salima laughed at Liz's comment. "A dish, hmm? I have not heard that phrase since I attended university in the States, and I think it was old-fashioned then. I heard it in an old movie."

Liz blushed. *Salima has no idea how often I use old-fashioned words,* she thought. *Mom heard that phrase in an old movie and it sounded new to her.*

Salima quickly arranged the scarf to cover Liz's hair before they walked into the tent covering the excavations on the tombs where they approached the area cordoned off with the cautionary tapes to keep people away from the 'cursed tomb.' As they assumed their positions to guard the tomb, Salima frowned. Frick and Frack continued dancing their way through the tented area towards the steps leading down to the cursed tomb of the Royal Queen.

"Oh, great, here come the Troublesome Twins."

"Fabulous. Who could ask for anything more on a day when we are supposed to have a curse removed from a 3500-year-old tomb?" whispered Liz.

Salima shrugged her shoulders and shook her head in disgust. The girls began working their way around the tent, dancing along the way. "What on earth are those idiotic girls doing?"

Liz groaned. "It's a popular dance from that silly Fortnite game. Ronan, my younger brother, plays Fortnite. This dance is called the Glyph It. The name is a play on 'hieroglyphics.' Good grief, could they have picked a worse time to come in here prancing around like brain-damaged fools?"

Salima looked around and paled. "Oh, no, and here comes the imam now."

Salima stepped away to greet the imam. She bowed slightly in respect for the religious leader. Elizabeth noticed Salima did not shake his hand. "Asalam 'alaykum, imam. We are thrilled and honored you could come out today to help resolve our little problem."

He waved a hand in the air. "Asalam alaykum, Salima. It is good to see you again. Has Father El Masry arrived yet? And what are those girls doing?"

Salima looked frustrated. "I have not seen Father El Masry yet, imam. The girls are tourists who are acting like fools. Please pay no attention to them. Allow me to introduce you to the young lady who discovered the name on the tomb, and the warning of the curse."

They started over to the cordoned-off area where Elizabeth stood keeping guard over the tomb. As they approached, the teens began dancing right in front of Elizabeth.

Elizabeth rolled her eyes in disgust. She could not believe the spoiled brats would behave in such an immature manner before an important ceremony. "You girls need to cut out the nonsense. Go play somewhere else. The ceremony is about to begin."

Marjorie nodded. "We know. We wanted to dance for the spirits. We thought it might help."

Elizabeth shook her head. "Oh, for the love of – listen, cut it out or I will ask Dr. Hassan to remove you two from this tent."

Christina danced closer to Elizabeth. "You can't make me do anything. You aren't the boss of me."

Elizabeth frowned. Christina, I'm warning you --"

As Christina danced closer to Elizabeth, the teenager kicked out. Her foot connected with the leg Elizabeth had previously broken. As her leg gave way, Elizabeth suddenly flew backward through the air.

"Oh, shit! What did you do, Chrissie?" asked Marjorie just as Christina's father ran up.

"What have you done this time, Christina? Oh, for heaven's sake, I told you to stay away from this tomb. Look what you two have caused this time."

Christina turned pale at the sound of her father's voice. "I didn't do it, Daddy. It's not my fault. She got in my way. I was just dancing."

"But you weren't supposed to be in this tent. Zain, I apologize. I think we should call for an ambulance. It looks like the young woman might be badly hurt."

Zain peered down to the top of the cracked tomb and paled. "I must fetch Ari and Levi right away. Gerald, call for an ambulance. Yes, it looks like Mrs. Hotep has been knocked unconscious."

Zain rushed to find Ari and Levi as Salima rushed down the steps to the tomb. Zain quickly explained Elizabeth had been knocked onto the tomb. Ari ran back to the tent with Levi and Zain right behind him. He took one look down at his wife before he rushed down the steps into the tombs. It looked like his wife had been seriously injured. She needed him now. As he reached the tomb, he stopped, stunned by what he saw. He looked up at Zain. "She cracked the covering to the tomb. What should we do now?"

"Get her to the hospital as quickly as possible. We already called for the ambulance. Gerald, you must take the girls away from the site. I will not allow either of them on one of my excavation sites again."

Mr. Moberley turned beet red and began protesting. "But Zain--"

Zain shook his head. "No. I told you yesterday to keep the girls away from this tent or someone could be seriously injured. Now, Mrs. Hotep has been knocked unconscious when your daughter knocked her five feet down onto this stone tomb. You need to get the girls away from here before the police arrive."

Gerald Moberley looked shocked by his words. After a pause, he turned to the girls. "Come on. You two little dingbats caused enough trouble for one day. We're leaving."

"But Daddy, I want to see the ceremony!" wailed Christina.

He shook his head. "That's too bad, Christina. You should have thought about the ceremony before you knocked poor Mrs. Hotep on the top of Queen Nefertiti's tomb. We are leaving. You, my dear, have been banished."

Chapter 18
Eighteenth Dynasty – Egypt
Elizabeth

I could sense chaos, rage, and fury all around me. It felt like my body catapulted through time and space. Through fire, and then through torrential rains. I felt restless... frightened... And then, with a gasp, I realized I was being carried.

"Where am I?" I gasped as I looked around, stunned by the exotic paintings and gold relief on the walls as much as by the pounding pain in my head. "Oh, my sweet Lord, my head hurts horribly."

The tall, handsome man carrying me stopped. "My beloved? By, Aten above, you are alive! I thought I had lost you. Praise Aten, you live!"

I tried to laugh, but the sound caught in my throat as I took in the sight of the man carrying me. He looked so much like Ari, but I doubted my Ari ever dressed like this in his life. Ari wore a shirt unless he was swimming or headed to bed. I had never imagined Ari in a kilt, and this one was of pleated white linen unlike any kilt I ever saw a person wear. I would have to remember this look for Krazy Kilt Karaoke Night. The man wore a heavy gold necklace decorated with lapis and turquoise and a matching gold and gem-encrusted belt. Better yet, his eyes were lined with green pigment, and I am confident Ari never wore eye makeup in his life. While Ari's hair was cut short, it was not shorn off. This man's hair was clean-shaven from his head. This man's face was shaved smooth with no trace of a beard or mustache. I slowly realized I never saw this man before, or any man dressed like this.

Except in the artwork of ancient Egypt. Oh, my merciful heavens.

I swallowed hard and slid a hand down over my body. Like the man, I was dressed in pleated white linen. A heavy necklace surrounded my throat. I would bet it looked a lot like the one the man wore. As my hand slid on down my body, it shocked me to discover my belly great with child. Wow, I did *not* expect to find myself pregnant.

The tall, handsome man who looked so much like my Ari raised his arms so he could kiss me. "It is all right, my love. Our baby is fine. Aten has preserved you both."

Oh, my god, I thought, the fickle bitch snatched my soul. Some thanks I got for finding her blasted tomb. I would bet anything I now lived in the pregnant body of one recently deceased, Queen Nefertiti. But how could this have happened?

Oh, yeah. Frick and Frack. The Troublesome Twins, as we jokingly called the teens. Christina Moberley must be a minion straight from the depths of hell. She was dancing that stupid Glyph It dance from Fortnite, and she somehow kicked me right over the edge of the trench and onto the lid of Queen Nefertiti's tomb. The impact must have cracked the blasted tomb open, and I forfeited my soul since I caused the tomb to be opened. So, help me, if I ever could get back to my own time, I would whup the snot out of one skinny little rich bitch from Savannah.

I forced myself to smile at the man carrying me. "Your prayers have been answered, my lord. Now, will you put me down and let me walk?"

He shook his head. "No, no, I will carry you, my beloved. We will go on to the alter in the temple and give thanks to Aten for healing you. I was headed there when you awakened."

We soon entered the inner sanctum of the temple. As he approached the alter, he bowed down, and gently laid me down beside him. I sat up, wondering what I was supposed to do next. I realized with a start the good queen was blind in one eye because I could see nothing from her left eye. Maybe her blindness is why the bust of her only has one eye. I kept my good eye focused on Pharaoh Akhenaten (words I had never expected to hear, much less to utter) and copied him as he knelt to pray. Like him, I held my hands up in supplication to Aten.

"Oh, lord most high, the one true god, I come today to give thanks to you for delivering our beloved wife from the illness which nearly claimed her life. Thanks be to Aten!"

Our beloved wife? Was he using the royal 'we,' or did his comment convey something else? It seemed like I should remember something Salima told me about Akhenaten's beliefs regarding Nefertiti, but for the life of me, I could not remember it right then. It was not like I was accustomed to awakening to find myself in the eighteenth dynasty in the arms of a long-dead Pharaoh. I wondered why I did not have her memories since my spirit was in her body. Things were not in any way normal. It surprised me to discover I could remember anything including my name or hers.

"How manifold it is, what thou hast made! Oh, sole god, like whom there is no other!"

As Akhenaten prayed, it seemed like I should say something, so I said, "Thanks be to Aten, the one true God!"

"You are in my heart. There is no other one who knows you, only your son, Akhenaten, whom you have taught your ways and told of your might. You are the giver of life. One lives by you."

Akhenaten's prayer continued for a long time. He would pause and I would repeat the last thing he had said, or say, 'We lift our voices in praise to Aten!' I thought I might die of boredom before it ended as he droned on and on and on. Finally, he realized I sagged against him with exhaustion. *Hey, man*, I thought, *you need to remember your beloved wife almost died a little while ago.*

Somehow, I held my tongue. I remembered Mom telling us how both Aunt Sassy and Grammy often said things that were poorly understood when they traveled back in time, and they did not go as far back as I had just traveled. Oops, my bad. I guess technically, little ol' Elizabeth Ann Winslow Hotep had not traveled back in time. My *ka* did. I would have to think carefully before I uttered a word in this strange new world, so intriguing and yet so foreign from the world in which I previously lived.

Akhenaten finally finished his prayers, after he praised me as the 'great Queen whom he loved, the lady of two lands, Nefer-Nefru-Aten Nefertiti,' who he said would live with him forever. Really? Forever? He gently lifted me again. He tenderly placed my arms around his neck, so he could get a better grasp on me. He bent and kissed my cheek as he softly murmured something to me in Egyptian. He might be a crazy religious fanatic, but the pharaoh loved the woman he held cradled in his arms with a passion I had rarely ever seen, well, except between Mom and Daddy or Ari and me. I laid my head against his shoulder and sighed as he carried me back to my quarters in the harem. My head hurt so horribly, and I was way past ready to rest.

I would have killed for some Ibuprofen about then.

My rooms were bigger than my entire apartment in Galveston. Heck, my rooms in this palace were bigger than Ari's entire house. Like the hallways we traversed and the temple, the walls of Nefertiti's rooms were decorated extensively with exquisite artwork and gold leaf. Where I expected one wall belonged was an opening out to a beautiful garden with a small pond. Linen drapes were pulled back from the opening. The drapes could be closed at night, if Nefertiti wanted it darker, or if she desired more privacy in her quarters.

A pretty, slender girl about fifteen years old and infinitely more mature than Frick and Frack came running up to assist Akhenaten as he entered the room with me. I noticed the girl wore a wig that looked like my goddess braids. Her braids hung down to about her collarbone. Her natural colored, linen dress hung straight down from her bodice without decoration. However, like Akhenaten, she wore eye makeup. I vaguely remembered Salima told me ancient Egyptians wore eye makeup to help prevent eye infections. I would have bet money I wore similar eye makeup.

"Miriam!" Akhenaten snapped terse instructions to the girl in rapid-fire Egyptian. The terrified girl bowed and backed away from him before she wheeled around at the door to rush to obey his orders.

Strange. I could respond to him in this language so much like Coptic, but when he spoke rapidly, I could not keep up with him. It reminded me of when I studied Spanish in high school and then we went to Mexico one summer. I could talk to people, but I had a tough time at first keeping up with the conversation until my comprehension improved and I learned how to think in the language. Like then, it looked like I needed to step up my 'A' game in comprehension of the Egyptian language if I was going to pull off whatever I was supposed to pull off, here in the body of Queen Nefertiti.

"You see, my love? If you are firm with the slaves, they obey you immediately." His full lips curved into a slight smile, his hazel eyes so much like my Ari's, and yet so infinitely different. He gently smoothed his hand across my forehead.

I blinked and swallowed hard. Oh, great. Now the daughter of a slave was the owner of slaves. That was just too creepy and way too close to home for this girl child. I took a deep breath and dared to be bold with him. I smiled and fluttered my eyelashes at him. "And yet, she came running because she cares for her queen. She responds well to kindness, my lord."

He laughed as he sat me down on the edge of a bed covered in linen bedsheets and a silken coverlet. "Yes, she does. She loves you, as do I. But must you always be right, my love?"

I inched up onto the down pillows before I lowered my – her – exquisite eyelashes. I felt her eyelashes flutter across my cheeks. Gosh, I wish I could grow long, lush eyelashes like this woman had. I gave a shrug of my shoulder with a playful toss of my head. If I had hair, I would have thrown it over my shoulder, but this poor woman's head was shaved smooth as a bowling ball, just like his was. I realized she was not wearing a wig. Oh, well, it would have made this horrible headache worse. "Only when I am right, my lord."

I thought Akhenaten would collapse laughing. He finally wiped a tear from the corner of his eye from laughing so hard and stretched out to lay down beside me on the bed. "I thought I had lost you. How would I survive without you, my beloved wife?"

I tried to smile as I ground my teeth and struggled not to pull away from this man who I barely knew. "I don't know, great pharaoh. However, my head still hurts terribly. And look how swollen my legs are. I am unsure whether my head or my legs hurt worse. What could cause this?"

He shook his head. "I don't know, my beloved. Your slave girl will bring some cool juice to soothe your throat and head. Here, my love. Let me wet the linen and bind the clay crocodile to your forehead again. It eased your headache before."

I tilted my head as I stared at him, struggling not to laugh. "Akhenaten, are you telling me a clay crocodile eased my headache?"

He grinned. "Of course not. I attribute no power to the little statue of the crocodile, my love. You know I believe in Aten, the one God, the creator of the heavens and earth. Only He can heal, just as He healed you today. I swear He brought you back from the brink of death. Yesterday, I wet the clay and used the dampened crocodile to help hold the linen to your forehead. You said the pressure seemed to ease your headache."

I nodded. "Ah. Of course. I wondered if you had suddenly reverted to belief in the old false gods. I could not imagine you had turned away from, uhm, the One True God. However, I think I would prefer some willow bark tea. It should help ease my headache."

He frowned. "You usually say willow bark tea makes you feel ill. Are you sure?"

I gulped and nodded. "Yes. My head hurts so painfully. I think willow bark tea will ease the headache."

"Well, it eased your headache yesterday when the court physician administered some to you. He mixed it with some wine."

"Then I definitely think I need some willow bark tea now. They should send a jug of boiled water as well. I could mix the water with the willow bark tea. The tea is more palatable if it is not too strong. And the cook could send me some bread. It might help me tolerate the willow bark tea better if I have something in my stomach. I have not eaten much today. Could you send word to the kitchen for Miriam to bring those things as well, my lord?"

He bent to kiss me again. "Of course, my beloved."

As he turned to give instructions to another handmaiden, I glanced downward and saw the pleated linen dress was pulled up. I stared in horror at Nefertiti's poor, swollen legs. I had a niggling idea what caused her edema. If I were correct, cool water might help to ease some of her discomforts, but I doubted it would significantly reduce the swelling.

Mom had edema with her last pregnancy. I vaguely remembered she had an accompanying headache. She took aspirin for it. Mom said two aspirin eased her headache and helped to lower her blood pressure. I hated to think how high Nefertiti's blood pressure was right then. If I was correct, the willow bark tea might help lower her blood pressure, too. Mom used to call willow bark tea 'nature's aspirin.' She told us aspirin was originally made from willow bark. I remembered our Grammy McCarron used to give Daddy willow bark tea to ease his migraine headaches. She said they gave aspirin in the future to help ward off heart attacks and strokes. "Oh, my heavens, my legs are so horribly swollen. No wonder my legs hurt. I am glad you carried me. I doubt I could have walked with my legs swollen like this."

He grimaced. "I thought the same, my beloved. I will bathe them in the cool water as well. It eased the swelling before."

I glanced into a bronze mirror hanging on the wall and winced. The beautiful face staring back at me was round as the moon from the edema. She had dark blue circles under her eyes. While I could see the ghost of the beautiful woman in the reflection in the mirror, the difference horrified me. This poor woman was dreadfully ill. "My face is swollen, too, my lord."

He leaned over to kiss my cheek. "You are still beautiful, my love."

Well, it was a sweet comment, but I was not fishing for compliments when I mentioned the swelling to him. I grew more concerned about the edema with each passing minute.

Mom is rarely physically ill since her heart surgery. I searched my mind. I thought future physicians would call this condition pre-eclampsia. Fortunately, Mom is married to one of the top cardiovascular surgeons in the world and he ensured she had excellent prenatal care.

Now, the best treatment available was cool water, a compress held in place on my face with a clay crocodile, and willow bark tea. At least none of the remedies available involved ingestion of crocodile dung or dried bat's wings – yet.

I realized with a shudder that poor Nefertiti did not have the excellent prenatal care available to women in the future. I was not sure they even knew what caused this condition until the nineteenth or early twentieth century. God alone knew what the so-called physicians in this era might have given Nefertiti to treat her medical condition. Probably something vile like bat dung or cat urine. I cringed at the thought of both. Her physicians did not know what caused her condition. *Oh, great*, I thought, *this condition nearly killed her. Correction. It killed her until the spirits or whatever brought me back in time to keep Nefertiti alive long enough to deliver her child. Correction again. The spirits did not bring me back in time.*

The bastards stole my ka. The essence of my soul. They needed it to keep Nefertiti's physical body alive long enough to give birth to this child. I can't 'hear' her thoughts because her ka has departed her body, or they would not need mine.

I hoped for poor Nefertiti's sake and mine that this blasted baby would be the boy Akhenaten so desperately wanted to be born of his Great Royal Wife. I blinked back tears as I realized poor Ari and my family might well think I was dead. *Please, my love, don't give up on me. I will figure out a way to come back to you. I promise.*

But could I go back to my life in the future? And could my soul keep the body of Nefertiti alive long enough to give birth to the son Akhenaten needed to be his heir? Or would my soul die when her body died?

Chapter 19
Egypt - Ari

"Elizabeth!" Ari shouted out her name as he rushed down the stairs to the tomb where she lay unconscious. He looked up to the horrified onlookers peering down at Elizabeth's crumpled body. "Call for an ambulance, right now!"

Levi rushed up behind his brother. "We already did, Ari. The ambulance is coming."

Ari crawled on top of the tomb, little caring about any blasted curse. His beloved wife was injured, in part because he insisted they come today and help Zain Hassan ride herd on those horrible girls. Ari's heart lurched as he noticed blood seeping from both of her ears and her nose. He carefully checked and found a pulse. He lifted an eyelid and noticed with alarm she did not respond to the penlight he pulled from his shirt pocket to shine into her eye. He checked the other eye with the same result. Zain rushed down with a stethoscope, and Ari felt relief wash over him as he found her heartbeat, loud and steady.

"She is unconscious. She has a steady pulse and heartbeat. However, her pupils are non-responsive, and she has bleeding from both ears and her nose."

"I'm not surprised she has the bleeding. She suffered a hard fall. I will be surprised if she did not fracture her skull." Zain's face was pale, and his hands shook as if he were disoriented by the accident.

Ari took a deep breath and nodded. He realized he needed to stay calm. "We need a paramedic team to carefully get her off this blasted tomb and transport her to the hospital right away. Her neck and head need to be immobilized for transport. She will need to have an MRI and an EEG to determine how badly she has been injured as soon as possible at the hospital."

Ari glared at Gerald Moberley and his brat. He pointed towards Christina.

"Get that blasted girl away from my sight before I throttle her. I might someday regret my actions. She caused this horrible accident. I never want to see your ill-mannered brat again."

Mr. Moberley huffed up as Christina looked like she might cry. "Now, hold on a minute. I don't know who you think you are--"

"No, you hold on, Moberley. I'm the husband of the beautiful woman who is lying unconscious on Queen Nefertiti's tomb. This would never have happened if your juvenile delinquent had done as Zain instructed this morning. Instead, your idiot daughter knocked my wife into this pit where my Elizabeth landed on a stone slab. Now, Elizabeth is unconscious and probably has a skull fracture. You damned better hope Elizabeth awakens, safe and sound. Now, get your little witch out of my sight."

Ari turned back to Elizabeth and gently stroked her face. "It will be all right, my love. I promise. Everything will be all right."

Ari knew his words might be a false promise of hope.

As soon as the ambulance arrived at the hospital, they rushed Elizabeth into the ER where the team immediately began working on her. Since her vitals were stable, they performed a skull x-ray in the ER before they sent her for an MRI and CAT scan. While they awaited the results, Elizabeth was moved to intensive care, where a neurologist conducted an EEG and a BAER test. While the specialist performed the various tests, Ari paced back and forth, nervous and upset because they would not allow him in the room to observe or assist.

Levi finally found his brother outside intensive care. He laid a hand on Ari's shoulder. "Are you alright?"

Ari looked around, startled by his brother's voice. "What? No, I'm a nervous wreck. I don't know what to do. They won't let me in there with her until they finish their testing."

Levi winced. "I hate to ask you this, Ari. Have you called her family?"

Ari started trembling again as he paled at his brother's words. "No, I thought I would wait for the results of the tests. Why? Do you think I should call now? Oh, dear God, she must recover!"

Levi looked worried as he laid a comforting hand on Ari's shoulder. "Perhaps you should let them know she has been injured and she is in the hospital. Her mother might want to come, and it could take some time to arrange a flight to Egypt from Texas."

Ari gulped. He did not want to make this call, but he knew it was inevitable, unless Elizabeth awoke in the next few minutes. "I guess you're right. Dammit, I hoped she would regain consciousness before I would have to make the call."

Levi nodded. "I understand, brother, but... I think you need to call her family. Or would you prefer I call for you?"

Ari laid a hand over his brother's hand. "As tempting as it is to say 'yes,' I need to be the one to make this call. They don't know you. My God, Levi. It took me four years to convince her to marry me. We finally get married, and now this. We haven't even been married a week--"

His voice broke off.

Levi pulled Ari into his arms for a brotherly embrace. "I tell you what, the phone call can wait. Let's see what the doctors have to say right now. I see Dr. Salah headed our way."

Ari took a deep breath and turned to face the doctor who was approaching them. "So, what is the verdict, doctor? How do the tests look?"

Dr. Salah shook his head. "She has a skull fracture, but it should easily heal. I cannot explain why she remains unconscious or why her pupils are non-responsive. Those things gravely concern me. However, she has brain wave activity. That is a good sign."

Ari frowned. "She has Stargardt disease and limited vision in her left eye. She was accidentally knocked about five feet down onto an old tomb by a girl. The tomb houses the mummy of Queen Nefertiti, and there was supposed to be a curse on the tomb. The imam and the priest were both about to perform the ceremony to protect those who would open the tomb when my wife was knocked onto it."

Dr. Salah looked horrified. "A curse puts a whole different light on everything."

Ari could feel his brow furrow with worry. "Why? What could it mean for my wife?"

Dr. Salah shrugged. "We have had similar cases before in which a curse was involved. I hate to say I might believe in such things, but... We will keep her in intensive care and maintain a close watch on her. Hopefully, your wife will return to us unscathed. In the meantime, pray for your wife. Perhaps the imam and the Coptic priest would come to the hospital and offer prayers as well."

Ari was already upset because Christina knocked Elizabeth into the tomb, but he had not worried about the alleged curse. Could a curse be valid? Wasn't the warning on the tomb simply a way to keep grave robbers out of Nefertiti's tomb? And how could a 3500-year-old curse damage a human being in the twenty-first century? For the first time, he worried about the words of the curse. Was it possible an ancient god snatched Elizabeth's *ka* to carry it back to Nefertiti so the queen could live past the date she originally died? What god or goddess could be powerful enough to steal Elizabeth's soul? Why would they want to hurt her? And if an ancient god stole her *ka*, how could Elizabeth ever free herself from the prison of Nefertiti's body to return to her rightful life?

Worse yet, how could he explain a curse had potentially snatched Elizabeth's soul to Dr. and Mrs. Winslow, let alone to Kirk O'Malley? He would have to talk to Johnny and see what he could suggest. Of course, he failed to follow Johnny's advice, and now Elizabeth lay unresponsive in ICU.

Kirk would throttle him.

Ari resumed pacing back and forth in front of Elizabeth's room.

Chapter 20
Eighteenth Dynasty – Egypt
Elizabeth

I awoke early the next morning while it was still dark. Mom calls that time 'half past dark thirty.' My head ached, and my legs, hands, and face still looked bloated, but I felt and looked better than I had the previous evening. And I was hungry. I felt like I had not eaten in a month of Sundays, as Mom used to say – or would say someday in the future.

The handmaiden called Miriam was nowhere to be found in the Great Royal Wife's quarters. I sighed and pulled on a clean caftan. I stuffed my swollen feet into a pair of shoes that looked a lot like flip-flops back home, except they were made of something covered in what appeared to be gold. I never imagined I would someday wear slippers of gold in an ancient Egyptian palace. I started down the intricate maze of hallways, but I soon found myself lost. At the next turn in the hallway, I stopped in front of a guard. "Could you point me in the direction of the kitchen, sir?"

The guard looked shocked I spoke to him. He fell to one knee and slapped his right hand over his heart. "Your Majesty, please allow me to guide you there."

I bit back laughter as the young guard arose and awkwardly hurried in front of me, embarrassed to have his back turned to me while still attempting to lead the way. After countless twists and turns, we finally arrived at the kitchen.

"Her Majesty, the Great Royal Wife, Queen Consort Nefertiti," he solemnly announced.

Everyone in the kitchen stopped what they were doing and bowed low before me.

I cleared my throat. "I am sorry to intrude. I awoke early and I was hungry. I hope it is not a problem I came to find a bite to eat."

The head cook looked startled and then snapped out an order to her assistants to bring out an assortment of foods for me. I bit back laughter again and smiled. "Oh, thank you, but don't go to so much trouble. Some bread and cheese would be plenty."

The head cook's face reddened at my words. "Your Majesty, it will never be said all I offered the Great Royal Wife to eat was bread and cheese as if she were a peasant. Here, please, sit down. We will bring you food from which you may make your selections."

I meekly nodded and sat down at the large kitchen table. Soon, the workers began a procession line past me to show off everything I could imagine eating for breakfast and then some. I finally selected two boiled eggs, a wedge of cheese, a chunk of fresh bread slathered with butter and honey, and some fresh fruit. However, when the cook prepared to salt my eggs, I slapped my hand over the plate.

"No salt. Please. I think it makes me retain fluids, um, to swell. We need to be careful not to give me anything with salt added to it for a day or two."

The cook looked shocked. "But, your Majesty, we must salt our food to keep from dehydrating in this heat."

I nodded. "I understand, but this unusual swelling concerns me. Let's cut back my salt intake today at least and see if I feel better. As it is, I already feel better than I did yesterday."

The cook appeared dubious but nodded and bowed low. "As you command, your Majesty."

I wasn't crazy about this situation, but it was nice to be queen if I had to be thrown back in time 3500 years.

As I began eating a bite of melon, Miriam rushed into the kitchen, her arms full of clean laundry. She shoved my clothing into the arms of another worker and bowed to the floor. "Please forgive me, my Queen. I was tending to --"

"My laundry, it would appear. There is nothing to forgive, Miriam. You were performing your job duties. I rarely awaken so early. Please, arise, and join me here at the table. If you wait for me, you can guide me back to my rooms. I became lost coming here."

Miriam's cheeks turned bright red. "Of course, your Majesty. It would be my pleasure."

The cook cleared her throat. "I cannot recall your Majesty ever visited my kitchen before."

I chuckled. "Perhaps not. That would explain why I could not find the kitchen without help. I felt ravenously hungry. It must be this child. I realize I have been with child before. This must be a sign this is a son for our Pharaoh, don't you all agree?"

I bit back a laugh as everyone quickly nodded in agreement with me.

Suddenly, they all quit laughing. The servants began bowing to the floor in obeisance. I glanced up, rolled my eyes, and sighed. Akhenaten had found me.

He frowned. I smiled. He glowered, clearly furious. "Why are you here?"

I struggled to keep from laughing. He looked so righteously indignant. "I awoke early. Poor Miriam had gone to launder my linens before I awoke at my regular time. When I awoke, I was hungry, so I came to the kitchen. Why?"

He shook his head. "The Great Royal Wife and Queen Consort does not walk to the kitchen to dine with the servants. It is inappropriate."

I could no longer hold back my laughter. "Oh, really? Why is it inappropriate? I was hungry. Let me correct myself. Our son was hungry. I came where there are all kinds of food. Look for yourself, my lord. Allow the staff to shower you with delicacies fit for the Pharaoh of Egypt."

He stared at me, and finally gave a small nod. He glared at a slave, who quickly pulled out a chair for him. I bit back additional laughter as Akhenaten deigned to seat himself at the kitchen table.

"Cook, please show his Majesty the fine assortment of foods you presented to me earlier. I am sure he will find something to pique his appetite."

The cook bowed again and snapped orders to her staff. Soon, they paraded by Akhenaten with an enormous variety of meats, eggs, breads, cheeses. Others paraded by with many varieties of fruits which included melons, dates, oranges, and pomegranates. Last, men walked by us carrying heavy urns of wine and beer. No wonder they looked at me so strangely when

I requested boiled water to drink. I could not identify some of the foods, but I would swear one was a whole peacock.

Akhenaten indicated which he desired, and soon began eating as well. I asked him to give me a bite of the peacock. I could not resist. I mean, how often would I ever get a chance to taste a peacock? Hopefully, rarely. I wanted to go home as soon as possible. I shook my head when he offered me the peacock's tongue. I thought I might gag. The idea of eating a bird's tongue was too much.

He finally smiled. "You may be right, my beautiful wife. This is a charming way to break our fast in the early morning. When we finish, we must go to the temple and thank Aten for this great bounty."

I stared in shock at Akhenaten. "Uh... am I dressed appropriately to go to the temple? I would not want to offend Aten."

He nodded as he chewed some bread and cheese. After he swallowed and belched, he replied. "Yes, of course, you must dress appropriately to approach Aten in the temple. The caftan is lovely, although it is not your typical attire to wear to the temple. We shall return to your quarters so Miriam can help you change into more appropriate attire."

I gulped and nodded. "Yes, I think it would be best if I changed my gown before we go to the temple. I would not want to make you look bad, or to make a poor impression upon Aten."

He smiled. "You could never make me look bad."

He leaned over to kiss me. I realized if I shut my eyes, I could pretend it was Ari kissing me, not this strange man who looked so much like my husband, and yet his personality was incredibly distinct from Ari.

How could one person look so much like another and yet be so different from him? Of course, how could I look so much like Nefertiti, and not be her? I could not wrap my mind around this conundrum.

We finished eating, wiped our hands with the squares of linen cloth the cook provided us, and then Akhenaten and I walked back to my chambers. Miriam had hurried back to put my things away.

"You should not have walked so far, my love. Your legs were so swollen yesterday. I cannot imagine how you managed the long walk."

I smiled and lifted the hem of the caftan to reveal my legs to him. "The swelling has gone down. My face and hands look better today, too. I told cook to withhold extra salt from my food for a few days. I think the salt is making me hold fluids. We eat salt in all our meals to help prevent dehydration."

He stopped and stared at me. "But you may become dehydrated without salt in your diet."

I laughed and pinched the skin on my arm. "No, look, my lord. I am not dehydrated. I will drink plenty of water and will make sure I don't become dehydrated."

He looked horrified. "But the water will sicken you."

I shook my head. "No. Aten revealed to me in a dream last night that I may drink water if it is well boiled first. I told the cook to boil the water for at least ten minutes and then to filter it through fine linen before bringing it to me in a jug. The water should be safe to drink if it has been well boiled and filtered. I can sacrifice drinking beer or wine with my meals, and I can avoid eating salty foods for a few days if it helps our son to be born healthy. Don't you agree?"

He still looked doubtful. "But the laborers in the fields sicken if they fail to eat salt with their meals."

I shook my head. "Akhenaten, I am not laboring in the fields. I am the Great Royal Wife of the Pharaoh of Upper and Lower Egypt. I think it will be fine for me to withhold extra salt from my diet for a few days. Besides, Aten revealed this to me in my dreams last night. He wants our son to be born healthy. He said, uh, I'm the Wife of Aten, and I must do this to give birth to a healthy male child."

He looked uncertain but he finally nodded. "Very well, since Aten revealed this to you in a dream. However, I will keep a watchful eye on you as well. You are extremely precious to me. I will not risk losing you because you cut salt out of your diet. Here, my beloved. Lean on me as we walk back to your chambers. Or if you wish, I can carry you."

I refrained from telling him the salt might have contributed to the near-death experience of his Great Royal Wife the previous day. "Walking is good for me, as long as I limit how much I walk. However, I will take you up on your gracious offer to allow me to lean on you. Thank you, my lord."

I leaned on his arm as we slowly walked back to my chambers. He wrapped an arm around me and pulled me close to his body. I must admit I was tiring rapidly as we reached the room. Miriam reached it before we did and had already put my laundry away. As I entered, she bowed low to Akhenaten and me. "Your Majesties."

Akhenaten waved a hand dismissively. "You may arise. Help the queen select an appropriate garment to wear to the temple this morning. We must give thanks to Aten for his message to her in her dreams, and for helping her health to improve."

She bowed again. "Yes, oh, great Pharaoh. My lady queen, here are three gowns I selected for you to make your choice. "

I saw she had three gowns placed artfully across my bed. The first looked much like the one I wore the preceding day, except it was made of cloth of gold. I arched my brows as I noticed it had a slit high up the thigh. The second gown, made of purple silk, crossed diagonally from the left shoulder to just below the right breast. Hmm, a bared breast would be a daring look to wear into a temple, especially for a pregnant woman. The third gown was a strapless sheath, created from linen dyed blue as the Egyptian sky above us. It dropped to the floor in countless pleats. Of course, being the lover of all things purple who I am, I selected the purple silk gown, the most unusual of the three. Miriam deftly applied my makeup, and then quickly helped me out of the caftan and into the beautiful gown.

It is hard to envision being in late pregnancy and looking not merely beautiful, but downright sexy. The soft purple fabric clung to my curves, accentuating first my bust line and then the curve of my pregnant body. I was relieved and pleased to see there was fabric to cover the right breast. I had begun to worry about going to the temple with one boob hanging out after I made my daring selection. As I turned to look in the bronze mirror, I was surprised and delighted to see Nefertiti's breasts were still firm and downright perky. She had already given birth to six children. I realized with a start Akhenaten probably insisted she use the services of wet nurses for her babies.

Miriam quickly brought me an exquisite gold collar studded with amethysts and citrines. She then slipped a heavy blue crown on my head before she slipped long, dangling earrings into my ear lobes which coordinated with the necklace. The weight of the blue crown alone was enough to give me another headache. Miriam next slipped matching cuff bracelets on my wrists. I realized with a start the collar and bracelets emulated the rays of Aten. Finally, she slipped my feet into the gold sandals which I irreverently called flip-flops earlier. Miriam lined my eyes with crushed malachite and stained my lips with henna, like I had seen in pictures of royal Ancient Egyptians. When she finished, the woman staring back at me in the mirror looked elegant and aristocratic. Queen Nefertiti looked fit to go to the temple to give praise to Aten for allowing her to live a little longer so she could deliver a son for Pharaoh Akhenaten.

It is a freaky feeling to be inside someone else's body looking at their reflection.

I guess I should say I looked like a queen, but it was Queen Nefertiti I saw in the mirror. Oh, yes, I could see I resembled her. I heard I look like her many times in my lifetime. It astounded me to see firsthand how much I resembled her. I had to remind myself again my soul was temporarily in her body. I was not looking at a reflection of me in the mirror. I was looking at a reflection of Queen Nefertiti.

I prayed this baby was the boy she craved so desperately, but I had serious doubts. I already knew a couple of co-regents would precede Tutankhaten to the throne. Sadly, no male child born of Nefertiti would become pharaoh.

"If you tire as we walk to the temple, I will summon a litter to carry you, my love." Akhenaten bent to kiss me.

I shook my head. "No, some walking is good for me. I try to walk every day."

Dammit, I needed my Fitbit watch to count my steps. I needed to walk at least a mile a day. I walked five miles a day at home in my body. I didn't want to tell him I hoped walking would bring on labor if I walked. The baby might be early, but prematurity might be better than to be born to a mom with full-blown toxemia.

He appeared startled and his elegant, slanted eyes narrowed speculatively. "I did not know this."

I laughed and placed my hand on his arm again. The lovely trill of her voice surprised me. I might be in her body, but I was still learning how she moved, spoke, and existed in her daily life. Now, if I could pull off acting like the Wife of Aten at the temple.

What the blazes are the responsibilities of the Wife of Aten anyway?

As Akhenaten began praying, I repeated the prayers at the end of each sentence, as I had done before. However, I silently prayed the rosary. My sister, Bella, taught it to me. We were raised Episcopalian, but she married a Catholic and joined the Catholic church.

I am not a Catholic girl, but I have found reciting the rosary calms me when I am stressed.

I began, *Hail, Mary, full of grace, the Lord is with you—*

And suddenly, I heard, "I hear you, my daughter. I shall not forsake you."

Okay, I must admit it freaked me out to hear her voice. I blinked. My mouth went dry. I finally whispered, "Who are you, my lady?"

I swear I could see her spread her golden wings as she answered me. "I am called Isis here in Egypt. Heket implored me to save her servant, Nefertiti. Your *ka* saved her yesterday. I have heard your prayers for the healing of my daughter, Nefertiti. I shall not forsake you, my beloved daughter."

My heart leaped with joy. I smiled, feeling renewed and encouraged by her words. I prostrated myself on the steps before the altar to Aten and silently thanked Isis for her promised help. "I shall urge Akhenaten to return to you, my lady."

I could feel the warmth of her smile she beamed at me. As I glanced downwards from my prostrate position, I noticed a little frog sitting beside me. I know it sounds odd, but I would swear the little frog smiled at me as well. Equally odd was the fact I felt no fear for the small frog. In fact, I reached out to gently stroke it as I whispered, "Thank you."

Wait a minute. Why was I thanking a frog?

Chapter 21
Egypt – Ari

Each hour seemed interminable. I sat by Elizabeth's side, holding her hand, talking to her. I reminded her of her love of life, of our love for one another, and our love of the things we enjoyed doing. I told her funny stories about our past and the future we hoped to share. I urged her not to let the little brats get the better of her. I begged and pleaded with her spirit to return to her body.

She groaned from time to time. She squeezed my fingers occasionally and I would see tears slip from her eyes to slide down her cheeks. I had never seen my Elizabeth so pale, so wane. Gone was her beautiful, golden-brown complexion which contrasted so vibrantly with her exquisite, gray eyes. My poor darling looked pale as a ghost. In fact, since I know a ghost, I must admit she was even more pale than Johnny, and that says something considering Johnny was white as a sheet as he hovered nearby.

Once, she nearly scared the daylights out of me. She sat straight up in the hospital bed and let out a blood-curdling scream. I rushed to her side, but she collapsed back onto the bed before I reached her.

Her parents arrived on the second day. Fancy Winslow, her mother, looked terrified. Her father, Kirk O'Malley, looked furious. "I told you to take care of her. You promised me you would."

I gulped and nodded. "Yes, sir. Believe me, if I could relive it, we would not have gone to the Golden City the day she fell on the tomb."

I lacked the nerve to tell him Captain Johnny tried to warn me not to take her back to the Golden City. Johnny was there when Kirk verbally attacked me. Johnny looked at me mournfully and shook his head but said nothing. I cannot express how much I appreciated his silence. I feared Kirk might have beaten me to a bloody pulp if Johnny revealed his warning went unheeded.

It appalled me to realize tears trickled down my face. Kirk's face first registered shock. After a moment's pause, the big man gathered me into his arms, and we wept together.

"We'll get her back, lad."

I nodded. I knew no words to express, 'if we can get her soul freed from whatever entity claimed it.' How could I explain to a man alleged to have been a pirate and who came from the eighteenth century to the present that his daughter's soul had been stolen by the Great Royal Wife and Queen Consort of Pharaoh Akhenaten? I have lived in Egypt all my life. My brother is an archeologist. It even sounded like some crazy cop-out to me. It would have to sound insane to them.

And yet, these people traveled through time. Maybe I failed to give them enough credit. Perhaps they would understand such things better than I ever could.

On the third day, her mother finally convinced me to take a break and go the hospital coffee shop for coffee. She insisted I needed to rest, and she longed to sit by Elizabeth's side for a while. As I hesitantly headed out the door, Fancy lifted Elizabeth's hand to her face and spoke softly to her daughter.

Minutes later, a nurse ran up to Kirk and me in the hospital coffee shop. "Your wife awoke. You need to return to the ICU right now."

Kirk and I looked at each other, delighted and shocked by the nurse's words. We grabbed our cups of coffee and ran back to the ICU with the little nurse. We didn't ask permission to enter Elizabeth's room. We simply rushed into it.

Fancy sat by Elizabeth's bed, pale and crying. She clung to Elizabeth's hand. "Honey, come back. We love you. Please come back."

My heart sank. "What happened?"

Fancy shook her head. "She opened her eyes and looked at me. She seemed startled to see me and clutched my hand. She glanced about furtively, as if afraid she might see someone she feared. And then, she whispered, 'I don't belong here. Help me, Mommy.'" Fancy paused as she wiped tears from her face. "She hasn't called me Mommy since she broke her leg."

"And then?" Kirk's voice sounded husky with unspoken emotions.

Fancy choked back her tears. "It looked like the life drained right out of her. She collapsed on the pillows again. She has been unresponsive since then."

I quickly dialed the number of our Coptic priest. I explained the situation and asked him to come back to the hospital that afternoon to say additional prayers of protection for Elizabeth. He agreed.

"Now what?" asked Fancy as she continued to stroke Elizabeth's hand.

"We wait." I sat my cup of coffee down and lifted my wife's limp hand to my mouth. I kissed it and prayed again. "Oh, lord God, creator of all that is and ever has been. Please bring my beloved wife, Elizabeth, back to us. We love her dearly. We all miss her. Our life as a married couple had just begun when she was ripped from my side. I love her with my whole heart. I need her. Please free her from the forces which dragged her to the past to give life anew to a dead woman. Elizabeth deserves better."

And then suddenly, Elizabeth opened her eyes again. When she spoke, her voice was soft but we all could hear her words. "Isis promised she will help me. She shall not forsake me. I know she will release me when the child is born."

She smiled at me and then her eyes fluttered shut again. She sighed and then appeared to slip back into the coma.

I stared dumbfounded at both her mother and father.

Finally, Kirk spoke, his voice hoarse with shock. "What the hell did she mean? What child? Is Elizabeth pregnant?"

I shook my head. "No, sir. However, she fell on the cursed tomb of an Egyptian queen long dead. Apparently, the poor woman was pregnant at the time she died. The curse on the tomb stated the queen would claim the soul of the person who opened the tomb. The priest and the imam were about to perform a ceremony to remove the curse--"

"A curse? Are you serious, lad? They were there to remove a curse?" Kirk sounded astonished. "So why was it not removed?"

I shook my head again. "I don't know, Mr. O'Malley. I know the whole thing sounds crazy. When archeologists find a tomb with a curse written on the outside, they perform certain rituals and recite specific prayers to protect themselves when the tomb is opened. Unfortunately, the prayers had not been uttered when Elizabeth was knocked onto the tomb. The force of her body cracked the slab covering it."

Kirk still appeared incredulous. "Oh, for the love of... who the blazes was in that blasted tomb anyway? Why would they want to curse my Elizabeth? Who could have been powerful enough to snatch her soul like this?"

I took a deep breath. "It was the tomb of Queen Nefertiti. She did not want to curse Elizabeth. She needed her *ka*."

Kirk still looked perplexed. "What the bloody hell is a *ka*?"

Both Fancy and Kirk looked confused.

I cleared my throat. *Okay, Ari, here goes nothing.* "The *ka* is the essence of a person's soul."

Kirk looked stunned. His voice trembled with emotion as he spoke. "So, you think this ancient queen stole my Elizabeth's soul?"

"No. Based on what Elizabeth whispered to Fancy, I think Isis stole her soul to reanimate Nefertiti. Apparently, Nefertiti needs to stay alive long enough to give birth to the child she is carrying."

Johnny surprised us then by speaking up. "Exactly, Kirk. I could not protect our girl against this. The goddess is too powerful."

Finally, Fancy spoke. "And you always say Elizabeth looks enough like Nefertiti to be her double, Kirk."

Kirk nodded, obviously shaken. "Aye. That explains a lot. Especially if Johnny couldna' protect her."

I frowned. "Why would it explain a lot, sir?"

Kirk shrugged. "Mayhap Elizabeth was Nefertiti in another life."

I went cold with dread. "Then her soul might be stuck there for a while."

Fancy shook her head. "Maybe not. She said Isis will send her back once the baby is born."

I shook my head and held my hands up in frustration. "You don't understand. Nefertiti never had a son. She had six daughters. There would be no reason to keep her there temporarily until another daughter is born."

Fancy smiled. "Maybe. And perhaps Elizabeth will enable Nefertiti to give Akhenaten the son he so desperately desired and craved from his Queen Consort."

"But the birth of a son from Nefertiti would change history," I protested.

"It wouldn't be Elizabeth's fault. It would be the will of Isis. Wasn't she reputed to have considerable magical powers?" asked Fancy.

I nodded, eager to grab the thin shred of hope Fancy tossed at me. "Isis was supposed to have greater magic than all the other gods. She was also said to be the giver of life. She protected pregnant women. She safeguarded the kingdom from its enemies, governed the skies and the natural world. She had power over fate--"

"Over fate itself," finished Fancy with a grin. "Isis is using our Liz to give Nefertiti another chance to change the destiny of Akhenaten and his heirs. There was a co-regency before King Tutankhamun. Wasn't Nefertiti thought to be one of the co-regents?"

I shook my head. "No one knows for sure. Nefertiti is shown in various archeological sites as equal in stature to Akhenaten, which was exceptionally unusual. She is illustrated smiting Egypt's enemies, riding in a chariot, and worshipping Aten the same way Pharaoh Akhenaten did. Her name then disappeared from historical records, and the name of a co-regent, Neferneferuaten, appears. Nefertiti might have been co-regent with Akhenaten because 'effective for her husband' is written in one of her cartouches. She may have been made a co-regent with Akhenaten when he was so involved in the development of his religion. Let's face it; someone needed to run the country. Some archeologists believe Neferneferuaten may have been a female Pharaoh after Akhenaten died. The co-regent may have been Meritaten, the oldest of their daughters, and she may have taken the name, Neferneferuaten, when she became co-regent. Levi swears Meritaten married someone named Smenkhare. I have heard other archeologists insist Nefertiti assumed the name Smenkhare when she assumed the role of the pharaoh, and her daughter, Meritaten, took the role of Great Royal Wife. Don't ask me how or even why they might have pulled off such a stunt. I believe there was a man named Smenkhare who married Princess Meritaten, and she took the name Neferneferuaten after both her parents died. We don't know who this Smenkhare was. He might have been a younger brother of Akhenaten. Interestingly, comments about this Smenkhare disappeared after only four years. He did not keep the throne when Tutankhamun came of age to take on the responsibilities as Pharaoh."

I took a deep breath before I continued. "Archeologists believe whoever ruled as Pharaoh after Akhenaten tried to control the damage Akhenaten's changes caused. As Zain Hassan puts it, the country was chaotic when Akhenaten died. The subsequent ruler re-instated the Ancient Egyptian religions with the priests of Amun-Ra. After his father's death, Tutankhaten was raised with the traditional pantheon of Egyptian gods and goddesses. He even changed his name to Tutankhamun. I understand Tutankhamun was only eight or nine years old when he ascended to the throne in Ancient Egypt, so he had a co-regent until he reached adulthood at about fourteen or fifteen. Tutankhamun then ruled the country for four or five years before he also died."

"And poor King Tut only reigned for a few years before he died, probably because of inherited problems associated with his incestuous birth," added Fancy.

I shrugged. "Perhaps. Pharaoh Akhenaten and the Royal Princess Kiya were his parents. Kiya was Akhenaten's full sister. They were both born to King Amenhotep III and Queen Tiye. And yes, Pharaoh Tutankhaten changed his name to Tutankhamun after his father died. Sadly, young Tutankhamun died when he was about eighteen or nineteen years old."

Kirk frowned. "Why did the pharaoh die when he was so young?"

Ari shrugged. "Good question. He may have died from injuries in a chariot crash. He had a club foot and scoliosis. Zain says it would have been harder for him to balance to drive the chariot than it would have been for able-bodied men. He used a cane to walk. There were many walking canes in his tomb to use in the next life. However, he was also trained for battle. His tomb included body armor, equipment for military campaigns, a chariot, and his bows. He would have been well trained in archery and I would imagine he was a better than average archer. He may have received injuries in battle, although some archeologists think his congenital deformities were too severe to have allowed him to actively take part in battles. They believe he was guided in military stratagems by his Vizier, Ay, who was the brother of his grandmother, Queen Tiye, and by Vizier Ay's foster son, General Horemheb. Some of Tutankhamun's injuries had not healed properly when he died, and he had necrosis of one foot. My brother says he also had malaria which might have caused his death. Vizier Ay became the next Pharaoh after Tutankhamun, and Horemheb became Pharaoh after Ay."

I paused. "You might recall there was a curse attached to the tomb of King Tutankhamun, also. No prayers fended off the curse when the tomb was opened. Several people involved in opening the tomb died within a brief period. Levi claims it was a coincidence, but the archeologists are careful to have prayers said before opening a tomb bearing a curse."

Kirk paled. "I don't believe in coincidences."

I nodded. "Nor do I."

Fancy cleared her throat. "But didn't people typically die much younger in the eighteenth dynasty than now?"

I nodded again. "Yes. People rarely live beyond forty if that long. Pharaoh Tutankhamun was extremely young when he died. Queen Tiye, Pharaoh Akhenaten's mother, was an exception. Archeologists examined her mummy and believed she was about sixty years old when she died. She still had beautiful, brown, curly hair. Pharaoh Akhenaten married Nefertiti when she was fourteen. Levi believes she was about twenty-seven when she died. He does not think she was the co-regent mentioned. Pharaoh Akhenaten was a few years older than she was. Levi thinks Akhenaten died a few years after she did."

"Incredible," muttered Kirk as he shook his head. "This whole mess is freakin' unbelievable."

"Not really. Girls married much younger when I was a girl, too. According to the Bible, Mary was only thirteen years old when she was betrothed to Joseph."

Kirk sniffed and shrugged. "Maybe so."

Fancy arched a brow at Kirk and snorted. "Oh, really, Kirk? You can't say anything except 'maybe so'? Remember how young Anya was when she gave birth to Liz?"

I remembered Anya was Elizabeth's mother who died following Elizabeth's birth. Anya was a teenager when Elizabeth was born.

Kirk blushed. "Oh, well, yeah. She was young, but she wasn't thirteen or fourteen."

Fancy smiled. "No, I think you told me she was sixteen when she gave birth to Liz. One in three women died in childbirth in 1780, the year Liz was born. It amazes me Queen Nefertiti successfully survived the births of six children 3500 years ago. Well, I always heard Egyptian physicians were advanced in their skills. They even performed brain surgeries."

"All girls. I wonder if the seventh child would have been a lad?" Kirk mused.

Fancy grinned. "Why else would Liz's soul have been hauled back in time to re-animate Nefertiti, unless it was to allow her to give birth to a son?"

"But like Ari says, birth of a son would change history," Kirk protested.

Fancy shook her head. "Not really. Think about it, Kirk. Isis had incredible power over the fates themselves. It would not be Liz interfering with history. It would be the great goddess Isis exercising her power over the fates if she chose to re-animate Nefertiti with Liz's soul and allowed the Royal Queen to give birth to her son."

About then, I heard a ghostly voice clear his throat. "But if Elizabeth's *ka* reanimated Queen Nefertiti to allow the Queen to give birth to a son, my dear, when would she allow our Elizabeth to come home?"

Fancy quit smiling as Johnny's words sank in. She gulped. "I don't know, Captain Johnny."

"It would depend on the agenda of the goddess. And only Isis would know what she plans for Nefertiti once she gives birth to the son of Akhenaten," I mused.

Chapter 22
Eighteenth Dynasty - Egypt
Elizabeth

In the following days, I walked as much as possible, watched my salt intake, and struggled to stay alive long enough to give birth to Nefertiti's baby. I understood Isis would not allow me to return home until Nefertiti's son was safely delivered. I prayed she would honor her promise to me and permit me to go home once this child was born, and she would let poor Nefertiti finally rest in peace.

I began experiencing maternal feelings for the child growing in the body my soul now possessed. I realized I referred to Nefertiti's body as my body more with each passing day. I would caress 'my' belly and talk to the baby growing inside 'me.' I made tiny baby clothes for the child and had many conversations with Akhenaten about what to name the child. I sometimes cried because I would never see Nefertiti's child take his first steps or hear him say his first words, much less grow up to become the pharaoh.

I visited the girls often. Meritaten, the eldest, and I frequently talked about her forthcoming nuptials with Smenkhare, who was the younger half-brother of Akhenaten. Smenkhare was a scribe studying to become a priest of Aten. He was an outstanding young man, and I prayed he would be a good husband to the girl I had grown to consider my daughter. Believe me, if I ever had a daughter, I would have loved for her to be as sweet, intelligent, kind, and loving as Meritaten.

We talked about 'our' loss when Metetaten died the year before at only nine years of age. We both cried as we remembered her sickness and death. As it was, I knew only Meritaten and Ankhesenpa'aten would live to be adults.

Ankhesenpa'aten would marry her half-brother, Tutankhaten. Their incestuous marriage still grossed me out, especially considering Tutankhaten's mother, Kiya, was Akhenaten's full sister, but it was a different world than the one from which I came – or the one into which I was born.

I also knew Ankhesenpa'aten would marry again after Tutankhaten died. I prayed the Hittite prince she would marry would prove to be a man who would treat her with the love, kindness, and respect she deserved.

As my time to deliver Nefertiti's baby grew near, I asked to speak with Kiya one day. I had learned Nefertiti and Kiya did not speak with each other frequently. The two women normally avoided each other. Kiya knew Nefertiti disapproved of Akhenaten marrying his sister. Royal Princess Kiya thought Queen Consort Nefertiti was jealous of the fact Kiya gave Akhenaten a son. Perhaps Nefertiti was jealous, but I like to think her revulsion was more basic than mere jealousy. I suspect Nefertiti did not approve of the fact a siblings married and had children together. Tutankhaten was not their only child.

I was in my garden when Kiya came to my quarters.

"Your handmaiden tells me you wish to speak with me." Kiya sounded guarded, wary, a bit hostile, and she held herself erect and stiff.

I looked up from my sewing and smiled at her as I patted the cushioned seat beside me. "Yes, please come in and sit down. We need to talk."

Kiya stared at me for a minute before she nodded and came over to sit on the edge of the seat, as she wordlessly awaited me to start talking.

Wow, these two women must have had one hostile relationship, I thought. I forced a smile upon my face. "Princess Kiya, I have an enormous favor to ask you."

Her eyes narrowed as she studied me. "No. I will not give him up, Nefertiti. We have discussed this before. I have a right to be married to Akhen, just as you do."

"Of course, you do. I did not wish to discuss your relationship with Akhen. I have a different question. As you know, this child will be born soon."

I laid my hand across my belly.

She stared at me before she responded. I could see confusion in her eyes. "Yes..."

I swallowed hard as I tried to choose my words. "I have serious concerns about whether I am going to survive this birth. I have had a difficult pregnancy. I am sure Akhen told you I almost died a few weeks ago."

She blinked as she stared at me, clearly not understanding where the conversation was going. "Yes, our husband told me the Aten saved you."

I nodded. "Exactly. However, I remain fearful my time on earth may be finished once this child is born. I asked you to come here today so I could ask an enormous favor of you. If something bad happens to me –"

My voice broke. I struggled to hold back the tears stinging at my eyes. She turned her head and spat to ward off evil, and then turned back to me. Kiya reached out and grabbed my hands. "Don't say that. Do not wish for trouble. Nothing bad will happen."

I clasped my hand over hers. "I hope not. But I need to know you will watch over my children if anything bad should happen to me. Merit will soon marry Smenkhare. Ankhesenpa'aten is pledged to marry your Tutankhaten when they are both of marriageable age. I know you will see that both girls are well raised until their marriages."

She nodded. "Of course."

I gulped as I struggled not to cry. "I pray you will also guard and protect our son, if I am safely delivered of a boy child, or our daughter, if it should be the will of our lord Aten. Please, Kiya, promise me--"

It shocked me when my voice broke off from unspoken emotions. This was not even my baby, and yet I was crying for the unborn child of a dead woman who had somehow caused my soul to be transported back through time so this child could be safely born. And of course, the baby shoved a foot against the side of my belly then. I rubbed the tiny footprint as I took a deep breath.

"Tutankhaten should still become the pharaoh after their father. But Tutankhaten will need strong supporters. He will need priests, physicians, even military leaders. If this child is a son, I would want my son to be raised to be his brother's strong right hand."

She blinked back tears. "Of course, Nefer, but you won't die. You are one of the strongest women I have ever known. You have lived through six births before this one. You will live through this one as well."

I smiled at her and patted her hands again. "I hope so. Then we can raise our children together for the best interest of our country. But Kiya, if I die, please promise me you will love my children and help them to grow up to be good people. Akhen will need your support, as will the children. I know Queen Tiye will do her best--"

"Mother will always do her best to help care for our children."

I smiled again. Queen Tiye was a 'force to reckon with,' as Mom would say. Tiye dearly loved her children and grandchildren. "Of course. And may I count on you to watch after my children as well, as if they are the children you birthed? I would protect your children if our circumstances were reversed."

She shocked me. As tears welled up in her eyes, she pulled me into her arms. "Oh, Nefer, of course I will. I would guard them with my life, as would Mother. But you will be fine."

Like Kiya, I could no longer hold back my tears. I wrapped my arms around my sister wife (I guess that's what you would call it since we were both married to the same man), as my tears streamed down my cheeks. "I pray you are correct. However, I will not fear this birth if I know you will help... in case..."

We talked a long time throughout the afternoon. About Akhen and our children. Between us, we had born ten children to the same man. About our feelings of jealousy when he would go to the bed of the other one. I could see I shocked her when I asked her to see to his 'needs' while I awaited the birth of this baby. "The physician says I should not engage in sexual activity with our husband right now. I pray you will succor his needs."

Her eyes grew wide with shock or surprise or maybe both. "Are you serious?"

Wordless, I nodded.

She pulled me to her again. "Oh, Nefer, I never dreamed the day would come when we could be friends, to truly be sisters. You have made me a happy woman today. I pray you live many long and happy years after this baby is born so we may continue this friendship. Of course, I will care for our husband during this time, just as you would if I were awaiting the birth of another child. And I will pray this child is a son. A man cannot have too many sons."

A cloud passed over her face and I realized she had lost a son. I struggled to hold back a new deluge of tears. I nodded.

As our conversation ended, there was a knock on the doorway leading out to the garden. We looked up and saw a frowning Queen Tiye standing there.

"Oh, please, your Majesty, come out here in the garden. We were talking about our husband and our children," I said.

She blinked, clearly surprised by my words. She nodded and came out to sit down across from us, stiff with a formality that made me want to giggle. I bit back my laughter.

"I am glad you came today. Princess Kiya and I were talking about plans for our children. I told her I fear I may not survive the birth of this baby. She agreed she will raise the child as if it were hers if anything untoward should happen to me."

Tiye shook her head and spat on the ground. "You must not talk like this, Nefer. You invite the bad spirits to steal your *ka*."

Nope, my ka was already stolen and brought here. I tried to smile as I shook my head. "No, Queen Mother. I almost died a few weeks ago. I am trying to be cautious, but I must be realistic. If any evil should befall me, I wanted to know Kiya will lovingly raise my children. I hope you will help her."

Her face softened as she struggled not to cry. "Of course, my daughter. I promise we would do everything in our power to protect Merit, Ankhe, Tash, little Nefer, Setenpenre, and this child."

"Thank you, Queen Mother. I hoped you would support me on this. You were a fierce, strong queen for Pharaoh Amenhotep. You raised Akhenaten to be a strong king and religious leader for our people. Princess Kiya is a wonderful mother and wife to our husband as well. I pray..."

My voice broke off. This was damned hard. I knew Nefer did not got along well with her mother-in-law. Now I was asking these two women to guard 'my' children if I died, which I knew would happen.

They surprised me. Each woman wrapped her arms around me in a loving embrace I am sure Nefertiti never felt from them while she lived. My hands crept up to clutch to the back of each woman. Of course, their kind attentiveness made me cry, especially when I felt a little foot press against my ribs again. I pulled Queen Tiye's hand down to feel her grandchild's little foot pressing against me.

Queen Tiye beamed at me through her tears. "Everything will be fine, Nefer. He is a strong child. You will see."

I hugged her close as I nodded, unable to verbalize a single word. She leaned her head against me, wordlessly comforting me as I clung to her again.

Miriam looked stressed as she entered my rooms with a tray of fresh fruits, little cakes, and a variety of foods to tempt me to eat. The pretty maidservant did this every afternoon, at the orders of my husband. She returned minutes later with beer, wine, and a fresh jug of boiled water for me. I noticed she chewed her lip nervously, as if waiting for a blow up. I figured those were common in the past among these three women. As the ladies ate the afternoon snacks with me, our mood lightened, and we began laughing and joking. Suddenly, we all quieted as a tall, angry man stormed into the garden.

"Her Majesty and I need to speak alone. Now."

I gulped as Princess Kiya and Queen Tiye arose to leave. Both kissed me on my cheeks, and then bowed to Akhenaten before they kissed him as well. They then left my chambers to leave me to face a furious husband alone.

I took a deep breath. "Miriam, please go to the kitchen and fetch Pharaoh Akhenaten a fresh mug of beer."

He shook his head. "I would prefer the sweet red wine."

She bowed low. "Of course, Pharaoh."

He waited until she left to speak. "Why were they here? Did they upset you?"

I tilted my head at him and frowned. "They were here because I invited them. Did I look upset when you came in? No. We were laughing and talking about our children. We were eating. We were having a wonderful visit until you barged in like an angry bull and ruined our time together. Why did you interrupt us, Akhen? Don't you want me to have a good relationship with your mother and sister? Can't you stand for me to have a good relationship with them? Do you want them to hate me?"

He stammered as his face reddened. "No, no, no, of course, not, my beloved. However, it has been too many times I have been warned they are in your gardens, and I arrived to find you sobbing as they attacked you with their words. I had no reason to expect anything different today."

I sniffed in disdain. "Oh, piddle. Perhaps you should look and evaluate the situation before you storm into my quarters. Next time, listen outside for a minute. Don't make a big scene if we are getting along well. Sit down and join us in our repast. We made more progress today in a half-hour than we made in all the years before today. You may have ruined it, Akhen. Your mother hugged me. My sister wife hugged me. We… we…"

And then like a big goober, I started crying again. Oh, I guess I should say like a typical, emotionally overwhelmed woman in late pregnancy, but I had never been pregnant before. Was I even pregnant now? Certainly, her body carried a baby, the only baby I figured I would ever come close to claiming as mine.

And then, dammit, it hit me. This baby would be born, and I would never see him take his first steps or hear him utter 'mama.' I would never see him grow to be a man. The thought I would never see this baby grow to manhood made me cry even harder.

Akhenaten pulled me into his arms. I laid my head against his chest and wept until I had no more tears to cry as he stroked down my back, murmuring sweet words of love to me. "You need to eat something, and you need to rest."

I took a ragged breath as I struggled to speak. "I was eating with them."

"Oh, no, don't tell me you would have eaten if I had not come into your rooms. Don't try to blame me because you are not eating now. You don't eat enough to feed a sandgrouse. You must eat to bear a healthy child. You must eat to have strength to give birth to my son. Come now, Nefer. Eat for me. And eat for our child."

I tried to smile. I took the bite of melon from his fingers. "Yes, my lord. For you. And for your son."

He beamed at me, no longer lost in his fury of a few minutes before. He possessed a terrible temper, but Nefertiti could be the tool to help him control it. He could be taught. I forced out another smile as I accepted another bite of melon.

Mom would have said I was on a coddiwomple. I figured I was on the coddiwomple of a lifetime as I traveled in a purposeful manner towards a vague destination. What would be my ultimate destination? Would I live to give birth to this baby? Would it survive? Would I then return to my rightful place in the future with Ari? Or would I be trapped here with a religious fanatic who would be known in history as a heretic and labeled the Betrayer?

...

The clock chimed again, ticking off another minute, hour, day. Would this be the day I would give birth? And if so, would this be the day I would go home?

Morning came far too early. I will never understand why Akhenaten insisted I must accompany him to the temple for the sunrise prayers that morning. I usually accompanied him to the noontime prayers. So, poor

Miriam dragged me out of bed at half-past dark thirty to get me ready to greet the sun when it would arise in all its glorious promise of another sun-drenched, hotter than hell, Egyptian day. If allowed to return home to my family in the future, I would never again complain Levi kept the air conditioning too cold in the house at Luxor.

First, Miriam scrubbed my body. Egyptians kept their bodies clean with daily baths. I bit back laughter as she fussed because I insisted on allowing my hair to grow. My new hair growth created additional work for the sweet, hardworking maidservant. Akhenaten said I spoiled her and let her have too much leeway, but I loved the girl, and so had Nefertiti before me. I hated the alien feel of a naked scalp. I held my tongue. There was no explaining my sudden aversion to baldness to the girl who had maintained my bald head for several years now. I thought all upper-class Egyptian noble women kept their heads shaved when I first 'arrived' here. I soon realized many upper-class women maintained their hair like Queen Tiye. She had beautiful brown curls I longed to emulate.

Next, Miriam wrapped my body in a plush linen towel, and pared my nails before she meticulously detailed my eye makeup with the crushed malachite Akhen preferred. She always made my eyes look absolutely fetching. My eyes took on a never-before-seen hint of green oceans when decorated with the malachite. I would have to remember how green eyeshadow flattered my eyes when Isis allowed me to return home. Miriam lengthened my lush lashes with something which must have been old-school cake mascara. It sickened me when she confided the mascara contained crocodile dung. I realized I should not ask questions if I could not handle the answers. Miriam then finished my makeup by applying henna to my lips. Next, she slipped an elegant, sunshine yellow, silk gown over my head. She smiled as the pleats fanned out over my enormous baby belly. I felt big as the side of a proverbial barn in the yellow gown, but she seemed exceedingly pleased with the resulting look. I figured I looked as big as the rising sun. I suspect she wanted me to look big as the pregnant Wife of Aten.

Miriam then affixed an exquisite gold collar adorned with inlaid turquoise and citrines. The extravagant collar draped deep into the 'v' of my cleavage. She added a striking black wig decorated with turquoise and citrine beads before she slipped a golden headdress over the wig. I had never seen much less envisioned anything like it in my life. It was crafted of cloth of gold, and then covered with small circles of gold. The circles reminded me of sequins, but I would not have imagined sequins existed long ago in the Eighteenth Dynasty. I was not sure how to keep it on my head until Miriam firmly affixed the gold headdress with a delicate circlet. Now, if the wig would stay in place, everything would be fine. Fortunately, it was all much lighter on my head than the heavy blue crown I wore on previous occasions.

She next slipped gold, citrine, and turquoise earrings into my earlobes. She added the gold bracelets which detailed the rays of the golden orb known as Aten. With a final touchup of color to perfect my lips, I was once again amazed at the transformation of Nefertiti into the Wife of Aten. Nefertiti was one fine-looking broad, even pregnant.

A girl could get used to attention like this.

As Miriam completed my toilette, I glanced around to see Akhenaten leaning against the doorway. He nodded his approval, and then grinned at me. "Like I said the first day I met you, your name should be Nefertiti, because beauty had come to Egypt from your homeland of Mitanni, my beautiful queen."

I felt my cheeks warm with color. He must have had three hundred women in his harem, many inherited from his father, girls sent as tribute from rulers of other countries like I had been sent from my father, the King of Mitanni. But this man knew how to compliment a woman and how to make her feel like she was The Only One. He called only two of his many wives his favorites, Kiya and Nefertiti, and only Nefertiti was his Great Royal Wife. Of course, Pharaoh's Great Royal Wife also served as his Queen Consort and as the Wife of Aten.

Miriam bent to slip my golden sandals onto my feet. I was pleased to observe the exquisite, golden sandals no longer pinched my toes. My self-inflicted salt restriction appeared to have reduced my edema and the resulting horrible headaches. I would bet my blood pressure was down from stroke level to just about normal. I held out my hand to Nefertiti's husband. Together, we walked to the Temple of Aten where Akhen would sing the morning prayers to the sun god called Aten.

"How manifold it is, what thou hast made! Thou art hidden from the face of man. Oh, sole god, like whom there is no other! Thou didst create the world according to thy desire, whilst thou wert alone: thou then created all men, cattle, and wild beasts. Whatever is on Earth, going upon its feet, and what is on high, flying on its wings…"

Akhenaten continued through his lengthy song of praise to the end. "The King who lives by Maat, the Lord of the Two Lands, Neferkheprure, Sole-One-of-Ra, the Son of Ra who lives by Maat, the Lord of Crowns, Akhenaten, great in his lifetime, and the great Queen whom he loves, the Lady of the Two Lands, Nefer-nefru-Aten Nefertiti, living together forever."

The words stunned me. I guess I should have listened more carefully to the whole song Akhen sang during his daily prayers. I had heard him sing this prayer repeatedly, but my mind often wandered as he sang it. I realized with a start his reference to Maat was not a reference to a goddess. He meant he lived by truth, justice, and he strove to maintain the cosmic order. Superman was not the first to strive to live by those tenets.

I had been silently comparing his song to Aten to one of the Psalms in the Old Testament although I could not remember all the words to the Psalm. There had to be some connection between the two compositions. I did not miss the mention of the Lord of Crowns, which reminded me of a song we used to sing back home in the future. The future hymn said, 'crown Him with many crowns.' Akhen's song of prayer also reminded me of a song about the Lord of Lords and King of Kings.

I had never realized he pronounced his great, eternal love for me at the end of his song of prayer. I swallowed hard. I finally realized why my soul had been dragged back through eons to give life again to Nefertiti. It was not so she could bear his son. It was because he had daily proclaimed his undying love for her for all times. Akhenaten insisted she be brought back to life.

How could I ever convince him of the error of his ways?

I could not fault his religion. If a man were to invent a religion to satisfy the scientific concepts of his day, scientists could not fault the correctness of Akhenaten's view of the solar system's energy, as known then. He certainly verbalized monotheistic thinking in his views and symbolism of Aten. His song was a beautiful statement of Akhenaten's doctrine of One God, an outpouring of emotion honoring Aten -- and of Akhen and Nefer, eternally together, forever in love.

I thought again of my strong, uncanny physical resemblance to Nefertiti, and my Ari's remarkable resemblance to Akhen. Could we have known each other through multiple lifetimes?

Many old religions stated kings were the sons of gods. Salima told me Akhenaten was the first to claim a close relationship between the Father God and his earthly Son. Likewise, Akhenaten was the first to assert only the Son knew the heart of his Father God. Akhenaten viewed himself as the Father's image on earth, with Akhen being the king on earth, and Aten the king in heaven. Akhenaten made himself a high priest, prophet, king, and divine as he claimed the central position in his new religion. Since only he knew his father's mind and will, only Akhenaten could interpret the will of Aten for all humankind with true instruction coming from Akhenaten.

My mouth went dry with shock at the realization. I suddenly understood how unusual it was that Akhen bought my story when I claimed Aten revealed anything to me in a dream. Perhaps he was merely humoring his pregnant wife, I mused. But then again, Nefertiti was the Wife of Aten. Perhaps she could channel dreams from Aten since she was His wife.

No wonder the old priests hated Akhenaten so intensely. Not only did he displace them and destroy their temples, but Akhenaten also claimed to be the only one who could understand the will of the one God, Aten. No wonder they would label him the Betrayer in years to come after his death. But was he the Betrayer? Or was Akhenaten the first to fully grasp God is God, and there is no God but God?

After the sun arose in all its beauty and glory, we stood at the balcony overlooking the street below. Akhenaten then spoke to his people, thanking them for their prayers asking for my safe delivery from my recent illness. He ran his hands over my belly and told them he knew Aten would bless us with a son because of the outpouring of prayers and trust in Aten. He then tossed down golden collars worked with discs symbolizing the Aten. "Aten told me to disburse these amongst my people in thanks for the many prayers raised on behalf of our Great Royal Wife."

A loud cheer arose from the waiting throngs below us. I could not believe he was tossing down golden collars as if they were trinkets made of mud and straw. Egypt would not remain a prosperous country long with antics such as this one. Salima told me one reason he was called the Betrayer was because Akhenaten nearly bankrupted the country while he was the pharaoh. Akhenaten pulled me close to him and handed me some of the collars to throw down to the waiting throngs below us as well. I pasted what I hoped was a gracious, regal smile on my face and tossed the golden collars down to the people. People reached up with greedy hands to grasp the golden collars given to them by their Pharaoh and the Wife of Aten. After we dropped all the collars, we both waved to the people until they disbursed. As the last walked away, I sagged against my husband.

"I'm exhausted."

He bent to kiss my forehead. "But you were magnificent. Aten is well pleased with you as am I, my beloved."

Well, it was good Aten was pleased, because I had a feeling Isis raged with fury.

It was one of those days when I felt as if I were waiting in a dream as I held on for just one more breath. I ached with longing to give birth to this baby and for this bizarre situation to end. Every day, I slipped more easily into the role of Nefertiti, and I would forget I was not her. It frightened me as it became easier to slip into the fantasy with each passing day. But I was not Nefertiti. I wanted my life, not the life of another woman long dead, no matter how much this man had loved her. Would I ever return home to the man I loved? And if I could ever return home, when would that fateful day occur? I longed for the touch of my husband, for his kisses and caresses.

Chapter 23
Egypt - Ari

"Ari, Ari, wake up. Elizabeth needs you. Now."

You wake up fast when the cold, dead touch of a two-hundred-year-old ghost grabs your shoulder and shakes you. I pulled myself up in the recliner in Elizabeth's hospital room as I shook off Johnny's grasp. "What's wrong?"

Johnny shook his head. "She is moaning, calling out for you. Her eyes are fluttering. She is attempting to awaken, but something is holding her back."

I rubbed the sleep out of my eyes as I rushed to my wife's side. Johnny hovered right by my shoulder as I grabbed her hand and started patting it as I began talking to her, urging her to awaken. "Darling, wake up. It's time to come home to us. Don't let them hold you captive there any longer. Come back to me, my love. Come back."

My heart lurched as her eyes fluttered open.

"Can't... yet. Soon..." she gasped out the words as she went limp, and her eyes rolled back into her head again.

I continued to stroke her hands and cheeks for several more minutes. Finally, I leaned against the bed as I struggled not to weep. I was convinced she needed me to remain strong. She did not need me crying at her bedside.

My beautiful wife had been gone for a month now. Miguel rushed to Cairo to direct Biozyme International while I sat by Elizabeth's side, day after exhausting day. The original plan was I would serve as the interim director until he would arrive from Boston. Elizabeth's horrific accident resulted in Miguel rushing to Cairo while I was on medical leave sitting beside my unconscious wife.

Fancy usually stayed with me. Last night, she looked like she was about to collapse from exhaustion, and I sent her to the house for a well-deserved night's sleep.

And then, this morning, I became furious. I turned and stormed out of the room. The charge nurse looked up in shocked surprise as I stomped past the nurses' station. Johnny came floating after me, calling to me to wait for him. I ignored nurses and the ghost as I hurried outside. I needed fresh air. Sunshine. The searing heat of the Egyptian day. Anything but the cold, sterile room where I had spent most of the past month with my unresponsive wife.

Why didn't I listen to Johnny the day we returned to the Golden City? Why did I take her back there? If we avoided going back to help guard Nefertiti's tomb, my beloved wife would still be with me. She would be learning Arabic and growing to love my country. Instead, I dd not know what was happening to her. Was I really supposed to believe her soul had been ensnared by an ancient goddess? When would Elizabeth be allowed to return to me?

Would she ever return to me?

I leaned my face against the cool exterior wall of the hospital and finally gave in to the sobs I had held back for weeks. She could not see me out here. Now, I could cry for my lost love.

Fancy found me there. I didn't realize she had walked up to the building, much less that she spotted me. But my sweet little mother-in-law marched right up to me, pulled me into her arms, and began speaking to me in a warm, loving, soothing voice. I gradually returned to conscious awareness and wrapped my arms around her as I sobbed even harder.

"It will be all right, Ari. She's going to come back to us. She really will, darlin.' You will see. You just have to keep the faith."

I nodded. "I keep telling myself she will come back to us. But, when, Fancy? Why can't she return yet? She has these moments of lucidity and then she is lost to us again for hours... days... sometimes a week. She can breathe on her own. She has brain wave activity. She just can't remain conscious. Why? What foul spirit ensnared her so tightly that she cannot return to those of us who love her most in all the world?"

Fancy looked uncertain. "She mentions Isis. But the first day, didn't Johnny mention someone he called the Betrayer?"

I looked down at the little spitfire of a woman and blinked. "Yes, he said the Betrayer wanted her. He demanded her return."

Fancy's lips narrowed into a narrow, resolute line. "Then we need to find out who the Betrayer was, and why he wanted Nefertiti so badly. That might explain how he has such a hold on our girl."

I blinked again. "They also called the Heretic Pharaoh 'the Betrayer.' He was the one who tried to eradicate the pantheon of ancient Egyptian gods. What was his name? Akhen...baba. No, that's not his name. I'm so tired. I'm not making any sense. I'm being ridiculous. Akhen... something or other. I can call my brother and find out. But, didn't Elizabeth say something once about Isis? I thought Isis was keeping her there for some nefarious reason."

Fancy nodded. "Liz said something about Isis would allow her to return when the baby was born. I figure Nefertiti was pregnant when she died. Who was her husband? Why would they have called him a heretic or the betrayer?"

I shrugged. "I'm the ophthalmologist, not the archeologist. I don't know. Let's call Levi and see what he can tell us."

I phoned my brother and explained our question. Minutes later, he rushed up to us where we had sought refuge from the unrelenting sun in the shaded area outside the hospital. "Nefertiti was Queen Consort and Great Royal Wife of Pharaoh Akhenaten. He was first known as Amenhotep IV. He changed his name when he became Pharaoh and revised the religious order throughout the Two Kingdoms."

"Of course. I don't know why I couldn't remember his name was Akhenaten," I replied, shamefaced.

"You're dead on your feet. You need some rest." Levi sounded anxious about me.

"What do you mean, Levi?" asked Fancy. "I mean about this Akhenaten fellow. By the way, I agree Ari needs some rest or he is going to wind up a patient in the hospital, too."

"Well, for starters, Akhenaten believed Aten was the only god. Aten was the sun god. He was also known as Aten-Ra. Later, Akhenaten closed all the temples devoted to other gods. In particular, he shut down the temples to Amun-Ra, and then he began dismantling those temples. He then set himself up as the only son of God, and the only intercessor to God. One could say he established himself as high priest, prophet, king, and the divine son of God. He claimed the central position in his new religion. We think there was a great plague in the country at the time of his death. Amun-Ra's priests knew how to work a crisis to their best interests and blamed Akhenaten's heretical rejection of the other gods as the cause of the plague. The plague may have resulted from the volcanic explosion at Thera or some similar eruption at another location in the Mediterranean. An explosion could have occurred hundreds of miles away in the Mediterranean, but the ash from the explosion would have affected crop growth adversely throughout the Middle East and Egypt for well over a year. It would have caused tsunamis and major flooding, also. The Nile delta would have been severely affected by the unusually high flooding. Amun-Ra's priests claimed Akhenaten's rejection of the traditional pantheon caused the Amun-Ra and the other Gods in the Egyptian pantheon to turn away from Egypt. The priests further contended Akhenaten caused the gods to punish Egypt via volcanic eruption, flooding, and subsequent plagues. The priests of Amun-Ra manipulated the situation to their advantage and proclaimed Akhenaten was the Betrayer of the Faithful. As a result, they tore down his city built to honor Aten, his mortuary temples, and as much as possible which recorded his life. When we found his body, his external genitalia had been removed. In fact, at first, we initially thought it was the mummy of a woman."

"Oh, my god!" Fancy exclaimed with horror written all over her face.

Levi nodded, his expression grave. "It is the only case we have ever found of what appears to have been intentional mutilation of a corpse's genitalia after death. Oh, yes, some mummies have been damaged when their tombs were ransacked. The body of Seti I was damaged when his abdomen was broken open when tomb robbers searched for hidden jewels. I don't know why they thought jewels were sewn up inside Seti's abdominal cavity. They also severed his head from his body. In other cases, arms or legs have been broken and severed by tomb robbers. Some think Tutankhamun's skull could have been damaged after his death. Initially, they thought the skull fracture might have caused his death. Anyway, we believe the penis, testicles and scrotum of Akhenaten were removed as he was being mummified. It was as if the priests wanted to deprive him of a future love life with Nefertiti."

I gulped. "Do you think she outlived him?"

Levi shook his head. "It would not have mattered to them. They believed the Pharaoh was incarnate and would be reborn as a man in the afterlife where he would be reunited with his beloved Nefertiti. If his external genitalia were removed and not placed in canopic jars, they intended him to be an incomplete man in his afterlife, never able to couple with his wife again. That's pretty cold."

I nodded. "Yes, it was harsh punishment, even if he had been responsible for the volcanic eruption, ash, tidal waves, and plagues, and I assume he was not responsible for any of those things. Anything else?"

He nodded. "Yes. Until we found this tomb, no one knew where the body of Nefertiti was buried. It had been hypothesized she might have gone to Spain or even on to Ireland or Scotland with another husband. I think one of her daughters might have been the one who moved far away. Ankhesenpa'aten changed her name to Ankhesenamun when she married to Tutankhamun. After the young king's premature death, we believe she later married a Hittite prince. They probably went elsewhere when her father and mother were reviled by the reinstated priesthood of Amun-Ra."

Fancy frowned. "What is the difference in Amun-Ra and Aten-Ra? Aren't they both names for the same thing, the Sun God?"

Levi smiled. "Ah, you grasp the big picture. Many people were so ensnared in the minutiae that they could not grasp the big picture. Aten was not a new god but was one aspect of the sun God. He was worshipped as early as the Old Kingdom. 'Aten' was the traditional name for the sun-disk itself. He was often called 'the Aten.' In the story of Sinuhe, Amenemhat I described soaring into the sky and uniting with Aten, his creator. During the New Kingdom, Aten was considered to be one aspect of the composite deity, Ra-Amun-Horus. Ra represented the daylight sun, or the Aten. Amun represented the sun in the underworld, or at night. Horus represented the sunrise. Akhenaten proclaimed the visible sun itself to be the sole deity. Some believe his religion was based on the scientific observation that the sun's energy was the ultimate source of life. The full extent of his religious reforms was not apparent until the ninth year of his reign. Akhenaten proclaimed the Aten to be the only God. He then banned the use of idols except for a rayed solar disc. He insisted the image of the Aten represented God. He realized God transcended creation and could not be fully understood or represented. This aspect of his faith bears a notable resemblance to the religion of Moses, and some people claim he may have been Moses. I believe the claim he was Moses is utter nonsense, but it is undeniable their versions of the Godhead shared similarities. Freud thought Akhenaten was the first monotheist.

Several hymns to Aten were written during his reign, and some are attributed to Akhenaten. They describe the wonders of nature and hail the sun as the universal lord of all lords. The Hymn of Aten has been compared to Psalm 104, which describes the wonders of nature and the ultimate power of God. Only Akhenaten and his immediate family were supposed to have a personal relationship with Aten. It does not appear the ordinary people took to the new religion but continued to worship the old gods in private. Before Akhenaten's reforms, there had been a vast pantheon of gods. There were priests and temples for each god and goddess. For Akhenaten, it was simple. The Sun God was supreme. The others did not matter. Everything came from the Aten. In a manner of speaking, he was correct. The Sun grows our food. We even get vitamin D from the sun. Without the sun, we cannot live."

"True," Fancy murmured as she shrugged.

"Queen Nefertiti was called the Wife of Aten. Her status placed her on a goddess level. Nefertiti could take an active part in the rituals in the temple with Akhenaten. No one else was allowed such a privilege. Later, it was suggested this proved he still clung some belief in Isis and equated Nefertiti to Isis on earth. I suspect he intended for Nefertiti to replace Isis. I also suspect if Nefertiti outlived Akhenaten, she suggested they bring back at least some of the old pantheon, such as Isis, who had been well-loved. That would explain why both Isis and the Betrayer wanted her restored to life."

Fancy frowned. "Elizabeth said Isis would enable her to return after the birth of the child."

Levi nodded. "I remember. We have completed the MRI of Nefertiti's mummy. She was not pregnant when mummified. The question, of course, is how soon did she die after the birth of the child."

"And was Elizabeth's *ka* allowed to return home after the birth of this child, or was her *ka* somehow kept there by Akhenaten," I mused.

Levi nodded again, clearly excited I grasped his meaning. "Exactly. So much about them was destroyed in the aftermath when the old priesthoods resumed power again. We did not even know where she was buried until her tomb was discovered in the Golden City. Right now, we are trying to establish an age for her at death. Her estimated age at her death might help us to know more about how long Elizabeth was trapped there after the birth of the child she mentioned."

My shoulders sagged. "So, she might be there for years to come."

Fancy smiled. "Not necessarily. Time does not move in a straight line."

Both Levi and I gaped at her. "Wh-wh-what do you mean?"

"Time is a fabricated construct. It does not actually move in a straight line. We plot it on a straight line because the concept is easy to understand. Time is more like a huge spiral. Sometimes, it seems to move at the same pace. At others, not so much. What has been three weeks here might have been three months there... or three years there. When I came forward in time, I was here for twelve years before Kirk found me. It had only been a few years there. When Richard went back in time, he was there almost two years. He was gone from here about seven months. Time did not move at the same pace."

Levi's eyes bulged out in surprise. "Are you saying…?"

She grinned. "I am, Levi. I'm talking time travel, which may also be why Elizabeth comprised the perfect choice for a soul to restore life to Nefertiti. Elizabeth came forward in time as a child."

"My dear God in heaven above." Levi crossed himself.

I felt the glimmer of hope. "What are you trying to say to us, Fancy?"

"Her soul may have already been there for years. Hopefully, she will return to us soon."

Levi's eyes narrowed. "Wouldn't her *ka* be searching for Akhenaten?"

Fancy shook her head. "Not necessarily. Nefertiti was Akhenaten's twin flame. Liz is Ari's twin flame. They may have been reincarnated during many lifetimes, but right now is Liz and Ari's time. The only way Akhenaten and Nefertiti can continue to live together, is in the past. Those dried up mummies are not coming back to life. Liz loves you, Ari. She won't remain in the past voluntarily one day longer than Isis requires of her once she enables this baby to be born."

Levi nodded, but I noticed he still looked grim. I felt my brow furrow as I stared at him. "What else did her mummy show?"

Levi hesitated. "I need to review the results with Zain before I tell you."

I felt the color drain from my face. "Is it bad?"

He nodded. "Yes."

Chapter 24
Eighteenth Dynasty – Liz

My back ached hideously as we returned to my quarters. I snapped at Miriam as she helped me change from the yellow silk gown into a more comfortable linen caftan. "Get me out of this damned thing. I'm burning up. I can't stand this silk another minute."

She nodded and quietly helped me into the other gown. "Perhaps you should rest awhile, your Majesty."

I nodded, as I trembled with exhaustion. My peevishness appalled me. I was not usually cross with the servants. It still embarrassed me to own slaves, and Miriam was one of my slaves. The young woman always worked diligently to fulfill my every whim. "Yes, I think I will. I was not made to arise before the dawn. Arising so early is hard enough under ordinary circumstances, but right now? Impossible. I don't know why we had to go to the temple so early today. My back hurts horribly, Miriam. I'm... I'm sorry I'm so ill-tempered today."

"Yes, your Majesty. Please do not worry about it. You are the finest mistress a girl could have. I am blessed to be your handmaiden. Would you like me to massage your back?"

I realized my hands were trembling. "No, thank you, but I think I will lay down. I'll rest."

"Of course, my Queen. I will keep everyone out of your quarters for you so you can have some peace."

I nodded as I rubbed my back again. "Thank you, Miriam. You are an excellent servant. I don't deserve you."

She smiled and hummed a soothing tune. She plumped a pillow behind my head and pulled a light linen blanket over my legs. "You are the best mistress a girl could have. Now, go back to sleep. This baby will come soon. You need to save your energy."

I sighed as I laid down on the bed. I quickly fell asleep, but I had strange dreams. Isis and Heket came to me to talk about my forthcoming birth of the long-awaited son Akhenaten wanted so desperately.

"You will have choices to make, you know," whispered the little frog.

I looked from Heket to Isis. "What does Heket mean, great goddess?"

Isis smiled at me. "Every woman has choices to make, my daughter. You will have choices, too. Will you stay? Will you go? Will you live? Will you die?"

I felt panic rise inside my chest. "You said I could return home to Ari after this child was born."

She nodded as she spread her wings. "Of course, my child, if that is your wish. You will have choices to make. Make them wisely. Your choices may affect many generations."

The little frog nodded. "Many generations may be affected by your decisions."

I grew so furious that I balled up my fists and shook one at them. "I had no choice in whether I came. You brought here against my will. Why give me choices now? Why put the burden of what happens to future generations on my shoulders? This is not fair."

Isis shrugged, and her wings spread wide. "Much in life is not fair. You read the warning on the tomb. You knew it would bring you here if you opened it."

"You know that was an accident!" I shouted.

She shrugged. "Was it? You opened the tomb. What will you decide when your child is born?"

"It's not *my* child. It's *her* child. You stole my *ka* to bring her back to life so this child could be born," I shouted.

"But now you are part of the child, and the child is part of you. He has part of your essence just as you have part of his," came her calm, serene response.

I shook my head. "I don't understand. How can he have part of my essence now? And how can I possibly have part of his essence in me?"

Isis smiled. "It is birth magic, my daughter. Part of the soul of the mother goes into the child as part of the soul of the child goes into the mother. You have choices now. Will you stay? Or will you go?"

I awoke, sweating profusely as my belly clenched into the worst cramp of my life. Oh, sweet baby Jesus, I realized to my horror, I was in labor.

I pulled myself up from the bed and gasped as another contraction hit me. I struggled to control my breathing as I called out for my handmaiden. "Miriam! The baby is coming."

She came running at once. She laid a hand on my contracting belly and smiled as she nodded. "You are correct. It is your time, your Majesty. I will send for the midwives."

My eyes must have widened in shock or horror as a warm rush of fluid gushed out of me and down my legs. I grabbed her hand. "Don't go. I don't want to alone."

Miriam's eyes widened in surprise as well. She nodded, but ran to the doorway and shouted, "Fetch the midwives! The Great Royal Wife is in labor!"

Things got interesting in a hurry then.

I was eight when Mom gave birth to Ronan. She underwent an emergency c-section in Atlanta. I don't remember her ever being in active labor around us. Bella miscarried at seven months when she had Covid-19. I was in Galveston, and she was in Boston, so I didn't even have experience being with her during that horrible time in her life. I had no experience with a normal modern labor and delivery, and now here I was in the eighteenth dynasty of Egypt, about to give birth to a royal child.

The midwives rushed in quickly to help me. Akhenaten was kept far away from my quarters. They stripped me out of the sodden gown, and we began walking. I had not realized walking was good for labor. It is. Finally, when my contractions were fast and furious, they sat me on a birthing stool and told me to push.

Hey, wait a minute! I thought Mom said you give birth lying down on a bed.

I figured it out as I hung on to the arms of the little birthing stool. As I squatted on the stool, I could feel the baby dropping down into place, so he could be born. The birthing stool put Nefertiti's uterus and pelvis into the correct position to deliver this baby. It also strengthened my contractions appreciably while it relieved pressure on my back. One midwife stood behind me, rubbing my back. Another stood by my side, holding my hand to encourage me. The third knelt before me, ready to catch the little bundle of joy as he would pop out. I must admit I wondered which midwife was the human form of Heket, the little frog goddess. For the first time all day, I felt better.

They didn't have to tell me when to push; Nefertiti's body began pushing all on its own. And I pushed. And pushed. And still no baby.

The midwives became worried. Nervous. They were fearful for their lives when I told them to call the physician. Minutes later, the court physician came rushing in.

Of course, I felt terrified by then, too.

"What is the problem?" asked the court physician.

"The baby won't come. He is too large. His head cannot pass through her birth canal," whispered the head midwife with a nervous glance at me.

I sat trembling on the little birthing stool as I tried to catch my breath between contractions. "She's right. I've been pushing and the poor baby can't come out. You are going to have to cut him out of me."

They stared at me in horror. "But your Majesty, you will die..."

I shook my head, impatient with their idiocy. "Well, if you don't, I will die anyway and so will Pharaoh's child. You must cut me. You must do it now before I change my mind."

I could hear Akhen yelling in the hallway, pounding on the door, demanding to know what was happening. "Tell him everything is fine," I urged, as I struggled to catch my breath. "Don't let him in. Don't tell him there is a problem."

The court physician frowned. "Your Majesty, he knows there is a problem, or I would not have been summoned."

I frowned. "Then tell him I am a silly, hysterical woman. Now, help me on the table so you can cut me and save this baby."

They helped me onto my dining table, and at my prompting, the midwives and servants held my arms and legs down. I told the physician to wash me off with soap and the boiled water from my jug. He looked at me like I was nuts, but he obeyed me. I next ordered the physician to boil his scalpel before cutting me. Another stunned look, but he did as I demanded and boiled the scalpel in water hung over the brazier in the room before he made his cut. One of the midwives gave me a rag to bite on while he cut. A rag is not much help when you are undergoing a c-section with no anesthesia, but I was just along for the ride in this body. Poor Nefertiti was the one who was in pain, not me. So, why was I crying? Why was I the one screaming in pain?

I could hear Akhenaten banging on the door again, frantically demanding to enter my rooms. I wept for the man who desperately wanted to see his beloved and who now stood outside her door, terrified the woman he cherished would die apart from him.

"Don't let him in," I begged as tears slid down the beautiful face of their queen. "Save his baby. I am here to bring this baby into the world. Save his baby."

And then through my pain, I heard the wailing cry of a newborn baby. My tears changed from tears of pain and terror to tears of joy. The baby was born. It was the long-awaited son. Soon, I could go home. Soon, I would be in my Ari's arms again.

"Here, Your Majesty. Your son."

I opened my eyes, surprised to see I was still alive in ancient Egypt.

"What? You mean I'm still alive?"

She tried to smile at me and held the baby out towards me.

I blinked as my exhausted eyes focused on the small bundle in the midwife's arms. I winced as she laid the baby on my stitched and bandaged stomach. I realized Egyptian physicians were tremendously smarter and better skilled than I had thought. I had to give them credit. They damn sure knew how to cut and stitch.

I lifted a weary hand up to gently stroke the cheek of Nefertiti's newborn son. "We did it, kid," I whispered. "You're born. Now, how will you grow to manhood and find your destiny?"

As he rooted about for a nipple, I lifted his little head to my breast. I gasped as he connected and suckled.

And then I wept as my hands gently fondled his beautiful little face. Golden brown skin, lighter than his father's Egyptian skin, darker than Nefertiti's Middle Eastern skin from Mitanni. Dark curls adorned the crown of the infant's elegantly shaped head. Dimples in his fat little baby cheeks. How could a newborn baby have such fat cheeks? I chuckled as he puckered his face as if he might fuss, but then turned his head back to my breast.

Oh, sweet baby boy, you have already captured my heart. How could I leave you now?

The door suddenly burst open, and Akhen came rushing to my side. Eyes wide, he stared from his son to me and back again. "By Aten, Nefer, you have given me a son."

I shook my head. "Aten helped, my love, but I think Isis helped with this more than Aten."

He looked shocked and then his shock turned to anger. "You must not say her name. There is no god but Aten."

I stared down Nefertiti's beautiful nose at him. "I just gave birth to a boy child for you. Do not presume to tell me what to do, Akhen. I know who we counted on for the six times I was previously with child. I know who promised me a son this time. It was not Aten. You cannot tell me who to worship, or you can give birth to your son the next time. You act as if you don't need the help of a woman now anyway. Let's see if your precious Aten will give you another son without a woman to bear the child."

Isis smiled and nodded.

Chapter 25
Eighteenth Dynasty – Elizabeth

We named him Neferkheprure.

Akhenaten and I were not speaking. He decided I was a heretic, perhaps insane. I knew which one of us was insane and it was not me. Of course, I could not tell him where I came from, or why I was there. I had a role to play while I remained in the Eighteenth Dynasty.

I will never figure out how I lived beyond such a traumatic birth. I will never know how any woman endures childbirth. I once read that childbirth involves more pain than the human body is supposed to be able to survive, yet women survive the pain of childbirth every day. Fortunately, most women did not have to endure a c-section absent anesthesia.

With each passing day, the baby known as Neferkheprure grew more important to me. I was caught in a neat trap laid by Isis and her frog. Some days, I cursed them for this adventure. Other days, I gave praise they allowed me to be a mother, if only for a split second in the vastness of eternity.

Somehow, my battered body began to heal. For the next six months I remained there, I knew my cesarean section looked like it had healed, but infection brewed deep inside me. I often suffered from excruciating pain in my lower abdomen. I told no one. I knew my days were numbered. I wanted to ensure the little boy I gave up so much to bring to life would live long and prosper, as they would say someday far in the future. So, for those six months, I made alliances and encouraged people to make me promises to protect my child – Nefertiti's child – whenever she might die. I worked feverishly to ensure the child I had grown to love would be protected when Isis allowed me to leave.

Meritaten and Smenkhare married the week after the baby was born. Such ceremonies were simple then. Their wedding ceremony was held in my garden to allow me to attend my eldest child's wedding.

I spoke with Merit privately before their wedding and told her I was troubled I might not live to see Neferkheprure grow to manhood. She laughed at the idea. I stressed to her if something happened to me, she needed to make sure her baby brother was safe from all danger. She grew serious and assured me she would care for him, but sweet Meritaten was only fourteen years old. She was well-educated and about to marry an intelligent, well-educated young man, but I did not think she fully comprehended the seriousness of my situation. I took extra steps to protect this precious little boy.

I had already spoken with Queen Tiye and Princess Kiya. While both promised to care for my son if anything happened to me, I understood Kiya's first concern would be her son, not mine. Queen Tiye would do whatever she felt was expedient to protect her dynasty and the pharaonic line which descended from her husband and her. She would always favor Tutti over my Nefru. In the meantime, while I remained in Nefertiti's body, my life was much more pleasant because I had made peace with those two women.

The pain continued to grow in my belly.

My best bet was through Nefer's sister, Mutmedjmet, who was married to General Horemheb. The General had been a military leader since the time of Akhen's father, Pharaoh Amenhotep III. Horemheb was older than my sister, but he loved her since we first were taken to Ay's home for Ay's wife and Ay to foster us until our marriages.

The original plan was both Mutmedjmet and I would marry the old pharaoh when we were sent to Egypt from Mitanni as young girls. When both Amenhotep and Thutmose died, Akhenaten had the right to marry both of us. Akhenaten was young and filled with a young man's passion. He fell head over heels in love with the girl he dubbed 'Beauty Has Come.' He saw no reason to marry her younger sister as well as Nefertiti. Horemheb petitioned to marry my sweet, amenable sister when she was of marriageable age, and Akhenaten permitted them to marry. Rather than becoming one of many wives in the harem of Pharaoh, Medj, as I called her, became the beloved only wife of the top military leader in the country. They never had children, a situation which caused my sister considerable sadness and depression.

Nefertiti's sister and she had not been close in years. Medj felt cheated she never had children and resented the attention and lifestyle Nefertiti received as Queen Consort and Great Royal Wife. Yet, she was the only wife of a man who adored and treasured her all the years of their childless marriage. Many men would have taken another wife when the first proved to be barren. Horemheb did not. He stuck faithfully by the side of the woman he loved. They had a prosperous life together in their home in Thebes. He had remained head of the military for Akhenaten, and I knew he would remain in that position of authority for many more years to come.

I knew the world would turn upside down within a few years after Neferkheprure was born. Akhenaten and Nefertiti would both die. Smenkhare and Meritaten would be co-regents until Tutankhamun reached an age considered old enough to rule. Under their tutelage and the wise counsel of Vizier Ay and General Horemheb, Tutankhamun would abandon his father's religion and would turn back to the traditional pantheon of gods. Unfortunately, the sweet boy I called Tutti would die early as well, because of a compound fracture of his leg. The country I had learned to love would again be torn apart for a while.

Although I emphasized that Nefru, as I called him, should be raised as a scribe or in the military to support his brother, the future pharaoh, I understood it was equally probable he could be executed as superfluous. It complicated matters if there were multiple sons entitled to become pharaoh when the old pharaoh died unless the father left specific directions on who was to follow as his heir. That was why Smenkhare became a scribe years before: it enabled him to escape possible execution. However, Smenkhare's mother was a lesser wife, not the Great Royal Wife. Smenkhare was not considered the threat to Tutankhamun a son born of the Great Royal Wife would have been. A son born to Queen Nefertiti could become a great threat to Tutti, the son born of Royal Princess Kiya, who was not the Great Royal Wife. Kiya was a Royal Wife but was not the Great Royal Wife. Likewise, she was not Queen Consort or the Wife of Aten.

I talked first to Mutmedjmet. I told her if anything bad should ever befall me and Akhenaten, I wanted Horemheb and her to take Nefru to Thebes and to raise him to be of service to his country. They should tell no one he was my son. He would be raised by them as their foster son if they did not want to claim him outright. I suggested they might then change his name to

Paramessu to hide his identity further. After much cajoling, they finally agreed, I think mostly to shut me up. I could tell it troubled Horemheb to contemplate the death of his pharaoh. He was an honorable man and a dedicated soldier. He could not foresee murdering a king or the child of a king even though he abhorred Akhen's new religion. Such things were not done in Horemheb's mind.

I knew Tutankhamun would not rule long before he died, and Vizier Ay would follow as Pharaoh for a few years. After him, Horemheb would be the pharaoh. Horemheb would diligently strive to destroy evidence of Akhenaten, Tutankhaten, and of me as I told Horemheb he should someday do. My suggestion shocked him, but I knew he would protect the child I called my son.

Horemheb had no sons. He would raise Nefru to be a scribe who Horemheb could trust like the son he never had, just as Ay raised Horemheb to be the son he could trust and upon whom he could depend.

Salima told me Horemheb would leave his kingdom to a man named Paramessu, who would be like a son to him. Paramessu would be known as Pharaoh Ramesses I, the father of Pharaoh Seti I, and grandfather of Ramesses II, believed to be descended from Pharaoh Ay.

Ay had no 'children of his loins.' His wife and he had three foster children who they loved as their own: Horemheb, Medj and me. Oops, there I go identifying as Nefertiti again.

After much cajoling, Horemheb and Medj finally agreed. If anything bad happened to me, and if anything catastrophic also happened to Akhenaten, so that my son needed to be rehomed, they would step up. My sister and brother-in-law would hide Nefru, raise him as their foster child, and never tell him he was the child of Akhenaten, born of his Great Royal Wife, Nefertiti, and entitled to become the Pharaoh in his own right. No, the boy would be raised with humility. He would love the people whom he would serve. He would turn away from his father's religion and would honor the ways of old among our people as he would be taught by Medj and Horemheb.

Huh. I just realized I thought of Egyptians as 'our' people.

Hopefully, Nefru would also be taught his birth mother loved him dearly.

Chapter 26
Eighteenth Dynasty – Egypt
Elizabeth

I began fantasizing about how I could be rescued from this hell on earth. One of my favorite scenarios involved a spaceship landing on top of the Great Pyramid and whisking me away. I loved to picture the spaceship hovering above the great, white pyramid topped with a crown of gold, and then the aliens would beam me up like Scottie used to beam up Kirk on Star Trek. The little green men were eager to remove me from ancient Egypt. I figured they wanted to probe me, but I didn't care. Probe away, just get me out of here!

A second fantasy involved me finding the Stargate. Carter grinned as he helped me through it. "Be quiet, Liz. We don't want to awaken Apophis."

I smiled. "Simply avoid Akhenaten. He worships the sun god, Aten. He renounced the rest of the Egyptian pantheon. They have turned their backs on him. None of them will aid him now. However, Isis must have sent you. She promised she would help me."

Another involved the Star Trek Enterprise arriving on the site. I looked up smiled, and said, "Beam me up, Scottie!"

And of course, he did. Then, Captain Kirk and the crew brought me home.

Another involved Darth Vader in a TIE fighter, coaxing me to come to the dark side. "I will save you from these heathens, my Queen."

"Thank you, Lord Vader."

I could never figure out if he thought I was Princess Padme Amidala, who he secretly married when he was a young Jedi knight. I would have preferred to be rescued by Luke or Han, but like Mom used to say, beggars can't be choosers.

No fantasy could have prepared me for my eventual departure from the Eighteenth Dynasty.

"No." I remember I frowned as I swatted at Akhen's grasping hands. "Don't, Akhen."

Akhen's hand stilled but he scowled, clearly displeased by the word I dared utter. "You dare to say 'no' to me? You must never say 'no' to your Pharaoh, Nefer."

I laughed until I realized he was serious. My lips narrowed into an angry slash. "Really? I'm no longer allowed to say 'no'? Since when? Get over yourself, Akhen. I have told you this before: I will not risk having another child. Giving birth to Nefru nearly killed me. You claim to love me. If you do, then you should not want me to die giving birth to another baby. I have given you seven children. You should treasure me, not torture me. You have over three hundred` women to choose from in your harem. Princess Kiya eagerly awaits your visits to her chambers. She would be delighted to satisfy your needs. I won't risk another pregnancy. You agreed to forbear future sexual attention to me when I was slit open from side to side. I will cuddle. I will kiss. I will perform other acts as you demand, but I will not risk another pregnancy. Why have you changed your mind? No, Akhen. Stop it, now."

I slapped his hands again as he glowered at me.

We had this conversation repeatedly. He wanted back in my bed. I wanted to avoid sexual intercourse with him like the plague. Nefertiti became pregnant at least seven times in fourteen years. God only knew if she had miscarriages or stillbirths besides those live births. I did not intend to get pregnant with his child now. I did not intend to engage in sexual relations with him. The whole idea made me think 'yuck.' I did not love this grasping man. My soul might still be trapped in Nefertiti's body, but I adored my husband, and I craved Ari's touch. I longed to go home to my husband. I wanted my life back.

I knew Nefertiti's days were numbered. I tried to tell Akhen she suffered from a lingering infection because her incision had not healed properly. He thought it was a paltry excuse to avoid intimate relations with him. It may have been an excuse, but it was certainly not paltry. My abdomen burned with the fire of infection. The pain would double me over, gasping in agony.

That day, Akhen's lips narrowed into a thin, angry slash. His dark eyes flared with fury as his hand lashed out across my face. I fell back, shocked by the slap. He had never struck Queen Nefertiti before, to my knowledge. My hand flew up to my cheek in horror. "Akhen, you never struck me before. Such behavior is unnecessary."

Cold shivers ran down my spine at his thin-lipped smile. With one fell swoop, he ripped my caftan down the front. "No? I think it was needed. I am your Pharaoh, Nefer. You shall submit to me now. You are my Great Royal Wife, and it is your wifely duty. I recall when you told me it was your privilege to couple with me. I have waited too long to enjoy the pleasures of your body."

"Who told you to behave like this? Why are you treating me like a common whore?" I gasped, still shocked by both the slap and the ripped bodice. He laughed again, the sound harsh and cruel, as I attempted to hold the caftan together. I had never heard such a note of manic hysteria in his voice before then.

I realized the all-too-perfect Queen Nefertiti never rebuffed the far-too-crazy Pharaoh Akhenaten. However, I am not a girl to take being slapped across the face lightly, much less to accept a marital rape. My lips narrowed into an angry line as I bounced up onto my knees and shoved against his chest. His eyes narrowed as he recovered from my blow, and he reached over to grab me.

And the fight was on.

I slapped. I pummeled. I kicked. I scratched. I bit. I gouged. He continued to pummel me with blows as I continued to scream, 'no,' to no avail. No one came to assist the Queen who dared to rebuff Pharaoh's advances. At the end of the fight, Akhen's hands closed tight around the neck of Nefertiti, his so-called beloved. "I shall kill you before I allow you to tell me 'no.' Do you understand me, Nefer?"

At first, I thought he was making an idle threat, but I soon realized this threat was not idle as my airflow became restricted. My God, the damn man was serious. He intended to kill me if I did not submit to his sexual demands. My feet kicked, as I struggled to escape his grasp. My feet slipped on the smooth-as-silk Egyptian linen. I tried to kick him to no avail. As my oxygen level depleted, I panicked. I could no longer control the reach of my kicks or the strength of my slaps. I reached out, hitting him with futile fists. He moved one hand long enough to slap me hard across the face and then resumed choking me.

Oh, yes, I understood. I must submit or die. I nodded I would submit, desperate to get free. Yet, Akhenaten seemed lost to his rage. He continued choking me. I realized he must know I was not his Nefertiti. The knowledge drove him to madness beyond control.

I became desperate to find something to use as a weapon as I realized he intended to kill me. My hands reached out in desperation. One hand finally landed on a statue of the Aten, golden rays extending from the circular orb. I grabbed it. As Akhen's hands continued to tighten around my throat, I saw the first spots of red dance before my eyes. Terrified, I concluded the capillaries in Nefertiti's eyes were bursting as he strangled her. As darkness welled up around me, I somehow summoned the strength to strike him repeatedly with the statue of his god. I was unsure where I struck, but I could feel a warm, sticky substance flow over both of us. I figured it was blood.

And then everything went dark.

Chapter 27
Eighteenth Dynasty

The guard could control his curiosity no longer as the shouts stopped. He pushed the door open with caution and peered inside. He paled at the horrible sight he beheld. As his knees shook, he shouted.

"Pharaoh and the Great Royal Queen have both been grievously injured! Summon the court physician immediately!"

Chapter 28
Luxor - Elizabeth

I felt cold.

I shivered and pulled the bed coverings up to my chin. I realized my teeth were chattering. Why was it so cold here?

And then it hit me. I was back in the twenty-first century, in an air-conditioned hospital room, or so it appeared. Tears welled up in my eyes as I reached a shaky hand over to stroke the back of the hand of the man I loved. I didn't know how long I had been gone, but he still awaited my return. Bless his heart, he slept with his head resting on his hands on the side of the hospital bed. As I stroked his hand, his eyes slowly opened.

I smiled. "Hi." I grimaced and rubbed my throat with my free hand. I cleared my throat and coughed. "Oh, gosh, I sound horrible."

He blinked, and then he sat up, stunned I was awake and talking to him. He grabbed my hands. "Don't go again, darling. Please, stay with me this time. I have missed you so much..."

My heart lurched as my big guy cried. I continued to stroke his hand. "I'm not going anywhere. She's dead now. Her death freed my soul to come home."

Somehow, he dropped the bar on the side of the bed, slid onto the edge, and pulled me into his arms. "I missed you so much. Thank God you are finally home."

I stroked his cheek in wonder. I was home. All I had to do was tell Akhen 'no' one too many times, so he could kill me. I swallowed and frowned as I rubbed my throat and coughed. "My throat really hurts."

He nodded. "You began murmuring throughout the night your throat hurt. Oh, my god, what happened to your eyes? The whites are red as blood."

I chuckled and then coughed. "Well, Doc--"

Just then, Mom walked into the room carrying a tray filled with cups of coffee and sweet rolls. "Ari, I brought – oh, my gracious, Liz! You're awake. My darling girl, you came back to us!"

I smiled and nodded. "I'm home."

I reached over and grabbed a cup of coffee. "Ooh, Starbucks? Uh, you guys wouldn't mind if I take a cup, would you? It's been a while since I had a good cup of Joe... or even a bad cup for that matter." I took a sip, closed my eyes, and sighed. "Oh, the coffee tastes delicious."

Mom and Ari looked at each other and then both started laughing.

Ari chortled. "She's been unconscious for six weeks, and the first thing she wants is a cup of coffee."

I shook my head. "Nope. The first thing I wanted was a kiss from you. Kiss me, mortal, or your life is forfeit."

He grinned ear to ear as he bent to kiss me. "Yes, my most beautiful Queen of Egypt. And allow me to prepare your coffee the way you prefer it."

He took the cup from my hands and added cream and fake sugar for me before he handed it back. I took another sip, sighed, and smiled. "Perfect."

My attending physician appeared stunned to find me sitting up, wide awake, talking and laughing with my family as I drank a cup of coffee when he made his morning rounds. The medical students accompanying him gawked like they were looking at the living dead. He kept me in the hospital another week to run all kinds of tests on me. He finally shook his head. "I was convinced you would never return to us. Your recovery is truly a miracle. I cannot explain it any other way. Even your vision has improved."

I smiled. "I agree completely. Ari thinks the month of sleep helped my eyes to recuperate somewhat. Now, can I go home? I'll be honest. I want to sleep in our bed."

I resisted the urge to say, 'next to my husband.'

He nodded. "Yes, of course, Mrs. Hotep. Stay well."

I lifted my hand in the old familiar sign. "Live long and prosper, Doc."

He chuckled as he shook his head. "You are incorrigible. Fine. Live long and prosper, Mrs. Hotep."

We flew home to Cairo. Ari had arranged to have the car taken back home when I regained consciousness. The hour-long flight was much easier than a six-hour car ride. We were home in less than three hours after my release from the hospital.

The cats went crazy when I walked in the door. I thought I would never get Macchi unwrapped from around my legs. Otto jumped into my lap, purring so loudly everyone could hear him as he rubbed back and forth across my body.

"They thought you would never return." Ari said with the faint hint of a grin flitting across his lips.

I rubbed my head against my cat's head, enjoying the silken sensation. "Yes, Otto, I love you, too. Oh, they knew I would come back. They just didn't know when."

We bought Mr. Maksoud's house, and he moved to Thebes to live with his daughter and her family. Contractors began knocking down much of the wall between the two houses so we could convert two small houses into one large home. We revamped Mr. Maksoud's living area and kitchen into a master bedroom with an attached bathroom. Let me tell you, I love my standalone soaking tub, and Ari loves the oversized, walk-in shower. Upstairs, we broke through the wall, and suddenly had room for three bedrooms, two bathrooms, and an office for Ari.

"I don't know why you want all these bedrooms." I stood studying the floor plans one afternoon as he came in the house about three months after I 'came back.'

He blushed, which surprised the heck out of me. "Uh, Elizabeth, my love, we need to talk."

I cocked an eyebrow at him. "Did I miss the memo I got pregnant or something? I swear I never had sex with that crazy man. He killed me because I refused his advances."

He grinned. "No. I assure you that neither of us is pregnant. However, you know I had a sister named Antigone."

I nodded. "I remember Levi and you have a sister named Antigone. Wait a minute – did you say you had a sister? What happened to her?"

His blush deepened. "She lived in London with her husband. They had a little boy. Unfortunately, she had cancer and died a little over two years ago. I thought you knew she passed away."

My eyes must have been big as proverbial saucers. "No, I didn't realize your sister died. I'm sorry. It must be rough to lose a sibling. I can't imagine if one of my siblings died. Hmm... What happened to the little boy? Where is he?"

He gulped. *Hmm, this should be interesting.*

"His father didn't want him. Antigone and Theo lived with me until she died. Egyptian Family Services would not allow me to keep Theo because I was single, so he went to live with Levi and Anna. Egyptian Family Services requires foster families to be related to the foster child. However, Anna is pregnant. Under Egyptian Family Services regulations, a foster family can only have two children in the foster home. They already have a daughter. Their baby is due in a few months."

I stared at him for a minute before I replied. "Why are they considered a foster family? Can't they adopt him?"

Ari shook his head. "Not under Shariah law. It's strange. His dad does not want him, but he has not agreed to relinquish his parental rights to Theo. And it gets pretty tricky to adopt under Shariah law anyway."

I didn't want an in-depth description of the oddities of adoption in Egypt, so I cut to the chase. "What an ass. I met Theo at their house when we stayed there overnight. Theo is an adorable child. What's going to happen to him?"

He cleared his throat again and ran a finger around the neck of his collar. *Oh, yeah, this ought to be good.*

"Well, my love, if a family member does not take him in as a foster child, he will go to live in the state orphanage."

My mouth fell agape at his words. "Now, wait a minute. They would put him in an orphanage instead of letting Anna and Levi adopt him?"

He nodded.

"That's bizarre. It's also wrong. I can't believe anything like this could happen in the twenty-first century. Heck, they were more advanced about adoption in the eighteenth dynasty than Egypt is today."

He blushed as he laughed. "That may well be true, my love, but you told me they also used crocodile dung for birth control."

I stroked the cat purring in my lap as I thought about the situation. "So... I guess you mentioned this because Theo needs a new home, right?"

Wordless, he nodded.

Have you ever felt caught between that proverbial rock and a hard place? I was in a hard place right then. What would I do? How could I become the surrogate mother for this precious little boy? His biological mother died, his father did not want him, and his foster parents could not keep him because the foster mom was going to have another baby.

And yet, how could I not accept such a sweet little boy into our home and my heart?

I sighed. I was going blind. I did not want children to have to grow up with a blind mother. I always said I wanted to be the best mom possible if I raised children. I had my tubes tied to prevent becoming a blind mother. I told Ari years ago I was not interested in adoption – although adoption was downright challenging to accomplish in Egypt. How could I be the best surrogate mom for Theo when I had Stargardt disease, even if my vision improved during my 'long sleep'?

I bit my lip as I thought about the situation. Nefertiti was blind in one eye, probably from what ancient Egyptians called river blindness. If it was river blindness, it was caused by a parasite in the water which managed to infiltrate her body. Of course, Nefertiti could have had Stargardt disease like I do. Yet, even partially blind, she loved her children, and they adored her. I knew they grieved over her death, although Nefru would not remember his mother in years to come. Hopefully, Medj would be the mother he needed to raise him to be a man of honor.

I laid my head on my hands. I realized with a start my hands shook ninety to nothing.

"Can I think about this a day or two? I mean, it's a lot to ask of me."

He nodded his head, but I saw the disappointment in his eyes. "Of course, my love."

I bit my lip again. "It just... I always said I didn't think I could be a good mom if – when – I go blind, Ari. You know how I feel."

He nodded. "I know."

I looked up with a start. "Did you know this when you came to Texas?"

He looked shocked. "Oh, dear God, no. I knew Anna was pregnant, but they had not been advised Levi and she could not keep Theo once the baby was born. I'm sure they knew it before, but they never mentioned it to me, probably because I was a single man. Levi mentioned it to me this morning, in a phone conversation. He said Anna is sick with worry about Theo. They do not know what to do."

I gulped and nodded. "Could we go there and visit him? Or could he come here and visit us? We need to see if I can cope with a child."

Ari laughed and pulled me into his arms. "Elizabeth, you were a wonderful mother with the children in the eighteenth dynasty. Why couldn't you do the same thing here?"

I frowned and pushed against his chest. "Ari, I had servants – no, let me be precise, I had slaves – who helped care for the children. Nefertiti had a mother-in-law who wasn't crazy about her, but Queen Tiye loved Nefertiti's children. It was not the same."

He kissed my cheek. "We could hire a housekeeper. Or a nanny if you prefer."

I sighed as I shook my head. "You don't understand, Ari."

He frowned. "I guess not. What am I missing?"

"I'm going blind. He's only five years old. How will I protect Theo? How can I keep him from running into the street? We live in Cairo. There is a lot of street traffic. How could I keep this precious little boy from getting snatched from me in the market? How will I--"

My voice broke, and I cried. Ari pulled me into his arms and kissed me again. "You're not blind yet. We train him not to run into the street. We teach him to stay with us when we are out of the house, and to never allow a stranger to take him. And then, someday, if you go blind— "

"When I go blind," I interjected.

He sighed. "Fine. When you go blind, he will be prepared. Children are adaptable, Elizabeth. He will cope with your vision loss better than you or I will. God willing, he will be grown or nearly grown before you lose your vision. And in the meantime, we will have had years of loving and caring for a child who needs us."

"Listen to me, Ari. This is the reason I had my tubes tied. I realized I could never be the mother I would want to be with this horrible disease. Does Theo really need a second mother with an incurable disease? How can I be a decent mother to this child? How can I ever be the mother Fancy Winslow has been to me? How..."

I cried even harder. Full-blown, all-out sobbing. Ari wrapped his arms around me and kept murmuring words of love to me. "We can do this, Elizabeth. You're a wonderful person. You will be a fabulous mother to Theo. You will see. Everything will be fine. Theo can visit a few times before he moves in with us. We can all get to know each other first."

"I'll see, huh? You don't get it. Ari, I'm going blind."

He kissed me again. "I'm sorry, darling. Bad choice of words. I reminded Levi you have Stargardt disease this morning. He said, 'Ari, a blind mother is better than no mother. Liz will be a great mother if she will only take the chance.' Tolkien said, 'around the corner there may wait a new road or a secret gate.' Elizabeth, this could be our new road, our secret gate. But it's up to you, darling."

I nodded. I knew I lost the argument when he quoted my favorite author.

The following Saturday, we drove to Levi and Anna's house. We all went to the Great Pyramid, where Levi gave us a personal tour. It is eerie going down the long, narrow stairway to the king's burial chamber. The corridor is dark and foreboding even with modern lighting. I could only imagine what it was like for the workers who built it with only torches to light their way.

And then, as we stood in the King's Chamber, a little hand took mine. I glanced down to see Theo clutching to my hand. His face pale, his beautiful, dark eyes wide with apprehension as his little hand trembled in mine.

I bent down to face him. "Are you okay, Theo?"

He gulped and shook his head. "It's spooky in here."

I cleared my throat. "I have to agree with you, Theo. Levi, Theo and I are going outside, if you guys don't mind."

Levi and Ari looked startled. Anna smiled. "No, that's fine. We will meet you outside."

Theo beamed up at me as we walked back up the stairs to go outside. It was a sunny January day with a beautiful 68 degrees Fahrenheit temperature. He skipped ahead of me as we exited the pyramid. We found a place to sit and wait for the others after I bought the child a bag of pistachios. As we sat nibbling the treats, I broached the subject.

"Aunt Anna will have her baby in a few months."

His little hand stopped halfway to his mouth as his entire demeanor changed. Gone was the relaxed, happy child of a few minutes before. Instead, his hands trembled as he looked at me with haunted eyes. "I know. The social worker says I have to move soon."

"Really? Where will you go?"

He shrugged. "I don't know. She said I might have to go live at the orphanage. My Mama is dead, you know. My Papa don't want me."

His little hand fell to his lap as his lip quivered. It took all I had to resist pulling him into my arms. I took a deep breath. "I have a question."

He looked up, startled by my words. "What is your question, Aunt Elizabeth?"

I took a deep breath. "How would you feel about coming to live with Uncle Ari and me in Cairo? I hear there is a rather good school near our house, and we have plenty of room."

He stared at me for a minute as his beautiful brown eyes filled with tears. I noticed his little hands began trembling again. "The Sphinx is fascinating, don't you think, Aunt Elizabeth?"

Too much, too soon, Liz. I took his little hand into mine and stroked it like Mommy used to stroke my hand to calm me. "Yes, it appears extremely fascinating. Would you like to have a closer look?"

He looked up at me and gave me a little grin. "Yes, thank you, ma'am."

We were still examining the Sphinx when he finally voiced his fears to me. I could barely hear him when he spoke.

"I'm sorry, Theo, I couldn't hear you."

He looked up at me, dread in his eyes. "But what would happen when you have babies? Where would I go then?"

I gasped as I fell to my knees and pulled him into my arms. "That won't happen. You would stay with us until you are grown. Unless you hate it there."

He stared at me for a minute and then threw his arms around my neck. "Then I think I would like to live with Uncle Ari and you, Aunt Elizabeth."

Ari found us there still crying and clinging to each other. He rushed up to us, dropped to his knees, and pulled us both into his arms. "What's wrong? What happened?"

Theo looked up at Ari through his tears and smiled. "Aunt Elizabeth says I can come live with you."

I could feel Aris tears splash on my cheeks and mingle with mine.

"Are you sure?" he asked, his voice gruff with emotion.

I nodded. "Like Levi says, a mama who might go blind is better than no mama at all. He needs us, Ari, and we need him. So, we will round this corner and see where the new road leads our family."

Theo went home with us that evening for the balance of the weekend.

We tucked him into the bedroom upstairs which was already finished at bedtime. About an hour later, a little voice called out to us from the doorway as he knocked on the door.

Ari looked up from his papers. "Are you okay?"

Theo shook his head. "No, sir, I'm scared up there. May I please come into your room tonight?"

The poor little thing sounded terrified. It was a new house and a new city. I held out my arms. "Of course, Theo. You may come into our room."

"What's wrong, lad?" asked Ari.

The tearful boy glanced back upstairs and shuddered. "There's a ghost up there in my room. He scares me."

"Oh, really? What does he look like?" Ari struggled not to laugh.

"He has a big mustache, white hair, and a big hat. And a ruffly shirt and an old-fashioned jacket. He's very scary," answered the frightened boy as he smushed the tears off his face.

"Would you be afraid to live here, in a house with a ghost?" asked Ari, his voice serious and concerned.

The poor child looked like he might cry again. He swiped at the tears on his face as he struggled to look brave for us. "No, I promise I'll be brave. I will be good. Maybe I can make friends with the ghost. He didn't seem mean, but he startled me. I never met a ghost before. I... I promise to learn to like him."

Ari glanced at me and shrugged as I struggled not to laugh. Theo could see Johnny. I wondered if they would become friends.

Of course, we let him climb in the bed with us, where he fell asleep that night.

We took him back to Levi and Anna Sunday night. On the way, we suggested he might not mention the ghost, or it would scare Aunt Anna and the social worker. He agreed he would not want to upset the ladies.

On Monday morning, we called the social worker from Ari's office. We both told her we would love for Theo to come live with us. Because Ari was a blood relative of his mother, we would become his foster parents. She insisted Theo visit with us several more weekends before he moved in our home with us. By then, we would have our Coptic church wedding, I would have my twenty-fifth birthday, as was required of foster parents in Egypt, and the construction on the house would be completed. We eagerly agreed.

We changed our home plans and built a second master bedroom with a master bathroom upstairs. The new plans moved my soaker tub and Ari's walk-in shower to the new master bathroom. Ari moved his office downstairs where our bedroom originally was going to be situated. The construction team worked night and day to finish the renovations by our wedding so the house would be ready for Theo to move in following the church ceremony.

Theo served as Ari's best man at our church wedding. My sister, Bella, served as my matron of honor. Mom stood smiling with Daddy. Kirk stood smiling with Melanie. I smiled as Johnny slipped into the back of the church and waved a ghostly hand.

Coptic weddings are extremely formal, but the receptions are crazy fun. Our reception was held at a banquet hall near the church. My family appeared stunned as the belly dancers circled the hall. I doubt any of them ever saw belly dancers at a wedding reception before that night. Ari's jaw almost hit the floor when Dara, Sara and I joined the dancers. His eyes twinkled with delight as I danced close to him in my reception ensemble. I chose the outfit with the low-cut neckline, bare midriff, and high-low skirt to show off my dance moves for my husband.

Once Egyptian Family Services allowed Theo to move in with us, we flew to Marsa Alam for our first family vacation on the Red Sea. Theo and I both fell in love with snorkeling over the coral reef. The marine life on the pristine reef amazed us. One of the highlights of the trip occurred when we swam with the dolphins at the Dolphin House Reef. The sea cows and giant green sea turtles at Abu Dabbab Bay were other big hits with us.

Ari told us he remembered Marsa Alam as a sleepy little fishing village where his parents brought them on vacations. He enchanted us with stories of Levi, Antigone and him snorkeling among the fish when they were children. He told about his first dive at Abu Dabbab and how the sea cows came up to nuzzle him and Antigone. Theo seemed thrilled to learn his mother loved the water and sea life as much as he did. It was not the first time I observed Theo listen attentively as Ari talked about Antigone. He craved those stories. Sometimes I wished Antigone had come back as a ghost to help protect Theo, but Johnny and the child were becoming fast friends.

"May we come back sometime, Uncle Ari?"

Ari chuckled. "Of course. How about this summer? It's even better in the summer. The sea is calmer and the water warmer."

Theo's eyes a lot with excitement. "Oh, yes, Uncle Ari! That sounds wonderful."

I agreed.

We went home two days before Ari returned to work. Ari and I were relieved Theo felt comfortable sleeping in his bedroom, no longer voicing fear of Johnny. It thrilled us when he reported the ghost no longer scared him. "Captain Johnny is my friend now. He will help protect me here in Cairo." Ari and I continued to sleep in our new master bedroom upstairs.

Theo began first grade at the Coptic School a few blocks from our home the following September. He loved his school and proved to be an excellent student. He worked hard to teach me Arabic, and he worked even harder to learn English.

Sometimes, I would hear him reading to Johnny. They always made me smile. Theo no longer showed any residual fear of our friendly ghost. I realized Johnny was becoming his dearest friend and closest confidant. Who could be better to tell the secrets of your heart than a ghost?

We rounded the corner and took an unexpected road, and we were blessed immeasurably by the addition of Theo to our family.

Chapter 29
Modern Egypt, Four Years Later
Elizabeth

It was a Friday night, around eight p.m. It surprised us when the doorbell rang. Ari looked over his book at me and arched a brow. "Are we expecting company?"

I dropped the book Theo and I were reading to my lap. "No. Bella said nothing about coming over tonight, and Anna, Levi and the children are in Thebes."

Ari shrugged, set his book down, and walked to the door. He left the security chain on the door as he opened it. "Yes?"

The man at the door attempted to push his way into the house and scowled when the security chain blocked his entry. "I'm Benjamin Williams, Theo's father. I'm here for my son."

Theo paled and slipped behind my back. I motioned for him to remain silent so Mr. Williams would not realize he stood right behind the door. I pulled my phone out of my pocket and began recording the conversation between Ari and Ben Williams.

Ari tilted his head at Mr. Williams. "Oh, really? I don't think so. Theo is a ward of Egypt. We are his legal foster parents. Unless you have an order signed by the presiding family court judge, I legally may not release him to you. Let's see… You abandoned Antigone and Theo when he was a year old when she told you she had cancer. Where have you been for the past nine years, Benjamin?"

Williams shoved the door again. The chain held, but Ari put his big, size thirteen foot behind the door to prevent the chain from breaking as he scowled at Williams. "Do not try to force your way into my home, Williams. You abandoned my sister and your son nine years ago in London. She divorced you and the court gave her sole managing conservatorship of your son. No one has heard from you since, and you damned sure never paid a penny of child support for your child."

"I didn't know where he was. This is bull. I want my boy."

"Yes, this is bull. You received service of Antigone's Petition for Divorce. You were also served with a certified copy of the Decree of Divorce when the judge finalized it. As her illness worsened, she decided to return home. Antigone notified the London court of her move. She tried to find you when she moved back to Egypt so she could notify you of the move. You never returned her calls. She sent a notice of her intent to move to the Court and one to your last known address. The letter to you came back as undeliverable because you had moved with no forwarding address. When she arrived here, she sent a notice of her new address at *this* home to the London court and you. That's how you knew to come *here*. I live three blocks from the hospital where Antigone received her medical care during her illness. When she died, I could not keep Theo, because I was single. Theo went to live with our brother, Levi, and his wife, Anna. They sent notice to the London court and your last known address when he moved to live with them. Of course, the letter to you returned because you never gave anyone your new addresses. Shortly before Theo turned six, Anna was about to have their second child. Family Services allowed Theo to come live with my wife and me. We notified the London court where he would live. You figured out where he lives, or you would not be standing outside my door tonight. According to Egyptian Family Services, under the prior orders of the London court, you have *no* right to visit Theo outside of the supervision to be determined by his mother, who is deceased, or by Egyptian Family Services. Unless you have an order from Egyptian Family Services allowing you to see Theo, I legally must not allow you to visit with him. I recommend you contact Mrs. Hadad at Egyptian Family Services on Monday and see what she says."

Williams threw his arm in the doorway as Ari started shutting the door. "This ain't finished."

Ari shook his head. "It is for tonight. However, if you wait a few minutes, I will make copies of all the documents pertaining to Theo for you. Now, if you will allow me…"

Ari slammed the door in Williams's face. I could see him shaking. "Are you okay?"

He shook his head. "No, I'm furious. Help me copy the papers. Theo, go upstairs to your room. You can open the window, but don't let him see you. Stay in the dark."

Theo nodded his head. "Yes, sir, Uncle Ari."

We quickly copied the divorce decree which gave Antigone sole managing conservatorship of Theo and the order from the Egyptian family court which named us to be his foster parents. Ari highlighted the part of the order which specified Benjamin Williams was Theo's father, but his whereabouts were unknown. He also highlighted the portion which forbade Williams any visitation or contact with Theo until further orders from the court. I walked to the door with Ari but stayed behind the door when he opened it wide enough to hand the documents to Mr. Williams. I turned on the phone conversation recorder again. "Here are the documents which show you have *no* right to visit with Theo. I added the name, phone number, office and email address for Mrs. Hadad, his social worker. Now, please write where you are staying, your home address, your business address, your phone number and email address for us."

I could hear Ben Williams snatch the papers from Ari. "No. I ain't giving you nothing. You never once attempted to contact me."

"That is untrue. With the permission of the Egyptian Family Court judge, we made two trips to London in the past four years to search for you. We could not locate you. The London Court had received no notification of your new addresses. Your former landlord did not know where you moved. He evicted you for nonpayment of rent. When we learned about your police record, we checked the different addresses cited on the arrest records. You no longer lived at any of those addresses. You had been evicted from each address listed on those with no forwarding address. We filed a request for a new address for you with the postal service. None was available. We even employed a private investigator to locate you. We did everything humanly possible to locate you. You did absolutely nothing to stay in contact with Antigone or find your son. Until now. You need to call the social worker. Good night."

"But--"

Ari shut the door in Ben's face again and then leaned against the door. I could see he was shaking. I reached around him and pulled him to me. "He can't take him, can he? It would kill Theo."

Ari shook his head. "I… I don't know."

I heard a little noise behind us and looked towards the stairs. I thought one of the cats had caught a mouse. It was not the cat or a mouse. It was Theo.

"You can't let him take me, Uncle Ari. Promise you won't let him take me. Please don't let that man take me."

We held out our arms, and he ran to us. We pulled him to us as he cried. He might be ten and say he is a 'big boy' now, but he was lost in grief and terror at the thought of being forced to return to live with Benjamin Williams. We both held him tight as we told him we loved him.

It was late when we finally got Theo settled for the night. As we went to our room, I heard him talking to Johnny, who was gravely troubled Ben had shown up. I bit back tears. The ghost who scared Theo so badly at first was now his best friend and comforted the child over his father's unexpected arrival on our doorstep.

Ari emailed the social worker and told her about Ben's unexpected arrival. The next morning, we called her. I could tell Ben's arrival in Egypt rattled her.

"He can't take Theo, can he, Julia?"

She hesitated before she answered. "This is Egypt. Fathers have a lot of rights here. I don't know what the Court will do."

"But he hasn't seen Theo for nine years," I protested. "Theo doesn't remember him."

"Yes, I understand Theo does not know his father. He was an infant when his father left them. I think his father's long-term inattention may be your saving grace. Plus, you two are exceptional foster parents. You love Theo, and he adores both of you. But I don't know what the court will do, Elizabeth, and I won't make promises. Just pray. We must all pray Allah protects Theo."

Ari called Miguel Vargas, who directs Biozyme Egypt. Miguel is married to my sister. He referred us to the lawyer for Biozyme, who then referred us to a family law specialist. Mustafa Maksoud graciously saw us Sunday afternoon. By Monday morning, Mr. Maksoud sued for us to get legal custody of Theo. The papers indicated no one could locate Benjamin Williams for nine years. It detailed all the steps taken to locate him since he abandoned Antigone and Theo. It also attached copies of Ben's London arrests and stated he had been evicted for nonpayment of rent at least three times. It further stated he never called, wrote, or emailed any of us about Theo since he walked out on Antigone Hotep Williams and their infant son when she told her husband she had cancer. Last, it stated Williams had never paid a penny of support of any kind since he abandoned both of them.

The papers asked permission to serve Benjamin Williams 'wherever he could be found.' The Petition stated Williams refused to give us his current address or phone number when he showed up demanding Theo. With permission to serve 'wherever he could be found,' we did not need a new order to serve him if we found him. A process server could serve him 'wherever' he found Williams, even if he were in a bar, brothel or borrowed room. Both Ari and I prepared affidavits to attach to the Suit Affecting the Parent-Child Relationship and to confirm all the facts in the pleading. Mrs. Hadad and her supervisor graciously provided affidavits as well.

We were elated when Judge Jawhara Mohammed was appointed to the case. She signed a temporary restraining order the same afternoon which stated Benjamin Williams could not see Theo pending a hearing. She further ordered Theo was not to be removed from our possession and control before a hearing on the matter. She set the case for a hearing on temporary orders two weeks later. We immediately carried a copy of the temporary restraining order to Family Services. Mrs. Hadad and her supervisor cheered with when we gave them a certified copy of the TRO.

Now, we needed to find Ben, serve him, and then go to court. Hopefully, the judge would not give Theo back to Ben at the hearing. Ironically, we were served with a counterclaim asking for custody of Ben and denying all our allegations on Wednesday before we served the elusive Benjamin Williams.

We continued to pray.

Chapter 30
Eighteenth Dynasty Egypt
Pharaoh Tutankhamun

"Queen Ankhesenamun and I thank you for helping with the smooth transition from the co-regency to my rule. Effective today, I hereby cancel Pharaoh Akhenaten's order which only permitted Aten to be worshipped. My people may worship whoever they please again, as has been the policy in Egypt for countless millennia. I will not tolerate religious persecution of any religious group."

"Yes, my lord."

"Now, as you know, we are moving the court back to Thebes. Move my father's remains from the tomb at Akhetaten to a hidden location in the Valley of the Kings."

Vizier Aye looked puzzled. "May I ask why, your Majesty?"

Pharaoh Tutankhamun nodded. "Yes. There has been significant looting of the city called Akhetaten. Move my father's tomb to prevent looting and destruction of his remains."

"Of course, my lord. Is there anything else?" asked the vizier as he wrote down the young pharaoh's instructions.

Tutankhamun nodded. "Yes. Move the remains of my Aunt Nefertiti to the City of Gold south of Thebes."

Vizier Aye frowned. "But your Majesty, your father was most explicit about burying her in the Valley of the Kings."

Tutankhamun glared at the vizier. "I am pharaoh now, not my father. Have the remains of Queen Nefertiti moved to the City of Gold."

"Shall her tomb be marked, my lord?"

Tutankhamun thought for a moment before answering. "Yes. It should show she was the Queen Consort of Upper and Lower Egypt and the Great Royal Wife of Pharaoh Akhenaten. It should also warn anyone who opens the tomb shall be cursed."

"It is already marked with those cartouches. But your father wanted the location of her remains to be unknown."

"My father is no longer the pharaoh. As I said before, I am Pharaoh now. My aunt was always most kind to my mother and to me. I realize Father claimed Aunt Nefertiti struck him and attempted to kill him. She did not kill him. He killed her. My aunt was a sweet, gentle soul. She adored my father. I cannot imagine she struck him unless it was to get him to stop choking her. His raving that Aunt Nefertiti had been possessed of a demon did not sit well with Mother or Grandmother. Mother was always afraid of him after father killed Queen Nefertiti. My father was wrong about many things. One was the way he attempted to force the country to renounce our gods for his. Another was in the way he treated the Queen Consort. A pharaoh should never lose his temper or act irrationally. Have her tomb moved to the City of Gold with all the honors accorded to a Great Royal Wife and Queen Consort."

Vizier Aye frowned but bowed to his young pharaoh. "Of course, my lord. We will attend to those changes immediately."

"Do it quietly. Do not make a big issue of it. Do not hold any ceremonies which are not needed to protect her *ka*. But get it done."

"Yes, my lord."

"My sister should be buried in the tomb next to her husband. They should be buried in the City of Gold as well. Perhaps they can be buried near her mother. I still cannot believe they are both dead of the plague, as are my grandmother and my mother. My Uncle Smenkhare taught me much about our religion. I made many of the changes back to our old ways because of his teachings."

Vizier Aye smiled. "Right away, my lord. Yes, that is an excellent idea."

"And I want the official record to show my younger brother died of the plague. Better yet, omit all records of him."

Vizier Aye nodded again. "Of course, my lord. And may I say, you are well within your rights to place the lad with his aunt and uncle."

Tutankhamun frowned. "From this day hence, we shall never mention the name the lad was given at birth, or that he has gone to live with your son and his wife. Do you understand?"

Vizier Ay nodded. "Yes, of course, your Majesty. There shall be no mention Nefru survived the plague and lives with General Horemheb and his wife. They plan to change his name to further avoid any connection of the child to Pharaoh Akhenaten and Queen Nefertiti."

"Excellent, Vizier Ay." Pharaoh Tutankhamun turned back to Queen Ankhesenamun who smiled at her young husband.

Vizier Ay ducked his head as he left the throne room. He finally allowed himself to smile. Things were going exactly as he and Nefertiti had planned.

Chapter 31
Modern Egypt, Two Weeks Later
Elizabeth

I had been a nervous wreck all week. I rarely have a sensitive stomach, but I could not eat without throwing up. Unfortunately, Benjamin Williams and anxiety adversely affected my stomach and my nerves. I figured I developed the nausea because of my growing anxiety about court.

I could barely think of food without feeling nauseated. I vomited Thursday morning before we left for court. I soiled the first outfit I planned to wear and quickly changed into a gray suit with a blue blouse. I carried a blue scarf to put over my hair in the car before we entered the courthouse. I changed to a pair of gray heels instead of the black ones I had planned to wear, and quickly changed my personal items into a matching handbag. I have a 'thing' about my shoes and handbags matching. Mom laughs and says it's an old lady habit.

Ari grinned at my new selection. "You look beautiful."

'I certainly don't feel beautiful. Come on, babe. We better go before I chicken out."

We dropped Theo off at school a little before 8. The principal knew the hearing would start around 9. We reminded him not to release Theo to anyone other than Levi, Anna, or us without additional written instructions from us or written orders from the Judge.

I was trembling when we reached the courthouse, but I deftly touched up my makeup, adding subtle lipstick and a quick flick of additional mascara. I then put on the scarf. I had grown accustomed to wearing one many places by then. I took a deep breath, and we entered the lion's den. I slipped my yellow lensed glasses on, and I held my hands tightly in my lap so Ari would not see them shaking.

When the Judge called the case, she noticed Mr. Williams did not stand up until his attorney told him to do so in English. She cleared her throat.

"Mr. Williams, do you speak Arabic?" she asked in English.

He looked flustered. "No, ma'am, I don't."

She frowned. "Mr. Harbish, did you arrange for a translator to be here today?"

He nodded. "Yes, your honor. She has been delayed in traffic, but she is on the way."

She shook her head as her frown deepened. "Did you advise her to be here at 9:00 a.m. sharp this morning?"

Mr. Harbish looked nervous as he ran a finger around his collar. "Yes, your honor. I apologize for the delay."

She looked up from her papers and smiled. "There is no delay. Mr. Hotep filed this suit. We will begin with his testimony. Mr. Maksoud, please call your first witness."

I cut my eyes at Ari. He winked at me and walked to the witness stand. He quickly and efficiently delineated how Theo wound up living in our home, why we wanted him to remain with us, how he was doing in our care and control, and what our concerns were about Mr. Williams. He described his job, salary, and our ability to care for Theo emotionally and financially.

At the end of his testimony, Mr. Harbish surprised us when he reserved the right to recall Ari later but did not propound any questions to him. As he returned to his seat, Ari shrugged. Mrs. Hadad testified next. She described everything which had happened involving Theo since his mother and he moved to Egypt nine years earlier. Mr. Harbish again reserved the right to call her back to the stand later. He frowned when the Judge allowed her to remain in the courtroom since Mrs. Hadad had been designated as an expert witness.

Mr. Maksoud then called me to testify. It did not go as smoothly as either Mrs. Hadad's testimony or Ari's testimony went. Once Mr. Maksoud passed me to Mr. Harbish, my worries came true.

"Isn't it true, madam, you used to run a bar?"

"No, sir."

He made an exaggerated stare at me. "Oh, really? What was Nefertiti's Bone Yard if it was not a bar?"

"Nefertiti's is a restaurant and club I own in Galveston, Texas."

"It's a bar, isn't it?"

"No, sir. it is not a bar. It is a restaurant and club," I repeated. "Bars don't serve food usually in Texas. Nefertiti's serves meals and drinks, like the restaurants in the high-end hotels here in Cairo and like other fine dining establishments in Galveston."

He made a dismissive motion in the air. "Semantics. How long did you own the bar?"

I bit back the urge to roll my eyes at the nimrod. "I have owned Nefertiti's for about six years now."

"And how did you come to name it Nefertiti's Bone Yard?"

I could feel my cheeks redden with embarrassment. "I didn't name it. My father named it. He says I look like Queen Nefertiti. He bought the property in an area of Galveston called 'the Bone Yard.' He named it Nefertiti's Bone Yard, because of my resemblance to the beautiful queen and regarding the neighborhood in which the restaurant and club were being built."

He nodded. "And where did you work before Nefertiti's Bone Yard?"

"I worked for about eighteen months at my father's restaurant, the Brian Boru, in Blue Ridge, Georgia."

"Isn't the Brian Boru a bar, also?" He smirked.

I shook my head. "No, sir, it is a restaurant and club, like Nefertiti's. It is the most popular eatery in North Georgia."

He frowned and shook his head. "Don't both locations serve alcoholic beverages?"

I nodded. "Yes, sir. It is legal to serve alcohol in the United States."

"Do you drink alcohol now?" he pressed.

"No, sir. I understand alcoholic beverages are not legally served in Egypt except in the high-end hotels which cater to tourists. We don't frequent those establishments. I don't drink alcohol here unless you include communion wine on Sunday."

The Judge laughed. Mr. Harbish looked fit to be tied.

"Oh, I drank a glass of wine and maybe two when we were on vacation in England last summer," I added. My hands began shaking, and I placed them in my lap out of his sight. *Bad girl, Liz. Don't tell him things if he does not ask,* I thought.

He smiled. "So, you drink alcohol."

"On rare occasions, sir, unless you include the thimbleful of communion wine I drink on Sunday."

"Do you believe the communion wine becomes the blood of Christ?" he asked with another smirk.

I blinked, surprised by his question. "I think Roman Catholics believe in transubstantiation. I've never been a Roman Catholic. I believe communion wine is nothing more than wine. We get about a thimble-full of wine at communion. It is symbolic of the blood Christ shed for us. I have never heard anyone other than Roman Catholics express belief in transubstantiation."

I joined the Coptic Church shortly before Ari and I married. Coptic Christians do not use the term 'transubstantiation,' but I knew the Coptic religion teaches that bread and wine are objectively changed into the body and blood of Jesus at communion. I could play semantics games, too.

Harbish frowned, shook his head, checked his notes, and pushed his glasses up before he asked another question. "Where did you work before your father's restaurant?"

"I worked in New York City," I replied.

He frowned again. "Do not be coy with me, Mrs. Hotep. Where did you work in New York City?"

"I worked for the Joffrey Ballet in New York City."

"And what job did you perform with the Joffrey Ballet?"

I gave him a quizzical look. "I was a ballet dancer."

"So, you were a dancer on the stage in the Big Apple. How decadent."

Mr. Maksoud stood up. "Objection. Side bar."

"Sustained." The judge frowned at Mr. Harbish.

He ignored her glowering at him and continued. "How did you fall off the stage the night in question? Were you drunk?"

I looked up at the judge. "Which question shall I answer, your Honor?"

"The first one. How did you fall off the stage?" she replied.

I took a deep breath. "I was doing a series of turns backwards across the stage from upstage left to downstage right. I was supposed to stop right on the edge of the stage and appear to be teetering there. Unfortunately, I was temporarily blinded by the lights. I miscounted and went off the stage."

"Were you drunk?" he asked again.

I stared at him a minute before I answered. This guy was a royal prick. "No."

"Please explain how you went off the stage." he insisted.

I took another deep breath. "It was an accident. People have accidents sometimes. I was doing backward turns across the stage. I miscounted. The lights temporarily blinded me--"

"Are you blind?" he asked.

"No."

"Are you going blind?" he asked with a look of triumph.

I paused for a second. "Maybe."

"What do you mean? Either you are or you are not going blind." He smirked.

My heart raced. "I have a congenital condition called Stargardt disease. It gradually reduces the central visual plane like macular degeneration."

"Doesn't macular degeneration cause blindness?" he pressed.

"Usually, but--"

"Objection to anything after 'usually,' your Honor." He flashed another smarmy smirk at me. I could really learn to hate this guy. I took another deep breath and looked at the judge.

"I would like to hear what else she was going to say." The judge smiled.

I gulped and smiled back at her. "Thank you, your Honor. I receive these shots – injections – into my eyes every month. They appear to have dramatically slowed down my visual deterioration."

"To what degree?" asked the judge.

I gulped again. "My husband is the ophthalmologist. He could explain it to you better than I can. Ari says the deterioration appears to have stopped and my vision has improved."

I glanced at Ari. He nodded slightly.

"Don't give her hints, Dr. Hotep," snapped the judge.

He stood up. "I'm sorry, your Honor. I did not realize I gave her any sort of a hint."

She stared at him for a minute. "I'll let it pass this time. Don't give her hints again."

The attorney smiled. "So now let's talk about the day you fell onto the tomb."

"Yes, sir."

He frowned. "Don't be coy, Mrs. Hotep."

I glanced at the judge before I answered. I gulped. "I must not be understanding the questions, sir. I didn't think you asked me a question. I was waiting for your question."

"He didn't ask you a question, Mrs. Hotep," said the judge. "Ask your question, Mr. Harbish, and stop playing your games with this lady. You know Arabic is her second language."

He stood up and gave a slight bow. "I apologize, your Honor. I tend to forget because she speaks Arabic fluently."

She rolled her eyes. "Of course. Her excellent fluency in Arabic must be why you asked about her experiences in the United States. Proceed."

"Answer the question, Mrs. Hotep," he snapped.

I looked at the judge in confusion. "I don't think he asked me a question, your Honor. Did he ask me a question and I missed it? What was the question?"

"No, my dear, he is toying with you. Harbish, I tell you again, quit this nonsense now. Ask your question or your cross-examination of Mrs. Hotep stops."

He flushed as he stood up. "Yes, your Honor. I apologize. How did you fall into the tomb?"

"I didn't fall into the tomb, sir. I was knocked onto the top of the tomb."

"Oh, really? Who in their right mind would knock a person into a tomb?" he snapped.

"I can't say if she was in her right mind or not, sir, but her name was Christina. I don't recall her surname. My husband might remember it. She was a teenager who acted like a fool. As she cavorted around the tent, she spun around and kicked sideways in her ridiculous dance. When she did, her kick struck me, knocked me off from the side of the trench, and down onto the tomb about five feet below us. The force of my body striking the top of the tomb cracked it and opened the tomb. I understand I suffered a serious skull fracture in the fall."

"Isn't it true you told people you went back in time to the eighteenth dynasty then?"

I hope I looked at him like he had grown another head. "No, sir. At least, I don't think I said anything of the sort. I was unconscious in the hospital in Luxor."

He rolled his eyes and let out an exasperated sigh. "Young woman, you are playing with me."

"Sir, I'm just trying to answer your questions." I reached up and rubbed my neck.

"Do you need a break, Mrs. Hotep?" asked the judge.

I shook my head. "No, your Honor. It's almost lunch time. I'll be okay until then."

She smiled. "Ah, lunch. An excellent idea. Let us break for lunch and return at 1:30." She stood up.

I glanced at our attorney and realized he stood up when the judge did. I stood up, too. After she left, I sagged against the chair.

Ari hurried over to me. "Come on. Let's get out of here."

I nodded. "Great idea. Let's go."

We went across the street to Mr. Maksoud's office where his secretary offered to fix us coffee and sandwiches for a working lunch. "My lord, Ben's attorney is horrible. He's a shark in the courtroom. Can he continue like this with me much longer?"

"He's a blasted arse. I can't believe he is behaving in such a scurrilous manner." Ari appeared livid.

I chuckled. "A blasted arse? Really, Ari?"

Mr. Maksoud chuckled. "You are doing fine. He wants to rattle you, to upset you. Stay calm. You will be fine. The judge is not going to put up with much more of his nonsense." He frowned. "Hmm... You told no one you traveled back through time to the eighteenth dynasty, did you?"

"No, sir, not to my recollection. However, I had some crazy dreams while I was hospitalized."

"She was unconscious for five weeks. Sometimes, she would awaken screaming nonsense about Nefertiti and Akhenaten," Ari interjected. "It's possible someone mistakenly thought she claimed to be in the eighteenth dynasty. However, she was right there in the hospital bed. But you must remember she fell on the tomb of Queen Nefertiti which allegedly cast a curse on the person who opened the tomb. Since Elizabeth fell on the tomb and broke it, she essentially opened the tomb before the prayers were said."

Mr. Maksoud shook his head. "He is probably trying to get to those facts. Do you remember what you said?"

"I don't have a clue, sir. Ari should know."

Ari nodded. "I heard most of it. Her mother heard other parts."

Mr. Maksoud sighed. "This may be a long afternoon. Keep asking him to repeat things and ask for breaks if you need one. Don't be afraid to ask him to clarify questions. He wants you to say things you don't remember. He wants you to admit what he wants you to say. People will often give up and say what he wants them to say to get off the stand. Don't tell him what he wants you to say. Just keep asking for clarification. I promise I will object the third time he asks anything."

I gulped. It sounded like this was going to be a horrible afternoon. "Yes, sir."

I was not about to tell him the whole *ka* stealing story. Ari surprised me when he did. "The tomb was supposed to be cursed. We were awaiting the imam and the priest to come to say the prayers over the tomb before it was opened."

Maksoud shut his eyes. "Wonderful. A cursed tomb. What did the curse say?"

"I'm not – I couldn't read the cartouche, so I can't really say."

He smiled. "Excellent answer. Now, tell me – not him – what it said."

"Salima said it warned the *ka* of whoever opened the tomb would be given to Queen Nefertiti to resurrect her."

"Oh, shit," said Maksoud.

"I take it that's not good?" I asked.

He shook his head. "No, it is not good. You were not drinking?"

I shook my head. "Oh, good lord, no, sir. Of course, I wasn't drinking. I had a cup of coffee and an apple for breakfast the morning of the accident. It was something like ten or eleven in the morning when the accident occurred. There wasn't any alcohol around if I wanted a drink."

He frowned. "Just say, no, sir."

I nodded. "Yes, sir."

I chewed on my lip.

"And don't chew your lip. it tells him you are nervous," he snapped.

I stopped gnawing on my lip and nodded again. "Yes, sir."

We ate our lunches and returned to the courthouse at 1:20. As we approached the courtroom, Mr. Williams suddenly came barreling towards me. "You lying heifer, you're going to tell the truth if I have to kill you to get you to tell it."

He bent over and ran towards me. I stared in shock, frozen in place, as he tackled me, knocking me to the ground. The man would have made a damned fine linebacker. As my head slammed into the marble floor, all hell broke loose just before the impact knocked me out.

I regained consciousness almost immediately and saw Ari had Ben Williams pinned to the ground. As two bailiffs ran to us, Mr. Maksoud helped me up from the floor. I rubbed my neck, winced, and then paled. I held out my hand to show Ari it was covered with blood.

"Ari, my head is bleeding."

I thought the bailiffs were going to have to pull Ari off Ben all over again. "You sorry, little, twatfaced bastard. Keep your bloody hands off my wife!"

"No, Ari! Please, darling, stop. He's not worth it. I'll be okay." I pulled the scarf off so Ari could check my head.

"It doesn't look serious, darling. I think you will be okay but leave the scarf off. The judge might want to look since your head bled a good bit."

I nodded and folded the scarf so the blood showed if the judge wanted to see it. We went into the courtroom to a furious judge. She looked sternly from Mr. Williams to Ari and back again before her eyes settled on me. She paled. "Call an ambulance. Mrs. Hotep needs to go to the hospital immediately."

I pressed one hand against the back of my neck and the other against my forehead. "I'll be okay, Judge. My head hurts, but the bleeding seems to have stopped."

She shook her head. "No, my dear, you need to be checked out. There is blood on your skirt."

I looked down, stunned to see blood seeping through the fabric of my skirt. I crumpled into Ari's arms as I swooned.

Chapter 32
Cairo, Egypt - Elizabeth

"She's pregnant."

Ari and I stared at the doctor in stunned surprise.

"But she had her tubes tied years ago," Ari finally said.

The doctor pointed to the fallopian tube shown on the ultrasound. "I would estimate she is about eight weeks along. Dr. Hotep, the fallopian tube was not severed. It appears to have healed after an incomplete cut. There is significant scar tissue there, but one little egg finally squeezed through the narrow opening. What we have here, Dr. Hotep, is a miracle. This is your miracle baby. I am keeping you overnight, Mrs. Hotep. We want you to safely deliver your miracle baby."

I leaned forward and ran my finger over the screen. "And the figure on the ultrasound is my baby?" I whispered. "It's so tiny."

He nodded. "Yes, my dear. Now, let us get you into a room."

Ari called Mr. Maksoud and put him on the speaker as he told him the unexpected news. "They are admitting her. My God, she is pregnant. They say this is a miracle baby and they don't want her to miscarry it."

"By the Prophet, this will be all over the news this afternoon." Mr. Maksoud sounded stunned by our announcement.

"I can come back as soon as they get her admitted, but I'm not leaving her until then," Ari said.

"No, no, no. I am sure the judge will say you should stay with your wife. I will let Judge Mohammed know the joyous news. I will call you later and tell you what she says."

Mr. Maksoud showed up an hour later looking like the cat your mama told you ate that poor canary. My mama called it a 'shit-eating grin,' although

I always thought her description sounded like it should be a nasty face. He handed me an exquisite floral arrangement.

I recognized the flowers from my stay in the eighteenth dynasty. "Lotuses. How beautiful, Mr. Maksoud. Thank you."

"You are welcome, my dear. The judge put Ben in jail. She passed court tomorrow. We will resume on Monday *if* your doctor says you are well enough to proceed. In the meantime, *if* Ben gets out of jail, he is to have *no* contact with Ari, Theo or you."

"If he gets out of jail? What do you mean?" demanded Ari.

Mr. Maksoud grinned. "The judge set bond at £1,000,000. I doubt Williams can raise it."

"Ol' Harbish must be royally pissed off," I said. I winked at Mr. Maksoud as I grinned.

"Exactly. He is pissed off, big time. Now, you get to feeling better. Don't you dare miscarry our miracle baby. I will check on you tomorrow," said Mr. Maksoud.

I waited until he left the room. Tears of joy and terror welled up in my eyes. "I'm pregnant."

Ari rubbed my hand across his cheek. "So, I heard."

My lip trembled. "What do we do?"

He smiled. "We have a baby, if you can hang on to it."

"But Ari–" I began.

He shook his head. "There is no 'but, Ari.' You heard the doctor. This is a miracle, my love."

I glanced around to make sure no one could hear me before I leaned towards Ari. I whispered, "Isis did this."

He grinned. "So, it would appear. The goddess of life was reputed to have great magic, you know."

I gulped. "I was praying when she first appeared to me. She said she would reward me if I helped Nefertiti give birth to her son. I never dreamed she would give me a miracle baby. Well, if I didn't believe it before, I believe now. It wasn't simply a dream."

Over the next two days, the obstetric specialists ran all kinds of tests on me. They were astonished to see my medical records from Texas showed both fallopian tubes had been cut and tied properly. The only explanation was 'it's a miracle.' By Friday afternoon, the uterine bleeding stopped completely. The attending physician released me on Saturday afternoon with a firm warning not to get into any more fights with crazy men at the courthouse or anywhere else.

Theo stood waiting for us in the lobby with my sister, Bella. When he saw me, he ran to me, sobbing as I pulled him to me. "It'll be okay, sweet boy. I promise. Everything will be okay."

"But you are with child," he lamented as he cried again. "I'm sorry. Big boys don't cry."

"It's okay, sweetheart. Everyone cries sometimes or other. But I'll be okay."

He shook his head. "But will the judge make me go with Ben because you are with child?"

I had not thought of the possibility. "Surely the judge would not punish us for having a miracle baby. We will all pray about it."

I swear we must have prayed all weekend. Our religion had become very important to me since Theo came to live with us. On Sunday, I stayed home in bed as ordered by the doctor, but Ari, Theo, Anna, Levi, and their children went to church. I understand the whole church spent much of the service praying for our unborn miracle baby and me, and for Theo's case.

Sunday afternoon, the Judge called and told us to come at 1:30 on Monday afternoon. "And bring Theo. I want to talk to him."

My heart must have dropped all the way back to Texas when she told us to bring Theo. I struggled to swallow. I finally whispered, "Yes, your Honor."

Mom and Daddy arrived Sunday evening. They would accompany us to court the next day, as would Mrs. Hadad, Bella, and Miguel. They were all prepared to testify at the hearing Monday.

We kept Theo home Monday morning. We prayed as a family, which helped calm Theo. The poor child seemed overwrought with anxiety. As we finished praying, I saw Johnny watching us. He sniffed, wiped his nose with the back of his ghostly hand, and then gave me a big thumbs up.

We called the principal at the Coptic School and told him the Judge wanted to confer with Theo. The principal had already been told by the priest. The principal promised us the entire school would assemble in the church at noon and would pray for us. They would hold a prayer vigil until the case ended for the day. I bit back tears as I thanked him for all their prayers.

Ari picked out a lavender suit for me to wear to court. I argued at first.

"It's your favorite color, darling. And your eyes look lavender when you wear it."

I sighed and put the dark blue suit I had planned to wear back in the closet. I wore a lavender scarf over my hair and fastened it with a small silver brooch engraved with a staurogram, an ancient symbol representing Christianity. I completed my ensemble with black patent pumps and a matching handbag. Ari and Theo both wore dark blue suits. Theo held tightly to our hands as we walked to the judge's chambers. She chatted with him for a second in her secretary's area before they went into her office. I trembled as the door shut, and then Ari and I went into the hall. Bella sat on the other side of me. We sat down, and I pulled out my Coptic prayer beads to pray.

Mom taught us all how to pray when we were little. We were taught to fold our hands in supplication to begin our prayer. Next, we were to lift our hands towards heaven to thank God for our many blessings. Next, we were to hold our hands open and upright to receive our blessings from the Lord. I shut my eyes tight and did not even realize I was doing the hand motions as I prayed.

I heard someone clear their throat, and I dropped my hands as I opened my eyes.

"Where did you learn to pray like this?" the judge asked as she studied me.

My cheeks reddened and I tried to smile. "My mother taught me to pray this way when I was a little girl. Why?"

"It is the way I was taught to pray as well. Was your mother Muslim?"

I shook my head. "No, ma'am. She is Episcopalian. Hmm... You know, Mom's grandmother immigrated to the U.S. from Africa. She might have been raised in the Islamic faith. My DNA says I'm part Egyptian, from my mother, and Irish, from my father."

She stared at me for a minute and then nodded her head. "Interesting. I imagine the Irish blood explains those pretty eyes. Please have someone watch Theo in my office while we go into the courtroom."

"Of course, Judge. Bella, please stay with Theo."

"Sure." She headed for the office with her baby and Theo in tow.

Ari gave me a quizzical look. "Are you ready for this?"

I took a deep breath and squared my shoulders. "I guess so. Let's go."

After everyone sat down, the judge frowned again. "I will allow Mrs. Hotep on the witness stand to answer some questions I have for her. Mr. Harbish, you may question her for fifteen minutes after I finish. That is all the time you shall have to complete your cross-examination. I hope you understand."

He turned red in the face and glowered at me. "Yes, your Honor."

She smiled. "Excellent. Mrs. Hotep, please take the stand."

I took a deep breath, stood up straight and tall, and walked to the hot seat. I was sworn in again.

"Mrs. Hotep, you had an accident Thursday and were taken to the hospital. What did you learn from the medical examination?" the judge asked.

I smiled. "We learned I am eight weeks pregnant, your Honor."

She nodded. "Congratulations. Are you still having problems?"

I shook my head. "No, ma'am. I am a high risk because of the problem Thursday, but my doctors permitted me to attend this hearing today."

She smiled. "Wonderful news. Mr. Harbish, this is why I am limiting her testimony today. She did not have to return. She returned voluntarily. When I finish with my questions and turn her over to you for your fifteen minutes of questions, I will not tolerate any verbal abuse of Mrs. Hotep."

He blushed deep red and arose from his seat. "Of course, your Honor."

She waited until he sat back down to begin her questions. "Mrs. Hotep, was this baby planned?"

I blinked as I realized she already knew the answers to these questions. "No, your Honor."

"Why not?"

"I had my tubes tied years ago because I have Stargardt disease."

She nodded again. "Why?"

"I did not want to bring a child into the world who might someday go blind."

She tilted her head at me. "And now?"

I smiled. "Judge, my doctors call this my miracle baby. I figure if the Almighty saw a reason to give me a baby now, then He, in His infinite wisdom, has His reasons. Who am I to question the will of the Almighty?"

I was not about to mention Isis.

"And what are your feelings about this pregnancy?" she asked.

I gulped. "Scared. It's a big responsibility, to be carrying a miracle baby. And scared because I want to be a good mother."

"And are you a good mother now?" she asked.

I blinked back the tears stinging at my eyes. I swallowed hard. "I think I am a good foster mother to Theo. I hope I am. I try to be. I…"

I stopped to try not to burst into tears. The Judge passed me a box of tissues. I pulled one out to daub at my eyes and tried to smile at her. "Thank you, your Honor."

"What else, Mrs. Hotep?" she pressed.

I took a deep breath. "I want to be a good mother to Theo and to this baby."

She smiled. "I will tell you Theo says you are 'the best mom a kid could have.' Since Allah has seen fit to give you this unexpected blessing, will you have other children as well?"

I shook my head. "No, your Honor. We know Egyptian foster families can only have two children in the home. This baby will make the second child. I will have my tubes tied again, and Ari will have a vasectomy after this child is born."

She tilted her head again. "Why?"

I tried to smile. "We would not want to do anything to endanger Theo being able to live with us."

She nodded. "I appreciate that. So, you say you had your tubes tied before. How did you get pregnant?"

"That's why I said it's a miracle baby, judge. The doctors say --"

"Objection. Hearsay," shouted Mr. Harbish.

The judge rolled her eyes at him. "Denied. Sit down, Mr. Harbish. Shut up and listen to her testimony. You might learn something."

He blushed again and sat down, clearly upset.

"Now, Mrs. Hotep, tell me what the doctors told you," the judge said.

"The doctors said apparently the tube had been improperly cut and healed back. They could not explain it other than it was a miracle." I tried to smile but I felt the corner of my mouth twitch like it does when I am nervous.

"You have not asked to adopt Theo. Why not?" she asked.

"We know it is difficult to adopt in Egypt if Mr. Williams would not sign a relinquishment of his parental rights. We thought it would be best if we simply asked to be named custodial non-parents of Theo, since his father reappeared in Theo's life."

She narrowed her eyes as she studied me. "If you could, would you adopt him?"

My eyes filled with tears again. "Oh, yes, ma'am. It's just…"

I struggled not to cry. Her face softened. "It's just, what, Mrs. Hotep?"

I took a deep breath as I tried to control my emotions. "We already had one miracle this week, your Honor. I could not imagine we would be blessed with another one today."

"Why not?"

I could not answer. My eyes began leaking again.

She handed me a Kleenex. "Take your time."

I wiped my eyes and blew my nose. I noticed out of the corner of my eye Mr. Harbish looked fit to be tied. I wished momentarily someone had hogtied him this morning to keep him from attending the hearing. "Mom taught me to count my blessings one by one. I've had one this week."

She shook her head. "No, my dear. You had one last week. Mr. Harbish, you may ask your questions now. Fifteen minutes. Not a minute longer. Do not endanger the miracle baby or his mother." She handed me another tissue. "Here, my dear. I think you might need this."

I smiled as I took the tissue. "Thank you, your Honor."

I wiped my tear-dampened cheeks.

Mr. Harbish arose slightly and nodded to her. "Isn't it true you told people you have been in the eighteenth dynasty?"

I shrugged. "No, sir, I don't recall ever saying any such thing."

He frowned as he scanned down his paper. "So, you deny telling people you are Nefertiti?"

I looked at him like he was a two-headed monster again. "Yes."

He rolled his eyes. "Why deny you said you are Nefertiti?"

I rolled my eyes right back at the old scoundrel. "Well, A, because I did not say it, and B, because that dog don't hunt."

I heard the judge choke back laughter as Mr. Harbish glared at me. "And what on earth is the meaning of this odd phrase, Mrs. Hotep?"

I smiled. "I'm sorry, sir. I used an old colloquial expression from the Southern United States. 'That dog don't hunt.' In the Southern United States, many people hunt and raise hunting dogs. If a dog won't go after a trail, we say, 'that dog don't hunt.' It means the dog is worthless as a hunter. We also say it about totally ridiculous questions."

He glared at me, his lips narrowed into thin lines. "Totally ridiculous questions? Why do you say my question is ridiculous?"

"Well, sir, Queen Nefertiti died 3500 years ago. I've seen her mummy. She's dead as a door nail. The eighteenth dynasty ended about 3400 years ago. It is a physical impossibility for me to either A, be Nefertiti, or B, to be living in the eighteenth dynasty. Like I said, 'that dog don't hunt.'"

The crowd in the courtroom audience howled with laughter. I noticed the judge struggled not to grin as she lowered her gavel. "We will have proper decorum in the courtroom. Mr. Harbish, you have five more minutes left to question Mrs. Hotep. Use your time wisely."

He frowned again. "How can we know you won't have additional children since you are suddenly pregnant with this 'miracle child'?"

I smiled. "The answer is simple, sir. I am under oath. I swore to tell the truth. I try to never lie, and I am most assuredly not going to lie under oath."

"Why not?"

"I would hate for God to strike me dead on this chair."

"Your time is up, Mr. Harbish. Mr. Maksoud, did you have questions of this witness?" the judge asked.

He stood up. "No, your Honor. May she be excused?"

The judge nodded. "Yes. Mrs. Hotep, you may stay in the courtroom if you wish, or you may go to my office to sit with Theo if you prefer."

"I would like to stay, your Honor."

"Call your next witness, Mr. Maksoud."

Mr. Maksoud arose and smiled. "I call Benjamin Williams."

Ari leaned over to me. "Are you okay?"

"I'm fine. I wouldn't leave now for anything in the world."

Over the next half hour, Mr. Maksoud verbally eviscerated Ben. He proved Ben knew about the divorce and the decree which awarded his wife sole managing conservatorship of Theo with no domicile restriction. He proved Ben knew Antigone moved back to Egypt as her health deteriorated. Ben admitted he knew Antigone and Theo lived with Ari in the home where we currently live. Ben confirmed he never gave the London court or his ex-wife notice of any of his changes of address. He also testified to our mystified delight he had been in prison for eighteen months.

Mr. Maksoud smiled. "And why were you incarcerated, Mr. Williams?"

He shrugged. "Drug charges, sir."

Mr. Maksoud had told me he never asked questions if he did not know the answer. He had to have known about Ben's conviction and imprisonment from the grin spreading across his face. "Will you please tell the court what drugs you were convicted of possessing, Mr. Williams?"

Mr. Williams cleared his throat. "Well, sir, it warn't no possession conviction."

"Please tell the court the nature of the crime for which you were convicted."

"Possession with intent to sell methamphetamines," Ben answered, as his face flushed red.

Mr. Harbish looked shocked.

"May I approach the witness, your Honor?" Mr. Maksoud asked.

She nodded. "Yes, Mr. Maksoud."

"Please look over this document, Mr. Williams." He paused.

Mr. Williams looked over the papers Mr. Maksoud had handed him. "Yes, sir, it's my conviction papers from the Birmingham courthouse."

Mr. Harbish put his head on his hand and shook his head as he sighed.

"I tender Petitioner's Exhibit 4, your Honor," stated Mr. Maksoud.

He started towards Mr. Harbish to hand him a copy of the document. Mr. Harbish arose. "Your Honor, my client has already admitted to the contents of the document. May I suggest we take a brief break so I may speak with my client, and then Mr. Maksoud and I may confer with you in chambers?"

"I hoped you would suggest a conference, Mr. Harbish. We will take a fifteen-minute break. Mr. and Mrs. Hotep, please go to my office to sit with Theo during the break while I consult with the attorneys."

I grabbed Mr. Maksoud's sleeve. "What's happening?"

He grinned at me and patted my hand. "Don't worry, my dear girl. Everything will be fine."

Ari put an arm around my shoulders. "They are going to negotiate a settlement in chambers, my love. Come on. Let's go to the office to sit with our boy."

I started shaking like a leave when Ari said, 'our boy.' I began shaking even harder as I realized I we might be about to receive another miracle. First, my pregnancy, and now it looked like we would get custody of Theo.

We sat in the office with Theo for about ten minutes. By then, Mom, Daddy, Bella, Miguel, and Mrs. Hadad had crowded into the office with us. At the end of the conference, Mr. Harbish exited.

"Well, that was interesting," said Mom.

"Why?" I asked.

She grinned. "That man looks like someone just kicked his dog."

The Judge came to the doorway and smiled. "Come in, please."

We arose and walked into her office with Theo. He and I were shaking like proverbial leaves during a hurricane. I held Theo's hand tightly as we sat on the couch in front of her desk.

"Mr. Harbish has extended an offer of settlement. Mr. Maksoud, would you like to present the offer to your clients?"

He smiled. "Indeed, I would, your Honor. Mr. Williams allowed his attorney to offer you two be named permanent sole managing conservators of the minor child, Theodore Williams, known as Theo. Mr. Williams would like to have monthly visitations with Theo."

Ari's eyes narrowed. "What sort of visitation are we discussing?"

The judge cleared her throat. "It would be under your supervision, on the first Saturday of the month, from noon until six in the evening."

Ari thought about it for a minute. "I would have agreed to this before he testified to his conviction for selling meth. Could we stipulate something about drug testing, your Honor?"

She smiled. "I shall make drug testing a requirement for Mr. Williams to visit with Theo, Dr. Hotep."

Ari gulped. He glanced at me, and I nodded my head like a bobble head fool. He smiled and lifted my trembling hand to give it a quick kiss. "Then we would accept, your Honor."

Theo's eyes were wide as saucers. "What happened?"

"Your dad gave us custody of you," Ari whispered as he pulled Theo close for a hug.

"Let's go back into the courtroom. Theo, come with your aunt and uncle," said the judge.

Tears filled his eyes, and I started my leaf-shaking routine again as I realized I was about to receive my second miracle. We arose and followed the judge back into the courtroom. After the judge took the bench, she spoke. "Mr. Williams, I would like to take this opportunity to introduce you to your son, Theo. Theo, this is your father, Benjamin Williams."

Theo made a slight bow towards his father. "Hello, sir."

Mr. Williams scrambled to his feet. "It's nice to finally meet you, lad."

They both stood there awkwardly, unsure how to react to each other.

The judge cleared her throat again. "Mr. Williams, I wanted you to have a firm picture of Theo in your head. I never want you to forget what this young man looks like, or who you gave custody to his aunt and uncle today."

He gulped and nodded. "Yes, ma'am."

"You may both be seated. It is my understanding the parties have come to the following agreement: Mr. and Mrs. Hotep shall be named permanent, non-parent, sole managing conservators of the minor child, Theodore Benjamin Williams, who is known as Theo. Mr. Benjamin Williams shall be permanent possessory conservator. I shall make an affirmative finding it is not in Theo's best interests to live with Mr. Williams. Mr. Williams shall have the right to visit with Theo on the first Saturday of each month, from noon until six p.m., under the supervision of Dr. or Mrs. Hotep, or an adult designated by them to supervise the visit if they are unavailable. I added the language allowing another person to supervise visits because Mrs. Hotep is pregnant. A visit might otherwise be impossible to hold if she were in the hospital. I would hate for Mr. Williams to travel to Cairo from London and not be able to visit Theo because of a medical situation. I am making the following requirements, also. Prior to beginning visits, Mr. Williams shall provide this court a clean urine test. He shall be tested for urine and hair follicle today at his expense to establish a baseline."

Mr. Williams looked ill. Mr. Harbish ran his finger around his collar again. "Yes, your Honor."

"Mr. Williams shall provide this court and the Hoteps with his current work and home addresses and phone numbers today. He shall also provide his email address to this court and to Dr. and Mrs. Hotep today. He is ordered to keep this court advised of any changes which arise in any of those."

Mr. Harbish nodded again as he jotted down her ruling. "Yes, of course, your Honor."

"Mr. Williams shall be required to provide seven days written notice to Dr. and Mrs. Hotep along with proof of a clean UA before any visit shall occur."

Mr. Maksoud bit back a smile. "Yes, your Honor."

"Mr. Williams may visit Theo by telephone every Wednesday evening between 7 and 8, for five minutes."

Ari cleared his throat. She looked up at him. "Did you have something to say, Dr. Hotep?"

Ari stood up. "Your Honor, we attend church on Wednesday nights. Could they talk by phone after 8, or on either Tuesday or Thursday nights?"

She nodded. "Mr. Williams, which night would be best for you?"

He stood up. "It don't matter, your Honor. Whatever."

She shut her eyes and shook her head. "Then we will change it to say you may call him on Tuesday nights between the hours of 7 and 8 p.m., for five minutes. The calls must be on the speaker phone so his aunt or his uncle may supervise the call. You may also email Theo, Mr. Williams, but be aware all email communications shall be through his uncle's email address. You may not contact the child directly."

He gulped and stood up again. "Yes, your Honor."

She smiled. "Fine. Then, let's see if I have covered everything. Conservatorship, possession, access. Drug testing. Ah, yes. Finally, Mr. Williams shall pay child support in the amount of two hundred British pounds sterling due every month on the first of the month, beginning next month."

Mr. Williams blanched.

Ari arose. "Your Honor, we did not request child support."

She shook her head. "But I require it, Dr. Hotep. It is the policy of this court for all non-custodial parents to pay at least minimum wage child support. Each party shall be responsible to pay their own attorney's fees. I covered everything. Entry shall be in two weeks. Mr. Maksoud, you will prepare the documents. I suggest you prepare them as quickly as possible so Mr. Harbish may get them to his client for review before he leaves Egypt. And if there are no further questions, court is dismissed."

Mr. Williams stood up. He wiped his hands on his pants and then sniffed as he wiped his upper lip with his sleeve. "I have a question, your Honor."

She rolled her eyes. "Of course, Mr. Williams. What is your question?"

He cleared his throat. "May I speak with my boy for a few minutes, ma'am? I got me a couple o' questions for the lad."

She frowned and took a deep breath. Finally, she nodded. "Fine. You may speak with him in my office in my presence. Theo, come with me."

I blinked and looked at Ari. "What is happening?"

He shrugged. "I haven't a clue. Do you know, Mr. Maksoud?"

"I have an idea, but we will wait and see. In the meantime, let us all pray."

We sat there huddled together, a Moslem attorney and his two Christian clients, praying until the judge and Theo returned to the courtroom. Judge Mohammed grinned from ear to ear. Theo looked bumfuzzled if I ever saw a bumfuzzled child. He sat down next to me, shaking, and struggling not to cry. I took his hand as we all arose. As he continued to tremble, I put an arm around his shoulders. "It's okay, Theo. This will all be over soon."

"We are having a change in our orders. Mr. Williams is executing an irrevocable affidavit of relinquishment of his parental rights to Theo as we speak. After he spoke with Theo, Mr. Williams stated he believes it would be in Theo's best interests for his parental rights to be terminated and for Dr. and Mrs. Hotep to be allowed to adopt Theo. He says he feels like 'a right fool' and a 'blasted eejit,' whatever an 'eejit' is, for having sought custody under these circumstances. Theo's right to inherit through his father shall not be terminated. His name shall be Theodore Williams Hotep, to further maintain a link with his father's family. I consulted with the senior judge, who states the adoption shall be allowed with those stipulations."

I began trembling as tears streamed down my cheeks. "Really?"

"Yes, Mrs. Hotep, really. Theo, would you like to say anything?"

He arose and nodded. "Yes, your Honor. Thank you for helping with this."

His voice broke.

The judge smiled at him. "Anything else, Theo?"

He nodded as tears coursed down his cheeks. He looked at both of us and took our hands. "She says I may call you Mommy and Daddy now."

I could not contain my sobs. Ari pulled Theo and me into his arms as he struggled not to give into to tears of joy.

The judge's eyes sparkled as she smiled at me. "Congratulations, Mrs. Hotep. Now you have officially had your second miracle for this week."

I smeared tears across my face and struggled to smile at her. Finally, I managed to respond. "Thank you, your Honor." I turned towards Mr. Williams as he walked back into the courtroom. "And thank you, Benjamin."

His cheeks turned scarlet again as he nodded towards me. "Just keep takin' loving care of him like you folks been doin' all these years. He's a good lad. He thinks the world of you two."

We were there about another half hour before we went across the street with Mr. Maksoud with a copy of the Affidavit of Relinquishment held tight in my hands. The original had already been filed. Mr. Maksoud's secretary was already preparing the Petition to Terminate Parental Rights and for Relative Adoption when we entered his office. She jumped up from her seat and hurried around her desk to hug me. "Congratulations."

I hugged her back, unable to speak, as my eyes filled with tears again. I cleared my throat several times before I could talk. "I can't believe it. This is like a dream."

Mr. Maksoud smiled. "A happy dream, I hope."

I beamed at him. "Oh, yes, sir. A wonderfully happy dream. A miraculous dream."

We signed the requisite affidavits, attached a copy of Ben's Affidavit of Relinquishment, and Mr. Maksoud efiled the Petition to Terminate Parental Rights and for Adoption by Relatives while we waited. I continued to cry intermittently.

Mr. Maksoud looked up at me and smiled again. "It's all right, Elizabeth. You won."

"I know. These are tears of joy, not sadness."

"This dog hunts, right?"

I laughed. "Yes, sir, Mustafa Maksoud. This dog definitely hunts."

Chapter 33
Nine Months Later - Cairo

Our daughter, Isis Antigone Hotep, was born seven months later. Six weeks after her birth, we went to court to complete our adoption of Theo. Benjamin Williams had been terminated a few days after he signed the Relinquishment of Parental Rights, at which time Ari and I were named to be the permanent, non-parent, joint managing conservators of Theo. As Judge Mohammed pronounced the adoption of Theodore 'Theo' Benjamin Williams Hotep was granted and signed the decree, our families cheered. My mother, Fancy Winslow, cried, as did my sister, Bella, my stepmother, Melanie, my sister-in-law, Anna, and I. Ari, Ari's brother, Levi, Daddy, Dr. Richard Winslow, my Poppa, Kirk O'Malley, and Bella's husband, Dr. Miguel Vargas, all beamed as they patted a beaming Theo on the back. Mrs. Hadad and her supervisor clapped with enthusiasm.

"I see you have a beautiful baby girl. May I ask how you chose her name?" asked the judge.

"All my family have Greek names, your Honor," stated Ari. "Our mother was Greek. Antigone was Theo's mother's name. She was my sister."

She nodded. "Yes, I remember. Why did you choose Isis?"

I cleared my throat. "We wanted an Egyptian name for her, too, your Honor. It seemed appropriate, considering my fall onto the tomb and all."

She nodded with a slight smile. "Will you try again for a boy, Dr. Hotep?"

He shook his head as he put an arm around Theo. "No, your Honor. I have my son."

He put his arm around Theo's shoulders. Theo beamed up at his dad.

She smiled. "Wonderful. I wish your family every happiness in the future."

We walked out of the courtroom arm in arm. We all laughed as Daddy and Poppa unfurled a sign which declared, 'Theodore Hotep: this dog hunts.' Cameras flashed and everyone talked in excited tones. We were all thrilled it was finally all over.

As we walked down the stairs, I nodded my head and smiled. "Thank you."

Isis spread her golden wings before me. "You are welcome, my daughter. Thank you for helping Nefertiti to be able to give birth to her son. She found peace subsequently. And thank you for naming your daughter after me. I am exceedingly well pleased. As an additional blessing, you will discover a bit of Nefru's essence is in your daughter."

She folded her wings and disappeared. I felt certain I was the only one who saw her.

I glanced over to the side at the sound of whispering. I was surprised to see Johnny standing there, with one arm around the shoulders of a slender, dark-haired woman.

"Come on, Jay. They will be fine. It's time we go now, darlin'," she coaxed in a low, soft voice.

"In just a minute, Tamsin, my love." He bent down to look into Theo's eyes. "Did everything work out like I promised?"

Theo nodded as a smile spread across his face. "Yes, sir."

Theo reached up to hug Johnny. Theo is the only person I ever knew who could hug Johnny. As their hug ended, Johnny sniffed, and wiped his sleeve across his face.

"Wonderful. Then Tamsin and I shall be off. Remember, Theo, I told you Tamsin and I were married when we were alive. She was your Grandmother Fancy's mother."

"I remember, sir. I will make sure she knows her mother and you are together again," answered my son.

Johnny nodded. "Tamsin tells me I many have things to do, and I am rather late."

Theo reached a hand towards his ghostly friend. "But Johnny! Will you ever return?"

Johnny shrugged. "I don't know, lad. It all depends on the Big Man Upstairs and what he decides."

They vanished from our sight.

Just then, the judge walked up to us. "To whom was Theo speaking?"

I smiled and cleared my throat. "To his guardian angel, your Honor."

'He was talking with his guardian angel' was easier to explain than 'he was talking to the ghost of a long dead pirate.'

"Ah, excellent. Everyone needs a guardian angel. It has been a pleasure working with your family. Now, don't you dare to come back here again!" She grinned as she shook her finger at me as if she were giving me stern instructions.

I laughed. "Believe me, your Honor, I never want to be back in this building unless it might be to take you to lunch sometime."

"Lunch with a friend would be a wonderful treat, Elizabeth. But you must call me Jawhara since now we will be friends."

I laughed. "Thank you, Jawhara. It would be an honor and a privilege to call you my friend."

The judge leaned over to kiss my cheek. "Take care of our boy and little Isis. Important things are in store for both children."

"Of course, Jawhara. After all, they are my miracle babies."

Her smile broadened as she leaned over to hug me. "Exactly."

Mom put her arm around my shoulders. "You know the ghostly woman with Captain Johnny was my mother, don't you?"

I nodded. "I thought so. Why?"

"She called him Jay. Did you realize Johnny's real name was Jay Fitz Simmons?"

I stared at the spot from where the ghosts had disappeared. "No, not until now. I always wondered why he was so devoted to our family. He would say he felt a tendresse for us because he was the person who fished my Poppa out of the drink after the hurricane."

"I suppose he wanted to make up for the way things started," Mom mused. "He convinced my Mama to leave me behind when they went to Ireland. Lord knows he was a real bounder when he was alive."

I smiled. "But he sure turned out to be one great ghost. My Captain Courageous. And to think I used to call him Captain Horrible."

We heard Johnny laughing as we walked away. "Yes, Tamsin, my love. I know I should have come back while we were both alive. I realize we should have taken little Fancy with us when we left Virginia to sail to Ireland. And, I understand I could have known our son all those years if I had returned. I was a stubborn fool. I've told you I'm sorry. Now, let's get on with this final reward matter."

He partially materialized and glanced at me one more time. "Take care, girl."

"I will, sir. We will miss you."

"And I shall miss all of you." He smiled at Ari. "Yes, I believe I can leave you now. Ari is a fine man. He will make sure Kirk's girl is well protected. Kiss the baby girl for me and watch over my young friend."

I leaned over and kissed his scruffy cheek. I meant to give him an air kiss and it startled me when I could feel the scratch of the scruffy beard on his cheek. I had rarely been able to feel him in the past. "Thank you for everything, Captain Johnny. I'm afraid I can't call you Jay after all this time. In my mind, you will always be my privateer, Captain Jolly Johnny English. And tell the Big Man if he needs a reference, I will be most happy to provide one."

He leaned over to brush a ghostly kiss on my cheek. "Thank you, my dear. I appreciate your vote of confidence more than you will ever know."

And then, they were gone.

Postlude

"Yes, my Lord, I realize I have been rather naughty -"

"Duplicitous," boomed the loud voice. "Adulterous. Murderous. You have been downright evil. Admit it, Fitz Simmons. You were a horrible human being."

The ghost formerly known as Jay Fitz Simmons and known until recently as Captain Johnny ducked his head. "Yes, my Lord. I admit it. I was a dreadful human being. But I have had my moments of greatness."

The Lord Almighty sat back on his throne. "Then I believe it is time for you to tell me your story."

"Well, my Lord, it all began when my father ran off with my mother, Mariah Constantine. She was still married to her first husband. Father fell in love with Mother and determined to marry her. When she told him she was *enceinte*, he took her to Ireland."

"Go on," encouraged the Lord.

Jay smiled his most beguiling smile. "I should have been able to inherit from my father -- Micah Fitz Simmons -- as his eldest son. Unfortunately, I was born out of wedlock, before her divorce was finalized from Lord Patrick Constantine. That meant my younger brother, Marcus Fitz Simmons, was the eldest legitimate male heir, not I. I must admit I developed an unreasonable hatred of Marc because of the circumstances of my birth, which was not something he caused. My mother and father caused it."

"You are correct." The Lord leaned forward. "Jay, did it never occur to you you were Lord Patrick Constantine's legal heir?"

Jay turned pale – if a ghost can turn pale. "His legal -- I beg your pardon, but how, my Lord?"

"Jay, all your evil manipulations were for naught. You sold your siblings into slavery to steal your brother's birthright. You did not realize you had a greater birthright through your legal father, Lord Constantine. He never renounced you even though he was not your biological father. Your brother, Marcus, gave his title to your son, Winston, with the permission of King George. Winston then became the Earl of Waterside. But, if you had returned within the three years stipulated by Tamsin's father, Lord Josiah Selk, Winston would have become the Duke of Ranscome when his grandfather died. You threw the opportunity away when you remained at sea rather than return home. Instead, Fancy's son, Charles, is the Duke of Ranscome. You missed the big picture."

Jay's forehead wrinkled. "I don't understand, Lord. Please explain."

The Lord God laughed. "Lord Patrick Constantine never remarried. He had no other children. Your legal father left his estate to the legal issue of his marriage to Mariah."

Jay blinked and then blinked again. "I don't understand, my Lord."

"Winston inherited from Lord Constantine, who left his entire estate to you, as his legal heir. Winston subsequently became the Duke of Somerset and the Earl of Waterside."

"I tried to tell you, darling. It all worked out in the end. You could have come home a long, long time ago," Tamsin said.

Jay looked stunned. "Well, I'll be hornswoggled."

The Lord laughed. "Now, I want you to tell me all about your life. In your own words. From your perspective. I am especially interested in hearing how Jay Fitz Simmons became the pirate, Captain Jolly Johnny English."

Jay perked up. "Well, Milord, I was a privateer."

The Lord laughed. "Oh, really? Tell me how a conman like you became a privateer."

"The ship was headed for Cape Town when the storm struck. The ship sustained heavy damage and sank. I managed to swim to shore, where I was stranded on the Skeleton Coast of the Namibian desert. I thought I would never see my sweet Tamsin again. My heart was separated from its beat. My rhyme was lost to my song. It seemed as if my soul was denied its essence. My light dimmed, weakened, and broke until you allowed us to be reunited. Now, our two halves are rejoicing again, as our two halves mirror one another."

The Lord frowned. "Balderdash. Give it to me straight this time."

Jay flashed the Big Man his most beguiling smile. "Of course, My Lord. It happened like this..."

About the Author

Sharon is a fourth generation Texan who grew up in San Antonio. She retired from her law practice, and now writes, quilts, and spoils her Skye terriers. She loves North Georgia, and her husband and she plans to build their retirement home overlooking the Cohutta Wilderness soon.

This is the second book about the *McCarron's Corner* kids. The next book will be a mystery about Sara before the series proceeds closer to moving the Cohutta Cherokees westward before the infamous Trail of Tears.

She hopes you enjoy the books. If you do, be sure to leave positive feedback. You can reach her at sharonmiddleton359@gmail.com if you have ideas about future plots or have constructive suggestions.

Note from the Author

I hope you enjoyed *Love You Forever*. If you did, I hope you will leave positive feedback anywhere you read or purchase books.

If you are new to the McCarron's Corner series, I invite you to read the other books, too. The story began with *Beyond McCarron's Corner*, which is the story of Sassy Winslow. All seven of the McCarron's Corner novels are free on Kindle Unlimited. I hope you will enjoy them all.

The McCarron's Corner stories are not yet finished. I expect there will be at least three more. Watch for the next story about this family in the first McCarron's Corner mystery. I am currently calling it *Eye of the Storm*. I am working on the one to follow it, tentatively titled *The Queen of My Heart*.

The last one, still forming in my head, will need to wrap up a lot of loose ends, and get the Cohutta Cherokees safely out west before the infamous Trail of Tears. A group of Cherokees from the North Georgia area moved west in about 1810 and are known as the Old Settlers. The final story remains untitled. The heroine has only begun to tell her story to me. If I have my way, it will be called *The Song of the Hummingbird*. 'Walela' is the Cherokee word for hummingbird. The Cherokee believed hummingbirds were the messengers of the gods. Believe me: Walela has a beautiful song to sing.

If you have story ideas or constructive criticism, please write me at sharonmiddleton359@gmail.com. You are also invited to drop by the Beyond Writing Group on Facebook, an open group where my readers and I discuss story ideas, clothing, and select my book covers. My readers urged me to write this story about Elizabeth. A contest was held to help me decide what story to write, and Elizabeth won. I also have contests occasionally to give away books and other goodies. I look forward to seeing you there!

Word-of-mouth is crucial for any author to succeed. If you enjoyed *Love You Forever*, please leave a review online—anywhere you are able. Even if it's just a sentence or two. It would make all the difference and would be very much appreciated.

Thanks!
Sharon K. Middleton

We hope you enjoyed reading this title from:

BLACK ROSE
writing™

www.blackrosewriting.com

Subscribe to our mailing list – *The Rosevine* – and receive **FREE** books, daily deals, and stay current with news about upcoming releases and our hottest authors.
Scan the QR code below to sign up.

Already a subscriber? Please accept a sincere thank you for being a fan of Black Rose Writing authors.

View other Black Rose Writing titles at www.blackrosewriting.com/books and use promo code **PRINT** to receive a **20% discount** when purchasing.